Trouble Tree

MACMILLAN CARIBBEAN WRITERS

Trouble Tree

John Hill Porter

**MACMILLAN
CARIBBEAN**

Macmillan Education
Between Towns Road, Oxford, OX4 3PP
A division of Macmillan Publishers Limited
Companies and representatives throughout the world

www.macmillan-caribbean.com

ISBN: 978-1-4050-7105-5

Text © John Hill Porter 2008
Design and illustration © Macmillan Publishers Limited 2008

Typeset by EXPO Holdings
Cover design by Bob Swan
Cover images by Corbis/Zack Seckler

Printed and bound in Hong Kong

2012 2011 2010 2009 2008
10 9 8 7 6 5 4 3 2 1

Macmillan Caribbean Writers Series

Few West Indian writers have featured the redleg community of Barbados. John Hill Porter's first work of fiction treats this inbred society from the insider's viewpoint, with respect, understanding and sympathy. And though *Trouble Tree* claims to be no more than a thrilling yarn, it contains almost Faulkneresque passages in its haunting descriptions of a child's early encounters with a virtually mute uncle, and an albino aunt who cannot leave the house. *Trouble Tree* is also unusual in its presentation, which instead of chapters takes the more realistic and immediate form of hospital notes, journal extracts, historical reconstruction and daily reports, to track damaged Ben Cumberbatch's extraordinary and dangerous search for the truth.

The Macmillan Caribbean Writers Series (MCW) is an exciting collection of fine writing which treats the broad range of the Caribbean experience. The series offers a varied selection of novels and short stories, and also embraces works of non-fiction, poetry anthologies and collections of plays particularly suitable for arts and drama festivals.

As well as reviving well-loved West Indian classics and presenting new writing by established authors, MCW is proud to introduce work by newly discovered writers, such as Porter, Martina Altmann, Deryck Bernard, Garfield Ellis, Joanne Haynes, Joanne C. Hillhouse, Margaret Knight, Graeme Knott and Nellie Payne. Writers on the list come from around the region, including Guyana, Trinidad, Tobago, Barbados, St Vincent, Bequia, Grenada, St Lucia, Dominica, Montserrat, Antigua, the Bahamas, Jamaica and Belize.

MCW was launched in 2003 at the Caribbean's premier literary event, the Calabash Festival in Jamaica. Macmillan Caribbean is also proud to be associated with the work of the Cropper Foundation in Trinidad, developing the talents of the region's most promising emerging writers, many of whom are contributors to MCW.

Judy Stone
Series Editor
Macmillan Caribbean Writers

ACKNOWLEDGEMENTS

The Bajan proverbs that appear in this book and its title are taken from the book *Bajan Proverbs* by Margot Blackman. Ms Blackman, a native of the parish of St John in Barbados, and a retired Professor of Nursing in her adopted home, Montreal, Canada, has compiled the definitive collection of these wise and pithy sayings. She garnered them, over the years, from the daily speech of her relatives and friends in Barbados

Some of the proverbs are unique to Barbados and the West Indies, reflecting the harsh realities of plantation life in times past. Others, borrowed from English culture, will be familiar to many readers, although they have been adapted to the Bajan dialect or modified to reflect the daily experiences and wisdom of the "strong, sincere, hospitable, cheerful and witty people" of this appealing island.

With regret, the author notes that with the passage of time and the influence of universal education and American television, the use of these proverbs is in decline. These sayings reflect a rural Barbados which is being significantly modified by the social and economic realities putatively called progress.

The author also must acknowledge the assistance he received in writing this book from the physicians, clinicians and medical staff of the Medical Center and the Medical School of the University of Pennsylvania in Philadelphia in understanding the treatment and rehabilitation of traumatic head wounds. Also, he wishes to thank the police departments of Philadelphia, New York and Barbados for their advice and guidance as well as my former associate Connie Fletcher's excellent resource book, *Pure Cop*. My interviews with patients and former patients who had suffered such head wounds were particularly useful in understanding the problems they have faced.

Most of all, I wish to thank my many friends and acquaintances in Barbados who, over many years, have generously shared with me their wisdom and understanding of the magical and delightful island nation of Barbados and the varied people who are privileged to live there. And the over three dozen Bajans who read my manuscript at various points in its development and gave me valuable insight into details of life in Barbados, past and present, as well as their insightful criticisms and welcome encouragement. To Dr Trevor Carmichael, my thanks for his advice and guidance regarding the intricacies of the legal system of Barbados. Any inaccuracies or oversights in this area are entirely the fault of the author. I wish to particularly acknowledge the assistance and counsel I received from Gilly Metzgen, whose patience and fine attention to detail helped me immeasurably.

Last, but by no means least, I wish to give my deepest thanks to my clever and skilled editor, Judy Stone, for her sage advice, encouragement and assistance, delivered with good humour and kindness. With her help, *Trouble Tree* has endeavoured to bridge the gap between North American English and English English. Any shortcomings in this effort are entirely of my doing.

If this book in any way misrepresents or puts a bad light on the people, institutions, organizations or culture of Barbados, the author says, "Can' help, ent do fuh purpose."

"Trouble tree don' bear no blossom"
Bajan proverb

Trouble Tree is dedicated to the women in
my life: my sister Cornelia Porter Ream,
my daughter Allison Porter and, most
particularly, my wife Louise Porter,
without whose patience, enthusiasm
and gentle criticism
Trouble
Tree
would
still
be
a
sapling

Contents

Foreword

Several friends of mine in New York and Barbados have urged me to write about the night of 3rd June 1996, and the related events which occurred in the months that followed. More than most who attempt this task, I owe my gratitude to others who have filled in the blank spaces in my memory: the surgeons and other medical personnel at Kings County Hospital, my sister Elyce Cumberbatch Downes, Lieutenant Tom Moran of the NYPD Arson Squad and, last but not least, Shannon Tierney Bradstock, who found a way to give me a working memory.

Ben Cumberbatch
Glenville
St Charles Parish
Barbados
West Indies

Prologue – Before Midnight

The elevator chimes as it reaches the lobby floor. It makes a small adjustment and the doors snap open. The elevator emits an irritating buzzing sound. A tall, slender man leans forward as he peers into the small, dimly lit hotel lobby. Satisfied that he is alone, he limps into the lobby, leaning on a heavy wooden cane. The night clerk behind the counter is watching a six-inch television. Dave Letterman has just begun his nightly comic dialogue.

The clerk glances up briefly and says, "Going out for a walk? Be careful, this is Brooklyn. You never know who you might meet at this time of night."

He returns to his television but then adds, "I wouldn't go into the park, if I was you. You'd be better off to turn right and go up toward Billington Avenue. More lights."

"Thank you for the advice," the man mumbles as he hobbles to the door.

"If you return after twelve, that door'll be locked and you'll have to use the night bell to get in."

The man looks over to locate the bell and then limps out onto the stoop under the small hotel marquee that has "Park View" scrawled on it in red neon. There he stands, savouring the cool spring air. He looks left, then right, scanning the street. Only one person is in sight. Twenty feet to his right, across the street at a bus stop under a streetlight, a young man waits, apparently totally engrossed in his newspaper.

Unwilling to risk even the most casual contact with this or any other stranger, the tall man ignores the clerk's advice and

1

turns left, away from the lights, into the safety of shadows in an empty street. Grimacing with pain, he walks stiffly to the corner, where he glances back at the bus stop.

No one is there! The young man has already crossed the street and, having just passed the entrance to the hotel, is coming along the sidewalk directly towards the tall man with the cane.

Wishing now that he could retrace his steps and re-enter the relative safety of the hotel lobby, the tall man instead turns into the side street. He limps hurriedly along and enters the small alley that leads to the back of the hotel. The dark brick walls of the hotel loom to his left. Fire escapes hang, well out of reach, above his head. To his right, a blank wall is lined with garbage and trash cans, waiting to be collected. A rat scurries down the alley and disappears under a stack of plastic bags.

He goes directly to the entrance at the back of the hotel, where a large grey door is illuminated by a small light-bulb in a wire cage. He grasps the handle but it does not move, the door is locked. Looking back to the street, he is relieved to see that no one has followed him into the alley.

Nevertheless, to be on the safe side, he continues to retreat into the shadows. As he moves further along he sees that a small white car is parked directly across the alley, in front of a windowless brick wall. With a sinking sensation, the man sees that there is no way out except the way he entered. He is in a cul-de-sac.

Again he turns and looks toward the entrance from the street, but this time, to his great dismay, someone is standing there. It is a man, his form barely visible in the soft yellow glow cast by the distant streetlight. From the size and shape it is almost certainly the young stranger from the bus stop.

Walking as rapidly as he can on his cane in the uneven alley, the tall man makes his way to the small car, hoping to find safe hiding there. He squeezes behind the car and crouches down. He can hear footsteps approaching rapidly, but then they stop.

The tall man straightens up enough to peer through the car windows. He can see his pursuer's form looming in the alley, not thirty feet away. At this moment a bright flashlight beam cuts through the shadows and sweeps the wall and the car. Startled, and not wishing to draw attention to himself, the tall man freezes.

The flashlight sweeps again, then settles on the car window. He has been spotted. He slowly stands and raises his hand, to block the bright light from his eyes and to shield his features.

But it is too late. His face has been seen.

To his amazement he hears his pursuer say, "My God, is that you? How did you get here? Why aren't you in the hospital?"

The questions briefly stun the tall man. How could this stranger know him? But he quickly perceives the danger implicit in this recognition and knows he must act at once. He steps from behind the car and draws a pistol from his pocket. Without a word he aims and fires at the shadowy figure behind the flashlight, but misses.

The shot ends any indecision; the stranger drops the flashlight and charges forward. A second shot rings out and again narrowly misses its mark as the distance closes. A third shot. This bullet connects with a dull thud, striking the forehead just above the right eye. As the bullet sinks home, the young man's knees buckle and momentum propels his falling body into the tall man, who is knocked back against the wall.

A scream of pain slices the darkness, followed by a groan. The tall man's already swollen knee and cracked ribs send excruciating signals to his brain. Slumped back against the wall, he holds his side and moans. The young stranger lies motionless at his feet, blood gushing from the head wound.

Despite the pain, the tall man tells himself that he must gather his strength and his will. He must get out of the alley before someone discovers him there.

Just then there comes a voice from the street end of the alley. "Hello, is anyone there?"

Two figures in the half-light move cautiously into the alley.

"Let's see what gives."

"Dis is crazy, man, let's get outta here!" argues a second voice.

"Don't be chicken-shit, this could be good."

Their voices sound young.

The tall man, desperate to put distance between himself and the bleeding body, drags himself towards the rear of the car. He crouches there and places his sweating face against the tail-light, praying that the intruders will not see him.

"There he is. Look, he's been shot in the head. The dude must be dead with all that blood."

"You're right. It's a drug deal gone bad, for sure. Don't touch him. Just get the stiff's wad or his wallet if he has one, and let's go."

Hearing rather than seeing, the man realises that theft of the dead man's money is the objective. The youths apparently find what they seek and their footsteps retreat rapidly up the alley.

Mustering his strength, the man locates his cane and, leaning on it, hobbles painfully up the alley to the street. He looks right and left, then makes his way to the corner and turns toward the red neon "Park View". He re-enters the hotel just before midnight.

"Have a good walk?" the night clerk asks.

Walking as straight as he can, the tall man crosses the small lobby, past the clerk. His pain is such that he dares not reply. When he reaches to press the elevator button, pain extracts a low groan. The clerk accepts this sound as a gruff answer to his inquiry.

Early the next morning, the man checks out of the hotel and takes a taxi to Grand Central Station.

Prologue – After Midnight

The door opens and a black woman in a white starched uniform squints and peers into the cave-dark room. Her heavy-set form partially blocks the light from the hallway. She nudges the door, encouraging a shaft of light into the room. The light falls upon a man sleeping on a narrow bed, his face to the wall.

"Dr Cawthorne, you better get up now. We got a gunshot coming in right this minute."

Her voice rises on the last three words, so that they become a command to the sleeping man.

Nick Cawthorne MD, the twenty-nine-year-old neurosurgical resident, is on duty at the emergency room of Kings County Hospital, the principal – and the oldest – public health facility in central Brooklyn. He groans and turns, with one hand shielding his eyes.

Nurse Naomi Lukens waits impatiently. She clucks her tongue and opens the door further to allow additional light to spill into the room.

Cawthorne's hand wipes across his face in an effort to banish the cobwebs from his mind. He stands up and grimaces at Nurse Lukens, then looks at his watch. 12.40.

"What do we have?" he asks in a husky voice.

"I heard the radio call," the nurse says. "A gunshot. Entry above the right eye; exit wound just behind the right ear. They think he's a cop, a detective. They'll be here in a few minutes."

The two hurry down the hall toward the operating rooms. Nurse Lukens's shoes tap a rapid staccato; Cawthorne's operating-room clogs slap a dull counter-rhythm. They find operating room 1 is in use by a thoracic team working on the crushed ribcage of a young motorcyclist.

The doors snap open and two emergency technicians wheel in a bloody man on a gurney. Cawthorne examines the patient and says, "Get him into surgery now."

Lukens turns on the lights in room 3 while Cawthorne begins to scrub up. Then the resident stops, his arms glistening with soapy water. Half to the nurse, half to himself, he says, "I'm going to call Guenther."

"You sure?" Nurse Lukens says as she enters the scrub area.

"Yeah, I am. I think we've got enough time and, if this guy is a cop, this one will get in the papers for sure. Plus, if we don't bring him back, this could end up as another nail in the coffin of this place. None of us needs that, and Guenther's told me to always call him for cases like this."

Dr Mark Guenther is not pleased when the telephone on his night table rings, but he is not surprised. He has the receiver in hand before it can ring a second time. He notes the time: 12.51 a.m.

His wife barely stirs as he slips out of the bed. Guenther puts on his metal-rimmed glasses and steps into the hall, closing the bedroom door softly behind him. He listens as the resident describes the situation.

"You're right to call. I'll be there shortly."

Guenther arrives and begins to scrub up. In the next room the patient is being prepped for surgery. A young blonde nurse and a tall black male nurse's aide have removed his bloody clothes and washed the blood and dirt from his face. The nurse is shaving his head.

"Jessie, is he black or white? It's hard to tell, he's got blue eyes," Nurse Elliott says.

6

The nurse's aide laughs, "You kidding, Elliott? We undressed the dude, didn't we? This one's a brother for sure."

Cawthorne comes over and peers at the patient – a big, strong-looking man who appears to be in his mid to late thirties.

The young nurse looks up from her task. "Let's save this one, Doc. He's real good-looking."

Nurse Lukens has just entered the small operating room and overhears the remark. She says sharply, "Elliott, you pay attention to what you're doing and don't you let Dr Guenther hear you kidding around or you're out of here."

Guenther has heard the exchange but he considers that Lukens has adequately handled the matter. In truth, Guenther is not nearly the ogre that the senior nurse represents him to be. He finishes scrubbing, enters the operating room and examines the patient.

"How long ago was he shot?" he asks Cawthorne.

"No telling for sure, but at least an hour, more like an hour and a half. A patrolman who rode in the ambulance says that some kids who called it in to 911 had heard shots at approximately 11.45. They had found him in an alley and thought he was dead. They had his wallet and said he was an NYPD cop named Cumberbatch."

Dr Guenther checks his watch and says, "This guy is running out of time. Much over an hour and a half and he's in trouble. What are his vitals?"

The resident reads a series of numbers from a chart. Guenther frowns and turns to look at the CT scan completed minutes before. It shows a jagged line running straight through the patient's head, from above the right eyebrow, slanting down slightly, ending behind the right ear. In the centre of the brain a large dark mass, the blood seeping from the broken vessels, is growing and exerting increased pressure inside the skull.

"We go in now," Guenther announces.

The surgical team expects this decision, they're ready. They know that time is critical; they must stop the bleeding and reduce the swelling of the brain soon; if they don't, the patient will die.

Nick Cawthorne watches the senior surgeon make three incisions in the newly shaved scalp and peel the skin back to reveal the right side of the skull. The resident then steps to the table and, using a small electric saw, cuts through the skull, starting behind the ear, going below the exit wound, up across the side of the head, over to the mid-point of the forehead, then back across the top of the head and down to where he started.

Very carefully, working together, the surgeons lift the loosened segment of skull bone to reveal the cerebral cortex, the grey matter of the brain that sets humans apart from less complex species. As the constraining skull is removed, the brain swells dramatically in reaction to the pressure from the internal trauma. Cawthorne, who has seen this reaction several times, is still in awe of the phenomenon.

Carefully, Cawthorne separates the grey matter to expose the bloody track of the bullet. For the next four hours, the two doctors take turns "zapping", using small electric needles to cauterise hundreds of bleeding vessels. Cawthorne, the less experienced of the two, is at times nearly nauseated by the odour of frying blood and charring vessels.

Finally, at five minutes to six in the morning, Cawthorne steps back with his hands raised, indicating that he believes all bleeding has been stopped. Guenther, who has been leaning on a nearby counter, comes over, examines the patient and concurs.

The temperature of the brain is then slowly lowered to further reduce the swelling and, an hour later, the missing piece of skull is reset in place.

"One more thing," Guenther says.

Into the top of the skull, penetrating the bone and touching the cerebral cortex itself, they place a small device called an ICP bolt. Until the patient is fully out of danger, this bolt will record the pressure the brain is exerting upon the inside of the skull.

The patient is moved to intensive care. There he will remain at least three days, closely monitored for any complications.

Dr Guenther turns to Nurse Lukens and says, "What about the family? We should speak to them if they're here."

"That's the funniest thing, his sisters have been here at Kings for the last two days. Their father is in our ICU. He was badly beaten, apparently the victim of a mugging. They're in the waiting room."

The surgeons walk down the hall. Guenther says, "Nick, you take the lead. It will be good practice."

Two tired-looking women are sitting on the small sofa. One of them, probably the older of the two, looks to be a light-skinned black. The other woman appears to be white.

Cawthorne asks, somewhat hesitatingly, "Excuse me, are you the sisters of Detective Cumberbatch?"

The older woman says, "Yes, we are." The second woman nods.

"Your brother's surgery has gone as well as can be expected but his condition remains critical. The next twenty-four hours will be decisive."

The women ask several questions, all of which are answered with variations of "It's too early to tell."

The surgeons leave the women with a less than reassuring promise: "We'll let you know if there is any change."

Kings County Hospital

23 June to 19 July 1996

Total darkness. I could see nothing and I could hear nothing. I seemed to be lying on a bed. Then someone came into the room. From the sound of the steps, it was a woman. At first, she fussed at the bottom of the bed; I heard a rustling of papers. Then she came to my side and took my arm from under the sheet. She held my left hand in hers and pressed her fingers lightly to my wrist. She was checking my pulse, I guess.

It was pretty clear I was in a hospital. But which one, and why? I tried to ask her, but my voice came out as barely a whisper.

"What happened to me? Am I alive?"

"Oh yes, and now you're conscious. This is wonderful. They'll be pleased."

The woman's voice was warm and caring. She went on, "You've had an accident but you're going to be all right."

She sounded middle-aged and very much a New Yorker. Somehow, I can't imagine why, this reassured me.

I had a splitting headache. I tried to bring my left hand to my head but it barely moved. My right hand worked better. I took it out of the covers and touched my fingers lightly to my face. I could feel fabric, what must have been bandages, going from my nose right up over the top of my head and down the back to my neck. No wonder I couldn't see.

"What's happened? Who are you? Where am I and why are my eyes covered?" My voice came out a little louder than before, but it was still slurred, hoarse and scratchy.

"You're in Kings County neurosurgical ward. I am Nurse Thompkins, and we've been looking after you for nearly two weeks. Before that, you were brought to the ER here at Kings, then in the ICU. You've had an accident, but the doctors will tell you about that."

Her footsteps receded as she went to tell the doctors that I was awake.

Next thing I knew, I was being awakened from a deep sleep. I had no idea how much time had passed – a minute, an hour, a day. Someone was touching my hand. Just a nudge, hand to hand. I moved my hand in response, signifying that I was present and accounted for.

A man's voice, professional and in charge, said, "Detective, I am Dr Guenther. I am your attending physician. I'm very pleased that you're awake. You had us worried there for a while. How do you feel?"

"I'm okay, I guess. But I've got a hell of a headache and I feel weak and dizzy."

The doctor reassured me that it was quite normal for me to feel that way, "after what you've been through."

"And what was that?"

"You were shot in the head with a small calibre pistol. The police found the bullet. It was a .24 calibre. The bullet entered above your right eye, went through the brain and exited behind your right ear. All things considered, you were most fortunate."

"When did this happen?"

"About three weeks ago; you have been under our care ever since. You were brought to our emergency room on the third of June; today is the twenty-third."

"Why can't I see?"

"That's just a precaution. Your left eye is fine. There has been some trauma to the optical nerve in your right eye. That should improve in a relatively short time. However, you'll probably find that you've lost some peripheral vision in that eye. It should get better over time and, if it doesn't, it can be improved somewhat with special glasses."

It struck me that the doctor was being somewhat offhanded about me and my condition. I felt myself getting angry at him for his attitude and, in general, I was angry about my situation.

I blurted out, "And what else do you have to tell me? What's wrong with my left arm?"

"You have a hemiparesis of the left side of your body. This is a partial paralysis as a result of the wound in your right frontal lobe. With a little therapy and some patience, you should regain complete use of the arm."

"How soon?"

"Hard to predict. You can look forward to seeing some progress in the next two weeks or so."

He patted my leg to add weight to his verbal reassurance.

"And, what else?" I didn't like what I was hearing.

"Along with the hemiparesis, you may experience some stiffness in your left leg and arm or, possibly, spasticity – sudden, involuntary jerking of your limbs. This too should subside over time."

He hesitated, then said, "And, ah …" and hesitated again.

"And ah what?" I said, too loudly, the irritation in my voice masking my fear and worry. I was surprised at myself. I'm usually pretty cool; this kind of anger wasn't really much like me, but then, I'd never been shot in the head before.

"You will have sustained some memory loss, but how much and for how long remains to be determined. We'll be conducting some tests in the days ahead to answer that question. It is also possible that you will experience some seizures, but hopefully you'll be spared that. If not, we will control them with medication."

12

With this less than reassuring news he concluded his visit.

I lay there, thinking about what he had just said. I couldn't see out of my right eye, I would have to wear glasses, I was paralysed on one side, I had lost my memory and I might have epileptic seizures. And he said that I was lucky! Just great! What would an unlucky person be like?

Dead, I guess.

As the days passed I grew physically stronger, but I still could not walk. I lay in bed and tried to understand what had happened. My mind was jumbled, I was having difficulty holding or completing a thought. But there was some good news; the longer ago something had happened, the better I could remember it. It was the more recent events where my memory was shaky.

Some things were real clear: my family; growing up in Brooklyn with my two sisters; going to Barbados to see my grandmother when I was young; being in the Army; joining the NYPD and becoming an arson detective. But I didn't know who had shot me or why. I couldn't even remember what was happening on the days before I was shot.

And, worst of all, I was even forgetting current things, everyday things that happened to me. For example, I couldn't remember what I had had for lunch, or even if I'd had lunch. It was like my brains had been scrambled by the bullet.

Now only the top of my head, from my eyebrows up, was bandaged. I had the use of my left eye and I had sight in my right, but it was blurry. They had me wear an eye patch on my right eye most of the time.

I received a big basket of fruit from the people at work, the Arson/Explosives Squad, NYPD. It was signed by Lieutenant Grover and a number of other familiar names, including that of my good friend, Tom Moran.

I asked the young doc, Cawthorne, if he thought that I'd be able to go back to police work. He ducked the question, saying that was not his department. I sensed that he was breaking it to me gently.

All my adult life I had been a cop. What in the world would I do if I couldn't stay with the police?

I was okay about the eye – what the hell, I still had one good one. And as for the physical stuff, the numbness and occasional twitching, that was getting better already, enough so that I believed the docs when they said that it would be gone in a few months' time.

What worried me most was my memory. Or, more accurately, my lack of it.

My first visitor was my older sister, Elyce. Dr Guenther told me that I could see her for only a short time and that I must not ask questions because her answers might confuse me.

He said, "You're getting better physically and, naturally, you'll want access to your memory. For a while, that's going to be a problem. It may take months and some hard work on your part but be patient, most of it will return. If you ask a lot of questions now, the answers you get will, inevitably, contain different information and ultimately will conflict with your own memories. For one thing, they won't be yours, they'll be from someone else's perspective, based on their view of the facts."

"Doc," I said, "what if I need to know something, something really important?"

"Try to find the answer in your memory, but if you can't, you'll do what you have always done, rely on someone else's information. But first and most important, work to rebuild your own memory as best you can."

I agreed to do it his way. I said that I would not ask Elyce a lot of questions.

I waited anxiously for my sister's visit. Would I recognise her? Would seeing her help my memory? I'd been warned not to expect too much.

The nurse looked in and then opened the door for a woman in her late thirties or early forties. Her skin was a light cream colour, like mine, and she had my colour eyes. She was not beautiful but she had very nice regular features and a no-nonsense air about her. She wore her dark hair short and her blue eyes were warm and intelligent behind her gold-rimmed glasses. She stood at the end of the bed and stared, smiling at me.

And I did recognise her.

"Elyce," I said in a husky voice.

She came over and we hugged. Elyce told me how worried they all had been.

"Margaret and I stayed here at the hospital until you were out of danger. When we were allowed into the room, you just lay there, unconscious, hooked up to tubes and monitors. We couldn't stay for long. Anyway, your head was bandaged and we couldn't even see your face. Margaret had to go back to her family upstate but she sends her love."

When Elyce mentioned Margaret's name, I remembered that she was my little sister and that she was married and lived in a small town near the Canadian border. My mother was dead, I remembered when she died. My memory of my father was coming clearer, too. I remembered him as a young man, taking us kids to the beach at Coney Island.

"When will Pa come to see me?"

Elyce stared at me. She reached over and held my hand.

"Ben, Pa is dead. He died here in this hospital two days after you were shot. He'd been mugged."

"What! My God! Where did it happen?"

"Just off the park. He was attacked in the street, not far from where we live. It happened a couple of days before you were shot."

"Have they caught the person that did it?"

"No, they say they're working on it but they don't have them yet. A detective named Jannetta has called me a few times, but I don't think they even have any suspects."

I was silent for a long time, thinking about my father.

Finally I said, "Have you told Grandma Dora and Pa's family in Barbados?"

"You and I talked about that before you were injured. If Pa did die, we had agreed that they would have to be told. But they don't have a telephone down there and you said that it would be too much of a shock for them to get the news in a letter. You said you would go down to break the news to them in person."

"I'm going to be tied up here for a while," I said with a sorry laugh. "Maybe you should go."

"Ben, I've never met them. Besides, I'm teaching summer school this year. I've missed so much time as it is."

Elyce pointed out that it had been well over a month since Pa died, so it was going to be old news anyway. We agreed to wait until I could travel to Barbados to tell them.

I started to ask her more questions about Pa's death, but Elyce reminded me that she had agreed not to discuss the period right before I was shot. But the doctors had said it was all right for her to tell me about Pa, otherwise I'd be upset that he was not coming to see me.

Elyce left with a promise to return soon.

I was beginning to walk a bit, if somebody walked with me and held my arm.

My second visitor was my best friend, Tom Moran.

Tom had a big smile when he came in the room.

"Well, Lucky, have you promoted any of these beautiful nurses yet?"

I waved one arm at him feebly, all the answer that he needed. Tom and I had been friends since we were patrolmen in the Seventy-Ninth Precinct, covering Bed-Stuy, one of the toughest parts of Brooklyn. That's where I got the nickname Lucky. Now we were both detective sergeants on the Arson/Explosives Squad, or Arson Squad for short.

Tom was pushing six foot two, maybe an inch shorter than me. He was slender, to say the least. He had no hips. Out of necessity, he had to wear suspenders, a belt wouldn't keep his pants up. At the Seven-Nine we called him "The Rail". Tom's broad shoulders made him look like an athlete but I don't think he ever played a game other than pool. But when it came to action, there was no one in the NYPD you'd rather have had at your side.

As Tom was about to go, I asked him the forbidden question.

"Tom, don't bullshit me, who shot me? I've got to know, doctor's orders or not."

"They told me not to discuss it with you."

"Tom, for Chrissake, tell me who did it."

"Lucky, I swear on my mother's grave, I don't know. The detectives investigating don't know either. You may be the only one on the police force that does and, right now, you can't remember."

"Where and how did it happen?"

He took my pitcher and poured himself a drink of water. You could see that he was debating with himself about how much to tell me.

"In an alley in Brooklyn, off Desmond Street. It was just before midnight on June three. Do you know where the Park View Hotel is?"

I nodded, I thought I knew.

"Right behind there," he continued. "Some kids said they heard gunshots. They waited, then they went down the alley and found you lying there. I think they thought you were dead. They took your wallet, but when they looked inside and saw your badge they called 911 to report you'd been shot. If they hadn't, you wouldn't be here now."

"What do they think happened?"

Tom shook his head. "Ted Pilkington is handling your case. Do you know him?"

"Not that I know of."

"He says he has no leads. But with both you and your father being attacked within the same week, within a few blocks of each other, it seems like a good possibility that the attacks are connected. What are the odds of a father and son both ending up in Kings County at the same time with head wounds from two unrelated incidents?"

"What are you talking about? What happened to Pa? Is he okay?"

"You don't know about Nate? Oh God, what have I gotten into? Elyce said she'd told you that he had died."

"Tom, I'm sure she did. In fact, now that you say it, I think maybe I do remember it. But that doesn't mean I knew it before you said it. I'm having problems remembering things, particularly things that happened around the time I was shot. Tell me what happened."

Tom looked at me carefully and then he said, "Nate was attacked before you were hurt. What do you remember?"

"Not much; nothing really, no details."

"Two days before you were shot, Nate was mugged on Procter Street, three blocks from where he and Elyce live. He was badly beaten with what looks to have been a metal pipe. He was here at Kings in intensive care when they brought you in. The

18

homicide detective working your father's case, Tony Jannetta, says that you and he talked about it. He said that you didn't buy it being a simple mugging. Your theory was that it might have been because of someone your father was seeing. But Nate died without regaining consciousness, two days after you were shot, and never told us who it was."

Tom added, "Both Pilkington and Jannetta want to talk with you but the doctors say you're not ready yet." He made a wry face. "I hope to hell I haven't screwed you up, telling you all this."

"Tom, thanks for telling me. Don't worry. I had to know what happened. It was driving me crazy. Damn it, I'm not just some guy shot down in the street, I'm a detective, supposedly a professional. I deserve to know."

A few days later I was sent to a neurological rehab hospital in Manhattan. It was called the Wickham Institute. There I began my rehabilitation in earnest.

Wickham Institute I
July to August 1996

A pretty, red-headed woman in her late twenties came into the room at Wickham where I had just arrived. Her nametag said she was "Shannon Tierney, MS".

Shannon explained to me that she was a neurophysiologist, part of the team who would be working with me here at Wickham. Today she was there to evaluate my memory. She warned me that she would be asking lots of questions.

She sat down and began to read from a multipage document attached to a clipboard.

"What is your name?"

"Ben Cumberbatch."

"Where do you live?"

"Brooklyn," I said. But, wait a minute, I don't live there now. "Can I change my answer?"

I felt foolish.

"Of course," she said with a slight chuckle. She repeated the question, "Where do you live?"

"In Manhattan, on West Twelfth."

"At what address?"

I drew a blank.

"How long have you lived there?"

"I can't remember."

"Where do you work?"

"I am a detective sergeant in the Arson/Explosives Squad with the NYPD."

"Where is your office located?"

I didn't know. I could see it, it was in Manhattan, but I couldn't think of the address. Then, it came to me. "Wait, I remember, it's at Police Plaza."

"How long have you been in the police?"

I remembered when I joined, I thought it was in July 1979, but I didn't know how long ago that was.

"Since 1979," I said, fudging my answer.

It went on like that. The questions were mostly general things, the kinds of things that anybody should know about themselves. Some I knew, some I didn't. The funny thing was that, with a lot of them, I did know the answers but I couldn't seem to come up with them at the right time.

Frustrating.

For example, I knew that my date of birth was July 22, 1958, and that my mother's maiden name was Mary Margaret O'Brien and my father was Nate Cumberbatch and that I had two sisters, Elyce and Margaret. But I didn't know other stuff Shannon asked, like who the President was or the day of the week or even the month of the year.

Shannon explained that at Wickham each patient was assigned to a team of specialists. In my case, there was a neurologist in charge of the team, Dr Lawrence Knight. He did my initial evaluation, but I seldom saw him after that. In addition to Shannon, there was a psychiatrist, Dr Fine, and a whole bunch of physical therapists and other medical specialists. Shannon had promised me that my days were going to be busy and they were.

I saw Shannon nearly every day. She always asked questions. Many of them were the same thing, over and over. Sometimes the questions were meant to evaluate my progress, mostly they were a form of therapy to stimulate the memory part of my brain.

After a month at Wickham, the paralysis on my left side was almost completely gone. My eyesight was better but the right eye

21

still got tired; it twitched and watered. And, as I'd been warned, I had lost my sight to the right, my peripheral vision.

The eye therapist fitted me with a special pair of glasses with prisms built into the right lens, but they didn't really work that well. What they did was bring things around so that I saw them in front of me, instead of where they really were. I still bumped into things. The damned glasses were more trouble than they were worth.

The staff at Wickham were great but, frankly, being cooped up with head cases like myself was depressing. Some had head gunshot wounds like me but many more were the result of falls or accidents in autos, motorcycles, bikes and, increasingly, in-line skates. Others were alcoholics and druggies who had fried their brains for years, losing their memories in the process. Believe me, every one of us at Wickham was a bit messed up.

My physical problems were getting better every day. I couldn't say the same for my memory.

Shannon explained it to me this way: "Ben, you have two kinds of memory loss. First, you have what is called retrograde amnesia, the loss of the period just before and including your injury. The second is what they call post-traumatic amnesia. This means that, since the trauma, your short-term memory and, thus, your ability to learn and retain new information, is impaired."

"Will it get better?"

"Absolutely, I guarantee it. We see progress already. You are my poster boy. Just hang in there and work with me in our therapy sessions and you'll get a whole lot better."

I would do anything that Shannon asked. She was flat out the best-looking female at Wickham. Not that the competition was too great there but Shannon would be a standout anywhere. It was a damned shame that she was engaged to marry a surgeon over at Columbia Presbyterian.

At least I had her to help me lick this memory problem. In my whole life I had never given two seconds of thought to memory. Good or bad, it was just a part of me. What I now realised was that without the ability to recall an experience, in effect, it might as well never have happened.

And I had another problem. It was difficult for me to learn something new. Here at Wickham, I would get lost going from one place to another, even though I had gone there many times. I forgot the simplest things. The staff reassured me that I was not stupid; it was just that that particular part of my brain was not yet working quite right.

Shannon suggested that I carry a notebook with me to write down everything that I heard or saw, no matter how trivial or obvious. I felt silly at first but I did it. At the end of the day I read my notes and I could remember what had occurred. It was useful and, apparently, according to Shannon, it was good for my memory.

Shannon said she had never had a patient who responded so well to this discipline. As I told her, note-taking came naturally to me. When I was a rookie patrolman, I had been taught to keep detailed notes of what happened on the job. Later, as a detective, my notes became even more important because, when I was called to court, I could refer to them and testify accurately.

One day Shannon asked, "Ben, why does Tom Moran call you Lucky?"

"Oh, that's a long story. It goes back to my first day as a rookie patrolman."

"What happened?"

I told her how I was being shown the ropes on my first day on the job by an old cop named Mooney, and how we ended up arresting three cop-killers. The papers wrote it up and quoted some precinct sergeant who said I was lucky to get such a collar on my first day. The name stuck.

Shannon kept pressing me for details, so I told her the whole story. It probably took me half an hour. I had always been able to keep pretty ladies interested by spinning a tale. Shannon seemed to genuinely enjoy my story and, in truth, I enjoyed having her company.

The next day I was watching a video with a dozen or so of my fellow inmates at Wickham. I had seen it several times. I must have been getting better; I could remember that the brother-in-law killed the woman. Shannon came in and tapped my arm.

I followed her back to her office. When we got there, she sat at her desk.

"Ben, I really enjoyed hearing yesterday how you got your nickname. You've got a real knack for storytelling."

"It kind of runs in my family. I spent a lot of time listening to my grandmother in Barbados. We didn't have TV or even a radio. In the evenings, she used to tell stories."

"What kind of stories?"

"Mostly about our family. Early days in Barbados, how she met my grandfather, stuff like that."

"Why don't you write about your family?"

"My Barbados family or my Brooklyn family?"

"Why don't you start with Brooklyn?"

"Dr Fine would love that. He told me that he thinks that I have 'unresolved anger' toward my family, whatever that means. If I'm going to have to tell all about my family, I'm going on *Oprah*."

Shannon laughed at my little joke.

"I'm not sure what Dr Fine has in mind, but why don't you just write whatever comes into your head?"

Shannon looked so pretty, and she acted as if she really did care; I couldn't refuse.

My Journal: My family

Brooklyn, 1955 to 1996

Growing up in a family like mine was an experience that you wouldn't wish on anyone. You've heard TV talk shows discussing families that are broken down, families that just don't work. They had to have had my family in mind.

My mother, Mary Margaret O'Brien, was born in Brooklyn. As a little girl she identified herself with the child actress, Margaret O'Brien. This similarity of name was her bad luck, because it had an impact on her whole life. My mother never really got a firm grasp on the world where the rest of us live. In her head she was always the lead in a technicolour wide-screen movie. Unfortunately, her life didn't turn out to be the romantic musical comedy she'd wished for.

She met my father, Nathaniel "Nate" Cumberbatch, at Coney Island the summer of 1955. She was just sixteen, and that next September would be a junior at St Kate's High School for girls.

You can understand why she was attracted to him. Nate was a handsome devil, and you can be sure he dressed better than any of the young men she knew. Plus, Pa always had a teasing, pleasing way with women.

He was twenty-two, five and a half years older than Ma, and he was a tall, slender, light-skinned black man with a lilting, intriguing accent. Also, he was from a faraway place called Barbados. Ma probably thought that he was Harry Belafonte.

Mary Margaret O'Brien had the milk-white skin that goes with being young, red-headed and Irish. Looking at her pictures, you see a pretty, buxom girl, with a mischievous grin that was at odds with the innocent look in her eyes.

She was the fifth of six children. Her father, my grandfather O'Brien, was a small-time contractor for the City, primarily doing minor street repairs: potholes and storm drains and other such jobs.

By all reports, growing up Ma had been obedient to her family and her religion, but that summer she was looking for something different. She was looking for romance. And she had to look no further than the boardwalk at Coney Island. Nate Cumberbatch was there and ready to oblige.

Ma went to Coney Island with her friends almost every night that summer. Like young people everywhere, the girls walked up and down the boardwalk talking, looking and flirting with young men. Pa was there too, filling one of the male roles in this familiar ritual.

They must have passed several times as they strolled up and down. This gave them several opportunities to glance, to smile, even to pass a quip back and forth. Anyway, something clicked.

But there was this racial barrier thing. They could look but they could not touch. They could talk, maybe even flirt, but they could never go out on a date because, in Brooklyn in 1955, so-called nice girls did not pair up with men of colour, no matter how charming and well-dressed they were.

However, my mother was never one to be limited by petty convention. One night she gave her friends the slip and met Nate under the boardwalk. They met there again on the next and on subsequent evenings. Soon they shifted their meetings to the privacy of Nate's one-room apartment.

This went on for the rest of the summer. Only Ma's best friend knew what was happening. But when September came, Ma had to go back to being a schoolgirl. Without Coney Island and her friend to provide cover, there was little opportunity for them to meet.

If Mary Margaret and Nate were to get together, it would have had to be a prearranged and publicly acknowledged activity; in other words, a date. But interracial dating was not on the social agenda, particularly not in Brighton Beach where the O'Briens lived. In fact, to have dated a "coloured person" would have created a major scandal.

Knowing Ma, this was probably half of the attraction.

They did not see each other, except at a distance, for several weeks. They yearned for each other. There seemed to be no way that they could be together. But this would change.

By mid-October, Ma knew for sure that she was pregnant. She could not bring herself to tell anyone. Not her priest, not her best friend, not her sisters, certainly not her mother. Not even Nate. In fact, no one knew about it until the nuns sent her home from school with a note suggesting that Mary Margaret see a doctor.

Naturally, the family was upset. But it had happened in the O'Brien family once before, to an older sister, so it couldn't have been that much of a shock. And that had worked out amicably enough when Uncle Dominick and Aunt Cathy married.

But when Ma, after many tears and much brow-beating, finally identified the father-to-be, there was a hell of a row. He was a foreigner, he wasn't Catholic, and he was black.

The O'Briens were regular church-going Catholics of the old school, so there was no talk of an abortion. A light-brown-skinned baby was going to be born into the O'Brien family. Grandma O'Brien swore that she would never leave the house again.

Nate was a steamfitter at the Brooklyn Naval Yard. He was making good money and, with the Cold War in full swing, the Yard was running double and triple shifts with lots of high-paying overtime.

Grandfather O'Brien swallowed his pride and went to the Naval Yard to see this Nate Cumberbatch, to ask him what he intended to do about Mary Margaret's situation. The old man hoped that Nate would pay some of the expenses for the birth, maybe even agree to pay a bit every month for the baby's upkeep. However, to everybody's surprise – even my father's, I think – Nate said that he would marry Mary Margaret.

I'm sure that wasn't the answer that Grandfather O'Brien was looking for, but that was the one he got.

You should see the pictures of the wedding. The only one with a smile was my mother, and that probably didn't last long. The rest of the wedding party, including my father, looked like they had just been sent up the river to the prison at Sing Sing.

My parents set up housekeeping in a racially mixed part of Crown Heights. Elyce was born in 1956. I came along twenty-six months later, in 1958, and my youngest sister, Margaret, in 1959.

My sister Elyce used to say that we were one-eighth black and seven-eighths white. Ma was white and Pa was a quarter black, with a white mother and a half-white/half-black father. As a young kid, I was so light-skinned that the black kids in the neighbourhood called me "Pork", "Snowman" and "Suntan". I was even called "Frankie Sinatra" because of my blue eyes.

"I wish we were more black," Elyce has said on more than one occasion. "I hate this being neither one nor the other. White people look at us and see the black; blacks look at us and see the white."

I am a few shades lighter than my father. "Coffee with extra cream," he called it. Elyce was similar to me, but our younger sister Margaret was the lightest of us all. She took after Ma. She had a ghost-like paleness to her skin. In addition, Elyce said, Margaret, growing up, used powder to accentuate her whiteness.

The funny thing is that Elyce and I have blue eyes but Margaret's are dark brown. I guess that old melanin in her genes had to find some place to reside.

I assume that the first few years in the Cumberbatch family were happy enough; at least, I have no witnesses who swear they weren't. But by the time I was four or five, things had begun to go seriously wrong.

My mother always said that she had never drunk a drop of liquor until she met my father. It was probably true since, after all, she was only sixteen. But, you can take it from me, she made up for any shortfall in consumption later in life.

As little kids, we didn't know exactly what was going on. We'd see Ma pouring herself half a glass of dark brown liquid at ten o'clock in the morning, but we didn't know what it was or why she drank it. Elyce also remembers that when Pa didn't come home for a few days our mother would cry, yell at us and spank us for any small offence.

When he eventually did come home, we would be locked in our room where we still could not escape the bitter words that they hurled at each other.

I was sure that all of Brooklyn could hear those angry voices. You had better believe the people around us heard them through the thin walls of our apartment. And in the summer, with the windows open, the whole neighbourhood was witness. It got so that I was ashamed to look our neighbours in the face.

But in some ways, those were the good days; at least they were talking to each other.

By the time I was ten, the fighting had more or less stopped. All of the emotion had been wrung out of the two of them. Love was long gone, but even the hatred and anger had been exhausted. What was left was nothing at all, unless you count apathy and mistrust.

An unhappy peace settled upon our family. My parents mostly ignored each other. My father had his outside ladies and my mother had her Bushmills Irish whiskey. There was nothing more to fight about.

Ma was never much of a homemaker, even when she wasn't drinking. The house was always an unholy mess and meals were pretty haphazard. Peanut butter with jelly was a gourmet meal at our house. Ma would try to cook something occasionally but, particularly if she'd been drinking, she'd burn it or ruin it by putting too much salt or hot sauce or something in it. The only decent meal we ever had was those rare times when one of my mother's sisters came over and prepared the food.

But, drunk or sober, Ma had a sweetness to her that was very appealing. She would cuddle us and sing Irish songs when we were little. She always insisted that we go to church on Sundays, learn our catechism and do our homework. And we had to give her a kiss when we went off to school and when we returned home.

A liquor store on the block delivered to good customers. We kids would try to interrupt Ma's supply by turning the delivery-man away at the door, but she always had a bottle in reserve and would order up more when we were at school.

We were fighting a losing battle.

In her heart, Ma knew that she was making a mess of her life, but she just couldn't pull herself together. We kids did what we could, but it was never enough.

Pa had apparently decided long ago that there was nothing to be done for Mary Margaret. It seemed to me that at least he should have tried. But Pa was a hard, unforgiving man. You didn't get a second chance from Nate Cumberbatch.

By the time we were teenagers, the drinking had gotten worse. On some days, Ma hardly got out of bed. Pa gave Elyce the money to pay the rent and to buy the groceries. The only money he ever gave Ma was to pay for her booze. Elyce and I begged him not to but he said that she would die if he didn't. He was probably right.

Pa was always a mystery man. He'd come home at four, if he

wasn't working overtime, change out of his work clothes and spend a few hours with us kids. He'd ask us about school and always wanted to see our report cards. He was nice to the girls and overly strict with me – at least, that was how I saw it.

I was into sports like basketball and baseball but Pa, being from the islands, didn't know or care anything about them. The only sport he professed to like was cricket. No one I knew had ever heard of that game.

Pa hardly acknowledged his marriage, only his obligation to us kids. He seldom stayed home in the evenings. About seven, he'd get dressed up and leave, saying, "I'll be spending the evening with some friends."

Pa was involved in an accident at the Naval Yard when I was nine; it messed up his leg and thereafter he walked with a slight limp. At first he was on crutches and then on a cane. After he got better he still carried what he called "my walking stick" if he was going to have to be on his feet for very long. When I think of him, I always think of that stick. It had a big knob, size of your fist, and must have weighed four or five pounds. Anyone else carrying it would have looked ridiculous, but not Pa; he made it look elegant.

Most nights, Pa would return in the early hours. Sometimes, on weekends, he'd be gone for two nights in a row.

It seems odd, but we never talked about these absences, nor did we ever ask him where he'd been. We just accepted his behaviour as the norm. For him, it was.

One thing Pa did do for me was to insist that I spend summers with his mother and family in Barbados. I was eleven the first time, and I went back there each of the next three summers, until I was fourteen.

Pa had to work extra overtime at the Naval Yard each year to pay for my airfare. But he said that it was important for me to know my family and to understand my heritage. It was important for me but apparently not my sisters, because neither ever got to go to Barbados.

It wasn't a great family but, looking back on it, we were probably luckier than some. At least we kids had each other and we still lived as a family. Pa brought home his pay, or at least enough of it to keep us afloat, and he was as good a father to us as he knew how to be. It was just that he was a lousy husband.

Not surprisingly, my sister Margaret and I got out of the house as soon as we could. I enlisted in the Army at eighteen and missed having to go to Vietnam. I was in the Military Police for three years, and for the last two years I was assigned to the special investigative branch of the CID, the Army's Criminal Investigations Division, in Washington. That's how I ended up in the NYPD.

Margaret, always a good student, went upstate to college on a New York State Regent's Scholarship. She met her husband there and lives in a small town. Her husband knows her background but, to the rest of the town, Margaret is as white as they are. She's told them that her dark eyes come from her "Italian grandmother".

Neither of us ever really returned to our parents' home.

Elyce stayed home to take care of Ma. She managed to earn her teaching degree at Brooklyn College while supplying the principal – and probably only – stable element in the Cumberbatch family.

After I left, Ma was in the hospital twice that I knew of. I think she would have liked to quit the drinking, but by then it was too late. She was committed to her bottle of Bushmills a day. Toward the end, she shifted to one hundred proof vodka. But it didn't matter what she was drinking, her health was already ruined.

Mary Margaret O'Brien Cumberbatch died of cirrhosis of the liver, plus complications, on July 19, 1988. She was forty-nine and looked seventy. She deserved better than she got from life.

Nate admitted that he felt bad about Ma, and he conceded that his way of life, his outside women, had been a factor in her drinking, but he claimed that there would have been a problem even if he had been a good husband all his life. Maybe.

"Your mother was never going to be happy," he said. "She wanted to live a life that the Queen of England would envy. Me, my work, you kids, we were holding her back. She wanted to be a star. Not just a movie star, she desperately wanted to be someone really special. But Mary Margaret had no way to make herself into that person. Your Ma never graduated high school. Plus, she inherited a good case of 'the Irish disease'. It was the drink that eventually got her mother, her father and most of her brothers and sisters. Mary Margaret, like most of the other O'Briens, was born with that weakness. She couldn't handle the drink and she couldn't leave it alone.

"I was never a vagabond," Pa said with some pride. "I married your mother and I saw that you children had a roof over your heads. I did what was right by everyone."

Maybe yes, maybe no. In my opinion, it would have been best for everyone if Mary Margaret O'Brien and Nate Cumberbatch had never married, or had gone their separate ways when we kids were still young.

But that's all over now.

Wickham Institute II

August to September 1996

My sister Elyce came to see me every week. She filled me in on what was happening outside, about our sister and her family upstate, about her own job as a schoolteacher in lower Manhattan and, most important, about a new man in her life. This was exciting news. Elyce had never dated much, never even had a serious boyfriend, as far as I knew. But now she had one.

Inevitably, at some point in her visit, I'd say, "How's Pa? When is he going to come to see me?"

Elyce would then say, "Ben, Pa is dead, he was killed by a mugger in the street."

I was saddened and shocked by the news every time, but then I would realise that I had already known that he was dead, I just hadn't remembered it. Either I couldn't remember it or maybe I didn't want to. Both, I guess.

I would give a sorry little laugh and say, "We've had this conversation before, haven't we?"

Elyce would nod and smile and reply, "Don't worry, Ben, you'll get better. Ms Tierney says you are doing very well. Then you'll remember it all, the happy events and the sad ones too, like Pa."

One day I got a message from Shannon that said, "Please come to the conference room on the third floor at three this afternoon."

I pulled myself away from *General Hospital*. There was never anything quite like watching a soap opera with a bunch of head cases who can't remember what has been happening up to now. The arguments were priceless. I hoped to make it back for *Oprah* at four. Depending on the subject, her show could produce even more interesting conversations among my fellow watchers.

At the head of the table was Dr Fine, the psychiatrist assigned to my team. He was tall and balding, about sixty and had a way of staring off into space that made you think that he was getting his instructions from another planet. He introduced me to a much younger man, a Dr Lamont, a new house psychiatrist here at Wickham.

Shannon told me that Dr Fine and Dr Lamont had read my journal about my family and they wanted to ask me some questions. At first, their questions were just general stuff, most of it clarifying what I had written in the journal.

Finally, Fine said to me, "How do you feel about your father at this moment?"

I thought for a long time, remembering Pa as he was. Then I remembered my last conversation with Elyce.

"Sad and angry," I replied.

"Why do you feel that way about your father?"

"Because he's dead. Somebody killed him and I don't know who. And I miss him."

They looked at each other, perplexed. Apparently they hadn't known that Nate was dead. I guess I never had said so in my journal. This wasn't on purpose, I wasn't hiding it, it just kept slipping out of my conscious memory.

Fine was upset. I think he had been planning to do a number on me about my father, probably as a training session for Lamont. He shot Shannon a dirty look.

"It's not Shannon's, I mean Ms Tierney's, fault," I said. "I've never mentioned my father's death to her. Probably when I do speak of him it's as if he's still living."

To cover his embarrassment, Fine asked me to do some more writing. He said that I should write about going to see my grandmother in Barbados. I didn't want to write anything if Fine was going to see it but, to get back to *Oprah*, I agreed.

Shannon caught up with me after *Oprah*.

"Ben, thanks for standing up for me with Dr Fine, but it wasn't necessary. Dr Fine really does care as much about you and your recovery as I do."

Right.

She added, "I want you to do what he asked and try to get more in touch with your own inner feelings. I know those summers you spent as a boy in Barbados were very important to you. See if you can explain why that time has meant so much."

I said that I would try.

My Journal: My first Bajan summer

Barbados, 1969

The Pan Am plane landed and taxied up to a squat cinder block terminal in the hot sunshine. Travelling as an unaccompanied child, I was the last passenger off the plane. The stewardess made me wait, then she took me to the arrivals area. It was all right; I got to go through a special immigration line with the crew while the other passengers stood, sweating, in long lines as officials slowly examined and stamped documents.

I was nearly eleven and tall for my age. I was wearing dark blue long pants, a white, short-sleeved shirt and a black bow tie. I must have looked like a tiny waiter. I had no idea what my grandmother looked like. We had never met and my father had only shown me a faded picture of her. All I knew for sure was that she was a white lady.

I walked into the waiting room where the baggage was being unloaded. My small bag was there. A Customs official waved me through a door.

Outside the terminal, it was crowded, hot and noisy. Anxious, peering faces, more of them black than white, were arrayed behind an iron rail waiting for passengers to emerge. I looked into the eyes of every white lady, regardless of age, hoping that she would be my grandmother. No one paid me any attention.

I waited. One by one the white ladies paired up with arriving passengers and left in their motor cars. Finally, there were no people waiting, just me and the baggage porters.

A tall, stiffly handsome Barbados policeman, in black trousers with a red stripe down the side, grey short-sleeved shirt with three stripes and a black hat with a red band, came over and asked if I was to be met.

"My grandmother is picking me up."

The policeman asked, "What is the name of your grandmother?"

"She's called Eudora Glenville and she lives at Glenville House, in St Charles parish." My father had made me memorise these details.

The information apparently explained everything.

"She coming. It be a long way. You just rest over here by me."

He gave me a small stool to sit on by his desk.

It is nearly seven miles to the airport from my grandmother's house. In Barbados, in 1969, that was a long way.

An hour later, or so it seemed to me, a donkey-drawn cart showed up. A middle-aged, heavy-set white man, dressed in overalls and wearing a broad-brimmed straw hat, was driving a mean-looking donkey. An older woman, with a hat tied under her chin, sat next to him.

She jumped down from the cart like a young person. She looked at me solemnly, appraising me, as I stood expectantly by the policeman's desk.

Then she smiled and said, "You must be Ben. Welcome to Barbados, Ben Cumberbatch. Sorry we weren't here to greet you but our truck wouldn't start."

She told me to call her Grandma Dora. This was OK with me. I called my mother's mother Grandmother O'Brien, so this seemed natural.

The man reached down and helped me up onto the seat next to him. Grandma Dora loaded my suitcase onto the wagon and then climbed to the seat next to me.

I listened hard to what Grandma Dora said, but her accent and some of the words were strange. I could understand maybe half. She said that the man driving the cart was my uncle, Clarence Glenville. He had yet to say a word. I was dying to ask him why he was Glenville and he was white and my father, his brother, was Cumberbatch and black. Nobody thought to explain this to me.

The sun was setting with an orange-gold glow behind us. Compared to the asphalt streets and brick multi-storeyed buildings of Brooklyn, Barbados was incredibly lush and green. The air was humid but surprisingly not nearly as hot as Brooklyn had been when I left. And the air smelled of flowers. But at times I would catch a less pleasant, pungent odour. I was to learn that this was fresh cow and sheep manure, recently spread on the fields.

Nearly all the fields were growing the same crop, a tall green plant with many long, narrow leaves and a banded stalk. It reminded me of the corn that our neighbour, old Mr Novelli, used to grow behind our apartment building, but this plant wasn't corn, it was much taller. And, in the wind, the crowded stalks rubbed together and made a soft, rustling sound that was pleasant to hear.

"That's sugar cane," my grandmother said, pointing. "That's what has made Barbados great."

Uncle Clarence never uttered a word but he watched to see how I reacted to what his mother said. If I said something in return, he smiled and mumbled a private comment to himself. His silence was strange, yet he had a twinkle in his eye and seemed kind and gentle.

As we entered St Charles parish, it was getting dark. That summer I would learn that, in the tropics, night falls suddenly, giving little warning. It goes from bright sunshine to dusk in minutes.

Soon it was dark, we could barely see the road ahead, but the donkey plodded along the familiar trail.

"It is not far now," Grandma Dora said.

If possible, the roads had gotten worse. The pleasant, cool breeze now carried a faint sound of crashing surf, and I realised that the broad green-blue sea I'd seen from the plane loomed somewhere in the dark not far ahead of us, out of view.

I could see lights burning brightly at a large white house, which was briefly visible down a long row of towering palm trees. I looked at the house, then looked quizzically at my grandmother.

"That is the great house of Savannah Plantation, one of the oldest and grandest plantations in all of Barbados."

She grasped my hand firmly and looked me in the eyes.

"But, Ben, listen to me. That is not a good place to go. You must promise me that you will stay away from there."

She uttered this warning with an ominous ferocity. Grandma Dora never used that tone of voice except when she spoke of Savannah Plantation.

I promised never to go near the mysterious plantation. Of course, my curiosity had been set in motion. In truth, I was not greatly committed to keeping this promise.

We plodded along past fields of dark, rustling sugar cane. We left the main road and the donkey slowly pulled the cart up a narrow, steep, rutted dirt road to our left. We entered a small village consisting of tattered but interesting-looking wooden houses. Grandma Dora called them "chattel houses". Some were painted in bright colours. Most of them were made of weathered boards and looked as if they would collapse with the next strong wind. And, like my neighbourhood in Brooklyn, some of the people standing around were white and some were black.

A sign declared this village to be Glenville.

We turned left off the street just past the last house. The donkey strained to pull up a small rise. A sign said that we were at our destination, Glenville House.

Glenville appeared to be much larger than the chattel houses in the small town. The two-storey structure was obviously old and had a wide, sagging veranda on all four sides. The next morning, I discovered that large, colourful vines grew up the veranda posts and a neat garden of flowers and strange plants filled the front yard.

The windows contained no glass. They were made of small wooden slats which Grandma Dora called "flaps". Between the slats of the window on the right I could see the soft glow of a single electric light.

We were met at the door by the third member of my Barbados family, my Aunt Emily. She stood waiting in the shadows inside the door. As we entered, Grandma Dora said something about food and that I was probably starving. It was true, I was famished.

Aunt Emily scurried into the lighted kitchen. Uncle Clarence brought my small suitcase into the living room and Grandma Dora, flashlight in hand, showed me the way up to a small bedroom on the second floor.

She called it "Clarence's room". I worried that I was taking my uncle's bedroom but Grandma Dora assured me that Clarence hadn't slept there in years. I would learn that Uncle Clarence now lived behind the main house by himself in a small shed. It was set in the garden so that my uncle had his privacy and, at the same time, could protect the ripening vegetables from enterprising visitors – either human thieves or, even more destructive, bands of Barbados green monkeys.

I unpacked, then went downstairs and into the kitchen, still the only room that was lit. Aunt Emily was peering into the pots on the stove and Clarence and Grandma Dora were at a round wooden table. I joined them, sitting between my grandmother and aunt and opposite Uncle Clarence.

When Aunt Emily turned I saw her face clearly for the first time; I gasped. Aunt Emily was white, white, white. Her hair was a sickly whitish-yellow. Her eyes were pale blue, nearly no colour at all, and her skin was the whitest skin that I had ever seen. She looked like she had never been in the sun.

Grandma Dora noticed my reaction.

"Ben, didn't your Daddy tell you that Emily is albino? Don't you be frightened like some ignorant folks around here. They say that our Emily is a duppy."

Emily shyly ducked her head and turned to the stove. Uncle Clarence laughed softly at the idea that his sister was a duppy. I knew what a duppy was because my father always says that when he is referring to a ghost. Sometimes he would say to Margaret, "Girl, you're as white as a duppy."

Grandma Dora pronounced albino as al-bean-o, three distinct syllables. I'd never heard the term. The reference to a bean made me think of a food intolerance condition. Margaret had one; she couldn't eat dairy products. Maybe poor Aunt Emily reacted badly to certain vegetables.

Nothing more was ever said about Aunt Emily's condition. I'm not sure that anyone knew anything more to say.

We had a good dinner of rice and peas and fried chicken and some vegetables I'd never seen before. It was all good to eat, and I would have liked to stay up talking with my newfound family but, with my stomach full, my eyes began to droop.

Grandma Dora lit the way upstairs for me with her flashlight, she called it a "torch". As she closed the door she said, "Nate has been promising to come to see us for years. I would love to see him but I am just as pleased that he has sent you to us. Sleep well, Ben Cumberbatch."

The next morning I woke before six with bright sunlight shining in my eyes. I lay in the narrow bed and listened to a symphony of unfamiliar sounds: the cries and chirping of wild birds, the crowing of roosters, screeching tree frogs and a strange low "chunk-chunk" which Grandma Dora said was the monkeys that lived in the gully nearby. It was all so new.

Grandma Dora showed me around Glenville House. There were four large rooms on each floor. Upstairs there was a big bedroom that was Grandma's; one nearly as big that was Emily's; and then the one that I had, the one that had been Uncle Clarence's. A fourth bedroom, the smallest, was being used as a sewing room.

Downstairs there was a formal living room in which we never did sit. On a table there was a photograph of a beautiful young woman. I meant to ask who she was but I forgot and didn't find out until later. There was also a dining room used only for Sunday dinners and for the four birthdays I would spend there, numbers eleven through fourteen.

The kitchen was the second largest room on the ground floor. It had the usual sink and a large wood-burning stove. There was a table on which meals were prepared and other kitchen work, such as canning, was done. There was also a round table with four chairs where we would eat most of our meals.

Behind the kitchen was a small room Grandma called her office. Mostly it was there that she kept her records and important papers, like the deed to Glenville House, her father's will, and her own will. These documents were kept in a square metal box secured by a hasp and lock.

Aunt Emily had put a big breakfast on the table. We ate fried eggs, home-made bread and fresh fruit. I ate my first ever mango. To me, it tasted like a peach with a huge pit, only better. The juice dripped down my chin and arms. Emily, with a shy smile, gave me another.

At seven o'clock we walked fifty feet uphill to where the garden began. It was the biggest garden I had ever seen. Grandma Dora told me proudly that it covered nearly two acres. Uncle Clarence began by hoeing weeds from between rows of green beans.

Everything grew there that you could imagine: sweet potatoes, English potatoes, yams, onions, carrots, beans, okra, cauliflower, beets, pigeon peas, belly pumpkin, eggplant and more. At the end of the garden were fruit trees. Some of these trees bore fruit I recognised – oranges, grapefruit, lemons, limes – and others I had never seen or heard of – guava, golden apple, pawpaw, shaddock and soursop.

We weeded and loosened the thick clay soil around the plants with our hoes until late morning. I asked questions incessantly and Grandma Dora patiently answered them. I suspected that Uncle Clarence knew the answers too, but he always waited silently for his mother to answer. And once, when she didn't hear one of my questions, Clarence answered. His accent was even harder to understand than Grandma's, but at least I now knew that he could talk when he chose to.

We returned to the house for lunch. Grandma Dora and I left our muddy shoes on the veranda by the door to the kitchen. Uncle Clarence was barefoot, but Emily had a bucket of water for him to wash his feet and a towel to dry them.

It was only eleven thirty but I was starving and the sun was getting hot. Emily had prepared a large meal and we all ate heartily. After lunch, we napped. Then we went back to do more gardening from three until five thirty.

A big cast-iron tank sat above ground in the middle of the garden. It held the water for the irrigation of the vegetables. Uncle Clarence showed me how the water ran off the roof into a big tank – he called it a cistern – under the house. From there, a small electric pump pushed the water through a galvanized iron pipe above ground, up into the cast-iron tank in the garden.

Once a week we loaded the small truck, if it was working, with boxes of vegetables to sell in Bridgetown, the capital and only city, fifteen miles away. Grandma Dora drove and I stood in the back holding on tight, watching to see that nothing fell off as we bumped over the rough roads.

The bustling market was a welcome change from the quiet, repetitive life at Glenville. Country people came here from all over the island to sell their produce to the residents of Bridgetown and to each other.

Virtually all of the people selling vegetables were women and Grandma Dora was one of the few of them that were white. Mostly they were big, jolly, rough-talking black ladies wearing long skirts with aprons where they kept their money in large wads of bills. They laughed and joked with each other and with their customers, black and white, but never with Grandma Dora. For some reason, she was left to her own. Out of respect? Out of fear? I never did learn why.

Life at Glenville House followed the same routine every week. Three of us worked in the garden from Monday to Friday and then Grandma Dora and I went to the market in Bridgetown on Saturday. Sunday was a day off, a day of rest, but not one of worship. The Glenvilles did not go to church.

In the evenings, after dinner, we sat out on the veranda to enjoy the breeze. At first, it would be just Grandma and me, but after a while Uncle Clarence and, when the kitchen work was done, Aunt Emily, would join us. I asked the questions and Grandma Dora answered them.

Church

One evening, I asked why they never went to church. At home, Ma made us go to the Catholic church. To tell you the truth, I was not all that keen on church myself but it would have been a welcome change from working in the garden and I might have gotten to meet some people my age. There was a beautiful small church on a hill, near Morton's Cove, not a fifteen-minute walk away.

Grandma Dora chuckled.

"Ben, I had my fill of churching when I was young. No amount of religion ever did me that much good."

Aunt Emily giggled and Uncle Clarence covered his mouth. Apparently religion was a humorous subject with the Glenvilles.

But I couldn't leave it at that.

"But, Grandma Dora," I asked, "what happened to make you feel that way?"

For a good minute she didn't say a word. I feared that I had offended her by asking her to explain herself. But it was not that at all. She was just reviewing how and what to say about the good Reverend Henry Hawthorne and his wife Martha.

"It was 1925, I was sixteen years old," she started.

"These two," she inclined her head towards Clarence and Emily, "were still in their nappies. He," she pointed at Clarence, "was under two and Em was just six months old. The Reverend showed up with a constable and a writ from the court saying that me and the children would have to leave Glenville and come to live in his house with him and his wife.

"Pa was fit to be tied. You see, I was his only child, and since my mother had died six years before I'd been keeping house, doing all the cooking and cleaning. We had big gardens then, but Pa was not one to do the work himself; he would hire the work out to our worthless cousins in the village. They'd hoe and weed and carry the water up to the field from the cistern. Pa and I would pick the ripe vegetables and sell or barter them in Glenville or Morton's Cove.

"I was strong and did what I could, when I wasn't tending the children. Pa depended on me for a lot of chores. But the constable made it very clear that there was no choice: the court's order had to be followed, me and the children would have to live with the Hawthornes. We ended up living with them for four and a half years.

"Henry Hawthorne was a Methodist minister with a congregation near Farley Hill, not too far from Speightstown on the West Coast. Hawthorne and his wife Martha were still young, barely in their thirties, and this was his first church.

"They had no children of their own, and maybe it was because of that sadness that the Hawthornes treated Clarence and Emily so good. I had my own room and the children were in a room across the hall. We ate the same food as the Hawthornes and, of course, we prayed a lot. Mostly we prayed for my soul and for those of Clarence and Emily.

"On Sundays we went to church. Before the service, I would put fresh flowers all around the church. Then the service would go on for hours. At a certain point, Martha would take the big children for Sunday school and I'd look after the little ones that couldn't read.

"Of course, I had to work for our keep. I'd clean the house and help the cook prepare and serve the meals. I also worked in their flower garden and, after the first year, I put in a small vegetable garden, although nothing as big as ours at Glenville.

"Clarence, as little as he was, helped me in the garden but Emily, 'cause of her al-bean-o, had to stay out of the sun. I could take her outside if I could lay her in the shade but mostly Martha tended to her inside.

"It was because of Emily that we ended up at the Hawthornes' in the first place," Grandma Dora continued. Clarence laughed and Emily hid her face and giggled.

"You see, word had gotten out about Em's al-bean-o and folks would come to Glenville to see her. Pa chased them away, but people talked and somehow word of it got to the Hawthornes.

"The Reverend Henry was a good man and, of course, very religious. He had it in his mind that I needed a lot of special attention from the Lord, so every morning and every night me and the babies would be prayed over. To tell you the truth, it got right tedious. Mrs Hawthorne was different. She left the religion to her husband and taught me things that she thought I ought to know, like cooking, taking proper care of the children and sewing and such.

"Also, she gave me some school learning. I'd had a few years at school up until Mama died but I barely knew anything about housekeeping and less about reading and writing. I guess I knew my letters and could count, but not much else. Martha, Mrs Hawthorne, taught me to read and write proper. Once I got the knack of it, I got pretty good at it, too.

"She had me reading all kinds of books. Of course, the Bible, but also other books. I read the history of Barbados and I learned how redlegs, like us Glenvilles, ended up here on the east coast like we did. And I read some of what Martha called her 'women's books'. They were novels, you know what I mean, love stories and adventures.

"Martha also taught me how to sew clothes, how to dress myself to look nice and how to fix my hair. She even showed me the way to use powder, rouge and lip colouring. But we never put it on or wore it in front of her husband. He would not have approved.

"Martha and me got to be real good friends, almost like sisters. And she was wonderful with my children, she loved them like they were her own. She had doctors come in to look at Clarence because he did not begin to talk when he should. He was four and he only had a few words.

"The doctors said that was just the way Clarence was, that he probably would never be much of a talker. Isn't that right, Clarence?"

Uncle Clarence nodded his head. That's the way it was.

Grandma Dora continued, "Martha told me that Clarence's problem, and probably Emily's too, was because we redlegs were all related to each other. It didn't make too much sense to me, but that's what she said.

"The Reverend Hawthorne was called back by his Church in 1930. We'd been living with them for over four years by then. He was to go somewhere else, to leave Barbados, to take over a new church. Martha wanted to take us with them, but the Church authorities would not hear of it.

"I was now twenty-one, Clarence was six and Emily was four. I hadn't seen hide nor hair of Pa for the whole time, over four years. But I knew that he'd gotten married to someone from the village. Anyway, the Hawthornes were leaving and the authorities sent us back to live with Pa.

"Martha Hawthorne and me had a good cry when we parted. I was most grateful for what they'd done for the children and for what I had learned. I would miss her, but I wasn't too sorry to be saying goodbye to her husband and all that praying."

I interrupted, "Grandma, is that picture in the living room Martha Hawthorne?"

"Oh no," she laughed, "that's a picture of me that the Hawthornes had taken in Bridgetown. They kept a copy and I was given a copy as a going-away present. They also gave me several books and Martha gave me most of her lightweight clothes. She said that where they were going, she wouldn't need them."

I later went back and looked at the picture again. It was Grandma Dora for sure. She'd been beautiful as a young woman. Her skin had become rough and red, she had lots of wrinkles and her hair was grey, not brown like in the picture, but I still recognised her.

Grandma Dora continued her story.

"Pa was glad to have us back but his new wife, Teresa, wasn't. Teresa Glenville was my cousin and was only a year older than me. I could see right away that Teresa and her Glenvilles, the ones that lived in the village down the hill, saw her marriage to Pa as a way for them to gain control of our house and land. Of course, this upset me because I was Pa's only child and I had grown up being told that I would inherit Glenville some day.

49

"Teresa and Pa had been trying to have a child and, if they had one, me and mine would have been out in the rain for sure. But she couldn't get pregnant and then Pa took sick. A year after we moved back to Glenville, he died.

"The will that Pa left said that I was to get Glenville and, upon my death, it should pass to Clarence."

Grandma Dora stopped, reached over and patted Clarence on the knee, as if to reassure him that he was up to the job of running Glenville. Clarence smiled weakly and then put his head down. I could not see his face hidden in the dark shadows on the veranda.

Redlegs

A few nights later I asked Grandma Dora to tell me why the Glenvilles were called "redlegs".

"Well, Ben, that's quite a story," Grandma Dora said. "You see, when the first English settlers arrived on Barbados in 1627, there was no one here in Barbados, no people at all. There had once been Indians, but they had left for some reason. The island had been named Barbados by some Portuguese sailors who'd passed by in a ship. The word 'Barbados' means 'bearded'. Some say they may have been referring to the bearded fig trees which are common here.

"The land was covered with mahogany and the other tropical trees so the first job for the settlers was to clear the land to plant cotton and tobacco.

"The white settlers were of two types, the high whites and the lesser whites. The high whites were the sons of the old wealthy class in England. They'd come out here to make their fortunes, and with them they brought the lesser whites to do the physical work. These poor souls were mostly Scots and Irish prisoners from the various civil wars in England, or they were debtors from the jails. It is said that they were called 'redlegs' because their fair skin did not take kindly to working out in the hot Caribbean sun.

"Most redlegs had been sentenced to work for a landowner for six or eight years, then, at the end, they were supposed to get a small plot of land of their own. Many poor souls died from the hard work, poor food and disease before their term was up. And for those who did survive, the owners usually found reasons not to honour their promises of land. The poor redlegs had little choice but to continue to work for the low wages offered by the landowners.

"To replace the ones that died, there were always more prisoners or debtors arriving from England's jails. At first they were all men, but later they started bringing in women. By 1650 Barbados was covered with small farms, owned by the wealthy families and worked by redlegs.

"Then something important happened, something that would change Barbados forever. Sugar cane was brought here from Brazil. It grew very well here and soon Barbados sugar and Barbados rum were commanding big prices overseas. The landowners became very wealthy and bought up and combined the small farms into bigger ones. These larger farms they called plantations and they were devoted full time to growing sugar cane.

"The redlegs were not able to do the heavy field labour required to grow sugar cane but the black man, being basically stronger and better able to take the heat, could. There'd been very few black slaves in Barbados up until then because they were expensive to buy. However, with sugar, the owners were now wealthy and they could afford to buy slaves from other islands and from the African slavers.

"Soon, most redlegs were out of work. A few found work on the plantations but others left Barbados for other islands like Antigua and Jamaica or for America. In fact they say that the first five Governors of the state of South Carolina in America were born here in Barbados.

"The Glenvilles, like many redleg families, stayed on. They were forced to come to this area of the island to live. All the good farm land was being used for sugar and only the steep land here on the east coast, between Hackleton's Cliff and the sea, was available. This land was judged worthless for planting sugar cane. The redlegs settled here, some fished and others scratched out a bare living farming." Grandma Dora swept her arm so that I would know that Glenville was part of this modest history.

"Glenvilles have been here on Barbados for well over three hundred years. Mostly we have remained poor and uneducated, shut off from the rest of Barbados, at least until recently. You see, redlegs only married other redlegs. I guess the high whites wouldn't have us and redlegs, stubborn and proud, wouldn't marry freed slaves. Because of our limited numbers, we had no choice but to marry kin, cousins, even brothers and sisters.

"After the slaves were freed, they looked down on redlegs. They called us 'backra-johnnies'. I think that 'backra' is an African word meaning 'white man' but, when they used it for us, it was a disrespectful term. They reckoned that they were better off and better educated than the redlegs and, in many instances, they were."

"Grandma," I asked, "What are people like me called, people that are both black and white?"

"Ben, they call you 'light-skinned' or 'red man'. But here we just call you our Ben. Don't you worry about it, just be what you are and be proud of it.

"Finally some Church people took pity and began to give us some education and looked after our children's health. Eventually, some of us found work in Bridgetown and today some of the most successful people on the island come from redleg stock.

"Unfortunately, the Glenvilles were not one of the families to have been so blessed, but we have been better off than most."

Grandma Dora ended her story there and she smiled at her two grown children. She also had a big hug for her half Irish, one-quarter light-skinned, one-quarter redleg, grandson from America.

Lester Cumberbatch

Every Sunday, we had our main meal at noon. Both Grandma Dora and Aunt Emily started cooking early in the morning. Sometimes Emily prepared some of the Sunday dishes on the day before. We would have chicken or duck or a leg of a blackbelly sheep for which Grandma Dora had bartered green beans and pumpkin at the market in Bridgetown.

After Sunday dinner Uncle Clarence and I would go for a walk. Usually it was along the windy coral cliffs of St Charles, above the crashing surf. Uncle Clarence, who was always barefoot, would climb down over the sharp coral to point out the nests of sea birds. Sometimes he would help me down the cliff; I never worried because he was so strong and steady.

One evening, I asked my grandma to tell me about my father's father, Lester Cumberbatch. I reckoned this way I would be able to learn why there were both Glenvilles and Cumberbatches in my family.

"Oh Lord, that man!" Grandma Dora laughed. It appeared that she had happy memories of my grandfather.

"The year after Pa died, my first year running Glenville, I nearly killed myself from overwork. I had nobody to help. You see, Teresa's family, my cousins, turned against me and wouldn't work for me, even for wages. And they discouraged other people from working for me, threatening to burn their houses if they did. Their plan, I am sure, was to have me fail or kill myself trying, so they could take over Glenville House and the gardens. They almost got their way."

Grandma Dora looked grim as she recalled those difficult days.

"My biggest problem was how to get the water from the cistern up to the garden. For years we'd carried it up, two buckets at a time. But with just me to look after the kids, the house and tend the garden, small as it was in those years, I couldn't also haul the water. I had neither the time nor the strength to do it. But we'd gotten electricity into Glenville village a few years before, so I looked into the possibility of using a small electric pump to get the water up the hill.

"The people in Bridgetown told me it was possible to pump the water but I would need pipe and some kind of a catchment in the garden to store it. That's where your grandfather, Lester Cumberbatch, came in. He was from St John parish, where he'd worked at Calverton Plantation as a boilerman in the sugar factory. It was the early 1930s and it was bad times all over the world. The sugar industry was hurting bad. Lester had been let go at Calverton and was out looking for work.

"One day I looked up and there he was. Over six foot tall, with a trim moustache and sideburns and a big smile that would charm birds from the trees. I told him what I needed: pipe plus a big metal catchment to hold the water.

"He told me what it would cost. Unfortunately it was more than I had. After paying for the pump, I wouldn't have the money to buy the pipe and materials for the tank and pay him. I was afraid that was that, but Lester said that he knew where he could get what I needed at a good price. I found out later that what he planned to do was 'borrow' the materials from Calverton Plantation.

"I still didn't have enough money, but I offered him a proposition. I'd buy the pump and pay him what I could towards the low price he'd quoted on the materials, if he would not charge me for making the tank and would help me in the garden for twelve months. In return, I'd give him one half of whatever we grew or made selling our vegetables.

"It doesn't sound like much of a deal for him now but, remember, Lester didn't have a job or any prospects. I was offering him the chance to sell me Calverton's iron plate and the other materials that he'd get at no cost, and he would end up with a job. Anyway, he took it. He told me later that the real reason he took it was because he admired my looks. The truth is, the admiration was mutual."

I swear that Grandma Dora blushed.

"We worked together in the garden for a year. He was always respectful and never overstepped his bounds. Prices were rock bottom at the market but we had bumper crops that year and we were able to sell some of the vegetables and barter most of the rest for what we needed.

"Lester had told me in the beginning that he had a woman and children up in St John. However, he spent most of his time here at Glenville. He slept on the porch at night and went to St John only on Sundays.

"Our arrangement was for one year. On the anniversary of the arrangement, I had all of his money, that which he had not drawn in advance, ready to pay him. I was unhappy to be losing him. Working together plus having the water for irrigation, we'd been able to expand the garden. I didn't know how I was going to get by in the garden without him, but at least now I had the new electric pump for the water and some cash to hire someone else, if I could find anyone who would not be threatened by the Glenvilles.

"Lester could see my unhappiness. He would have ended our arrangement in a second if he had a job to go to, but Calverton's was still not hiring. Lester said to me that he would be agreeable to extending our arrangement for another twelve months but only if he didn't have to sleep on the porch.

"I knew right away what he meant. He wanted to move into the house with me. Now you know that Lester was light-skinned, and that redleg families like the Glenvilles had not mixed their blood with that of coloured folk. We were supposed to only marry other redlegs but, as I told you, the Hawthornes had warned me that this mixing with relatives was the reason that some of the redleg children had problems."

As she said this, Grandma lowered her voice and glanced to see if Clarence and Emily were following what she was saying. Neither of them moved nor blinked an eye, but I would bet that they were listening very carefully.

She continued, "I knew that if Lester moved into Glenville House that there would be children. What they call 'mulattos' some places, but here in Barbados we call them 'light-skinned children'. And, as if they needed any more reason, I would be completely outcast from my relatives and the rest of the redleg families. But I wanted more children in my life and I didn't want there to be any problems. I sure didn't fancy any of my Glenville cousins, particularly since they had all sided with Teresa against me. Anyway, Lester was the handsomest man I'd ever seen. He moved in that night.

"We were together for over five years and we had four children. Your father, Nathaniel, was the eldest. He was followed by twin girls, Alice and Amy, and then the youngest, my little Thomas."

This was the first time I had ever heard that my father had a brother and sisters. Why had I never known of them?

"Every month Lester would go up to St John to see his other family. I wasn't happy about that but I tried to be understanding. He had obligations there that had to be met.

"Our twins died when they were two, of the diphtheria. This nearly broke Lester's heart. He loved those little girls. He loved them all, but he had a special place in his heart for those two.

"By now it was 1938. Things were picking up because of the world war that was brewing. Lester went back to his old job at

Calverton's. But the machinery at the sugar factory was old and rusted from disuse, so that a gauge stuck on the boiler. Your grandfather was working on it when the boiler split and scalded him. He lived for a month but died of pneumonia in the hospital," she said sadly.

"Your pa, Nate, was four when Lester died, and Thomas was just walking. Emily was twelve and she was a lot of help with the children and keeping up the house. Clarence was fourteen and big for his age. Since he didn't go to school, he was home and able to help me in the garden. I hired help as I needed it, just as we still do, but Clarence and I were able to take on most of the work ourselves."

I asked, "Where is my Uncle Thomas? Does he live here in St Charles?"

Grandma Dora looked real sad. "My Thomas was lost to me years ago. He followed Nate to England and has never been home again. And, as you know, your father went on to America and I have never seen him again either, though he does write occasionally. Ours has not been a happy family. We have a saying hereabouts, 'Trouble tree don' bear no blossom'. There was Lester's and the girls' deaths, but it goes back before that, to my mother and father, and even sweet Emily and Clarence have not been spared. Ben, I hate to tell you this, but our family is that trouble tree, and as for the blossoms – happiness and success – we haven't had much of them either."

Uncle Clarence

That Sunday, when Clarence and I were on a walk over to Ragged Point lighthouse, I asked him to tell me about his pa.

He didn't answer me right away but this was not unusual, Clarence frequently didn't answer until he had thought about what he wanted to say. I waited and waited, but time passed and it began to look like Clarence wasn't going to answer at all. Maybe he'd forgotten, so I asked him again.

"Uncle Clarence, tell me about your pa."

Clarence finally spoke. All he said was, "No Pa, Grandpa."

I had no idea what that meant, but I couldn't get another word out of him on the subject.

Glenville House

Grandma Dora's everyday language was laced with what she called "country sayings", like "Too long honest, too long poor", and "If greedy wait, pot will cool". She said that she had heard these and other proverbs all her life, both from redlegs and from the black folk. For example, when I was upset because I couldn't drive the truck, she said, "Ben, don't fret, every man's day does come." When I asked her to explain something, it was "Remember, common sense was born before book." And on her favourite subject, the family, she would always say "Water does run but blood does clot."

There were many other proverbs. Some were funny and made me laugh, and some were sad. Grandma Dora said that they reminded us of how hard life had been in the old days on the plantations for poor people, slaves, freedmen and redlegs. I remembered a lot of them in later life and from time to time I would even use them on the job, when appropriate. For example, I'd say, "Softee softee catchee monkey" when I thought we were rushing an investigation, and in the not infrequent instances when one crook stole from another I'd say, "When thief thief from thief, Satan laugh." My friend Tom Moran used to tease me about them. He would call me "the Bajan Aesop".

Some of Grandma Dora's stories I had heard many times over the years. Probably the stories were true – at least, I know that all of us sitting on the veranda at Glenville House believed every word. Sometimes they would be delivered with a great deal of description; sometimes she'd let us fill in the details from our memories and our own imaginations.

You'd have to say that Dora Glenville was a natural storyteller, and that she was at her best when someone like me was there, an audience, someone in addition to Clarence and Em.

Every summer, I'd hear the stories. My favourite was the one of how the Glenvilles got their land in the first place. I can write it as I heard it, all those years ago.

The first Glenvilles came to Barbados in the 1640s. Nearly two hundred and fifty years later, by the 1880s, Grandma Dora's great-grandfather, Frank Glenville, and his wife and three children, were living in a small house in Morton's Cove.

Frank had been a fisherman but he'd lost his boat in a storm. Having no land to cultivate, he scratched out an existence by gathering and selling the coconuts, breadfruit and other edibles that grew wild on the steep slopes of St Charles parish.

One day he was working on the hillside above where the steep slopes of St Charles parish levelled out to meet the broad, flat fields to the east. He was climbing coconut trees and, using his cutlass, chopping coconuts loose. After which he would come down and gather the fallen coconuts into piles, intending to collect them later with a cart.

He had shimmied up a tall coconut tree on the brim of the hill, from where he overlooked all the fields of Savannah Plantation. They were planted in sugar cane, much of it soon to be ready for harvest. He also saw the single track of the narrow-gauge railway that ran along the edge of the plantation to the small railroad siding serving Savannah Plantation. It was bare except for two large empty molasses barrels which had just been returned from a rum factory in Bridgetown.

The railway connected the rural parishes with the port and businesses of Bridgetown. The train came twice a day, carrying passengers and finished goods to the plantations and shipping the raw sugar and molasses from the plantations' sugar factories back to Bridgetown for processing and export.

Frank noticed that on the far side of the nearest cane field three men had surrounded a woman seated sidesaddle on a horse. They were on the cart track that separated this field from the next.

One man was talking to the woman and laughing. Frank watched to see what would occur next.

The woman seemed angry; she pulled her reins and turned her horse as if to leave but another man grabbed the bridle. The horse reared and Frank could hear the woman shout for the man to let her horse loose. As her horse spun around and around, she struck at the man with her riding crop but to no effect. Then the third man, a big man, reached up, grabbed the woman from behind and hauled her roughly from her saddle to the ground.

Now Frank's view was limited, partially obscured by the tall canes. Hardly knowing why, he climbed down the tree and, cutlass in hand, worked his way down the hill and across the field. The cane was thick but he could clearly hear angry voices, male and female.

As he approached the edge of the cane, Frank stopped and peered through the long green leaves. To his left, a man stood holding the horse. Another man, the largest of the three, held the woman's arms from behind. A third man, his back towards Frank, seemed to be taunting the woman.

Frank could see she was young and very frightened. He assumed that she must be someone grand from Savannah Plantation. He'd had little exposure to her kind but he judged her to be no more than sixteen or seventeen. Her grey riding dress was torn, probably when she was dragged from her saddle. He also saw that though frightened she remained defiant; her eyes glistened with anger and tears.

The men were dressed like the sailors he'd seen come ashore in Bridgetown. He wondered what they were doing in a cane field way out here in St Charles.

What Frank would not know until much later was that the trio had come ashore from a British merchant ship, the *Covenant*, early the day before. They'd gone directly into the Union Jack, a pub catering to sailors, located in a dilapidated street just off the Careenage in Bridgetown.

Mac Squint, the smallest of the three, was their leader. His real name was Bill MacMahon, but aboard the *Covenant* there was another sailor of the same surname so, to avoid confusion in giving orders, the taller man was called Mac Long and Bill was Mac Squint – so named for his left eye, permanently at half mast since his childhood in Glasgow, after one too many blows to his head by the senior MacMahon. Aboard ship, Squint was adept at keeping a low profile and doing as little hard labour as possible. But once on dry land he could be counted on to lead his friends to trouble, if there was any trouble to be had.

In physical contrast to Squint, Walt Damon was a mountain of a man, six and a half feet tall and weighing nearly three hundred pounds. His strength was legendary and the officers and bosuns used it to good effect on the *Covenant*, where he was always given the heaviest tasks. But the big man was slow-moving and slow-thinking. "Damon the dimwit" he was called, and was often the butt of jokes by his shipmates, including Squint. However, ashore Squint was always happy to have Damon at his side when trouble arose.

The third member of this unpromising group was Tom Malley, a barrel-maker and joiner. Malley, a competent enough member of the *Covenant*'s crew, was, like many sailors, a heavy drinker and brawler when off the ship and was known to have a violent temper when challenged.

The three came into the pub out of the bright midday Barbados sun, unable to see anything in the dark, low-ceilinged

61

room that was both a store and a bar. There, seafaring men bought tobacco, canned goods and sundries to take back to their ships. However, for the most part, the Union Jack thrived by dispensing good cheap Barbados rum by the glass or the bottle to thirsty sailors.

As their eyes adjusted, the sailors saw a large British flag, painted on a wood panel, mounted on the wall behind the bar. The proprietor, a red-faced, beefy man in a white apron, leaned forward and asked, "What'll it be?" as he slapped a large bottle of clear liquid on the bar.

Soon they were into their second bottle of white rum and Squint was looking for trouble. Two stevedores, redlegs in their twenties, came into the Union Jack to get a drink or two of rum before they completed offloading the *Covenant*.

Squint engaged them in an innocent conversation. Under Squint's calculated guidance, the conversation escalated from ribald jokes to obscene slurs and, finally, to heavy-handed insults.

The two bandy-legged Bajans were angered but reluctant to start a fight. They were outnumbered and wisely wary of Damon's size, plus they feared that a brawl might cost them their jobs as stevedores. They needed the pay they would earn by this day's end. They left the pub pursued by Squint's acid and obscene remarks and the mocking laughter of his companions.

When the day's labours were finished and they had been paid, the two Bajans returned to the Union Jack. This time, however, they were accompanied by four other stevedores, all friends or relatives.

There were few preliminaries; the fighting began as soon as the Bajans came in the door. Squint and his companions were drunk enough to welcome the fight, and nearly experienced and tough enough to win it, despite being outnumbered. But by the time the police constables arrived, the sailors were being worn down by the sheer number of their opponents. The constables admonished the locals and marched the *Covenant* troublemakers off to jail. There they would sleep off the effects of their first day ashore in Barbados.

In the morning, hung over and surly, the three were fined, released and ordered to return to their ship or face rearrest. Going back to the ship was the last thing they wanted to do. They still had another day of shore leave and, if they returned early, the bosun and the captain would know for sure that they had been in trouble. The captain had warned them as they left the ship that they would be "beached" at the next port of call – the tiny island of Bequia – if they caused any trouble in Bridgetown.

Malley, who had a wife and family waiting for him back in Bristol, said, "Squint, we can't go back to the *Covenant* or there'll be hell to pay."

"You're right, but we have to be careful."

Squint was wary of the tough-talking Bridgetown police.

They each bought a bottle of rum from a street vendor and then walked over to the train terminal. There they paid sixpence each for tickets on the newly-built Barbados railway.

There was a two-hour wait for the next train. In order to stay out of the way of the constables they sat, out of sight, on the bank of a dry creek bed that ran behind the station. There they drank rum and talked endlessly of the Union Jack brawl and other fights. The train was late, and by the time it arrived all three were drunk.

Squint and his friends lurched onto the train noisily, under the suspicious glare of the conductor. For the first hour, they just drank and enjoyed the passing scenery. Growing bored, they began to sing and to poke fun at country women walking with heavy loads of goods balanced precariously on their heads, and at the farmers tilling their fields with sturdy brown oxen. The sailors' loutish behaviour irritated their fellow passengers. The conductor several times asked them to be quiet, but they mocked him and continued.

The train made frequent stops as it turned inland and chugged through miles of sugar cane plantations. Frequently it stopped to offload empty molasses barrels and to onload full ones. The conductor used one of these stops to rid himself of his unwanted passengers. He called the engineer and the two labourers who handled the freight and, armed with clubs and cutlasses, the four men forced the sailors off the train.

The offloaded trio found themselves at a deserted siding; a small sign said "Savannah Plantation". The conductor told them that the train would be back the next morning.

"And, if you're sober and prepared to behave yourselves, you can get back on and return to Bridgetown."

The train moved off and was soon out of sight.

The sailors looked around. All they could see was tall, green sugar cane, towering far above their heads.

The young woman who had the bad luck to run into Squint and his friends was Barbara Mount, the eighteen-year-old daughter of Augustus Mount, owner of Savannah Plantation. Sent to England for schooling at the tender age of seven, she had returned to Barbados for the first time the previous year, to be at the bedside of her ailing mother. Since Mrs Mount's subsequent death, Barbara had been the mistress of Savannah Plantation. She was nominally in charge of the house servants, and was expected to be at her father's side when visitors called at Savannah.

This was not a job to her liking. She missed the gaiety of life in London and looked forward to her older brother's return from Oxford, when he would start to learn how to manage the plantation. Then she would be free to resume her former life and to take her rightful place in London society.

Barbara Mount was bored with plantation living and angry with her father for forcing her to remain in Barbados when there was so much to do in London. So, in defiance of her father's specific wishes, she had set out to ride across the fields unaccompanied.

Augustus Mount was in Bridgetown on business for a few days. Mistress Barbara, as she was called, assured the groom that, "My father said that it was perfectly all right for me to ride alone as long as I stay within earshot of the plantation yard."

Reluctantly the groom had agreed. Once through the gate, Barbara completely ignored her own fictitious parameters and set off at a canter along the various cart roads that separated the fields. Her ride eventually brought her to the last cart road. There she was accosted by the sailors.

Frank continued to watch from the canes and was shocked when the small sailor who'd been taunting the young woman suddenly struck her across the face. She stood wide-eyed, stunned by the insult as much as the force of the blow. Her face was bright red except for a white area on her cheek where Squint's hand had landed.

Then the sailor grabbed her collar and ripped her jacket open. Under the jacket, in deference to the heat of the day, Barbara was wearing only a light white cotton top – what Grandma Dora called a "Miss Betty".

"Let's see what you've got," Squint said.

Roughly he tore open the flimsy top, exposing the young woman's breasts.

Frank saw the sailor's face as he turned and grinned wildly at his companions. His left eye, half-closed, gave his leering countenance a sinister cast. A bright red scar ran from his eyebrow, down his cheek and under his chin. His face glistened with sweat as he turned back to stare greedily at Barbara's womanly breasts.

Squint reached out and touched the girl. She twisted away and screamed in anger and fear. Frank, who had come down the hill with no specific plan of action, was shaken by the terror and rage in the girl's face and the horror that her scream conveyed. He would never know why, but the young woman's scream spurred him to action. He pushed the last of the canes aside and stepped out into the cart road.

"See here," he said loudly, but without the degree of forcefulness that might have impressed the sailors, "Leave that young lady be."

Malley stared open-mouthed at the bold intruder just as the horse the sailor was holding, startled by Frank's shout and sudden appearance, reared and pulled free. It bolted down the cart road toward the plantation house. Malley, cursing, chased the horse a short way, in vain. Massive Walt Damon, not budging, kept his hold on the squirming, now wide-eyed, Barbara Mount.

Squint turned and saw a slight and unimpressive young man in a tattered shirt and trousers, holding a nasty-looking field knife, who had suddenly appeared from nowhere. Once he was sure that the stranger was alone, Squint drew a large knife from his belt and went into a crouch, moving from side to side with the knife thrusting closer and closer to the interloper. By this action, Squint signalled that he was a veteran of many such a fight and that he gladly accepted the challenge implicit in this man's sudden appearance.

There was a problem here. In addition to his being outnumbered, Frank was not really much of a fighting man. There'd always been plenty of clashes among the fishermen in Morton's Cove but Frank had stayed out of them, as best he could. But now this was beginning to look like a fight that could not be avoided.

Squint jabbed out with his sharp knife. Frank responded awkwardly. The scarred man's knife slashed Frank's leg and drew first blood. The pain from the cut, just above his knee, shocked Frank and caused him to assess his situation. It was clear that shouting and bluffing, his only actions so far, were not going to get the job done. These toughs would not be easily frightened and they didn't look to be the type that you could talk to. He was going to have to do something decisive, but what?

It didn't look good, Frank thought; in fact, it looked bad. He was outnumbered three to one and, in truth, any one of the sailors was more than a match for him in a head-to-head battle. Clearly, the wisest course was to retreat, if he could, but these sailors were hardly about to let him walk away now. If he turned tail, they would surely chase him down and kill him.

Reluctantly, he saw no alternative but to stay and put up a fight, relying on the hope that when the lady's horse got back to the plantation yard help would come. Frank decided to delay the sailors as best he could and, if possible, avoid getting killed in the process.

Frank relaxed his stance and put his hands up to signal that he meant them no harm. However, his gesture may not have had the desired effect because his right hand continued to hold the sharp cutlass.

Whether Frank's gesture of reconciliation was recognised or not, Squint chose to ignore it. He was a bully by nature and enjoyed having a reputation as a dangerous man in a knife fight. Squint wanted this fight, he wanted to add Frank to the small list of people he had killed, further to enhance his reputation. Plus, he liked these odds. With three of them against this scruffy farmer, it should be easy.

Squint jabbed his knife at Frank again and again, and then on one particularly vigorous thrust he briefly lost his balance and stumbled to his left.

It was at this moment that Frank realised his opponent was drunk; and probably all three of them were drunk. He thought to himself, maybe he had a chance to get out of there alive after all.

Squint continued to step from side to side, shifting his knife from hand to hand. Clearly he was enjoying himself, and was further bolstered by the encouraging remarks of his shipmates. Laughing and leering, he dared his quarry to make a move.

Each time the sailor jabbed, Frank fell back, barely out of harm's way. He made no overt effort to attack Squint, indeed he looked and acted as frightened as he no doubt was.

Given Frank's timid response, Squint grew supremely confident that the unimpressive young man would soon be at his feet, spurting his life's blood. But, try as he would, Squint could not cut his quarry again.

Tiring of Frank's dodging and retreating, Squint lunged at him with the knife extended, determined to make contact. But this time, instead of retreating, Frank moved sideways and easily avoided the thrust.

Startled by this new tactic, and briefly off balance, Squint stumbled forward. Frank instinctively recognised this as an opportunity he might not see again. He slashed his cutlass sideways and down upon the sailor's exposed forearm with full force.

The heavy cutlass was razor-sharp and Frank, though small in stature, was strong from years of hauling sails and fishnets at sea. The cutlass completely severed the sailor's arm three inches above the wrist.

The hand, still holding the knife, dropped quivering to the ground. The sailor stared at his hand in shocked disbelief. He felt nothing yet, but when his stump of an arm started to pump blood, he finally comprehended what had happened. Horrified, Squint turned and, holding his arm, ran screaming down the cart road towards the cliff above the sea.

Frank turned to the second sailor, the one who had held the horse. Malley did not have a knife but produced, from inside his shirt, a metal belaying pin, nearly as long as Frank's cutlass. In the hands of an experienced man such as Malley, a belaying pin became an effective weapon. It could be thrown or used as a truncheon. Even a glancing blow from a belaying pin could shatter a man's arm.

Meantime Damon, as always slow to react, had at last reached the conclusion that he too should join this fight. He clubbed the woman behind her head with his fist. She sank to the ground, unconscious. Damon then drew his knife and moved behind Frank, preparing to help his comrade.

Frank knew that he had little chance fighting two men at the same time. His only hope was to deal with one quickly, then turn to the other. But the man with the belaying pin was in front, no more than ten feet away, standing his ground. Frank dared not take his eyes from him for fear he would throw his weapon. Malley continued to hold the heavy pin in his right hand and tapped it ominously into his left palm. Meanwhile, Damon was closing on Frank from behind.

Frank was aware of the approaching giant and, when Malley's eyes shifted their focus from Frank's face to over his shoulder, Frank spun to his left and slashed blindly with his cutlass.

This quick move caught Damon off guard. The sharp cutlass cut deeply into the side of the beefy man and the blow sent him down on his right knee. Damon cursed and cried out in surprise, anger and pain. He tried to stand but the pain forced him to stay where he was. Malley, briefly transfixed, stared at his kneeling comrade. Then, with a snarl, he rushed Frank with his blunt weapon raised. Frank turned just as Malley reached him and braced his wrist. The sharp cutlass rammed deep into the exposed chest of the on-rushing man.

The blade split the chest and hit the heart. Malley died instantly. But his belaying pin had found its mark, crashing down on the front of Frank's head, cracking his skull and knocking him unconscious. Frank lay, out cold, pinned to the ground by the bleeding body of the dead sailor.

A minute later, the overseer and three plantation workers rushed down the cart road carrying weapons. They could hardly believe the scene before them, the entire area appeared to be bathed in blood. The young mistress lay unconscious, half naked on the ground. One man, bleeding profusely, was moaning and holding his side as he sat on the ground. Nearby, with unseeing open eyes, another man lay with a cutlass blade protruding from his back. Under him was another man, either dead or unconscious, his face streaked with blood oozing from a bruise on his forehead. The men rolled the dead sailor's body to the side and found that the man beneath, Frank Glenville, was still alive.

Then they saw a hand clutching a knife lying on the ground, and noted a ragged line of blood running down the track that led toward the cliff. While the overseer looked to Mistress Barbara, two men followed the trail of red. There, at the top of the cliff, they found a sailor's body. The dead man was missing a hand.

The bodies of the two dead men were roughly bundled onto a cart. The unconscious man with the bruised and bloody forehead and the wounded giant were put in chains and transported to a small building in the plantation yard. There they would remain under guard until Augustus Mount returned.

By the time her father returned that evening, Barbara Mount had regained consciousness. Her last memory was of a man emerging from the canes, battling with and wounding one of the sailors.

Barbara told her story to her father. He was furious at her for having wilfully disobeyed his wishes and, at the same time, he was relieved and grateful that she was relatively unharmed.

Barbara insisted on going with her father to the shed where the two prisoners were being held. She identified the big man as one of her attackers and the other man as her saviour.

Augustus Mount had Frank's chains removed and the still-unconscious man was brought into the main house. Mount called for the district doctor. Frank remained at Savannah Plantation, under the doctor's care, for a week.

Frank had a bad concussion and periodically would suffer severe headaches for the rest of his life. Nevertheless, in everyone's opinion – Frank's included – this incident was the best thing that ever happened to him.

Augustus Mount was not by nature a generous man but he was a proud one. His first instinct was to offer Frank Glenville a job at Savannah as a reward for what he had done. But Frank did not want to work at the plantation. He preferred it up on the Morton's Cove cliffs with the rest of the redlegs, where he and his family had always lived.

Barbara continued to pester her father to reward the brave man who had saved her from "a gruesome death". She insisted that her father do the "right thing". She swore that if he did not, she would "never forgive him".

Naturally, the word of this event had gotten out and everyone was talking about it. The *Clarion*, Barbados's leading newspaper, devoted its front page to a full account of what had occurred, and continued to have articles about it for days and weeks to come. Frank Glenville was, briefly, the most famous redleg on the island.

All of Barbados waited to see what Frank's reward would be. Some planters privately urged Mount not to be too generous for fear that he would set an unwise precedent. Others let it be known that they expected Mount to give Frank a reward that justly compensated him for his bravery, for risking his life and for his injuries.

"We never know when we might need one of the blighters' help ourselves," one influential planter said. "It would not do to be too mean."

Speculation centred on money as a reward. The consensus was that fifty pounds sterling, a substantial sum, would be appropriate. But Augustus Mount, always short of ready cash, hated to part with that much. Then he had an idea.

In the late seventeenth century, when Savannah Plantation was being formed from several lesser estates, one small segment of land had been added to the plantation. Just over four acres, it was up on the hill overlooking Savannah Plantation's fields. Appropriately, this land contained the coconut tree from which Frank had first viewed the sailors and the woman on a horse.

The original deed, which my grandmother would show me on more than one occasion, used the old English land measurements – acres and perches – to describe the land. Lord Mount, the first owner of Savannah Plantation, had acquired this particular segment of land in 1680 because it contained an active spring. A large well was dug there and for over fifty years, from approximately 1680 to 1730, this well, together with another well below it on the edge of the property, supplied all of the water needed to cultivate the six hundred acres of Savannah Plantation.

But, following a series of severe droughts in the 1720s, the two wells mysteriously went bone dry. Apparently, the underground spring which had fed them both had shifted. The rains returned but the water did not reappear in the wells. Such things were known to happen, particularly when the wells were located in hilly areas.

By 1883, these wells had been dry for over 150 years. This small piece of hilly, arid land was unsuitable for growing sugar cane, and since the Mounts were interested only in growing sugar, this land was of no value to them. Thus, it was announced that this land would be deeded to Frank Glenville and his family, "in perpetuity".

A ceremony was held at the land on 13th June 1883, to transfer the title of the four-plus acres from Augustus Mount, Gentleman, of Savannah Plantation, St Charles Parish, to Francis Glenville, place in society unspecified, of Morton's Cove, also in St Charles.

Present at the ceremony were Frank Glenville, his wife and three children; Augustus Mount; his daughter Barbara; the local Anglican priest and perhaps as many as two hundred other interested parties – redlegs, plantation owners and former slaves – including a reporter from the *Clarion*.

Speeches, always integral to such a ceremony, went on and on. Finally, with a flourish, Augustus Mount signed the deed and handed it to Frank. A small military band, brought all the way from the garrison near Bridgetown for the occasion, played a stirring martial tune.

Frank modestly murmured his thanks and turned, amid cheers, to show the deed to his family and relatives. Then, when everyone thought that the ceremony was over, Barbara Mount stood and said, "I would like to say a few words."

There is no record of her exact words but the reporter wrote that her speech "moved the audience to tears". Barbara then added, apparently without her father's foreknowledge, that along with the land the Mounts would build the Glenvilles "a substantial house" on the property. Her father was nearly apoplectic but there was little he could do, under the circumstances.

For a year, overseeing the building of this house was the principal occupation of the young mistress of Savannah Plantation. When finally finished, Glenville House was judged one of the loveliest houses in Barbados. People came all the way from Bridgetown just to view it.

Frank Glenville never returned to the sea. He and his family cleared their new land and planted tropical fruit trees and vegetable crops. Their hard work assured that the subsequent proprietors of Glenville House could always have a comfortable existence, if they continued to keep up the garden.

The Glenvilles were never wealthy, but they were well off compared with most other redlegs. They were secure in a fine house and had a steady supply of good food. And, as long as they were willing and able to work hard, they could produce enough crops to barter with their neighbours for fish and meat and to sell for extra income.

As was generally the case in Barbados, where central registration of land did not exist until the 1970s, my grandmother had in her possession the original deed of transfer of the land, signed by Augustus Mount, and the various wills by which the Glenvilles had passed ownership of the house and land to succeeding generations.

Grandma Dora showed the documents to me, Emily and Clarence every year. They were very beautiful, with fancy printing and lots of stamps and ribbons and blobs of red wax bearing official-looking seals. Her will was there too, although she never showed that to us.

Grandma Dora explained that to avoid splitting the property among his heirs when he died, Frank Glenville had left everything – the land, the house and its furnishings – to his oldest son, Wilmer. The other Glenville children were left nothing. They either settled down in the little chattel house village that had sprung up nearby or emigrated from Barbados to North America or England.

Frank Glenville's will dictated that subsequent owners of Glenville must always leave their estate to their eldest son. It also warned of the necessity of having a formal will, "writ by a Bridgetown solicitor," to ensure that the land would remain in the family and not somehow be stolen from its rightful owners.

Lance Glenville inherited Glenville from his father, Wilmer, in 1918. When Lance died in 1931, he left his inheritance to his only heir, his daughter Eudora, my grandmother.

Grandma Dora was only twenty-two when she came into her inheritance. Lance's will also stipulated that the land ultimately pass from Eudora to her son, Clarence Glenville. Thereafter, the land should continue the tradition of being passed to the oldest living male unless, as in Grandma Dora's case, there was no male heir; then it should go to the eldest female child.

My grandma's will was never unrolled. It was a holy document, like the others in the box, to be treated with care and reverence. The succession of the house and land, generation to generation, was the most sacred responsibility of a Glenville. Given that it was the only thing of value that the family had ever possessed, had ever called their own, this was understandable enough.

Home to Brooklyn

When I got back home to Brooklyn after that first summer in Barbados, I felt myself a changed person. The hard work and good food had made me taller and stronger. My clothes from the spring were now too short and too tight. And what I'd seen and learned in Barbados had made me feel very special and grown-up.

Pa wanted to know everything. So, on the next night, the family gathered to hear all about my summer. I was not used to being the centre of attention and it wasn't easy for me to remember everything that I'd experienced. So much had happened and much of it had been just "feelings" or smells or sounds, things that are not normally talked of easily by eleven-year-old boys. The entire account of my trip didn't come out at one sitting, but in several sessions over a two- or three-week period.

While I directed myself primarily to Pa, my mother and Margaret sat and listened, interested and attentive. But Elyce was not there. She was in a pout in the next room, pretending not to listen, still angry because, as the eldest, she believed that she should have gone to Barbados, not me. She had a point. But when I told her about working the garden in the hot sun every day but Sunday, I really laid it on about how hard it had been, and she became less vocal about her desire to have been there in my place.

I told them all about Grandma Dora, Uncle Clarence and Aunt Emily. Margaret didn't believe me when I described Emily, and said that our aunt was so pale and white because she had a food allergy, and for that reason could never go out of the house into the sun. Pa interrupted to say that Emily was an albino and that she had been born that way. Even Ma said that she had seen more than one albino herself, although usually they had been boys and men, not women. She also said that even black people could be albinos, but I found that very hard to believe.

Of course, I later found out that it was all true.

Pa was particularly interested in knowing how the house looked. He said that, growing up at Glenville, he'd thought that he was living in a mansion. I told him that it still looked good but, in truth, I didn't tell him that, even to my eleven-year-old eyes, it was becoming rundown and shabby from age and termite damage.

Grandma Dora had given me a letter to bring to Pa. He read it aloud to us. In it, his mother begged him to come to visit and also asked if he had heard from his brother Thomas.

Pa said to us, "I haven't seen or heard from that boy since I went into the British Navy in 1951. When I got home, Thomas had gone off to England. I've never heard a word from him since."

I told them how Frank Glenville, our great-great-great-grandfather, had saved the lady from Savannah Plantation and won Glenville House and land for our family. I did a good job telling it, Pa said, but he still couldn't help but jump in and add details that I had forgotten. Everyone sat spellbound throughout. Even Elyce forgot her pout and came into the living room to hear the end of the story.

I also told them how Grandma Dora, Uncle Clarence and Aunt Emily had gone to live with the Hawthornes. Pa didn't have any comment or anything to add to that story.

A few evenings later we gathered again and I told them what Grandma Dora had said about our grandfather, Lester Cumberbatch. Pa said that he had no memory of Lester, which is not surprising, since he was only four when his father was killed. But he said he knew that his father's death "broke my mother's heart".

I also mentioned my conversation with Uncle Clarence about his pa and his mysterious reply, "No Pa, Grandpa." My father offered no explanation for it, although I did see him lock eyes briefly with Ma.

For some reason which I didn't understand at the time, Elyce laughed.

A few days later, Elyce and I were in the house after school, and Ma was asleep in her bed. I said something about Barbados and that started us talking about it. Elyce returned to her favourite subject.

"Next summer, I should be the one to go. I can work just as hard as you, and at least I'll know what it is that people are telling me."

I disagreed with her on both points.

I said, "I am stronger than you and besides, I already know what to do in the garden. You'd probably just stay in the house with Aunt Emily. And I do too know what people say to me. Pa says I did a real good job telling the stories I'd heard."

Elyce said, "Well for one thing, you didn't even know what Uncle Clarence meant when he said, 'No Pa, Grandpa,' did you? Don't you see?"

She had me there. I had no idea what Clarence's comment had meant.

"What he was saying, dumb bunny, was that his grandpa was his pa. That's why he and Emily are a little strange and I suspect that's why they had to go live with the Hawthornes, so Dora's pa would not give her any more children."

I was flabbergasted. I couldn't grasp the principle of what she was saying. How could someone be both your father and your grandfather at the same time?

Elyce became quite explicit about it and, finally, I understood.

And, as I thought about it later, it all made sense. Of course she was right.

Wickham Institute III
October 1996

I was having my lunch in the Wickham Institute's cafeteria all by myself. My usual companions had already eaten. I'd been in the gym working out and had barely made it to the chow line before they shut it down. I was feeling better physically and trying to get back into shape. In a lot of ways, the rehab place was worse than the US Army. Except for one thing: the army never had anybody like Shannon Tierney. She made the whole experience almost bearable.

I was thinking about her, and then I looked up and there she was in front of me.

"I was passing by and saw you sitting here by yourself. Ben, do you mind some company?"

Of course, I was only too glad to have her join me.

"I was fascinated by the stories in your journal about visiting your grandmother in Barbados. What were the subsequent years like?"

"Well, in some ways they were much the same. We worked in the garden all day, but eventually I did make some friends and got out to see more of the island on my own."

"Ben, Dr Fine and I would like you to write more about your time there. Clearly Barbados is very important to you. But this time, write about your own experiences and less about the stories that you heard from others. It is great therapy for you and, to tell you the truth, I am looking forward to reading it."

Okay, for Shannon I'd give it a try.

My Journal: The last Bajan summer

Barbados, 1972

I spent my next three summers, up until I was fourteen, in Barbados. It was hard work and a lot of it was repetitive but that experience has held a special meaning for me all my life. I guess what Pa said about it being important for me to understand my heritage, where I came from, was right. At least, it was for me.

There was never a shortage of work to do in the garden, but in subsequent summers I didn't have to wait to be told what to do, I could see what needed doing and knew how to do it. And since I was getting bigger and stronger and more experienced with the garden tools, I could do more of the jobs that Uncle Clarence used to have to do.

However, I was also getting older and was no longer content to limit my social life to the Sunday walks with Uncle Clarence along the cliffs. I started to explore the countryside on my own. I went to Glenville and Morton's Cove to find friends among the young people my age, both redlegs and coloured. There were two people – a light-skinned boy a year older than me, Oliver Shorter, and his younger sister, Annie – who became my closest friends. And, despite Grandma Dora's continued stern warnings, I finally did go to see Savannah Plantation for myself.

Savannah Plantation

Grandma Dora had just told us the story of her great-grandfather rescuing Barbara Mount for the umpteenth time. I couldn't help but feel that I had a hereditary right to visit this plantation; after all, was I not a direct descendant of the heroic Frank Glenville?

One Sunday I didn't go with Uncle Clarence. I said that I was seeing friends in Morton's Cove. I walked down the path to the fishing village but I didn't enter. Instead, I veered to the right and took the road that led to the sugar cane fields of Savannah Plantation. I didn't run into a single person. This encouraged me, so on the following Sunday I again made an excuse and was soon retracing my steps of the week before, but this time I set off down the cart road between the first field and the second, determined to find the very spot where the famous fight had occurred.

I followed the cart road to its end, out to the cliffs above the sea. I could only guess where along the road the fight took place, but at the cliff I was sure that I had located the spot where the handless sailor bled to death. I even thought that I saw dark stains of his blood on a rock.

I walked out to look at the sea from the top of the rocky cliff. The area was much like where Uncle Clarence and I had our Sunday walks, but here the coast faced east and the wind blew directly in your face all the way from Africa, three thousand miles away.

A heavy surf steadily pounded the cliffs, continuing its efforts to undercut the coral face. Huge slices of coral, in various stages of sliding into the sea, were proof of its strength and persistence.

Light green water constantly surged against the coral at the base. Fingers of white sea foam beckoned to me and then retreated into the next wave. The continuous roar of the pounding surf was punctuated occasionally by the boom of a much larger wave. Following these larger waves, spray filled the air and the sun, shining through the drops of water, produced a tiny rainbow. The colours remained before my eyes for only a few seconds, then disappeared, leaving me in awe of what I had just seen.

Sea birds gliding overhead pierced the air with their shrill cries. A cool stiff breeze blew steadily from the east. It smelled pleasantly of the endless sea that stretched to the horizon.

I stood for what seemed an eternity, storing in my mind for the future the sense of being alone in someplace special.

Further along to my right, I could see the Savannah Great House where it presided on top of the white coral cliffs. I knew that this was where I must go next.

A few Sundays later, after our midday dinner, I set out to see the Savannah Great House. Again I told Uncle Clarence that I wouldn't be joining him, that I would be with my friends in Glenville. Then I headed directly where I'd been warned repeatedly never to go.

I walked along the main cart road that led to the plantation yard and the house. I passed three large fields of recently harvested sugar cane; then I entered the last field, the one that bordered the main house. It had not yet been cut. I moved through the canes, working my way carefully among the long green leaves that formed a thick canopy over my head. It was hot and humid, but I enjoyed being there.

The wind caused the canes to rub together so their soft noise muffled any inadvertent sound I might create. They towered high above my head; I was confident that my presence would be undetected by anyone at the Great House.

I finally reached the end of the cane field. I stood at the edge. In front of me there was a grassy strip, maybe fifteen feet wide, which separated the field from a six-foot fence made of coral blocks. The grey and black barrier completely surrounded the looming plantation house. About ten yards to my left there was a heavy wooden door in the wall, apparently a side entrance into the plantation yard. I saw broken glass imbedded in cement on the top of the wall. The message was clear: visitors were not welcome at Savannah Great House.

Then I heard voices, but I couldn't hear what they were saying, nor could I see anyone. The speakers had to be on the other side of the wall. But then, to my surprise, the gate swung open and two white men – one short and pudgy, the other quite tall and lanky – turned left out of the gate and walked down the grassy strip directly towards me. A large black and tan dog trotted behind them. The dog's pink tongue hung out from the side of his mouth.

I wanted to melt back further into the canes but I feared that the slightest movement on my part would draw attention. I decided that the best thing to do was to stay where I was. I slowly kneeled, lowering my head, and hoped that the men would pass without noticing me.

No such luck. The dog barked and ran right towards me. In fear, I stood up. The dog was at my feet, barking, ready to leap at my throat.

The shorter man shouted at the dog to stop and then said to his companion, "Pull that Rottweiler away or we'll have a dead boy on our hands."

The tall white man, dressed in riding gear, breeches and high leather boots, grabbed the dog's collar with one hand and with the other he pulled me roughly out of the canes and into the grassy area. The shorter man, who was similarly dressed, watched with a strange smile.

Then he spoke in a soft voice.

"Isn't he a pretty one."

Grasping me tightly by my shoulder, the tall man shook me and asked, "Just who are you?"

I was afraid to say my whole name for fear that it would get back to Grandma Dora, so I merely said, "I'm Ben."

"All right, Ben," said the shorter one, obviously enjoying himself, "it looks like we will have to call the constable and have you locked up for trespassing on private property."

I'd meant no harm but I did know that just coming on someone's property was a crime. I blurted out, "I am sorry, I meant no harm. I'm not from around here, I was lost."

They must have known by now, by my accent, that I was not local. This may have piqued their curiosity.

"Who are you then and where are you from?"

I used the last name of one of the families in the village.

"My name is Ben Hoad, I am visiting my uncle in Glenville. I am here for the summer from America."

The short pudgy man said in a low voice, "He'll do nicely."

"I'll lock him up," the tall man said. He let the dog go and took me roughly by one arm and led me through the gate into the plantation yard. The dog sniffed at my legs and made walking difficult. The shorter man trailed along behind us with an odd grin on his face.

Once we were through the gate, I could see that we were in the work yard of the plantation. I guessed it was maybe one hundred feet each way, surrounded on three sides by small buildings and sheds where equipment and animals were kept.

As I was being half led, half dragged across the yard, out of the corner of my eye, I could see a middle-aged man cleaning a horse's stall. He looked away as we passed, as if he didn't want to see us. I thought I recognised him from Morton's Cove, but I was not sure.

I was shoved into a small stone building with a dirt floor. I could hear the lock click shut in the wooden door. There were no windows and, with the door shut, the only light was that which leaked in under the eaves. I felt along the walls to see if there was any way out, other than the heavy locked door. I found nothing. I was stuck there until someone let me out. I was as scared as I have ever been in my life.

As my eyes adjusted to the dark, I could see that I was in a square, totally empty room, maybe ten feet by ten. From the smell of human urine, I felt certain that I was not the first person to have been kept here.

Who were the others, and what had happened to them? Why was I here? Were they really going to turn me over to the constables or was something else going to happen to me? Why had I not listened to Grandma Dora? She had warned me time and again not to come here and now I knew why. "Don' trouble trouble till trouble trouble you" she used to say, and she was right.

Two or three hours passed, I didn't know how long. However, the light was beginning to fade, so I guessed it was getting on for six. Then I heard the scrape of something moving outside the wall.

A hoarse voice whispered, "Boy!"

Then something heavy hit the floor. My hand went down and I lifted a large, wooden-handled screwdriver.

"Whoever it is out there, will you help me out of here?" I called out.

"Shush, boy!"

It was a man's angry voice. I knew it had to be the man I'd seen cleaning the stall. Who else could it have been?

He whispered in a husky, guttural voice, "You stupid boy. You gonna be hurt, and maybe ruined like some others around here, if you don't get away now. I am taking a hell of a chance as it is. So you've got to get out on your own. You just use that screwdriver and see if you can force that old lock. Now get busy while you got time."

"Thank you. What is your name?" I asked.

"Never mind. My name don' matter, just you get outta here and don' never come back."

For several minutes I used the screwdriver as a lever to try to remove the metal plate on the inside of the old door. I finally bent the plate but I couldn't break it free. However, in the course of working on the plate, the point of the screwdriver had sunk into the old wood of the door frame. I gave up on the lock and concentrated on the door frame. I was finally able to chip out enough wood to free the latch and pull the door open.

It was now pitch dark, with only the canopy of stars above me to light the yard. I crawled up onto a cart and, from there, scaled the wall, scraping the heel of my hand on broken glass in the process. Then I ran non-stop back to Glenville.

I made up a story as to where I had been.

I never did tell Grandma Dora of my visit to Savannah Plantation. And, having gone there, having satisfied my curiosity, I was now quite ready and willing to follow her wishes.

I never knew for sure what would have happened to me at Savannah, had I not gotten away, but, from what I've seen and learned in my years in the NYPD, I'm glad that I never did find out.

Annie Shorter

There were twenty-seven homes in Glenville village, not counting ours. Eleven were owned by redleg families, mostly Glenvilles and their kin, and the rest by black Bajan families.

I tried to make friends with my Glenville cousins in the village, but they were wary of me, particularly if any adults were around. The ones near my age talked to me sometimes, but apparently the old distrust between the residents of Glenville House and the village still ran deep. The only good friends I had were light-skinned like me, a brother and sister, Oliver and Annie Shorter.

Oliver was eleven months older than me, and Annie was a year younger. Oliver was strong and worked part-time on his uncle's fishing boat out of Morton's Cove. I was taller but Oliver could usually beat me when we wrestled. We were good friends but we frequently argued about silly things. It seemed to me that

Oliver resented never having been out of St Charles parish, never even having been to Bridgetown. All he had done was to go out to sea with his uncle. When I talked about things at home in America, things I had seen or done, Oliver got angry.

Annie was different. She liked me to talk about Brooklyn and life in America. She was always asking me questions.

You could tell that Annie was going to be a real good-looking woman. By the time she reached thirteen, the last summer I was there, grown men in the village and the fishermen from Morton's Cove were beginning to take notice of her.

Annie was tall and she moved slowly and gracefully, and you knew that she was aware that eyes were upon her. Her hair was full and she wore it pulled back in a long ponytail. And, that last summer, Annie's body was rapidly filling out, taking on the softness and curves of a woman.

Oliver and Annie lived with their mother in the smallest and most dilapidated house in Glenville. Their mother, a widow, must have weighed over two hundred pounds. I concluded that Annie and Oliver had gotten their good looks from their late father, a Morton's Cove fisherman.

After my ill-fated trip to Savannah Plantation, I asked Oliver who the two men might have been.

He said that, from my description, the short man had to be Edgar Mount, the master of Savannah Plantation. The other man was almost certainly his overseer, Vincent Lewis, an Englishman from Trinidad.

"What do you know about the overseer?" I pressed.

"Lewis came to work at the plantation a few years ago. The men hereabouts who work at Savannah have nothing good to say about him."

"What do you mean?"

"He treats the men bad, mostly when Mount is not around. Also too, his morning words and his evening words don't agree."

Oliver explained that the men considered Vincent Lewis to be a liar and not to be trusted.

"What about Mount?" I asked.

"From what I hear, you just want to stay as far away from him as you can."

Huh. Oliver sounded just like Grandma Dora. I asked but he wouldn't say anything more about Mount.

Oliver was gone most of that last summer, out on the fishing boat with his uncle. So I spent my free time with Annie. At first I missed Oliver's company, but not for long.

You see, Annie and I had a "thing" that summer. Mostly just holding hands and kissing. We would walk out along the cliffs and find a place back among the trees, away from prying eyes. There we would lie down and hug and kiss and, when Annie would let me, I would fondle her newly sprouted breasts. She let me touch them only from the outside, through her clothes. My sly efforts to slip an inquiring finger into her sturdy brassiere were always firmly rejected. Nevertheless, the whole thing was memorable for me, I had not even touched a girl's breasts before. And Annie claimed that I was the first to touch hers, but I don't think I believed her.

On the last night before I was to return to Brooklyn, Annie and I planned to meet to say goodbye. I'd been hoping for days that something very special might happen on that evening. My fervent wish was that, to mark our parting, Annie and I would go "all the way". I'd been thinking and dreaming about that possibility for days.

It is funny, I still occasionally dream about that night, even though my erotic fantasies and fevered expectations were never fulfilled. I have never quite been able to get Annie out of my thoughts. She remains my romantic ideal. Whenever I grow tired of a woman, I find myself comparing her to beautiful, innocent Annie. And Annie always wins.

I arrived at Annie's around six thirty that evening. Being so close to the equator, in Barbados the sun sets around six, winter and summer. By six thirty the sun was already down over on the west coast, and here on the east coast all we could see of it was the golden glow in the sky at the top of the cliff. Dark shadows were gathering beneath the towering trees that surrounded Glenville village.

Old Mrs Shorter was sitting on a broken-down sofa on the veranda giving me the "fishy-eye". She clearly did not trust me to be alone with her ever-more beautiful daughter, particularly not on this, my last night. She had intuitively come to the same conclusion I had about the potential for this evening. Her instincts were irritatingly accurate.

"You don't be out late," she said sternly to us both. "I want she back here on this veranda by eight o'clock."

Mrs Shorter gestured at her daughter with her finger which she then pointed at me.

We promised to be back by eight, anything to get out of there, and then we hurried off. Our objective was up the trail along the top of the cliff above the sea, a ten-minute walk. There, past a stand of trees, a small trail went to the right into a grove of casuarina trees. Among the trees was a clearing, not visible from the trail. The ground was covered with generations of long soft needles fallen from the towering casuarinas. It was our favourite spot.

We sat and looked at each other expectantly and then I gently pushed Annie back and we eagerly started hugging and kissing, surrounded by a symphony of Caribbean night noises. We could hear the surf pounding the base of the cliff below, making a dull thump. As the land cooled, the wind picked up and a soft whispering breeze rustled the trees above. Tiny tree frogs kicked in with their shrill screech, beseeching the skies for rain. And we heard the sharp cries of the grey and white king birds – which the locals called "pee-whitlers" – as these feathery acrobats swooped down to gather their nightly meal of flying insects.

Annie stopped kissing me and burrowed her face tight against my neck. I drew her closer to me, pressing my body against hers. Then I realised that my neck was getting wet. Annie's silent tears were soaking my shirt. I didn't quite know what to do. I had seen women cry – my mother a lot, my sisters, some – but I had never seen someone from outside of my family cry.

I patted her head, hoping to soothe her, to make her stop her tears, but it didn't help. In fact, the crying went from tears to deep sobs. I panicked, I knew that I had to be the cause of her crying. I felt guilty but I was uncertain how to get her to stop.

"Annie, sweet thing," I said, "please don't cry. I'll come back, I'll be back next summer, you'll see."

Either I was lying or I had, for the moment, forgotten that Pa had said that I would not be coming to Barbados next summer. It was, he said, time for me to start working and contributing to the family.

My words seemed to help, for Annie's crying subsided and, finally, stopped.

In a tear-stained voice she said, "Ben, I can't live without you. You can't imagine how bad it is here, living with my mama, particularly now with Ollie gone so much. Since our papa was lost at sea, she does nothing but eat, cry and make my life miserable. You're the best thing that ever has happened to me."

In the spirit of the moment, I began to rub Annie's breasts with fervour. She moaned softly and turned towards me and we kissed again. She pressed her body to mine. I still managed to keep my hand clasped upon her breast; I slipped my thumb into her blouse and probed into her brassiere. Finally, with a bold move, I managed to touch her nipple. Annie did not push my hand away. She lay there, her body shivering each time my thumb stroked her breast.

Annie threw a leg over mine and our clothed bodies moved back and forth in unison. My male member, of course, responded and I thrust it against Annie's body, simulating and mimicking what, I hoped, was about to happen next.

But just then, coming down the path, we heard voices. Several boys and girls our age, from Glenville and from Morton's Cove, were approaching. They were carrying a flashlight and if they saw us they would tease us unmercifully.

We lay unmoving, clinging together, hoping that no one would shine the light our way. The group passed us but then stopped just a short distance up the trail. There they sat on a small rocky promontory that jutted off the trail out above the sea. The young people call this spot "Lover's Leap".

They were sitting maybe forty feet away from where we were. We listened as they laughed and teased one of the younger boys, urging him to jump from Lover's Leap because he had been rejected by a girl they all knew.

Confident that they had not seen us, I tried to re-establish the mood and activities from before but, unfortunately and to my great disappointment, the moment had passed. Annie pushed my hand away when I tried to regain my coveted position inside her bra. It soon was clear that nothing more was going to happen on this evening. I sadly reconciled myself to the fact that my big moment had come and gone.

Our arms around one another, we whispered about our lives apart and, in the future, together. We promised to write to each other and I swore, faithfully, to return to her the next summer.

I got Annie home almost on time. Mrs Shorter was sitting on the darkened veranda waiting, arms folded. She ignored me and hustled her daughter inside. I stood outside in the dark, hoping to get a glimpse of Annie again, but the single light remained turned off.

Early the next morning, Grandma Dora and Uncle Clarence took me to the airport in the old truck. Annie was seated on her veranda, crying as we drove through the village. I waved to her but she buried her face and did not wave back.

Annie wrote me twice but, somehow, I never did get around to answering her. I guess I didn't know what to say, because by now I was fully aware that I would not be going back that next summer. And I didn't want her to keep writing to me. I hated being teased by my family about my girlfriend in Barbados.

Anyway, I never did return to see Annie as I had promised. And I felt guilty about it.

To tell you the truth, I still do.

Wickham Institute IV
December 1996

I finally got to see my whole therapeutic team at one time, the first week of December. They convened a meeting to discuss how soon I could leave Wickham as a full-time patient. They appeared pretty pleased with my progress, considering that it had been just six months since I was shot.

They reviewed the status of my vision. I got the impression that they thought it was about as good as it was going to get. I would never recover peripheral vision in my right eye and, since I refused to wear the damned special glasses, I would have to compensate by "scanning", meaning periodically looking to my right to see if there was anything there. I still occasionally bumped into things, but I was getting the hang of it.

My other physical problems had largely disappeared. My co-ordination was ninety per cent of what it had been; that was not bad when you remember that four months before I couldn't tie a shoelace. And, they said, it would get marginally better, over time. Of course, I was quite a bit weaker than I used to be, but I had been working out in the gym with weights and running on the treadmill, and my strength was improving.

I still had a nasty-looking scar on my forehead where the bullet went through my brain. It was red but it would fade, with time.

My memory had definitely improved, thanks to Shannon, the therapy and writing my journal. I had pretty good recall up to a couple of months before I was shot. After that, things were still a bit muddled. Sadly, I did remember that my father Nate Cumberbatch was dead. Not that I was remembering the event, what I did remember was being told of it time and again by Elyce and Tom Moran.

The doctors told me that the odds were I would never remember anything about my own shooting but that I should continue to work on it. They gave me the old, "Some further progress is possible."

But, the doctors said, my biggest problem was my short-term memory. This was why I continued to forget things and to get lost in the halls at Wickham. It was better than it had been but it was still not good enough.

After the meeting, Shannon and I talked about my memory problem. She had an interesting idea, one that has helped me a great deal ever since.

"Ben, this short-term memory problem is going to be with you for a long time, possibly, to some degree, for the rest of your life. But I believe that you can overcome it and that you are uniquely qualified to do it."

"What do you mean?"

"In the first case, you're a trained detective; trained to observe details and to gather information by asking the right questions. And you told me that you had been taught to keep written notes, and that you would later refer to these notes in the course of an investigation, or when you were asked to testify at a trial."

"That's true. I used to pride myself on the clarity and accuracy of my notes. It's definitely a learned skill and not something that just anyone can do well."

Shannon smiled at me and put her hand on my arm.

"Ben, that's why I think that if you work with me you can conquer this memory situation."

She continued, "I have seen you making notes around here, just as you did in the meeting with the team this morning. What

I want you to do is to expand your note-taking. Make it something that you do automatically all the time, whenever you hear or see something, something that you think may be worth remembering. You will quickly learn to differentiate between those facts or events which are valuable or useful to remember and those which are not. But err on the side of too many notes, because something that seems minor at the time might later prove to be very significant.

"And then, and this is most important, at the end of the day, or at the first opportunity you have, summarise your notes in a narrative. Eliminate the really unimportant things and link together and analyse those bits of information that are most significant and that you especially wish to remember. What you will be left with is, in essence, a story of that day. We know you are a good storyteller from your journals about Barbados. Now you will be writing a daily journal about what is happening around you.

"Your story will be your memory of that day. But whereas the rest of us depend on being able to dredge up what we need from our memory, you will have yours right there in hard copy in front of you."

"What if nothing happens, like here at Wickham? Everything in this place is pretty routine, except you."

Shannon laughed and blushed slightly.

"Ben, this is your memory. You decide what is worthy of being noted and then written up at day's end. I know you can do it and do it well. Additionally, and here we are in unproven territory, I believe that there may be a therapeutic aspect to this exercise. Taking notes on a regular basis may actually help you to recover your memory. At least that's my hope."

That's why I started carrying a notebook in which I put down everything that happened. Then, later, I would go back over my notes for the day and write them up. Often I looked back at what

I had written from days or weeks before. This way, not too much of importance got away from me. It didn't replace having a well-functioning regular memory, but it allowed me to get by.

Apparently Shannon had told Dr Knight about my note-taking. He stopped me in the hall and asked me how it was going.

"Pretty good," I said. "It takes a little practice but I definitely can see the benefit of it."

"I'd like to hear how it is progressing. Ms Tierney is quite optimistic about it. And, if she is right about the therapeutic aspect, we may have hit on something that could help a lot of other people."

He shook my hand, then he added, "And, oh yes, Ben, how would you like to go home for Christmas? You can be with your family for the holidays and then you can start coming here as an out-patient after the first of the year."

I loved the idea of getting out of Wickham for a while, not that Christmas at the Cumberbatches' this year was going to be any great shakes. There would just be Elyce and me and she had said she would be spending Christmas Day with her boyfriend and his kids.

What had me worried was that my father had been dead for six months and his family in Barbados still didn't know about it. I felt I should fly down there for the week between Christmas and New Year's to tell them the unhappy news. Then at least I would have that obligation off my mind.

I knocked on the open door of Shannon's office. She was on the telephone and beckoned me to come in and sit down. As she wrapped up her conversation I sat there and admired her. Shannon looked fabulous. She had just had her hair cut in an interesting and flattering way and, under her professional white coat, she was wearing a great-looking dress.

"Hello, Ben. I wanted to see you this afternoon. I know you're checking out tomorrow morning and I wanted to wish you merry Christmas and let you know how much I've enjoyed working with you. Once you start as an out-patient we'll probably not see as much of each other as we have while you've been a resident."

"I've enjoyed working with you too. You've really helped me," I said, and I really meant it.

"Shannon, I've got to tell you, you look terrific. Are you going out on the town tonight?"

"They're having their Christmas party over at Columbia Presbyterian. It starts at six," she said softly, her face turning a nice pink colour.

It seemed that everyone in New York was getting into Christmas this year. All of the patients at Wickham who were medically able to leave would be getting out for the holidays. There would just be a skeleton staff in residence.

I would be leaving in the morning, Elyce and I would have our "family Christmas" at her place on Christmas Eve, and we were both to spend Christmas Day at Elyce's boyfriend's house out on Long Island. I was booked to fly to Barbados the next day. No one at Wickham knew of my travel plans. I was afraid that they might object.

"How are you feeling?" Shannon asked.

"Great. I really do think I am ready to move on to the next level. And your note-taking and the daily report writing idea is a good suggestion. The only problem is that there is nothing much to write about here at Wickham. When I get on the outside there will be more to see, more to remember and to write about."

"I know you can do it. You've made outstanding progress." Shannon smiled at me, then tilted her head, looked at me quizzically and said, "Ben, is there something the matter?"

"I don't want to bother you with it; it's nothing, I'm sure."

She kept looking at me but didn't press me. Neither of us spoke for a moment.

Finally I said, "There is something. I keep remembering … it's like I'm seeing a picture in my head. It's a flash of something, I guess it's a memory, but not a real one. It only lasts a few seconds but it's always the same, the same thing over and over. It's got to be one of those 'false' memories that you warned me about, because what I remember could not possibly have happened."

"Tell me about it," Shannon said.

"As I said, it's crazy. I am in the alley behind the Park View Hotel, that's where I was shot. I see a tall man in the shadows. I speak to him but I don't know what I say. He turns, and I can see that it's my father. Suddenly he has a gun in his hand. I approach him but then he starts shooting at me. Then blackness."

"How do you feel about it?" Shannon said quietly.

"It scares me. It reminds me of how close I came to dying. But I know it can't be real. Pa was in the ICU at Kings County, fighting for his life when I was shot. He'd been mugged two days before and never recovered. Nevertheless, it seems very real."

"Remember what I told you about how to tell a real memory from a false one," Shannon said. "If it's a real memory, you would recall details like how your 'father' was dressed, what the weather was like and such."

"That's the problem. I think I do remember some detail. I can tell you what he was wearing and I even think I know what make the gun was."

Shannon looked at me curiously. I decided not to say anything more. Shannon had to be right: it was a false memory.

I wished her a merry Christmas, she gave me a nice sisterly kiss on the cheek.

The next morning Dr Fine dropped by. He said that Shannon had told him about my false memory.

"It's fortunate that you know it could not have been your father. However, it is possible that what you are having is what is called 'a leak from the past'. In other words, you are remembering the real event, when you were shot and nearly killed, but you have substituted your father's face for that of the person who actually shot you.

"Freud and a French contemporary of his, Janet, wrote about such incidents." Dr Fine was warming up to his subject. "These 'leaks', or 'flashes' as you call them, happen primarily when one is remembering a moment of terror. And the person that harmed you and your father are linked in your mind. That's interesting, we'll have to explore that together."

Over my dead body.

"I don't remember being terrified," I said grumpily. I didn't like to admit that I had ever been terrified, certainly not to Fine.

"Everyone, even the bravest or the most foolhardy person, knows fear," Fine commented. "Being shot in the head would be reason enough to terrify anyone. It is nothing to be ashamed of."

Dr Fine was in his element; he was the great shrink and I was his little subject.

"Maybe we can use hypnotism to help unlock the real memory of this event. Come see me when you get back after the holidays," Fine urged.

Not going to happen. I had no intention of being hypnotised by Dr Fine.

Shannon was right the first time. This was just a false memory.

The Daily Reports

Daily Report 1

Date of Events: Tuesday & Wednesday, 24 & 25 December 1996
Place: New York City: Brooklyn, the Precinct
Summary: Jannetta on Pa; Pilkington on my shooting; Christmas

On Christmas Eve morning I went from Elyce's apartment in Brooklyn, where I was staying, to Manhattan, to get her a Christmas present. At Saks Fifth Avenue, I got some perfume, a colourful scarf and a handbag. They were nice and I didn't have to worry about sizes. I always messed up on women's sizes when I was functioning OK, so I was not taking any chances now.

Elyce deserves all of this and more; I owe her a lot. Elyce practically raised me. She tended both my parents and she looked after me at Kings County and, for over five months, at Wickham. She is a wonderful person. And now she is in love. I couldn't be happier for her.

Next, I went out to Brooklyn to the Precinct to see Tony Jannetta, the detective who had been assigned to investigate my father's death, and Ted Pilkington, who was looking into my shooting. They both had wanted to talk to me, but up until now the doctors had kept them away. Now I could meet with them on my own.

I found my way down a dingy hallway to a room with four desks, only one of which was occupied: Jannetta's. It was the usual cops' work area: dozens of file folders, loose pieces of paper, telephone slips taped to light shades and crime scene photos covering the walls.

I was lucky that Jannetta was there. The other detectives were out, probably doing their last-minute Christmas shopping.

Jannetta was short, stocky and losing the battle with his waistline. His handshake was firm and his eyes reflected an active mind. He had a reputation for being a good detective. I had known him slightly in the past; we were at the Police Academy together, in the same class.

Quickly we got down to the details, cop to cop.

I explained why I hadn't been able to see him for all these months. Jannetta told me that we actually did meet twice in the days between the time my father was attacked and when I was shot. I told him about my memory problem, and that I still had no recollection of that period.

"Fill me in on what you know," I said, taking out my notebook. "Assume that I don't know anything, because the truth is, I don't. Let's start with the attack itself."

"Your father was attacked on Procter Street. He was hit on the head several times with a heavy blunt instrument." Jannetta's hand chopped up and down in imitation of repeated blows. "From the extent of the damage and the wounds, it looked like it was either a steel or lead pipe, eighteen to twenty inches long. He was struck approximately fifteen times. The skull was crushed and his face badly beaten. The damage was so bad that your sister had some trouble identifying him at the hospital."

"Were there any defensive wounds?" I asked.

"Several blows to both forearms and shoulders. It appeared that he had put up a hell of a struggle."

That sounded like Pa. Although he was over sixty, he was fit and strong. He walked everywhere and he was vain about his figure, so he kept himself in shape with regular exercises, push-ups, sit-ups and such. Plus, Pa was streetwise and he always carried a stout walking stick. It was hard to imagine that some stranger, a mugger, could have gotten close enough to him to do that much damage.

"From the direction of the blows, it appeared that they came from the front and that the killer was left-handed, or at least used that hand to strike your father."

Jannetta showed me pictures of Pa's body and he was correct. Clearly the blows had been directed upon the right side of his head and he had used principally his right arm to ward them off. He had received one hell of a beating.

"When did it happen?" I asked. I was recording every detail in my small notebook.

"Between eight fifteen and eight forty-five on the first of June. It was a cloudy day and it was already dark. That's a relatively deserted block at that time of day."

Detective Jannetta checked his notes and continued, "It was on the west side of Procter, just off the park."

I knew the area, a five-minute walk from where Pa and Elyce lived. I told Jannetta that Pa regularly went for a walk in the park after dinner and they always ate at seven sharp. He nodded his head and indicated that he knew this.

I said, "Given the time, eight thirty or so, he'd probably had his walk and was on the way home."

Jannetta agreed, he had found two regulars in the park who confirmed that they had seen Pa there that night, walking alone.

"We've interviewed up and down Procter and nobody admits to seeing anything that night," he added.

"Was he robbed?"

"His wallet was empty of money, it was lying there. But all his papers and credit cards were untouched, that's how the patrolman knew to contact your sister. There were no fingerprints on the wallet and there was no physical evidence that we could link to his killer. We swept the area good."

"What about his walking stick? Did it have any blood or hair from his attacker?"

"We never found it. Your sister confirmed he had it with him when he left the apartment and the people who saw him in the park also mentioned it. We think that the person or persons who attacked him must have taken it. Although I can't imagine killing someone for a walking stick."

"I agree. Did it ever show up?"

"No. You know, when we met last time, right after the attack, before you were shot, you were focused on that missing walking stick. I got a picture of the stick and we showed it around but we got no good leads. Lots of people remembered seeing Nate with that stick, over the years. A couple of people even thought they remembered seeing him with it a day or two after the attack. When we showed them your father's picture, they identified him as the person they'd seen with the cane. But they must have been confused."

I said, "Doesn't really sound like robbery was the motive, does it?"

"No. Robbers don't usually hit their victims fifteen times. They just threaten them, and if the victim does resist, then the mugger may use force. But usually not like this, not so violent. And you can see that your father put up quite a struggle. Two people in the neighbourhood did say that they thought they heard a scuffle going on. But no one called the police, and even if they had it's doubtful they would have gotten there in time to save your father. Maybe Nate knew his attacker or could identify him; but maybe not. Unfortunately we've got people out there who are crazy or hopped up on amphetamines or something else. Sometimes they kill just for sport. And sometimes a victim may be killed violently even if he doesn't fight back."

"Tony, generally this kind of wounding, multiple blows, is associated with a crime of passion. You've got to really hate somebody to hit them that many times."

Jannetta said to me, "Do you know anyone who would have hated your father enough to attack him like this?"

I told him, without humour, that potentially half of Brooklyn would have liked to do him in. I explained that Pa had been chasing ladies for years, and that it's entirely possible that he had finally crossed the wrong person in the pursuit of his favourite pastime.

"You had told me that before and, of course, when I made inquiries about your father, I came up with the same story from his friends. You gave me some names of women and I developed some others. I started checking. Old Nate was quite a guy. I've never seen so many good-looking, mature coloured women in my life. Most of them were from the islands – Jamaica, Barbados, Trinidad, Dominican Republic and others. But you know, none of the ones I talked to were mad at Nate. They genuinely liked him, they thought he was fun. Several said how much they missed him. I got the impression that these women were on to Nate's act, but they weren't holding any grudges."

"I'm not worried about them. It's a jealous boyfriend, husband or even a relative of theirs that worries me."

Detective Jannetta asked me for names of the women that Pa had been seeing over the years. I gave him the names that I could remember from the past but he said that they were all ones I'd given him before and he'd seen them all plus others. He said that he had asked each of them if they knew anyone who might have gone after Nate, but they all said no.

"But, nevertheless, I believe you're right, your father knew his assailant."

Jannetta said this in a way that made it obvious he was probing me for a lead.

"Quite possible," I said. "I agree that seems more likely than that it was a complete stranger. But I don't have a clue who it could have been. My only theory was the jealous boyfriend and you've already looked into that one."

Jannetta then asked, "Can you think of any explanation that might connect the attack on your father with your shooting?"

"I really can't," I said. "I haven't seen that much of my father since my mother died several years back. For a couple of years I didn't speak to him at all, but my sister got us back together. I saw him every three or four months, usually with my sister, at their place, but our lives rarely touched. The timing and location of the two attacks would suggest a connection, but I can't imagine what it could be."

Jannetta was sharp and he had done what he could up to now to find Pa's killer. But, regrettably, isolated murders like this, with no apparent motive other than robbery, often go unsolved. He promised to keep me informed of his continuing investigation and said that I should stay in touch.

On the floor above was the office of Ted Pilkington, the detective assigned to investigate my shooting. We had never met before.

I found him at the soft drinks machine. Pilkington was six foot, blond, had blue eyes and looked to be around thirty. He borrowed two quarters from me.

"I'm glad to meet you at last," he said. "It was touch and go there with you at first. It's good to see you up and about."

We walked back to his office. It was similar to Jannetta's: four desks in a space better suited for one or two. Pilkington's area was tidy, unlike the other three.

"The docs wouldn't let me see you," Pilkington said, shaking his head. "That was frustrating. When we have a shooting victim survive, particularly when it's a cop, they usually can give us the shooter's name and address or, at the very least, a good physical description. But the doctors said that you couldn't tell me anything. Say that isn't so."

"I wish it wasn't true but I have no recall of what happened. I lost that piece of my memory when I was shot in the head."

I pointed to the scar above my right eye.

He pursued it further.

"Why were you in that alley that evening? Did it have anything to do with any case you were working on?"

"I just don't know. It's all a blank."

"It was only a couple of blocks from where your father had been mugged. Could it have been related to that?"

I could only repeat the sad story of my lack of any memory of that period of time, and for several weeks up to and including my own injury. I told him that Jannetta thought my father might have known his attacker.

I asked him what he had found out in his investigation. He had to go to a cabinet to get the file. I got the impression that my case was no longer on the top of his list, if it ever was. Since I have survived, it was technically not a homicide. But since I was a cop, they kept my investigation here. Pilkington had obviously been hoping that I would wake up one morning and tell him who to arrest.

He looked at the file.

"At 12.23 a.m. on June 4, Emergency Medical gets a call from some kids saying that a detective has been shot and is probably dead in an alley behind the Park View Hotel. A cruiser went right there and saw that you were still alive, but barely. Within five minutes an ambulance arrived and took you to Kings County. The crime scene area was cordoned off. I got there just after 1.00 a.m. A forensics team was searching the area. They came up with the spent bullet that hit you, a .24 calibre. We didn't find another shred of evidence."

He continued, "I was able to interview the kids who called EMS. We had a hell of a time finding them. They had split after calling 911. Fortunately, they had your wallet and one of them had tried to use your bank card to get money. We ID'd him from the tape. At first we thought that the kids had done it, but we concluded it was unlikely. If they had, they never would have called it in. And, face it, their call saved your life.

"The kids, two boys fourteen and fifteen, said they heard what they thought were two or three gunshots shortly before midnight. They walked over to the alley and looked in but could see nothing. They waited a few minutes until they were sure that whoever'd been shooting was gone, then they went in and found you. They took your wallet and ran. Not until later, when they saw your badge, did they decide to call it in."

Then he told me what else he had done.

"We canvassed the neighbourhood, but no window looked down into the part of the alley where you were shot, except for a few in the hotel. Those rooms were not occupied and apparently no one in the hotel heard or saw anything. The night clerk was watching TV. He says a guest, an older man, went out for a walk shortly before you were shot, but the clerk was sure that the man walked east, towards Billington. That's the opposite way from where you were found."

"Did you interview the old man? Maybe he saw something as he came out of the hotel."

"He'd checked out before we got there the next morning." Pilkington checked his notes. "He paid cash. He was registered as P. LeBlanc, gave an address in Montreal, but it was either bogus or his handwriting was so bad that we couldn't make it out. I called the cops up there to see if they could help us find him but they were worse than useless. Apparently, LeBlanc is a big name up there and 'P', for Paul or Pierre, is a very common first initial. We talked about sending someone up there but, as you know, travel money is tight and it didn't look like much of a lead anyway."

I was a little miffed that the Department didn't make a bigger effort to find out who shot me, but this guy was right about travel money. There was a new mayor and money was scarce. And, in truth, there was little chance that the old guy saw anything; I was shot down in the alley behind the hotel, he had gone out the front door and turned the opposite way.

"What else did you do?"

"We put out the word to the network of informants in Brooklyn to see if anyone was talking about the detective who was shot around midnight on June third. A couple of things were fed back but they too proved to be bogus."

Pilkington had nothing else. There didn't seem to be much going on. I left.

I went to Brooklyn to spend Christmas Eve with Elyce and, on Christmas Day, we went to Freeport, Long Island, for me to meet her new boyfriend. Nice guy, a bit older than Elyce, a widower with grown kids but a good match. He loves Elyce and she loves him. I left after dinner because I was off to Barbados early the next day, the day after Christmas, the day known as Boxing Day in Barbados and other parts of what once was the British Empire.

The above is my first daily report of activities outside of Wickham, primarily drawn from the notes I took of my meetings with Jannetta and Pilkington. Shannon was right, it was easy for me to do this, given my background and training. However, it was ironic that my first such report was mostly based on police work.

Daily Report 2

Date of Events: Thursday, 26 December 1996
Place: Barbados: Glenville, St Charles
Summary: On Uncle Clarence

In my hired white Nissan I turned up the small hill to Glenville House. The same old Glenville House sign was there, but its letters had faded and it hung sideways, supported by only one nail. The bougainvillea, primarily red and white, which when I was last here had circled the veranda posts, now grew high on the roof. It totally obscured the windows on the second storey.

The veranda roof sagged from the weight of the bougainvillea, and probably from termite damage and the ravages of time as well. In front, where flowering plants had neatly grown, weeds now ruled. Only the hardy crotons still splashed their colour on the scene.

I parked my car and walked up to the front door. No one was in evidence. I rapped on the door and heard a familiar voice, Grandma Dora's, coming from upstairs.

"Just a minute. I'll be right there."

A few moments later, she appeared at the door. I knew her right away. Of course, she has aged in the twenty-four years since last I saw her. She's now in her eighties, but her blue eyes still sparkle in her wrinkled face. She was wearing a faded pink dress. It looked like, and may well have been, the same "best dress" as she had had twenty-four years ago.

She didn't recognise me, and how could she? When I last was in Barbados, I was an awkward fourteen-year-old boy, and now I am a grown man of thirty-eight.

She looked at me quizzically, waiting for me to state my business. Then she said, "Sir, you've come at a bad time. What is it that you want?"

I said, "Grandma Dora, it's me, Ben."

Her hand went involuntarily to her mouth and she gave a slight squeak. Whether it was a sound of surprise, joy or some other emotion, I couldn't say.

"Oh, thank God you've come. But Ben, how did you know he was dead?" she asked in a quavering voice.

I stopped, confused. I had come all this way to tell her of my father's, her son Nate's, death. And yet, she seemed already to be aware of it and, for some reason, was wondering how I knew.

Then it struck me, she wasn't talking about Pa, it must have been somebody else. The only "he" at Glenville House was Clarence.

I asked, "Grandma Dora, don't tell me Uncle Clarence is dead?"

"Oh yes, oh yes, our Clarence is dead. He had an accident. We've just come from his funeral at St Charles parish church."

I held my grandmother in my arms as she sobbed. I felt an overwhelming sadness. First my father and now his half-brother, my uncle Clarence. How much grief could these people take?

How small Glenville House looks now. In my memories the rooms were large and airy. In fact they are tiny and dark. The rambling bougainvillea blocks what little sunlight filters through the surrounding trees.

Although the house is smaller than I remembered, Grandma Dora is still formidable. Her hair is thin and grey and her face a sea of wrinkles, but she still moves gracefully and steadily and her voice is strong and clear. It appears that the years of labour in the garden have helped spare Eudora Glenville the usual infirmities of her age.

Time has been less kind to Aunt Emily. She is paler and thinner and more duppy-like than ever. Her light blue eyes still smile shyly at me, but she has shrivelled physically. Her hands appear to be crippled by arthritis and her voice is a barely audible whisper.

Grandma Dora was impressed by my size and that I am now a mature man and a policeman at that. She was sorry to hear that I have not yet married but, she assured me, "the right girl is out there waiting for you."

I told her that I can only stay until Monday. I have to go back to New York on 30th December. The next flight available isn't till 4th January. My out-patient therapy is to begin on the second, but I didn't tell her about that.

The principal topic of conversation was, of course, Clarence's death. They told me that he had died last Monday in a fall from the top of the cliff. It was an accident. That's what the police told them.

The death of Clarence had taken an emotional toll. Emily shook as if she had a fever and Grandma Dora, from time to time, when she allowed herself to focus on Clarence's death, moaned and wrung her hands in anguish. Their lives had been so simple up until now.

Grandma Dora said that Clarence had remained strong and active to the day he died. I can still picture him in my mind working steadily in the garden all day, every day but Sunday. He seemed tireless.

Grandma Dora said that, as she grew older, Clarence had shouldered more and more of the day-to-day work of the garden. Of course, the garden is much smaller now than when we all worked there. The Glenvilles had long since given up selling their excess produce at the market in Bridgetown. The old truck had died and there was no money to replace it. The garden now produced just enough for their own table and to barter with neighbours for fish and chicken.

I asked Grandma Dora, "What do you know about what happened to Uncle Clarence?"

"He had said that he was going back to the cliff. The garden is much smaller these days and your uncle only worked there in the cool of the morning. He would often go for a stroll in the afternoons. He said that there was something he had seen there on Sunday and he wanted to check on it. It was probably a newly-hatched nest of sea birds. Clarence loved that walk and all of its creatures," she related sadly.

This was the same walk I had taken with him many times. I remember him climbing the rocks barefooted, as sure-footed as any mountain goat. But, on this day, somehow, he fell to his death on the rocks in the sea below.

"When Clarence didn't return to the house from his walk, Emily and I assumed that he'd gone right to his cottage in the garden to get an early night's sleep; he'd done that before. It wasn't until he didn't appear for breakfast on Tuesday that we became concerned."

Grandma Dora looked at Emily. Aunt Emily buried her face in her crippled hands. My grandmother continued, "His body was discovered later in the morning by fishermen from Morton's Cove. Clarence's body was taken by the police and sent to a funeral home. Our Clarence was buried at St Charles parish church earlier today, in the Glenville family plot."

Today is Thursday. Clarence wasn't discovered until Tuesday. Just three days; pretty quick for a burial under these circumstances, in my experience.

Grandma Dora said, "Your uncle was always nimble. He was by no means as swift as in the past – after all, he was over seventy years old. But he had always led an active life. He was still strong and free of the arthritis which cripples Emily. It is hard for me to believe that he would just fall off the cliff."

We sat in silence and contemplated the mystery and the tragedy of Clarence's death.

That silence seemed to be an opportunity for me to do what I had avoided until then, tell them of my own father's death. I hated to add to their burden of sorrow, but Grandma Dora was Pa's mother and Emily his half-sister, they deserved to know. They'd have to hear about it, sooner or later, and there wouldn't ever be a good time to break the news. Since I'll be here in Barbados for only a few days, I thought I'd better get on with it. And, who knows, maybe it would be better for them to have all the bad news at one time.

I told them as gently as I could. I attributed Pa's death to a senseless act of violence, so common in a big city like New York. Grandma Dora and Emily certainly don't have to know that Pa may have gotten himself killed by chasing the wrong skirt.

I explained that it had happened several months ago and I felt it was necessary to come to tell them in person but I had had a "bad accident", and I'd been unable to travel for several months. I pointed to the scar on my forehead but didn't burden them with any more detail.

They were shocked at Nate's death; they sat in silence. I wished I could somehow have avoided telling them at all. Their lives had been free of such traumas for so long that I feared the piling of one death upon the other might have been too much for them.

You could see that they were saddened and depressed by what I had said. Although it was only five thirty and still light, they both went up to bed.

I boiled some water and took them each a cup of tea. Emily was asleep, or at least pretending to be, so I left the tea on her bedside table, with the saucer on top. Grandma Dora was awake, lying in her bed, the creases in her face filled with tears.

I sat down on the edge of the bed and patted her on the shoulder.

She said, "Oh Ben, how much more can I take? My boys are gone. What am I to do?"

She was shocked by these deaths, and I suspected she was also concerned about what the future might hold for her and Emily. Of most immediate concern, how would they survive without Clarence to tend the garden?

I tried to reassure her as best I could. I stayed with her until she finally fell asleep. Then I went back downstairs and made myself some tea. As I drank it, I mentally went over the events of the last few days.

The coincidence of the deaths of Nate Cumberbatch, in Brooklyn, and his half-brother Clarence Glenville, in Barbados a half-year later, rankled in my police-trained brain. And, don't forget, there was a third event: I was shot in the head and left for dead.

I long ago learned that, when it comes to crime, similar events, although seemingly unconnected, can often prove to be related.

An old detective once told me, "Crimes usually fit into a pattern. The art is to be able to see that pattern. It is not always an easy thing to do."

That's what detectives do; we try to make logic out of the illogic of criminal activity. Professional criminals – not always your most intelligent individuals in my experience – often repeat themselves. They do what they know has worked for them before. The police call these repetitive activities the criminal's modus operandi or, for short, their "m.o.".

If you spot a familiar m.o. it's like seeing an artist's name written on the bottom of a picture. And when you catch a criminal, you go back to review unsolved cases to see which other ones might bear this signature.

Two unnatural deaths, possibly two murders, in the same family, would be most unusual. One might think that they could be related. For example, that there was a single killer, or possibly two different killers, each with the same motive for the killing.

But it seems unlikely in these cases. Six months separate them and Brooklyn and Barbados are nearly three thousand miles apart. Plus, my father and my uncle had not seen each other or been in touch for forty years. Pa's death, on a dangerous street in Brooklyn, and Clarence's, possibly an accident, many months later on a rocky cliff in St Charles, don't seem to form a pattern.

And I can think of no reason why anyone would want them both dead. Who could conceivably benefit from their deaths? No one that I can think of. Maybe, in this instance, these deaths really are a coincidence. Such things happen. But as long as I am here, I should check it out further, to satisfy my own curiosity, and to maintain my self-respect as a cop.

Daily Report 3

Date of Events: Friday, 27 December 1996
Place: Barbados: Glenville; District C Police Station; Hinds Funeral Home, Oistins
Summary: Enquiries re Clarence

This morning I asked Grandma Dora if there was any reason to think that someone might have wanted Clarence dead.

"Oh no, Ben. You knew Clarence, he was one of the gentlest, kindest men in the whole of Barbados. He seldom left Glenville land except for his afternoon strolls. I can't imagine that he ever ran into anybody. If he did, Clarence would have been shy of them and would certainly have gone out of his way not to give offence."

Grandma Dora declared this with such conviction that I had to agree that the thought of Clarence having an enemy was hard to imagine.

"What about the Glenville kin?" I asked. They had once been anxious to cheat Dora out of her inheritance.

Grandma Dora said, "Most of them have either moved away or have died off. There are only a few kin left in Glenville village and they're either old or infirm. All of them together couldn't have pushed Clarence off the cliff."

And, frankly, looking around Glenville House and grounds, it was hard to imagine anyone killing Clarence to gain this decrepit home and its modest, overworked garden.

I then asked her if there had been anything out of the ordinary which had happened of late. Grandma Dora said that she couldn't think of a thing.

"Has there been anything at all involving Uncle Clarence?" I pursued the subject.

She shook her head slowly, then paused and said, "Well, this is pretty far-fetched, but a few months ago a Mr Lewis came by and asked me if Glenville was for sale. I explained that it was not mine to sell, that it had been willed by my father to Clarence. Lewis asked to speak to him but Clarence wouldn't even come out of his little house to discuss the subject. So, Lewis went away. He did appear to be irritated."

Lewis, Lewis. Wasn't that the name of Edgar Mount's overseer, I asked Grandma Dora, but she didn't know.

"What did he look like?" I asked.

"Ben, I don't know what to say. He was a good-looking man. A white man. Tall, like you. He had grey hair and a moustache. He was probably in his fifties. He drove a big green car, it looked like a military vehicle."

She said that Lewis seemed to be inquiring on his own behalf since he never mentioned Edgar Mount or Savannah Plantation. He said that he lived at Rosewood Plantation in St Philip. From her description of him, it could well have been the same man that I remember from my visit to Savannah Plantation all those years ago.

I next asked Grandma Dora if she had heard of any unexplained crimes in the area – my thought being that perhaps Clarence had the misfortune to run into a local serial killer. Grandma Dora said that she had heard of none, but admitted that she didn't read the paper regularly and that she and Emily only listened to music on the radio and, in hurricane season, to the weather reports.

The name of the policeman who had come to tell Grandma Dora of Clarence's death was Constable Norman Greenidge, from the District C police station in St Philip.

My little car chugged up the steep Station Hill to the District C station at around ten thirty this morning. Several large white buildings, looking like the military fort that they once had been, perched on a ridge overlooking a broad plain of sugar cane fields and small villages. From here the District C police oversee their area of responsibility: the rural parishes of St John, St Philip and St Charles.

Greenidge was not there when I arrived, but he was due to report in thirty minutes. I spoke with a Sergeant Brathwaite, the senior policeman present. I explained that I was Clarence Glenville's nephew and that I was a policeman in New York City.

Brathwaite examined my badge and credentials carefully. Then, satisfied that I was who and what I claimed, he told me that he had been on duty when the telephone call came from the fishermen about Clarence.

He checked his log and said, "It was at 9:18 a.m. on the Christmas Eve Tuesday. Fisherman calls in. He says that they had spent the night in Oistins drinking and were returning in their boat to Morton's Cove in the early morning. We have confirmed their whereabouts. They spotted a person floating in the rough sea in a place they call 'The Cauldron'."

I know the area, Uncle Clarence and I walked the cliff above there many times. Below, large rocks form a turbulent pool that is stirred up in all but the calmest weather. It's probably the roughest stretch of water on that coast.

Brathwaite continued, "No one swims in that place so they know that whoever it was, he was either in trouble or already dead. When they got closer, they could see the body face down in the water. Your uncle was a big man. They could not lift him out of the sea, so they use their fish net and bring him on board.

"The fishermen knew at once he was Clarence Glenville. They know the man from when he come to Morton's Cove to trade his vegetables for fish. As soon as they got to Morton's, one contacted us while the other stayed on the boat with the body."

Just then Constable Greenidge came in, reporting for duty. He looked to be around twenty-five or so. He was just under six foot and had the slim waist and broad shoulders of an athlete. I waited while the constable checked the duty roster and turned in some paperwork. Then Sergeant Brathwaite told him who I was and pointed to a table nearby where we could sit to talk. As usual, I was making detailed notes.

We were within easy earshot of the sergeant. I think that our positioning there was not by accident; Sergeant Brathwaite wanted to hear just what we said. Although he pretended to be reading reports, I could tell he was listening carefully to every word.

Constable Greenidge also appeared to be aware that our conversation was being monitored. He was stiff and formal. His answers to my questions were succinct and he gave me the minimum of information.

"I was in the area, not far from Morton's Cove, when the boat came in with the body," he said.

"Why were you there?"

"That's my area. I patrol that part of St Charles parish, both on foot and bicycle."

He told me that he periodically checked in with the station. He had called in at ten o'clock. The sergeant had instructed him to get over to the fishing village as soon as possible.

"The body was still in the boat, lying in the fishing net. No one had touched it. I oversaw the fishermen as they hoisted the net and set the body on the pier."

The constable said that Clarence Glenville appeared to have drowned after having fallen from the cliff above.

I asked him to describe the body.

"His head was bloody."

"Anything else?"

He didn't answer so I asked him a different way. "Were there any other injuries?"

"The fingers was bloody and broken."

"How do you think these injuries came about?"

"I don't know."

"Give me your best estimate."

"He slipped. His head was bloodied up from hitting rocks on the way down or at the bottom."

I asked him, "Please describe how the injuries to the head looked."

The constable again didn't answer except to mumble something that sounded like, "Just a wound from a rock." Then he looked out of the corner of his eye at the sergeant.

Sergeant Brathwaite leaned over and said, "We examined the body here."

He said that the body had been brought to the District C police station and examined there and, "it confirmed what Constable Greenidge say."

"How long was the body here?"

"Two hours, then it was taken to a funeral home to be prepared for burial."

I asked, "Who conducted the examination?"

Brathwaite said, "I did."

So there had been no examination of the body by a coroner or any other medical authority. It was hard to believe that a decision on whether or not to call in an expert would be left to the discretion of a desk sergeant at a rural precinct, even here in Barbados.

When I asked him why no coroner had been called, the sergeant said, "It's not necessary in the case of an accident."

I didn't see anything to be gained by arguing with him.

Clarence had been discovered on Tuesday morning and buried yesterday afternoon, Thursday. The more I thought about it, the more two days seemed an incredibly short time. And yesterday was Boxing Day, a major holiday.

"Why was there such a rush to dispose of the body?"

Neither Brathwaite nor Greenidge commented when I asked this.

When I pressed the point, the sergeant said dismissively, "This is the tropics, man. A body can turn fresh real fast. We got no place to store a body here. And this was Christmas Eve. You wouldn't expect the undertaker to work on Christmas Day, would you? So he had to be buried yesterday."

I have heard my grandma use the term "fresh" for fish that has gone bad and smells, the term meaning just the opposite of how we use it in America. And the sergeant had a point about Christmas. I had no choice but to accept this explanation.

I got the name of the undertaker and then left the policemen with my thanks. But I did leave with the feeling that Constable Greenidge might have told me more if I could have spoken with him away from his sergeant.

The undertaker is located in Oistins, a large fishing village on the south coast, over ten miles from Glenville. It seemed strange that a funeral director from there would be called by Grandma Dora. Surely there were funeral homes closer to Glenville than Oistins.

The Hinds Funeral Home was large and prosperous-looking, located on the hill above the town. In addition to being a funeral home, it also doubled as a taxicab company. An ancient black Cadillac hearse, polished to a bright sheen, sat in the driveway along with three large four-door American cars with small plastic signs identifying them as taxis.

The director of the business, Vere Hinds, met me at the door. He confirmed that he had prepared my uncle for burial.

I asked him, "How did you come to be hired by my grandmother?"

"Very simple, very simple. I was not hired by her. I was hired by Goodman Griffith, not by your grandmother."

"Who is Goodman Griffith?" I asked.

"Everyone in Barbados knows Goody Griffith. He is a big politician and the Member of Parliament representing the parish of St Charles. He is also the Minister of Tourism and Development, second in power only to the Prime Minister in this Government."

Hinds said this smugly as if he was in the know, at the right hand of Griffith and other movers and shakers of the island. I, obviously, was a know-nothing. Worse, I was a know-nothing-know-it-all Bajan Yankee – which is what the locals call the Bajans that come down from America and act superior to their island relatives.

He was partially right. There is a lot I don't know about Barbados. But I would be real surprised to learn that the politicians here on the island routinely pay for the funerals of their humbler constituents.

So I asked him, "Do politicians often ask you to prepare a constituent's body for burial?"

Hinds was suddenly cagey and didn't answer. Finally, he stuttered a bit, then said in a chirpy voice, "Well, it does happen, you know. Goodman Griffith is a very generous man and, ah, I guess he knew that your family could not ah, ah, afford the kind of funeral that a person such as your uh, uh, uncle deserved."

I was not convinced that this Goodman Griffith was motivated by pure generosity. If so, he was not like any politician I ever met in New York.

Hinds said that he had done the work on Uncle Clarence right away, "cause it was Christmas Eve and they was planning for a funeral on Boxing Day."

I asked Hinds to describe the extent of my uncle's injuries. Generally, what he said conformed to the description that I'd

122

received from the constable: the fingers torn and the head crushed.

"On which side?" I asked, taking notes.

Hinds hesitated, staring at my notepad and poised pen, then finally declared, "The whole head, it looked to me like he hit his head on rocks several times as he fell."

"How did my uncle die?" I asked him, purposely not looking at him.

Hinds didn't answer me right away. The question seemed to confuse him so I clarified it.

"Did he die from the hit on his head or did he drown?"

Then he said, "I don't know, I just prepared the body for burial. It was not to be an open casket."

"But surely you would know whether he had died from drowning or if he was already dead when he hit the water?" I pressed him, staring right into his eyes.

Hinds seemed to be growing more and more uncomfortable with my questions.

"You must see people all the time who have died from drowning, am I not right?"

Hinds nodded his head slowly in agreement.

"Well, was this a drowned man or not?"

Hinds again said that he didn't know how Clarence had died. The police had told him that the man had drowned and he had no reason to question it.

When I got back to Glenville House, I reviewed my notes to see what I had learned. I started with the parallel deaths of my father and my uncle, nearly seven months apart and, apparently, both caused by blows to the head.

I know that Pa was murdered by a left-handed, pipe-wielding killer. This killer may have been a mugger but the ferocity of the attack suggests that the killer had motivation other than simple robbery. He either hated my father for personal reasons or he wanted to be damned sure that Nate was dead.

Uncle Clarence apparently also sustained one or several blows to his head, whether that was what killed him or not. Everyone has said that Clarence's wounds were the result of having struck rocks as he fell from the cliff. However, if these blows had been from a weapon, not a rock, it should have been apparent to anyone experienced in seeing victims of violent death, such as the police or an undertaker. Both the police and Hinds have been quite consistent in their belief that his wounds were from hitting a rock or rocks. But I'm not sure that what I've been told is the whole truth.

I've decided that I have to get a look at Uncle Clarence's body before I leave Barbados. But there's not nearly enough time to get permission to open the grave. In fact, even if there was time, I doubt the authorities would grant such permission to me, an outsider.

Clarence is lying in a freshly-dug grave at St Charles parish church; although Grandma Dora and her children didn't attend services there, Clarence was a Glenville and this graveyard is the family's historic burying ground. Even here in the countryside, you can't go into a graveyard in broad daylight and start digging up a body. I have a plan, but both Grandma Dora and Aunt Emily will have to agree with what I want to do. I wouldn't want to upset them more than they already are.

And tomorrow I will find Vincent Lewis and ask him why he wanted to talk to Clarence about buying Glenville House.

Daily Report 4

Date of Events: Saturday, 28 December 1996
Place: Barbados: The Barbados Museum; the Garrison; the Garrison Club
Summary: Meetings Hugh Brodeur, Vincent Lewis

A rum shop in Morton's Cove has a telephone. I borrowed a telephone book. Vincent Lewis was in the book as an unlisted number, but there was a listing for his home, Rosewood Plantation. I placed a telephone call there. A woman answered the phone. She sounded English.

"Rosewood Plantation," she said.

"Is Vincent Lewis there, please?"

"No, he is not here at present."

She slurred her answer slightly. "Present" came out as "preshend". It was only ten o'clock in the morning or I might have thought that the woman, presumably Mrs Lewis, had been drinking.

"Do you know how I might be able to reach him?"

The woman laughed but did not answer. I was not sure that I got the joke.

"Would you have a number where I could reach him sometime today?"

"What day is it? Saturday? This Saturday you can catch up with him at the Garrison Club at lunch time." Her voice sounded bitter.

I got the distinct impression that all was not going well on the domestic home front for Mr Lewis.

I thanked her. I presumed that I could find the address of the Garrison Club in the phone book. Wrong. It was not listed – not in the white pages and not in the yellow pages under "clubs", where the listings were primarily athletic clubs for cricket and football. I concluded that either this club was awfully exclusive or it was brand new. It turned out that I was right on both counts.

I know that the Garrison is what people call the large open area, formerly the site of the British Army's principal operational base in the Caribbean, on the coastal road south of Bridgetown. The British had a large military presence here in Barbados for over three hundred years and, on this site, they had trained and outfitted the soldiers who protected and controlled the British West Indies.

The British flag was lowered in Barbados thirty years ago and the open grassy area is now used solely for a handsome new horse-racing track. Many of the old colonial military two-storey red brick buildings surrounding the race track have been converted to other purposes. Some are government buildings and one is the site of the Barbados Museum. It seemed logical to me that a place called the Garrison Club would be located in this general area. I decided to drive there to see if I could find it.

It was nearly eleven thirty by the time I arrived at the Garrison. I knew that in Barbados horse-racing was a big, well-attended activity, and it was normally held on Saturdays. This was Christmas week, the height of the tourist season. I had expected to see crowds already gathering to attend the races that afternoon. But, to my surprise, there were no magnificent horses and jockeys, no owners, no well-dressed spectators nor hard-core bettors. Today the track and the stands were empty.

I drove slowly past the buildings, looking for some indication of where the Garrison Club is located. I did a complete circle around the Garrison but I could find no sign of it. Maybe I was mistaken. Perhaps it was named for the Garrison but was actually located elsewhere?

I went into the one-storey building that states it is the Barbados Turf Club, thinking that surely they would know where the Garrison Club is. But they didn't, or at least the people I talked to acted as if they had never heard of it. I did learn why the track was empty. This week's races took place two days ago. During Christmas week, I was told, racing is customarily held on Boxing Day, not necessarily on a Saturday.

I visited several other buildings asking people for the Garrison Club, with the same result. Finally I went into the Barbados Museum. The young lady selling tickets suggested that I inquire at the Museum Library upstairs.

I walked up to the second floor, past bookcases bulging with old books and magazines. I saw a woman at a desk.

"Excuse me, would you happen to know where the Garrison Club is located?"

"Do you mean the Turf Club?" she asked, in a withering tone.

"No, I've been there. I mean the Garrison Club. This is different; I think that it is a private men's club where business people meet and have lunch."

"Let me handle this, Mrs Johnson," said an older gentleman seated nearby. He was lanky, balding, with white hair and a moustache.

He introduced himself. His name was Hugh Brodeur. He was an Englishman by his accent but, he was quick to tell me, had been a resident of "this blessed island" for nearly sixty years.

Brodeur invited me to join him at the large, cluttered library table where he had been working.

"May I inquire how you heard of this Garrison Club?" he asked.

I was not about to tell him my business.

"I was told that I should meet someone there at lunch time."

"May I ask who you are meeting there?"

127

I ignored his question and said, "I would just appreciate it if you could tell me where it is located."

"I wish I knew. The existence of a new club has been rumoured for months, but this is the first time that I have heard an outsider refer to it, and it is the first time that I have heard it called the Garrison Club."

I must have looked confused.

He continued, "For years there has been a businessman's club in Bridgetown, called the Broad Street Club. I happen to be a member there myself. It is located in the Barclays Bank building on, not surprisingly, Broad Street. Until I retired, I was an officer of that bank.

"The Broad Street Club has fallen on bad days," Brodeur went on sadly. "Most of its members are older now. Most of them, like me, have retired. The principal activity there is lunch and the odd game of bridge. The really important people of this island, the large landowners and the men that own the rum factories, hotels and trading companies, are members but they are largely inactive. Frankly, without their support, the Broad Street Club will soon have to close its doors."

Brodeur was clearly unhappy about this prospect.

"It has been said that the most important people, the dozen or so people that control the economy of Barbados, have set up a new club of their own and that this club meets only once a week. From what you say, this club is calling itself the Garrison Club and may be meeting today."

"I take it that you don't know where it is," I commented, "but I'm sure you know the area well enough to give me an educated guess as to where it might be?"

Brodeur thought for a bit, then he said, "If I was looking to set something like this up, I think I would do it in the old Army NCO Infirmary building. It is a small two-storey building that can only be reached from a side street. It doesn't face the main

Garrison ring road. Members could come and go there without being noticed."

Brodeur explained to me how to get there. I thanked him and got up from the table to leave. He said, "If you do find it, I'd appreciate it if you would tell me where it is."

I promised that I would, but I had no reason to think that our paths would ever cross again.

I was able to find the side street that Brodeur had suggested. It was residential, a mixture of wooden chattel houses and the newer, more substantial concrete block variety, what the locals call "wall houses". On the corner there was a small rum shop, whose open door provided a good view of the courtyard of the old Army Infirmary building. A sign, posted by the Barbados Historical Society on the coral block wall outside the courtyard, confirmed that this building was indeed formerly the Non-Commissioned Officers' Infirmary.

It was nearly noon. Only one customer, a small old man, apparently a fixture in the place, was seated on one of the three stools nursing a Banks beer. The owner, a tough-looking, heavy-set man, appeared from the back and gruffly asked, "What would you like?"

"What is your best seller?" I said.

He poured me a three-ounce shot of a clear liquid. When he put the bottle down, I could see that it was rum. None of your fancy, caramel-coloured rum. This was the real thing, clear as water. I took a cautious taste and sat down to watch whatever might happen across the street.

Over the next half an hour, fourteen cars arrived. They were, without exception, big and powerful cars, no doubt reflecting the persons driving or being driven within them. Interestingly, not all these persons were what I had expected. I had assumed from what Brodeur had said that these people would without exception be white males. And most were but, to my surprise, an Indian or Pakistani woman arrived in one of two Rolls Royces, and two of the men were black while another appeared to be an oriental. Whatever else you cared to say about it, the Garrison Club was integrated. That's good news, I guess.

At twelve thirty, I drained the last of my white rum and crossed the street to the courtyard where the British Army's ambulances had once stood. As I moved out into the midday sun I could feel the rum in my belly. It glowed warmly, and I felt the slight euphoria that is the reward – or punishment – for having a stiff drink on an empty stomach and then walking in the sun.

Fourteen cars and a large catering van were squeezed into the courtyard. I could see why the membership was limited; there wasn't room for even one more vehicle. One of the vehicles was a green Land-Rover with a P before the numbers on its licence plate. I knew that this meant that this car's owner resided in St Philip. Vincent Lewis's home, Rosewood Plantation, was in St Philip. I also assumed that this Land-Rover was the "military vehicle" that Grandma Dora had mentioned.

Good, Lewis was here. Maybe I would get some answers.

Nowhere in sight was there a sign that said "The Garrison Club". A small sign on the wall next to some steps leading to the second floor said "Private". This was all the signage I was going to find.

I mounted the stairs. At the top was a set of new, heavy mahogany doors with shiny brass fittings. A small brass plate repeated the assertion, "Private".

I anticipated that a warm welcome might not be waiting for me inside.

I started to knock and then I thought, *What the hell*. I grasped the doorknob and pushed. To my surprise, the door opened to my touch. I found myself in a small reception area. A heavy blast of air-conditioning chilled the room. To me, warmed by my drink of rum and the walk in the sun from the rum shop, it seemed way too cool.

No one was in sight.

Through an archway on my left, I could see a bar and several overstuffed leather chairs. From behind heavy, gleaming, solid-wood double doors on my right I could hear the rattle of cutlery and plates set against a background of voices in serious discussion. At one point, a voice raised in anger, another voice cursed and then there was general laughter from many voices. It sounded like the entire membership of the Garrison Club was in that room.

From out of a door behind the bar, a slender black man in a white shirt, black pants and bow tie emerged holding a platter of soup bowls.

"What you doin' here, mister?" he said. Then he turned, put down the tray and called into the doorway behind him, "Clem! Come here, we got us a visitor. Did you forget to lock that door?"

Clem was bigger and younger than his companion. He looked out of the door and, when he saw me, he ducked back inside. He re-emerged with a cane-cutter's cutlass which he held menacingly. Clem appeared to be ready and able to use this weapon, should I present any sort of problem.

"I am here to speak with Mr Vincent Lewis," I said, in my most official tone of voice.

The two men stopped and exchanged glances. I got the impression that "Vincent Lewis" might be magic words here at the Garrison Club.

"My name is Benjamin Cumberbatch, I am the grandson of Dora Glenville. I know that Mr Lewis would wish to speak with me."

I knew nothing of the sort, but it was worth a shot.

The older man walked carefully past me, knocked on the double door and entered. A full two minutes passed. I could hear the vague buzz of conversation.

The man re-emerged and said, "Mr Lewis will be with you in a minute. Please sit over there." He pointed to a small leather sofa.

The door eventually opened again and a tall, grey-haired man entered the reception area. He was wearing a light tan suit and a regimental tie. I recognised him as an older version of the man from twenty-four years ago at Savannah Plantation.

Lewis moved purposefully and appeared fit and athletic. His face had the hard expression of someone who expects to control every situation. He fixed a cold stare on me.

"Ah, Mr Cumberbatch, from New York, I believe?"

I nodded and he continued, "How did you find me here? Not too many people know about this little club. And why would you know to look for me here on a Saturday? We normally convene only on Thursdays."

"Your wife told me and …"

"Of course," he interrupted me. "That was naughty of her, but no matter, I welcome the opportunity to meet you. Incidentally, I was sorry to read of your uncle's death."

"That is why I am here to see you," I said, getting right to the point. "My grandmother said that several months ago you came to Glenville House and wanted to buy the property but that my uncle, who stood to inherit the land upon my grandmother's death, would not even speak to you."

A look of anger briefly flared in Lewis's eyes. The memory of my uncle's refusal to speak with him apparently still irritated him. Such a rejection was probably a rare occurrence for the exalted Mr Lewis. But surely it wouldn't have made him so angry that he would have wanted to kill Clarence – or would it?

"That is true. But it was of no consequence. It was a very preliminary inquiry, I assure you," Lewis said very casually.

I made no comment so he continued, "As you may know, I own a good deal of land in the eastern parishes. I just wanted to know if there was any possibility that Glenville would be for sale any time soon. It was clear that your uncle was not interested in selling and that was the end of it." He spoke quickly, as if it was a matter of little importance.

Lewis continued, "Please express my sympathies to your, ah, family. It may seem insensitive of me but I can't help but wonder, with the death of your uncle, perhaps your grandmother might now wish to sell the land?"

I had no idea what Grandma Dora was thinking about the future. In all likelihood, she hadn't focused on it at all. I certainly didn't want Lewis coming around and bothering her about selling Glenville.

"We have not discussed it. I doubt that my grandmother has even considered it. However, I will speak to her before I leave the island and if there is any interest at all on her part, I will let you know."

Lewis then shook my hand, not in friendship but as an act of dismissal from his presence. He strode across the room and returned to the meeting behind the heavy double doors. Clem and his companion continued to keep a careful eye on me as I made my way out the front door.

What have I learned? That Lewis is an arrogant and tough son-of-a-bitch. And that he is still interested in acquiring Glenville. Interested enough to have had Uncle Clarence removed from the picture? That remains to be seen.

I also now know about the Garrison Club, something that's not widely known in Barbados. I know that the real movers and shakers of Barbados meet there on the sly. To do what? Not to play cards, I'll wager. Probably they meet to settle their differences, apportion the turf and carve up the rest.

What part could Glenville House's little four acres play in their plans? I suspect that if and when I find out what happened to my uncle, I will know that too.

Daily Report 5

Date of Events: Saturday, 28 December 1996 – night
Place: Barbados: St Charles parish church
Summary: Examining Clarence

An unlikelier group of grave robbers you could not imagine. My eighty-seven-year-old grandmother, my seventy-one-year-old albino aunt and me, a walking wounded New York police detective with a memory problem.

Grave robbing is hardly one of my normal investigative techniques but I don't see that I had a choice. There was little likelihood that a formal request for disinterment would be granted. In any case, I don't have the time to pursue that route. I'm here for only one more day.

When I explained to Grandma Dora what I intended to do, to go to the graveyard and open Clarence's grave to examine his injuries, I feared she would be offended by the idea and would forbid me to do it. If she did, I would have had to honour her wishes.

I explained to her, "If I can determine that Clarence did not die in an accident but he was killed like Pa, it might mean that the same person killed them or they were killed for the same reason. This could help us to know why they were killed and to see the guilty person or persons are brought to justice."

She was clearly distressed by the idea that the grave would be opened but Grandma Dora understood why it had to be done and, to my relief, agreed.

"You are a policeman, Ben. I am sure that you are right."

In fact, Grandma Dora then insisted that she and Emily come along with me to help me locate the correct grave.

We waited until well after dark. About ten o'clock we drove over the hill to St Charles parish church. When we got within a hundred yards of the church, I turned off the lights and pulled my rented car off the road, out of sight.

St Charles parish dates back to the 1600s, but the church building itself has been destroyed by hurricanes on more than one occasion. The current structure dates only from the 1870s. The graveyard, of course, survived the storms and includes grave markers and family mausoleums from as early as 1657. Tour buses regularly visit it to see the graves and the lovely church.

The main graveyard is a jumble of moss-covered headstones, with a dozen family names, including Glenville, predominating. It is virtually full, and in recent years most new graves have been sited in a new graveyard a few hundred yards down the road. However, Clarence was buried in one of the last available spaces in the Glenville plot in the old graveyard, next to his father/grandfather and other Glenvilles.

The graveyard is surrounded by a low stone fence. Large, old, malformed mahogany trees grow amid the gravestones and create a dense canopy. Tree roots have pushed some gravestones at odd angles but, in general, the graveyard appears carefully tended.

A gate, open during the day, is closed and padlocked at night by the churchwarden, presumably to discourage unwanted visitors in the graveyard and the church. But the stone fence is only waist high and presents no real barrier to entry.

I put the shovel and pick over the wall and then easily vaulted over after them. I reached back and lifted over first Grandma Dora and then Aunt Emily. Grandma Dora was not heavy but Emily was lighter yet, a feather. As I grasped her waist, I could feel nothing but skin and bones.

I'd been called upon to do some unusual and sometimes dangerous things in the line of duty, but this was my first effort at grave robbing. I wondered how the women would react.

I need not have worried. Although Grandma Dora was not a woman of the world she had survived for a long time in a demanding life under difficult circumstances. She seemed to take the situation in stride. But Emily had lived an extremely sheltered life, in every sense of the word. She seldom even left her house. Until Clarence's funeral, she had not been seen in broad daylight for many years. I was amazed at Aunt Emily's reaction to being there. I could see in her eyes that she was frightened but also excited by what was happening, and ready for whatever would occur. I think Emily was more up for what we were about to do than either her mother or me.

We had my flashlight, but we didn't want to use it for fear that someone would see us before we had completed our task. Emily took me by the hand and led me to Clarence's grave. Then, she and her mother went to opposite ends of the fence to watch for anyone who might be coming. Grandma Dora was at the end of the graveyard by the road, the most probable direction for an interruption, and Emily, at the opposite end, was closest to the rear entrance of the old church.

The newly dug earth was easy to turn. It's late December, the beginning of the dry season, and no significant rain has fallen since Clarence's burial two days ago. But the clay soil was surprisingly heavy and soon I was sweating. Four feet down, I finally struck a plain wooden box, the simple casket of Clarence Glenville.

I uncovered the entire lid and could see that the wooden cover was nailed shut in four places. I made the hole larger so I could use the point of the pick to pry the lid open.

Grandma Dora came to see what was taking so long. I chanced a short beam of light from the flashlight to show her the coffin lid. She watched, her hand to her mouth, as I pried the lid up and then freed it from the last nail.

Grandma Dora drew in her breath as she looked into the coffin.

Uncle Clarence lay there peacefully, arms folded and eyes closed. He was dressed in an old brown suit that Grandma Dora had provided, but relatively little other preparation of the body was in evidence. The funeral director had merely dressed Clarence and stuffed him into his simplest pine box. Vere Hinds had done the minimum amount of work for his fee.

Several severe bruises were in evidence on Clarence's battered face. It looked like he had been beaten with a blunt instrument, with most of the damage to the top and right side of his head. This was in contradiction to what Hinds had said. I am not a forensic pathologist, but in my opinion these bruises could not have been caused by crashing into rocks as the body fell down the cliff; they were too regular in shape.

Then I looked at his fingers. The fingers were not torn on the underside, as they would have been had Clarence been clawing at rocks as he fell. Instead, they appeared to have been smashed from above, as if he had been hanging on and someone had pounded his hands to make him let go. The backs of his hands were similarly bruised.

Surely the Barbados police would have understood the implications of these wounds, yet they had insisted that Clarence had fallen. Clearly, they did not want me to know the truth. Were they just lazy or were they covering for someone? And Hinds, the funeral director, had also lied; or possibly he had spent so little time with my uncle's body that he did not know the answers to my questions.

At that very moment the vestry door opened at the back of the church. I could see, framed in the light, a stocky, middle-aged man holding a flashlight. I assumed it was the churchwarden. Someone must have seen us come over the wall and summoned him. He had entered the church from the front and had come out of the back door to see what was going on in his graveyard. I was holding my flashlight down near the body. I turned it off and quickly pulled myself up out of the open grave. I grabbed Grandma Dora and we ducked behind a nearby monument.

The churchwarden shone his light around the graveyard. At first he saw nothing, for we were hidden from his view, but then he heard a noise. It was a mouse-like squeak of fear from Aunt Emily, standing only a few feet away from him, to his side.

The warden swung his light toward the noise. The beam illuminated Emily, who froze like a deer blinded by a car's headlamps. She was too startled to run and the bright light rendered her weak eyes momentarily blind. Frightened and bewildered, Emily slowly lifted her arms toward the warden, palms out, nearly touching him. She silently beseeched him to divert his light.

Aunt Emily's pale eyes, white skin and whitish-yellow hair were made even more luminescent by the harsh flashlight. Understandably, her ghostly appearance startled and frightened the old man. He turned and ran, crying, "Oh Lord, oh Lord, a duppy. The dead have risen. Heaven save me. Help! Help!"

I couldn't help but laugh, but I knew it wouldn't be long before others came to see this apparition, so I left the casket open and the shovel and pick there. I gathered Aunt Emily and Grandma Dora, hoisted them over the wall and we beat a hasty retreat to the car.

Fortunately the warden's description hadn't encouraged the villagers to come right away. And when they finally did, they would have found nothing but our tools. We got clean away.

When we got home, Emily was still shaking from the experience but Grandma Dora saw the humour in it; she laughed at the warden's fright. But, upon reflection, both women were upset that we had left Clarence's body exposed to the elements. I assured them that the warden would soon return with others and find the open coffin; and that they would close Clarence's grave for us.

I asked Grandma Dora if she knew the reason why Goody Griffith had paid for Clarence's funeral preparations, modest as they had proven to be.

She said, "No, I couldn't believe it when the minister mentioned at the funeral that he'd done that. We don't know Griffith and we are not even supporters of his political party. The minister said that Griffith had done it out of Christian charity."

A politician dispensing Christian charity? Not likely. I suspect that Goodman Griffith paid for the undertaker because he, and probably others, wanted my uncle's body in the ground and forgotten as soon as possible.

One thing they had not counted on, for sure, was a busybody Bajan Yankee nephew coming in to stir things up.

Daily Report 6

Date of Events: Sunday, 29 December 1996
Place: Barbados: Glenville; District C Police Station; Police Headquarters, Bridgetown; The *Clarion*
Summary: Ollie's warning; *Clarion* reports

I woke early with the sun. I reminded myself that I had only a bit more than one day left in Barbados. I am not going to get to the bottom of what happened to Uncle Clarence but at least I should be able to get the Barbados police to reopen the case. I reviewed my notes from yesterday, then I made my plans for today.

My next step would be to go see Goodman Griffith. The Glenvilles, like most redlegs, had been ignored by the Barbados establishment for three hundred and fifty years. Why is attention suddenly being paid to them by a leading politician? Why them? Why now?

After I'd seen Goodman I would go to police headquarters in Bridgetown to tell someone in authority what I had found in Clarence's grave. I realised that there was some risk in so doing, because the police were probably out scouring the countryside now looking for the person or persons who opened Clarence's grave last night. They probably thought it was just a thief looking to rob the grave of valuables.

But the churchwarden saw Aunt Emily, even if he did think she was a duppy. When he calmed down, he'd probably remember her from the funeral. If he told the police, I reckoned they couldn't help but put two and two together. Unless they were total incompetents, they would eventually figure that the Glenville family had something to do with last night's activities.

That would bring them here to Glenville House and they would probably focus on me, rather than frail little Emily or my elderly Grandma Dora. I counted on the fact that as a blood relative of the deceased, they would not prosecute me for grave robbing. And when I told them what I had observed about Clarence's wounds, it probably wouldn't be a problem. The worst thing they could do, I figured, was deport me, and I plan on leaving Barbados tomorrow anyway.

Just then a vehicle pulled up outside Glenville House. It was only six forty-five. Grandma Dora and Aunt Emily, who normally awoke with the sun, were still sleeping after their big night. I could see that it was a blue and white Land-Rover, a police vehicle. These guys were sharper than I had thought.

Four policemen got out of the Land-Rover. There were two constables plus a sergeant and an inspector. I recognised both Constable Greenidge and Sergeant Brathwaite. The other two officers were new to me. The inspector was wearing a sharply starched tan uniform with two pips on each shoulder. He had a clipboard under his arm.

I quickly slipped on my pants and put on a clean sports shirt, my last. The police were rapping on the door as I came downstairs. The noise had awakened the women. I called to Grandma Dora that I would take care of it and that she and Emily should stay upstairs in bed.

I opened the door and the officer asked, "Are you a relative of Clarence Glenville?"

I explained that I was his nephew, Benjamin Cumberbatch.

He then said, "We regret to inform you that your uncle's grave has been broken into."

His tone of voice was not sympathetic. It suggested that the policemen had come to our house in the belief that it contained the grave robbers. My lack of surprise at their news no doubt confirmed their suspicion. The two constables noticeably shifted into position as if to grab me should I start to run away.

The inspector said, "Can you account for your whereabouts last evening between ten and eleven o'clock?"

This wasn't working out at all as I had planned. Instead of me going to the police and voluntarily admitting that I had dug up Uncle Clarence and getting them to reopen the investigation into his death, I was finding myself about to be arrested and charged with grave robbing. However, an outright admission at this time probably would not have been in my best interest so I decided to try to bluff my way out of the situation.

"I believe that everything that happened can be adequately explained, but there are more important issues at stake here. First, I want you to know that I am a detective sergeant in the New York police department, with nearly eighteen years of service."

No one appeared to be very impressed with this news. Of course, Greenidge and Brathwaite already knew this and they probably had already told the others. It seemed to me that, rather than the usual professional courtesy cop to cop, the Barbados police resented my presence. And, I now realised, they probably saw my efforts to examine my uncle's body as an implied criticism of their investigation. No policeman likes that.

I decided to take a different tack. These guys thought that their professionalism had been insulted so they were not about to cut some wise-ass NYPD cop any slack. But I should get a better hearing from a senior officer, someone not directly involved with the bungling of this case up to now.

"I would like to speak with a senior officer. I believe that there have been significant procedural errors in the investigation of Clarence Glenville's death and these must be addressed."

Again, nobody was impressed. They ignored my request. The inspector instructed the two constables to put me in handcuffs, which he called "manacles". They did that and then they escorted me, none too politely, into the police vehicle.

Grandma Dora had come downstairs and watched as I entered the vehicle. I assured her that this was a "small misunderstanding", and that I would return shortly. She, wisely, said nothing.

Initially, I was taken to District C station house where I was placed in a holding cell. No one talked to me. After an hour, a larger van showed up and I was transported to police headquarters in Bridgetown. There I was fingerprinted, processed and again put in a small cell, all by myself.

At midday I was given a meal of something and rice. I ate some of the rice and left the something.

At exactly one o'clock, a burly police sergeant unlocked my cell and took me, still manacled, up two flights of stairs.

We waited in the hall for several minutes. The questions I asked the sergeant went unanswered. Then a door opened and I was led into an office.

A name-plate on the desk proclaimed that this was the office of Chief Inspector O. P. Shorter. Before I could even speculate on whether or not this was some relative of my old friend Ollie Shorter from Glenville, the inspector himself walked in. He looked somewhat like the Ollie I remembered, but of course he was older, broader and more imposing.

I decided that it was not Ollie. My friend was well on his way to being a fisherman when last I saw him. But this impressive-looking man could have been a relative of Oliver's and Annie's; I believed I could see a family resemblance.

The sergeant sat me in front of the inspector's desk. The manacles were removed and the sergeant left the room saying, as he left, that he "would be right outside".

The two of us, the chief inspector and I, sat in silence for a good two or three minutes.

Finally he looked up and said, "Cumberbatch, you blue-eyed devil, you always were trouble."

"Ollie!" I said. "I hoped it was you but I wasn't sure."

"It's me all right, but don't expect that our acquaintance from many years ago will do you any good."

His tone of voice walked a fine line between firm and downright harsh.

I was getting the impression that this new Ollie Shorter was a serious man.

He went on, "The government of Barbados considers the unlawful tampering with a grave to be a significant offence. You will be lucky if you do not spend several months in our Glendairy prison. I warn you that you would not find that a pleasant experience."

I could tell that he was not necessarily committed to re-establishing our old friendship. In an effort to remind him of better days I asked after his sister.

"How is Annie?"

"She is married and doing well. Now, tell me, why did you do this despicable thing?"

"I came to Barbados on Thursday to tell my father's family that my father, Nate Cumberbatch, had been killed – murdered in New York last June. When I arrived at Glenville, I was greeted with the news that my uncle had died under mysterious circumstances. I am a New York police detective with eighteen years' experience. It appeared to me that everyone, by which I mean the local police out in the country, a prominent politician from that area and an undertaker, seemed anxious to have my uncle's body buried and forgotten. I wanted to see why. I had neither the time nor the expectation that I could get permission to disinter his body, so I took the situation into my own hands."

Ollie was not looking at me. He was studying his own hands, letting me have my say. I continued, "I apologise for my actions. I meant no disrespect to the laws of Barbados, but I believe what I saw in the grave justifies my actions."

The chief inspector looked up and said, "And what did you see?"

"My uncle appeared to have been beaten on the top of his head with a blunt instrument as well as having sustained blows from rocks as he fell. In my opinion, there was no way that those wounds occurred solely as the result of his falling from the top of the cliff. In addition, the injuries to his hands were on the tops of his fingers and hands. They too appeared to have been beaten by the same blunt instrument."

"Is there anything else?"

"Yes," I said, beginning to warm to my subject. "I believe that a politician named Goodman Griffith may be involved somehow. At least, he paid for a very quick preparation and burial of my uncle, seemingly in an effort to thwart any further investigation. I believe that the Barbados police should initiate a murder investigation into the death of my uncle. There is another thing. I also think that there is at least a chance that there is a tie between my uncle's death and that of my father."

Ollie now sat with his eyes closed and the tips of his fingers lightly touching in front of him. When I was at last finished, he looked up and said calmly, "You are completely mistaken. You have piled one poorly conceived assumption upon another. Our investigation has proven that Clarence Glenville, old and infirm, fell to his death through mischance. It is gross speculation on your part to tie this accident to your own father's death, months ago, thousands of miles away."

Shorter continued, but in a more personal tone, "I extend to you and your family my sympathies on both of these unfortunate deaths. But, frankly, trying to relate a simple accident here with your father's death in America is ridiculous, in fact it is irresponsible and unprofessional. Incidentally, it sounds to me as if your father's death was just another violent street crime in that jungle that you call your home, New York."

He spat out the name of America's largest city as if it was an unredeemable sinkhole of crime and corruption. Although I might at times criticise my hometown, I sure didn't appreciate hearing this starchy bastard's assessment of it and I didn't appreciate being called "irresponsible and unprofessional".

The inspector then said, "Finally, your efforts to implicate Goodman Griffith in this situation are absurd. He is one of our leading citizens and will probably be our next Prime Minister. I do not want to hear that you have continued these assertions or that you have gone anywhere near him.

"One other thing," Ollie continued. "I was told that you went, without having been invited, to a private businessmen's club yesterday. The members were extremely offended by your unwarranted intrusion. You are warned never to go there again."

Oliver paused to let these warnings sink in and then changed to a more conciliatory tone.

"I have ample reason to keep you in custody. However, in light of your recent personal losses, and your lack of familiarity with our laws and customs, I am prepared to take a chance. I will release you from police custody on the strict understanding that you cease your insulting and irrelevant investigation and that you are on the first available plane going to New York."

Since I would have to be on that plane anyway, it was not that much of a concession on my part. But before I agreed I said, "Oliver, Inspector Shorter, I thank you for doing this. I know that you do not have to do it, but I do have one favour to ask."

He nodded his head, agreeing to hear my request.

"Whether you believe it or not, in the last six months two members of my family have been murdered. Maybe these were separate, unrelated incidents or maybe they were not, that remains to be seen. But if a crime has been committed, the person or persons responsible should be brought to justice. I would think that the Barbados police would want the same thing. At the very least, would you have an experienced investigator, or better yet a pathologist, examine Clarence's body?"

Oliver stared at me and slowly nodded his head but whether it was in agreement to my request or not, I could not tell.

Then I added, "Meanwhile, my grandmother and my aunt are still here on the island. They're not young and now, with my uncle gone, there is no one to look after them. I don't believe that they are in any imminent danger, but I can't be sure. I would very much appreciate it if you could have someone you trust look in on them from time to time."

Oliver agreed.

"Cumberbatch, I'll have someone keep an eye on them. I guess I owe you that from the old days. I am sure they'll be fine, you needn't worry. Regarding reopening the investigation, I'll look into it, but I can't make any promises."

He leaned across the desk and shook my hand.

Moments later the sergeant appeared, summoned how I don't know. He escorted me down the stairs and out to the street. I hailed a cab.

I gave up the idea of seeing Goody Griffith. I doubted that I could find him and I knew that if I did, I risked Ollie's further wrath. He was very specific about my not approaching the politician or pursuing any other avenue of investigation. If I did manage to see Griffith and it got back to Inspector Shorter, I might yet see the inside of Glendairy prison.

But I was not totally ready to walk away. Clarence had definitely been beaten, in a manner not unlike the attack on my father. And a lot of people here, important people, seemed dedicated to keeping me or anyone else from finding out what had happened.

I still didn't know enough about what was going on. Why would some white landowner like Vincent Lewis be interested in buying Glenville? What could be happening that would make someone kill my uncle?

Then I had an idea. I told the cab driver to take me to the offices of the *Clarion*, Barbados's leading newspaper.

I spent the rest of the afternoon skimming three years of back copies of the *Clarion*, looking for any information of possible relevance. I looked for any news about the St Charles area and about its political leader, the honourable Goodman Griffith, Member of Parliament.

My time was not wasted. I took notes on several articles of interest and their dates of publication.

In January 1995 an article appeared saying, "A group of businessmen, representing both overseas and local interests, has awarded a contract to study the feasibility of building a world class resort and golf course in St Charles."

The article explained that for years Barbados had had only one really good golf course, the one at the Sandy Lane Hotel. Recently another high quality golf course, called the Royal Westmoreland, had opened on the west coast, near the Sandy Lane. The opinion of tourism experts was that, if Barbados was going to continue to attract the high-end tourists, at least two more such golf facilities were needed.

Given the availability of land and other factors, an additional golf course was to be located in the southern region of the island, at the site of an earlier failed golf course. And a fourth course was now to be constructed on the east coast in St Charles. This new course was hailed, in a glowing editorial in the *Clarion*, as "an ideal programme for the often neglected rural parishes of St Philip, St John and St Charles".

An article in June of 1995 announced that Savannah Plantation would be incorporated into the new golf resort in St Charles, and that the effort would henceforth be known as the Savannah Project. Letters to the editor appeared in support of the concept that the Savannah Project include a gambling casino. They pointed out that several other Caribbean islands had casinos. Barbados, which currently had horse-racing, two lotteries and slot-machine gambling, had so far drawn the line at casino gambling – unwisely so, according to these letter writers.

This issue was subsequently debated, pro and con, in the papers and, as reported, from the pulpits of Barbados. The preponderance of letters to the editor, from both private citizens and ministers, opposed the casino. But articles in the *Clarion* from "tourism experts" said that Barbados's tourist industry had been and would continue to be handicapped by the insufficiency of superior golf courses, and by the absence of a high-class casino gambling facility. They said that Barbados was losing important segments of the well-heeled tourist market.

Other articles quoted various estimates of the number of additional tourists that would come to Barbados and the millions and millions of dollars they would spend, if an additional golf course with casino gambling was available.

St Charles's own Goodman Griffith said that the Savannah Project's new 300-room hotel would be a great boon to his constituents. He claimed that there would be thousands of construction jobs created and "at least 800 permanent jobs will be created, long term, by the facility and related activities." Griffith purported to have in his possession a survey showing that "there is overwhelming public support for the project in St Charles."

Religious leaders spoke out against the casino, as one might expect. However, the current government seemed to be neutral on the subject, or maybe it was on both sides, for and against. From reading the various government statements in the paper, it wasn't easy to tell where they stood. Even the political opposition, which seldom passed up an opportunity to attack the government, was seemingly ambivalent on the issue.

However, in late September 1995 headlines appeared pronouncing the project's death knell. The Barbados Water Board had declared there was "insufficient water available in the immediate area to support the project". Alternative water sources were proposed but the Water Board shot each of them down. There had been no further mention of the Savannah Project after December 1995.

So why would Vincent Lewis still be interested in buying Glenville House if the Savannah Project is not going ahead? Something's not right here, but what could it be? But there's no way I can find out, I'm leaving here in the morning.

At five thirty that evening, bleary-eyed from skimming hundreds of pages of newsprint, I hailed a taxi and paid the sixty Barbados dollars for the trip to Glenville.

Daily Report 7

Date of Events: Sunday, 29 December 1996 – night
Place: Barbados: Glenville
Summary: Annie

After dinner Grandma Dora, Aunt Emily and I sat on the veranda and reminisced about the summers I had visited Glenville. I asked my grandmother if she had ever heard anything of a friend of mine, a girl from Glenville named Annie Shorter.

"Was she a tall, skinny, pretty girl, a little bit more dark-skinned than you?" she asked.

"Yes," I said. That was a reasonable description of Annie at age thirteen. There was no telling how she had turned out. At least she was married, according to her brother. And Oliver certainly had come a long way, from a deck-hand on his uncle's fishing boat to a senior officer in the Barbados police. I hoped that Annie had fared as well.

"She came around here every few months for a year or so after your last visit. She was always asking when you were coming back. Poor thing, I think you must have broken her heart," Grandma Dora said with a kind smile. Aunt Emily giggled at the thought of young Ben breaking a girl's heart.

Two and a half hours after dark, still not nine o'clock, the women went upstairs to bed. My arrest that morning and my long absence had given them a stressful day. Besides, they were used to going to bed early and rising with the sun.

I sat on the veranda in the dark trying to understand what had happened, going over what I had learned and what, if anything, I could hope to accomplish the next day before my plane left. I knew that once I got back up north, there would be very little investigating I could do from there.

I had another of my "false memories", the brief flash of a man in an alley, presumably the alley behind the Park View Hotel in Brooklyn where I was shot. I spoke to the man. He turned to me and I could see that it was my father, Nate Cumberbatch. Suddenly he had a gun in his hand. He shot at me and missed. That was all I could remember. The memory ended. It seemed real enough but, as Shannon had explained, it was not. It couldn't have been. At the time Pa had been in the hospital, barely alive.

My plane was leaving tomorrow mid-afternoon. My first priority had to be the wellbeing of Grandma Dora and Aunt Emily. I couldn't believe that they would be in any danger, no one would hurt such gentle and harmless souls. Plus, Ollie had promised that the police would keep an eye on them. I hoped that I could trust him.

Nevertheless, I did discuss the subject of their personal safety with Grandma Dora tonight. She said, "Don't you be silly. Nobody is going to come around here to bother us. Nobody ever has and, if they do, I'll scare them off."

"Scare them off, how?" I asked.

"I'll show you," she said. Grandma Dora went upstairs and returned with something wrapped in an old towel.

"With this," she said proudly, and unwrapped the towel to disclose a huge old pistol.

I took it gingerly from her hands. It appeared to be an old military pistol, probably from World War II, maybe even older. It had no bullets and the mechanism was totally frozen with rust. It couldn't have fired, even if it had had bullets.

"Where in God's name did you get this thing?" I asked her.

"Your Uncle Clarence found it in an old trunk he dug up on one of his Sunday walks. The British Navy used to have lookout stations on the cliffs during the war, watching for submarines. Anyway, Clarence found it and brought it home to us."

I handed it back to her and said, "It won't do you much good."

"Oh, of course I wouldn't want it if it could shoot someone. I would only use it to frighten them off. Only a young person would be foolish enough to think there was something worth stealing at Glenville. The sight of an old lady waving a huge gun would surely scare them off."

I had my reservations about the whole idea of my grandmother with a weapon but I didn't think that they were in any danger and it seemed to offer her some sense of personal security. My primary concern was with their financial and emotional wellbeing.

I told Grandma Dora, "I ran into that Vincent Lewis. Apparently, he is still interested in buying Glenville. Do you have any interest in selling? You would get enough that you and Emily could live out your years in comfort."

"Ben, where would we go? I've lived here all my life and Emily too. I've thought about it but there really isn't any place that I would be as happy as I am here. I'd like to continue to live here as long as I can."

We had discussed their financial situation and I knew what their needs were; frankly, they were quite modest. Grandma Dora swore that they needed only eighty Barbados dollars a week – forty US dollars – to support themselves. She already had a small savings account at a bank at Six Roads, not that far from Glenville. I said that I would wire money there each month for them to draw on.

I could easily find enough for them from my salary for now. And longer term, after I retired, I could send that much from my pension. When I had fully recovered I would get a job and probably earn more money than I did in the police. Then I could send them even more, if they needed it.

Suddenly my thoughts were interrupted by a low, soft, metallic noise, like change jingling in someone's pocket. I peered into the dark shadows and could see someone walking up the driveway toward where I was sitting. I remained quiet. I decided not to reveal my presence until I knew who it was.

I could not yet make out the approaching figure. It was hard to see any detail, the thick trees overhead blocked the small amount of light filtering down from the stars and the sliver of a new moon.

Whoever it was stopped. I still had not moved.

A woman's voice called my name.

"Ben, Ben Cumberbatch. Are you there?"

The voice was soft and musical. It sounded familiar but, for a moment, I couldn't imagine who it was. Then, with a start, I did know. I stood up and walked toward the shadowed figure.

"Annie, it's you, isn't it?" I said, and reached out. Our hands clasped.

Now I could see her face. It was Annie all right, but not the skinny, pretty girl I remembered. She had grown up to become an incredibly beautiful woman, fulfilling all the promise that she had held and then some. Her hair was brown and soft and it hung to her shoulders. Tall and slim, as always, she now had the woman's figure to complement her face.

Her light brown eyes were alert and intelligent. Annie appeared to be years younger than the thirty-seven that I knew she was. She was wearing a stylish, light-coloured dress, made of silk. It clung alluringly to her shapely body. On her wrist was a silver bracelet, apparently the source of the noise I had heard. She wore high heels. I estimated that in her stockinged feet, she would be an inch or two under six feet. An exotic scent, Annie's perfume, blended deliciously with the soft breeze of the Barbados night.

The total effect was overwhelming. Tall, slim, beautiful, exotic and sexy, Annie exuded an aura of competence, confidence and invincibility.

I was captivated by her. All my expectations for her were more than fulfilled and my teenaged fantasies were rekindled. I told her that I had been asking about her this very evening and that she had always been an important part of my memories of Barbados.

Annie said, somewhat sadly, "You have always been important to me too. You were my first love. For years I hated you for deserting me, for leaving me here in this ugly little town." She gestured behind at Glenville village.

"But in time I realised that you were barely fourteen and could hardly have been held accountable for not returning to me."

I was glad that she had forgiven me. I wish that I had been able to forgive myself. I've always felt guilty about not returning and, even more so, for not having written her, as I'd promised.

"I saw Ollie today," I said, changing the subject.

"I know, that's why I am here. He tells me that you're leaving tomorrow, is that so?"

"I'm afraid it is. He made it very clear that I should leave then but, to tell you the truth, I had to go back at that time anyway. But I am glad that at least we have had a chance to see each other."

We sat on the veranda of Glenville House and remembered how it had been to be young and in love, if that was what we were. Annie asked me if I was or had ever been married. I laughed and said no, but I told her that Grandma Dora had promised me that the "right girl is out there waiting".

Annie said that she had been married for eleven years and had one child, a daughter, Clara. She didn't say anything about her husband, her marriage or her life. Whenever I asked something about them, she changed the subject to the past, our youth and our time together.

I told Annie about my injury, that I had been in Wickham for nearly six months and that I still had a few problems – my peripheral vision and certain aspects of my memory. I told her that I might have to leave the NYPD. She reached over and gently touched the scar on my forehead and murmured sympathetically.

She stayed for about an hour. The time passed pleasantly but too quickly. She said that her husband was out for the evening, but that she had to get home to her daughter.

I asked if I could drive her home, but she said that she had a car nearby.

We kissed goodbye and she hugged me tightly for a few seconds, then she turned and left. Her scent lingered behind.

I was reluctant to be parted from her. I waited a few moments and then I followed her at a distance, just to make sure that she got safely to her car.

At the bottom of the Glenville entrance she turned left, rather than going right, into the village.

A hundred yards or so down the road, a large car was parked. Someone, a short, wide male, got out from behind the wheel and opened the back car door. I could hear Annie say something about going home. She called him "Malcolm".

She got into the back seat of the car, which was one of those big four-door Jaguars; Malcolm appeared to be the chauffeur. Without turning on its headlights the car pulled away with a low, powerful, purring sound.

Whoever Annie Shorter is, she must be doing all right for herself. I am very glad of that.

Six-Week Report 168

Date of Events: 11 May to 28 June 1997
Place: USA: Manhattan hotel; Miami, Florida; Freeport, New York
Summary: Farewell NYPD; holiday; Elyce's wedding; Ollie's message

They had a farewell party for me in May and it was a blast. There must have been a hundred cops, all of them I have served with at one time or another. Plus, Tom had invited practically every girl that I have ever dated seriously. And, to his surprise and mine, most of them came.

You would think that a party with a dozen or more former girlfriends, most of them long since married, would be a fiasco, but they all got along together just fine. After all, they had two things in common, a former relationship with me or with both Tom and me and the fact that they were, with a few notable exceptions, very nice people.

Tom Moran, now Lieutenant Moran in charge of the Arson Squad, had gone to a lot of trouble organising this party. He had put together "This is your life, Ben Cumberbatch". I couldn't believe who he came up with.

Of course both of my sisters were there, plus a couple of people from our old neighbourhood in Brooklyn. Shannon Tierney from Wickham was there with her fiancé, who turned out to be a really great guy. I had been recently discharged from Wickham as an out-patient but I was supposed to check in with them every month or so or let them know if I was having any problems.

But mostly it was people I had known on the job – cops. Tom had even found Mooney, the old cop who was supposed to show me the ropes on my first day, the time that we ended up arresting the three cop-killers. Mooney was now in a nursing home in New Jersey. He had emphysema and carried a bottle of air with him but he was actually funny, standing at the podium and telling, between gasps of oxygen, how I had stolen all the glory for his arrests.

There were guys from my police academy days, from my days as a patrolman in Bed-Stuy and as a Vice detective. Tom even came up with a couple of women who claimed to be former hookers and who said that I had arrested them. The stories they told were neither repeatable nor, I swear, were they true. However, they did get a good laugh at my expense.

However, most of the people and the stories were from my days at the Arson Squad. Norman Price and the forensics people gave me a do-it-yourself arson investigation kit, complete with hatchet, shovel, rubber boots and a flashlight. Pendergast gave me an old TV set, which he swore came from the Soh case, the Korean electronics store fire in Brooklyn.

Everybody got good and drunk, as is appropriate on occasions like this. Woodrow Grover, my lieutenant, who retired in February, gave a fifteen-minute stand-up monologue that was actually unbelievably funny. Everybody was laughing so hard that we missed some of his best lines. In seven and a half years I had never heard the man make a joke.

Finally, Tom spoke. He started with a number of funny stories about our lives together, on the job and in some social situations. Some of these stories were true, some of them were, shall we say, loosely based on the truth, but why ruin a good story by insisting on accuracy?

Then Tom changed gears and spoke of the night I was shot. He talked about how much our friendship had meant to him, and how my near-death had been the most traumatic event in his life.

There wasn't a dry eye in the house, mine included.

Tom then gave me a going-away present, from the entire Squad. It was a pen – by all appearances an ordinary ballpoint pen. Admittedly it was a nice-looking pen, but it was not quite what I had expected.

"Sergeant Cumberbatch looks a little disappointed with his going-away gift," Tom said. The people from the Squad, who were in on the joke, hooted and hollered. I looked at Grover but he just shrugged his shoulders. Everyone else, including all the old girlfriends, shared my disappointment: a lousy goddamn ballpoint pen!

Tom then said, "Most of you know that Ben has been in therapy, working to get his memory back in full working order. Those of us that know Ben, know that it will be only a matter of time until he is fully recovered. But, for now, part of Ben's therapy is to take notes, recording events and information throughout the day and then recording the important information in a written summary, not unlike the reports that we all write on the job.

"Ms Shannon Tierney, that beautiful lady over there" – he pointed at Shannon and everyone whistled and cheered – "who until recently had the task of working with Ben at the rehab, told me that this approach has not only provided Ben with a working memory system, it is also helping him to regain his full faculties."

Tom continued, "However, Ben has shared with me his frustration that there are times when note-taking is difficult and it may be hard to write down all the important details. So we chipped in and got him this."

Tom held up a small box, the size of a pack of cigarettes. People murmured, "What the hell is that?"

Mack Pendergast said, apparently on cue, "Very generous of you, Tom, Ben doesn't even smoke."

Again, only the people from the Squad laughed.

"This is in fact a state-of-the-art tape recorder."

Tom opened the box to disclose the small machine.

"That pen in Ben's hand is a voice activated microphone, capable of receiving a normal speaking voice. Ben will be able to carry the microphone-pen in his pocket and can even use it to write. This device," he again held up the recorder, "can be in his pocket or in the next room, anywhere within one hundred yards. It will record up to two hours and forty minutes of conversation."

I had heard about these gadgets but I had never seen one. It was a great gift. I knew that it had cost them a lot of money. Good friends.

Of course, I had to say a few words. I was feeling pretty emotional about the whole thing by now. I thanked them for the gift and then I paused and looked around the room. I didn't want me crying and blubbering into the microphone to be the last memory my old friends had of me. I had seen that happen at too many of these farewell parties; what else would you expect with all these Irish and Italian cops? But I was determined not to go out that way, so I had prearranged with Tom for an exit line.

I asked, "Are there any questions?"

Before anyone could think of one, Tom spoke up.

"Detective Sergeant Cumberbatch, there is one thing that I have been meaning to ask you. What are the most important things that you have learned during your eighteen years on the police force?"

I had prepared a monologue that got back at all my friends who had been making fun of me. It was gentle humour, some of it a little on the risqué side but we were all adults. Of course, I forgot half of it and mixed up some of the punch lines but, what the hell, I was among friends. It brought down the house and allowed me to get away from the podium without crying and making a bigger fool of myself.

At the party Elyce told me that she and her boyfriend, Hayden Downes, were going to get married. The wedding was scheduled in six weeks, on June 28. She asked me if I would give her away. I said that I would be honoured to do so.

I took a break from writing my daily reports and took off for Florida for ten days with a lady friend. We had a great time, played golf, went deep-sea fishing and to the track, both the horses and the dogs. She won at the horses, I won at the dogs. But we both lost at jai alai. We decided that the jai alai was fixed. Our conclusion: never bet on a human being.

It was a very nice wedding. Small, very traditional and done in excellent taste, as you would expect from Elyce. As I said at the rehearsal dinner, the wedding ought to be well done, she had had about forty years to plan it.

Margaret was the matron of honour and Margaret's daughter, Carolyn, was one of the four bridesmaids. Hayden had four children from his previous marriage. They were all grown and were in the wedding too, three as groomsmen and one as a bridesmaid.

The reception was held at Hayden's house in Freeport, Long Island, where Elyce and Hayden were going to live. Also, at last, I found out what it is that Hayden does for a living. It is both extremely lucrative and legal. He has a company that invests the cash that the teachers' union collects from its members each month. He invests the money in what he calls "cash instruments". He only has it short term, for just a few weeks or even a few days. But investing the cash for even this short period, there is enough interest earned in total that it makes big money for the Union. Hayden takes a tiny little commission on each transaction but so great is the volume that he does very well.

At the reception, Elyce told me why the marriage was so sudden. She's going to have a baby. She's over four months pregnant. Incidentally, they have just learned that the baby is a boy. She said that they plan to name him Benjamin, for me.

When I got home after the wedding, there was a message on my answering machine from Oliver Shorter.

"There has been a fire at Glenville House. You had better get down here as soon as possible."

Daily Report 169

Date of Events: Monday, 30 June 1997
Place: Barbados: Police Headquarters, Bridgetown; Glenville; Bathsheba
Summary: Ollie; first inspection Glenville House

This morning, I took the American Airlines nine o'clock direct flight to Barbados. I arrived in the early afternoon, picked up a cheap rental car – the tourists' favourite, the low-slung Moke, open to the air – and headed to Bridgetown to find Oliver. At five minutes to three, I arrived at police headquarters.

Ollie's reception of me was quite different this time compared to last. He was waiting for me at the top of the stairs and he wasn't stiff and distant. Ollie greeted me like an old friend. He appeared genuinely upset by what had happened.

I feared the worst.

He gestured for me to sit and then he said, "I have bad news and there is no way to make it any easier for you. There was a fire night before last. Glenville House burned to the ground and I am afraid that your grandmother and aunt died in the fire. At least, we believe it's them. There were two women in there. Their bodies were burned beyond recognition."

Since I had received his message I had been preparing myself for some such news. And, having been involved professionally with fires over the years, I had no difficulty visualising their shrivelled and twisted bodies.

It hit me. First Pa, then Clarence, and now this. I was buffeted with all kinds of thoughts. Should I be concerned for Elyce's and Margaret's safety? And what about the attempt on my life? Might that not have been a part of this as well? Was there somebody out there who wanted us all dead? Why? What sense did it make?

The overwhelming sadness I felt about Grandma Dora and Aunt Emily began to give way to anger. I found that I was standing, with my fists clenched at my side.

Oliver came around the desk and put his hand on my shoulder to comfort me. My mind was racing from thought to thought. Oliver had better not try to tell me again that this was just another one of a string of unconnected events!

He didn't. In a low, sympathetic voice, Oliver said, "Even though I doubted they were in any danger, I did instruct the local constable to keep an eye on them, just as you had asked. He reported to me every other day and said that they were just fine. He had even arranged for someone to take Mrs Glenville to the bank at Six Roads. I guess you were sending down money to her there."

I sat down and took out my notebook in order to record the details of what he was telling me.

"What was the name of the constable?" I asked him gruffly.

Oliver paused, then said, "Greenidge, Norman Greenidge, I think it is."

The same constable as before.

"I'll be speaking to him," I said, with forceful determination. Not Oliver nor anyone else would stop me from pursuing this investigation. He didn't try.

I regretted that I had allowed myself to be backed off from further investigating Uncle Clarence's death. If I had stayed with it, my grandmother and aunt might still be alive.

I asked where the bodies were being held. Oliver told me that they were in the police morgue, over at the Queen Elizabeth II Hospital.

"Do not let the bodies be touched or moved anywhere until I have had an opportunity to look at the fire scene."

Ollie promised that the bodies would remain untouched for at least forty-eight hours.

Then I said, "I'd also like to meet with your arson people. I might be of some use to them."

Ollie looked at me.

"Man, this isn't New York. We don't have arson people here. We may or may not have arson but, up to now, the police haven't counted it as a major area of crime. We do have one sergeant who spent three weeks on an arson course with the Miami Police Department but, the truth, I don't think he knows much."

He then added, "The fire service is the one that is usually called on to look into fire-related problems. Much of their work involves cane fires that have been started by disgruntled workers or greedy planters. They sent one of their senior fire officers over to see Glenville today. He declared it an accident. Frankly, they seldom ever call a house fire arson unless someone actually witnessed the fire being set."

I began to feel that I had to get out of this place. Ollie meant well, and he was trying to be sympathetic, but I couldn't help but think that it had been his attitude, at least indirectly, that was responsible for these deaths. However, I couldn't afford to alienate him. If he wanted to, he could make it harder for me to find out who had done this. But for now, he was just in my way. I thanked him for contacting me and told him that I was anxious to go to Glenville to see the situation for myself.

It took me half an hour to manoeuvre my way through the late afternoon traffic in downtown Bridgetown and to find the right road to St Charles. On the way, I couldn't help but be impressed with the handsome modern buildings both in Bridgetown and the surrounding areas. Gas stations and auto dealerships looked every bit as modern as they did in the States. On the street, there were numerous well-dressed men and women, apparently leaving their offices for the day. The roads were soon clogged with up-to-date cars, mostly Japanese makes but also BMWs, Mercedes and Jaguars. Whatever else had happened in Barbados, the economy had prospered and the prosperity had been shared by a large segment of the population. I just hoped that the gentle, kind and fun-loving people I remembered were still here.

It was nearly five forty-five by the time I got to the Glenville village turn-off.

The entrance to Glenville House was roped off. A yellow police "Do not Trespass" sign hung from the rope but no one was there. I parked by the rope and ducked under it.

Where Glenville House had stood there is now only a pile of scorched bougainvillea to be seen. The charred ruins, what there is of them, have fallen down into a massive hole that is the cistern beneath the floor.

I pulled the thorny bougainvillea back, pricking my finger painfully in the process, to look into the half-full cistern. Ashes and pieces of charred roof timbers were floating on the top. It was impossible to tell what else might be under the murky water.

I had a flashlight in my suitcase, part of Norman Price's joke gift, the farewell arson forensics kit. No one would possibly have imagined that I would be using it for that purpose so soon. With it I could see that the house had collapsed in on itself. In my experience, this suggested two things: that this had been a particularly hot fire and that the centre of the house had burned before the exterior walls.

A hot fire like that usually means that an accelerant – probably petroleum-based – has been used. Most likely, given the ferocity of this fire, it was gasoline. Also, with the centre of the house burning so quickly, the accelerant had probably been ignited in the middle of the house.

Even in a few minutes, I had seen enough to convince me that Glenville had been destroyed by arson, an intentional fire set for malicious or criminal purposes. But I knew that it would take more than just my opinion to prove it to the Barbados police.

I needed to get down into the cistern to see what I could find.

But it was getting late and dark. I would need some equipment and I would have to find a place to sleep. I decided to stay there on the east coast, at one of the small, inexpensive hotels that cater to the surfboard crowd. The nearest one to Glenville is the Wavecrest, down on the water, west of Morton's Cove, in an area known as Bathsheba.

I didn't have any problem getting a room at the Wavecrest as it's only half full. It looks to be mostly college-age kids, here for a tournament. I'll drive into Bridgetown to a hardware store in the morning to get what I need.

Daily Report 170

Date of Events: Tuesday, 1 July 1997
Place: Barbados: Glenville; airport; police station; Oliver Shorter's office & home
Summary: Collecting and dispatching evidence

I had to go to two hardware stores before I could get everything. I bought a shovel, heavy rope, chain, a hacksaw, a crowbar, a snorkel and mask and several large plastic storage containers.

It was after eleven in the morning when I got back to Glenville. I was alarmed to see that the police rope had been lowered and that a pick-up truck was parked inside. I saw two men in blue overalls poking at the debris floating in the old cistern.

I recognised one of the men as Constable Greenidge from the District C police station. The other – older, shorter and broader of girth – I had never seen before. I approached them quietly. Intent on what they were doing, they didn't notice me coming.

I heard the older one say, "Let's haul the big pieces out."

The constable was down on his belly, attempting to tie a rope to a large section of tin roof which was poking up out of the water.

I said, "Are you looking for something, Constable?"

Greenidge, startled, turned and looked at me, his mouth partly agape. The other man, clearly senior, stepped toward me and said, "This is official police business. You got to get out of here or face arrest."

Greenidge said quickly, "No, no, Sergeant. This is the man that Inspector Shorter say we might see. He is kin to the people that lived here and he is some kind of fire specialist police from New York."

Sergeant Daniel Butcher was the older man's name. He was the officer who, at taxpayers' expense, had spent three weeks on an arson course taught by the Miami Police. He said that Inspector Oliver Shorter had contacted him this morning and told him to come here to see if he could be of any help in this investigation. They'd just begun tugging at the debris when I arrived.

I thought, *thank you, Oliver, for wanting to be helpful. And thank the good Lord that I got here when I did or these two might have destroyed more evidence than they recovered.*

I explained that the first thing we had to do, before we started pulling things up, piece by piece, was to see what was below the surface of the water.

"How you gonna do that?" the sergeant asked.

I held up the snorkel, mask and flashlight. I had my trunks on under my pants. I quickly stripped down to the swimming gear. Then, carefully, I eased myself down into the murky water. It was cold and smelled like all fire scenes do, sour and unpleasant.

I was very careful as I got into the water. I didn't want to come down on a submerged sharp object and do permanent damage to a vital part of my anatomy. I adjusted my snorkel and mask and ducked my head under the water. As I expected, the reason that we couldn't see beneath the water was that ash and charred debris floating on the top were blocking our view. Beneath the surface, the water was perfectly clear.

The shapes of various pieces of the structure, plus the heavier-than-water non-flammables, were clearly visible. I shone my flashlight and identified the old cast-iron stove, the bath tub, the sink and various pieces of broken bric-a-brac.

What I had hoped to see but, so far, had not, were partially-burned floorboards. Although the old pitch pine floorboards, soaked with gasoline, would have burned quite readily, my hope was that some might have fallen into the cistern water before they were completely consumed by the flames. If so, they might contain the proof that the fire had been started with an accelerant. And ninety-nine times out of a hundred that was a sure sign of arson.

I surfaced and told them what I had seen, then started a series of short dives to recover various objects of interest. I passed these up and told my helpers to put the items carefully into one or other of the plastic boxes.

Next I attached a rope around a large section of the burned tin roof, so that the two men could carefully pull it up and out of the cistern. This would make it easier to examine and extract the debris still in the water.

My helpers attached the other end of the rope to the bumper of their pick-up truck and slowly inched the vehicle back. The roof section began to shift, and I thought for a second that it was going to crush me to the side of the cistern. Then it rose up until it was held suspended precariously above the water. As I had hoped, several charred floorboards floated up from where they had been pinned underwater by the roof section.

I grabbed two of the boards. On one I could clearly see evidence of a "pour pattern". I pointed this out to the two policemen and explained that when an accelerant, like gasoline, is poured on a wooden floor, it soaks into the wood and, when ignited, will explode, giving the wood an appearance visibly distinct from wood that has been charred or burned by the fire. I told them that forensics would be able to confirm that and could even identify the type of accelerant that had been used.

Sergeant Butcher said, "I knew that." And maybe he did.

My helpers secured the roof section and then, with a little manoeuvring, I was able to grab the rest of the boards. We put them into one of the boxes and marked it "floor".

I was looking for two metal objects. One, the old pistol that my grandmother had shown me, and the other the square metal box where Grandma Dora had kept her important papers. I eventually found the gun, but the metal box was nowhere to be seen. It might still have been hidden under debris, but it could not have burned.

I continued to look for the box and other items of interest but, by now, so much ash and char had been stirred into the water that it was difficult to see anything.

I explained to the two policemen what I'd been doing. I told them that there might be more potentially useful evidence under water. We agreed that it was going to be difficult to see anything in the water for now, but if we could get a portable pump to drain the water, we could do our job a lot better and faster.

Sergeant Butcher said that he knew where to get a pump. He took the pick-up truck and went to borrow the pump from a friend who worked at a large sugar plantation in St George parish.

While we waited for the sergeant's return, Constable Greenidge and I had a chance to talk without someone listening in on our conversation. I did not come on strong at first, not wishing to put the young constable on the defensive.

I started out by telling him that he had done a good job and thanking him for his help. He was pleased. Next, he asked me to tell him about the crime of arson. He said that it had never even been discussed in his training.

I explained to him that arson was "setting a fire on purpose with malicious or fraudulent intent". I gave him some examples.

"'Fire-for-profit', usually setting a fire to a failing business to collect the insurance money. Another possible motive is using fire to inflict harm or to destroy property as an act of revenge, or intimidation."

"Like cane fires?"

"Right, like cane fires. But with all the building that's going on here in Barbados it won't be too long before someone 'sells his building to the insurance company'; in other words, decides that he can make more money by collecting the building insurance rather than running a hotel or renting office space.

"There are other reasons for arson, too. Criminals sometimes use fire to try to hide their crime. And there are serial arsonists, what we call 'fire bugs' or pyromaniacs, usually seriously disturbed persons, who light fires because they like the excitement."

"What do you think we have here?" the constable asked.

"Good question. But let's wait until we have gathered all the evidence before we start shooting in the dark."

Now that I had him relaxed, I directed the conversation back to the first time we had met, at the police station.

"As I recall," I said casually, "you described the wound on my uncle's head as a 'heavy blow'."

Constable Greenidge began to squirm. He seemed nervous about the new direction of our conversation, but he nodded his head in confirmation that that was what he had said.

"I assumed, from that, that my uncle had only been hit once, or twice," I said. "Just one or two massive blows, like he'd hit his head against rocks as he fell, right?"

The constable didn't answer. He kept his eyes downcast.

I continued – but now my tone was purposely less casual – "But, as you know, I had opened my uncle's casket and, to me, it appeared that he had been struck several blows with a blunt instrument, not just glancing blows as he fell."

Greenidge was looking quite miserable but I was not going to let him off the hook.

I said, "No way were those wounds caused by bouncing off rocks as he fell. You and the others must have been able to see that. Why would you tell me something that you knew was not true?"

Greenidge's eyes were wide and he was beginning to sweat. It was clear that my questions had put him in a tight spot.

"Please, don't ask me. I can't tell you. You gonna spoil me in the police," he said, shaking his head in denial.

He was so pitiful that I couldn't help but feel sorry for him. But I needed to know why he had lied to me. If I could get that answer, it would be corroboration that someone was covering up the facts of Clarence's death.

I continued firing questions at Greenidge. At one point he started to get up to move away but I grabbed his arm and sat him down, hard.

Finally he broke. He began blubbering his explanation.

"I was only doing what I was told, just what I was told. I was to see that nobody got too interested in the old man's death. I was told that he truly died from the fall, that he'd been drinking but also he had been in a fight that same night, before he fell. The man that fought him is a friend of someone important and I was told there was to be no further lookin' into Clarence Glenville's death. Better for all to think it was just a simple accident."

"Did you believe this story?" I asked him.

"It wasn't important whether I believed. It was a direct order and I got to obey."

"OK then, Constable. Who gave you the direct order?"

Greenidge was now in real distress. He definitely did not want to say the name. Instead he said, "You know he. You already know he."

Who the hell do I know?

"You mean Sergeant Brathwaite?"

This was the logical person, he was Greenidge's direct superior.

To my surprise, the constable whispered, "No, no, not the sergeant."

Who could he be talking about?

"Was it that inspector that arrested me at Glenville that morning? I don't even know his name," I said, raising my voice.

The constable didn't look at me. He shook his head slowly and then he raised his hand up and then up again. I suddenly understood what he was saying; it was someone further up the chain of command. Way up.

The problem was that I didn't know anybody higher up in the police except Chief Inspector Oliver Shorter. It couldn't be Oliver. He was my old friend, the man who had been so sympathetic to me the day before, the man who had sent Sergeant Butcher to help me with the arson investigation and the man who must have known that I could be talking to Constable Greenidge right now.

I said, not really wanting to hear the answer, "Certainly you're not talking about Chief Inspector Shorter?"

Greenidge nodded his head slowly, miserably, and then buried his face in his hands, convinced that his police days were through.

I had a few questions to ask Chief Inspector Shorter.

Sergeant Butcher returned with the pump and we slowly drew the water out of the old cistern. It took us about two hours. Then the sergeant and I got down in the muck and started filling plastic boxes with what we found. I had pounded nail holes in the bottom of the plastic boxes so the water would drain out of them. When the boxes eventually get to the forensics lab, they will contain just a bit of dry ash and the debris from the fire.

When we finished, we had nine big boxes of muck plus the one with the boards and another with the pistol and various other small items that I had found. I never did find the metal box with the papers. I concluded that almost certainly someone had taken it; the same person who had killed my grandmother and aunt and set Glenville afire.

I went to the airport on my way back from St Charles, to look into shipping the boxes to New York by air, but I was told that it would cost me well over two thousand US dollars to air-ship. Frankly, I couldn't afford it, so I located a freight forwarder to handle the paperwork and I sent the boxes by sea. It would be at least five weeks before they arrived in New York, but it was a lot cheaper.

I called Norman and told him what I had done. He promised to get his people working on it as soon as the boxes arrived. If they concluded it was arson and found something useful about the fire or who had set it, it would be well worth the effort. I know that no one here in Barbados is prepared to take my word that this was arson. They have put me down as an excitable outsider, too close to the case to make a valid professional judgment. But they will find it harder to reject this finding when it comes from the NYPD, particularly when it comes over the signature of Norman Price, a world-renowned expert in arson forensics.

My next stop was at the police station to fill out the papers to claim the bodies of Grandma Dora and Aunt Emily. They said that I can pick the bodies up the day after tomorrow. I let them believe that I am going to bury the bodies here in Barbados, not letting on that my real intent is to ship them to New York. With luck, they will be on the same boat as the evidence boxes from Glenville. Norman will have the Squad's pathologists examine the bodies. At the very least, they will be able to determine how my grandmother and aunt died, and whether they were killed in the fire or were already dead before the fire began.

I then went to Oliver Shorter's office to ask him why he had obstructed my investigation into Clarence's death and why he was now being so co-operative. It was nearly six o'clock. Ollie's office was locked and there was no one around. I asked at the front desk if they had an address or a phone number for Inspector Shorter. The guard looked at me with half-veiled eyes and said something about not being able to give me that information.

So I asked if I could see a phone book, the regular Barbados phone book. It was sitting on his table, right in front of us. Reluctantly he handed it over and I turned to the letter "S" and found Oliver's name, address and home telephone number. Somewhat sarcastically, I thanked the guard for his help and asked if I could use his telephone. He refused.

Ollie's street address was familiar. I had seen a sign pointing to it just off the ABC Highway in a hilly suburban neighbourhood not far from the campus of the University of the West Indies, north of Bridgetown. I decided to drive there to see if I could find him.

I pulled up to an attractive house on a side street. It had a commanding view of Bridgetown harbour. A handsome woman wearing glasses answered the door.

I explained that I was there to see Inspector Shorter. The woman, as I suspected, was Oliver's wife, Elvira. She said that Ollie was not home and was not expected until late. She asked who I might be.

When I told her my name, she invited me to come in to have a cup of tea. Shortly, her two teenaged sons arrived, quarrelling good-naturedly about the merits of a certain fast bowler from Antigua who had just been dropped from the Windies, the West Indies' cricket team.

I gathered from Elvira that she was on the faculty of the university. She told me that she and Ollie had first met there in 1980, when they were both students.

When I had finished my cup of tea, I got up to leave. Mrs Shorter promised that Ollie would contact me that evening or first thing in the morning at the Wavecrest.

Daily Report 171

Date of Events: Wednesday, 2 July 1997
Place: Barbados: Glenville; Ollie's home
Summary: Ollie's explanations

Ollie called me at eight this morning.

"Did I wake you?" he said.

"No, I've been up since six. You and I have to talk. I've been hearing some things about the investigation of Clarence's death that have me upset. And I think you owe me some explanations."

"You're right, I do need to explain some things," Ollie replied. "I can't do it today. I'm tied up with official business. But why don't you come by here this evening? I should be home by eight o'clock."

It was agreed, we would meet at his home at eight.

I spent the day at Glenville House, searching for clues and talking with the people in the village. Nobody had heard or seen anything the night of the fire. Or at least, that's what they told me.

This time, when I pulled up to Ollie's house, his official blue Rover sedan was parked next to Elvira's Suzuki. Elvira answered the door and Ollie came down the stairs to greet me. He was wearing casual slacks and a Banks Beer tee-shirt.

"I'm glad you're here," he said, "we've got to talk. Come on upstairs."

On the way he opened a cupboard and got an imperial quart of a mean-looking rum from Guyana. Ollie held the bottle up, showing me the label, and said, "You don't even want to know the alcohol proof of this stuff."

We walked upstairs to a patio on the roof of the house. A cool breeze blew gently down the hill from the east but our view was toward Bridgetown, to the southwest. Night had fallen and the lights of office buildings of Bridgetown and hotels on the southwest coast were visible in the sky. Below us, the deep water harbour contained a large multi-storey cruise ship. It was lit up like a giant birthday cake.

To the right the Caribbean, silent and black, formed a void; only the running lights of an occasional fishing boat pierced the dark. Later, the monstrous tourist liner, lights blazing at every level, silently glided out the harbour to the sea.

Oliver poured us each a healthy three fingers of dark golden rum over ice. He took a good belt and then he said, "Where do I start?"

"Anywhere," I said, "but just tell me the truth."

I took out my notebook and started making notes, as I always do these days. But I also had my recording device in my pocket. I reached down and switched it on. It's a good thing I did because, I guarantee, between my memory problem and the rum, I would have forgotten much of what I was about to hear.

Ollie looked at me and my notebook sceptically and then said, "I imagine you got an earful from Constable Greenidge."

"Don't be hard on him," I urged. "The kid is a good man. You've put him in a hell of a spot."

"Don't worry. I just hope I can make it up to him some time," Oliver said contritely.

"Do that. Let him know that he is not in trouble because, right now, he's very worried. He might do something foolish, like quit the police," I replied, remembering Greenidge's dejected looks.

"I'll find a way to let him know that he's OK." Then Oliver said, "First off, let me apologise to you again for not doing a better job protecting your family. Of course, neither of us ever really thought they were in any danger, but it appears that we were wrong. And of course, you know that your uncle did not just slip from the top of the cliff. Whether he was killed in the fall or whether he was already dead from his beating is not clear. But either way, the beating that he had received was certainly a significant factor in his death."

I interrupted, "Did you know this when I came to see you?"

"Initially, I did think that your uncle had just fallen. But I admit, by the time you showed up in my office I had seen the body, and I strongly suspected that it was not an accident."

"So why instruct Greenidge and Sergeant Brathwaite to mislead me? And why did you pretend that Clarence's death was an accident, even after you'd begun to have doubts?"

Oliver paused and then poured himself another stiff drink. It was clear that he was stalling for time to collect his thoughts. Finally he spoke.

"I wanted to keep you from stirring up any problems. Initially, I'd agreed to do this as a favour for someone to whom I am deeply in debt. I was asked by this person to discourage any further investigation of the case."

Once again, he paused.

"If it is any help," he then continued, "let me say that I deeply regret having done it and I would not do it again, not for this person, not for anybody. But there is more you need to understand. Let me go back to the beginning.

"As you know, Annie and I lived in Glenville with our mother after our father disappeared at sea. I last saw you, when was it, the summer of 1972? I was almost fifteen, you were fourteen and Annie was a year younger than you. Do you know that when you went away that last summer, you broke my sister's heart? But, don't worry, she got over it," he added with a small laugh.

"I was already working on my uncle's boat. To everyone else, we were a fishing boat but, in truth, the fishing was just a cover. We were actually smuggling."

"Was it drugs?" I asked.

"No, not in those days, although we probably would have done it if we'd thought there was a market for it. No, it was mostly contraband goods. Whiskey, cigarettes, televisions, tyres, auto parts. Whatever people wanted and did not want to pay customs duty on. I worked for my uncle on weekends and summers while I was in school and then full time from the time I was sixteen until … it ended.

"Meanwhile Annie was growing up to be a stunningly beautiful young woman. Too beautiful, if you know what I mean. The men, all ages, started hanging around our little house in Glenville. Our poor mother was going crazy trying to keep Annie from getting involved with the wrong man and getting pregnant. In 1975 Momma gave up. With no husband and her son, me, away at sea, she couldn't protect her daughter. She sent Annie, aged sixteen, to Toronto to be with her sister, our Aunt Clara.

"I never met the woman but, according to Annie, Aunt Clara was something else. She was a teacher in a high school in Toronto, and she made Annie go to school and learn. Apparently Clara was totally committed to Annie's wellbeing, and this included real serious book-learning. It was hard for Annie, but she was smart and quick to catch on.

"As a newcomer at the school in Toronto, new to city living and new to Canada, Annie had much to learn. Fortunately she was adept at fitting in, making friends and capturing admirers. Of course it didn't hurt that Annie was more beautiful, innately sexier and more worldly than any of the other girls.

"Aunt Clara, like Momma, worried that Annie's beauty would get her in trouble and she was undoubtedly right, it could have. Since Clara couldn't make Annie less beautiful, she decided to teach her to use her beauty to her benefit, to make something of herself. Aunt Clara urged Annie to enter beauty contests all over Canada and even some in America. For two years, from 1975 to 1977, Annie competed in contest after contest. She won many and placed highly in most of the others.

"It seemed to have accomplished for Annie what Clara had wanted. Annie graduated from high school, has had a largely successful life and has turned out to be a nice person."

You could tell from the way that Oliver talked about his sister that he was very fond of her.

"Annie came back to Barbados in 1977, she was eighteen by then. Our mother had just died so she went to live with another relative in Bridgetown. Annie was just back three weeks when she heard about the Miss Barbados beauty pageant. She entered and, at a big ceremony at the Hilton Hotel, she was crowned Miss Barbados. She then began to compete in regional and finally international beauty contests. It was all tied in to the Miss World thing.

"In August, Annie went to Monaco and there she was selected to be one of the finalists for Miss World. No girl from Barbados had ever got that far in a major international beauty contest."

Oliver filled my glass and his and said, "You can't imagine what excitement there was in this small country. Everyone was following the competition. Annie didn't win, but she was the first runner-up. That was just about as good as winning as far as Barbados was concerned.

"When Annie returned home, thousands of people were at the airport to meet her. For a year, she was practically the only model that photographers in Barbados would use. Her face, and her body in a swimsuit, were in every ad, on every billboard, even on TV.

"Meanwhile, things were not going well for me. The Coast Guard had caught my uncle's boat with everything imaginable on board, including me. His boat was confiscated and he was given three years in prison. Because of my age and because I was just a deck-hand, I was not sent to jail, but the judge said that I had to go into the army for two years. Annie had won the Miss Barbados contest six months before I got out of the army.

"The Prime Minister of Barbados at that time was Aubrey Tudor. You might remember him. He was young, in his late thirties, handsome, about your colouring, and he was what you Yankees call 'charismatic'. Everybody loved him, particularly the media. I'll say this, Aubrey was damned smart and he was as handsome as any movie actor.

"Tudor had a white wife but he had a big place in his heart for all women. It wasn't long before my sister had become his primary lady friend. He was seen everywhere with Annie on his arm. I don't know what he told his wife, if anything, but the public loved it, Aubrey and Annie, Annie and Aubrey. Everyone, that is, except for a few church ladies and ministers. Bajans, for the most part, like to think that their politicians have an active sex life. Kind of like your Presidents Jack Kennedy and Bill Clinton."

I said that it was not quite the same thing, but I am not sure that I could have explained the difference.

Anyway, Oliver went on with his story.

"When I get out of the army, Annie asks her good friend, the Prime Minister, to do something for her brother. They decided that I should go to university so I could become something other than a fisherman or a smuggler. I hadn't seen the inside of a school since I was sixteen, so Annie hired me a tutor from the University of the West Indies. He beat some education into me and I started classes at the University in September 1979 at the age of twenty-two.

"What saved me was that I met Elvira, early on. She'd graduated from the University the year before and was studying for her graduate degree in education. With her help and inspiration, I got through university in three years.

"In my last year at university, 1981, Aubrey Tudor had a heart attack and died. He was barely forty years old. I had already been accepted for a job with the police by then. But now Annie had a problem: she had lost her 'special friend'. Suddenly nobody wanted to see her or hear from her, at least not in public. Anybody or anything that had been associated with Aubrey Tudor was now off everyone's agenda.

"Annie disappeared from sight for nearly eighteen months – to where, I couldn't tell you. She has never said where she was or what she was doing and I have never asked. She may have still been on this island, for all I know, but I don't think so.

"Elvira and I married in 1980 and we had Michael and then Hudson, our two sons. Elvira was and is still teaching at the University. She constantly makes me read and better myself, and now we've got involved in our church. I must say, my life has turned out a lot different, a lot better, than I ever imagined it would when I was working as a deck-hand for my uncle, smuggling hi-fis and auto tyres.

"Annie finally contacted me in the spring of 1983. She was now living in a nice house up on Thrustons Hill, three bedrooms and all of the modern conveniences. She had servants and a fancy car. Also, she was not working. Elvira and I had no alternative but to assume that she was a rich somebody's kept woman.

"I love my sister and I owe her a lot for helping me in life. I was not going to sit in judgment on her or put her on the spot by asking her who was keeping her."

Ollie stopped his narrative at this point and poured me and then himself another healthy drink. It was his fourth, my third.

Each had been at least a triple. The big bottle of rum was almost two thirds gone. My face was beginning to go numb and either Ollie's words were slurring or the battery in my recorder was running down.

"But Barbados is a small place," Oliver continued. "Sooner or later, everyone knows everyone else's business. Rumours said that Annie's 'friend' was a big planter from the eastern part of the island, Vincent Lewis."

I interrupted Ollie and said, "The same Lewis that was the overseer at Savannah Plantation when we were boys?"

"Yes, that same one, and the same one that you went to see at his club at the Garrison. Incidentally, you were lucky you got out of there alive, going there uninvited."

"What was going to happen to me? A couple of middle-aged bartenders and some overstuffed businessmen didn't scare me."

"You are naive. Every one of those businessmen was armed, including that woman. They all carry guns with them, wherever they go. Any one of them might have shot you and never thought a thing about it."

I was amazed.

"Why would they shoot me? What are they afraid of?"

"Us. You and me and the other 240,000 people of colour on this island."

"You're kidding! Grown men in fancy cars are carrying guns?"

"All the time. While they travel, in church, at work, probably in bed. Most of them have small calibre pistols, either in an ankle-holster or in their belt. There is nothing the police can do, they're all registered. There are probably more weapons at a Yacht Club dance on a typical Saturday night than there are in the Army's arsenal down the road."

"Are they really in danger? Do they have to protect themselves?"

"Not really. Not from the everyday, honest, God-fearing Bajan. Every once in a blue moon somebody gets robbed or roughed up by a criminal, a black criminal, and this, in their minds, justifies them arming themselves to the teeth. I guess they're just paranoid. Tell you the truth, I kind of feel sorry for them; they're a minority in their own country. Their grandfathers ran this place with an iron fist and now they have to share some of it with us. Although, I'll give them this, they're pretty damn good at hanging on to the best parts for themselves and their kind."

Barbados was turning out to be more complicated and more dangerous than I had thought. Not just your everyday friendly little island in the sun.

"Tell me more about Vincent Lewis."

"He came to Barbados from Trinidad over thirty years ago. Lewis was only in his twenties when Edgar Mount hired him to run things at Savannah Plantation. Mount was interested in things other than raising sugar cane, if you know what I mean?"

I didn't know what he was talking about and said so.

"Edgar Mount is the end of a long line and it's just as well, I might add. The Mounts have been one of the most prominent of the English absentee plantation owner families. For centuries, these people have taken huge profits from the land and people of Barbados and given damned little back.

"Some people say that Edgar was not really too bad a person when he was young and growing up here, but by the time he was in his thirties he had become a big problem. All he wanted to do was to have sex with young boys, particularly young boys of colour."

Oliver said this with obvious disdain. As the father of two young boys, you could see that this idea was particularly repugnant to him.

"Mount was still living at Savannah but Lewis pretty much had free rein to do what he wanted with the plantation. Lewis, as part of his job, saw that Mount had all the young boys he wanted. Things went on like that for several years. Everyone knew it. I'm surprised that your grandmother didn't warn you, I know my mother did, all the time."

"She did," I said, remembering my grandmother's frequent but nonspecific warnings, "only I didn't understand what she was saying at the time. But I later nearly found out the hard way."

"Oh yes, now I remember. You were lucky, luckier than another friend of mine. Anyway, the powers that be in Bridgetown tried to ignore what was going on out in St Charles because they didn't want to have to deal with it."

He continued, "In those days, the old families could do just about anything they wanted and get away with it. But by the mid seventies the situation had got so bad that the countryside around Savannah Plantation was in an uproar. There was talk of burning the old plantation house and Edgar Mount with it.

"Finally a deal was struck. Mount was forced to leave the island in 1976 and told he could never return. Lewis was left to run the plantation and to forward profits to Mount in England. From what I understand, there have been damn few profits to forward."

"So how did Lewis become so rich and powerful?" I asked.

"With Edgar Mount in England, Vincent Lewis did whatever he wanted with Savannah. Basically he ran it for his own profit. He leased other land and raised sugar cane. His operations were more profitable than most because Lewis used the labour, machinery and material from Savannah on his other lands. With the profits he earned, over time, he bought other plantations. As a consequence, he has become one of the largest landholders and wealthiest men on the island. Meanwhile, Edgar Mount kept sending him more and more money every year to keep Savannah Plantation going."

Oliver paused and poured the last of the rum into our glasses. I was not certain that I would be able to stand up.

"Elvira and I occasionally go to Annie's for Sunday dinner. She is a gracious hostess and always has nice gifts for our boys. By late 1985, it was apparent that Annie was going to have a baby. It was a girl, Clara, named for our late aunt in Toronto. She was born on Easter in 1986. She has just turned eleven.

"Just one look at Annie's baby and you knew that she was Lewis's. Very light skin, and her hair almost blond. Today, she's a beautiful young girl and all the boys and half the men in Barbados are already in love with her. She has green eyes and her skin is a golden colour. I swear, it glows. She has a bit of the kink in her hair but it has a blond sheen. And amazingly, even with all her beauty, she is one sweet, nice girl."

He stopped and reflected upon his niece. Then he added, "The truth is, Clara is going to be even more beautiful than her mother, God help us!"

"Does Lewis say Clara is his child?"

"No, and that's a further measure of the man. When Clara was born, Lewis had begun an effort to socialise with the rich on the West Coast. He wanted to break into the top ranks of Barbados society. He was afraid that having a lightskin child on the side, an occurrence not totally unknown in Barbados mind you, would not further his social ambitions. Also, we can only guess what was going on at home with his English wife. They have three children of their own. Not only has he not given Clara his name, he insisted that Annie get married to provide some cover for their relationship.

"He came up with someone for her to marry, an ambitious politician from St Charles named Goodman Griffith." Oliver saw my reaction. "Yes, the same Goody Griffith that we talked about. He is, technically, my brother-in-law."

Ollie made a face, suggesting that he did not care much for Annie's husband.

"Goody and Annie were married when Clara was a young baby. Everyone was told that Griffith was the father. She is called

Clara Griffith, but nobody with half a brain thinks that she is Goody's. He's too ugly to have ever fathered a child that looks like her.

"Annie stayed on in her big house. Goody has a room there but he actually lives with another woman in St Charles. Annie has been with Lewis, it must be thirteen, fourteen years by now. In the meantime, Lewis has become extremely wealthy and powerful, one of the three most powerful white men on the island.

"Annie has everything that she might want. She has a big Jaguar with a chauffeur, beautiful clothes, travels to Miami, New York and London at the drop of a hat. And Annie has been accepted into some of the top homes on the island. I hear that she makes the wives nervous but the husbands enjoy having her around. She is still a damned good-looking woman.

"As payback, Lewis has thrown his support, financial and otherwise, to Goody Griffith. I hear that he even brought in American political consultants to help Goody define issues and to teach him how to handle the media. Anyway, it seems to have worked, people are now talking about Goody for the next Prime Minister, if their party stays in power. The current Prime Minister has hinted that this will be his last term in office."

"Tell me, how does all this fit in with what they call the Savannah Project?"

"Oh, yes, the Savannah Project." Ollie spoke the name with an edge in his voice, then he drained the last of his rum. He got up unsteadily and said that he would get us more to drink but I said, "Not for me", so he sat back down.

"Savannah. Lewis is in back of it, everyone knows that. After years of being neglected and misused, Savannah Plantation was semi-derelict. Lewis hits on the idea of using it, together with adjacent lands of his own, as the site for a golf course and resort hotel. It was the right size and in the right place, also the old

Great House could be fixed up to be a great addition to the resort.

"The plantation, of course, is still owned by Edgar Mount in England. Lewis went over there to get his agreement to the idea. He was shocked to see Mount, he was obviously very ill and probably doesn't have long to live.

"Mount said yes, Lewis could include Savannah in his project and, moreover, he would give him an option to purchase Savannah, exercisable at the time of Mount's death. But there was a catch. Edgar Mount wanted to return to Barbados. The happiest days of his life had been spent here and Mount wanted to live out his final days at Savannah. Mount told Lewis that his option on Savannah depended on Lewis getting the ban lifted.

"Lewis agreed. He really had no choice. He wanted Savannah Plantation and, besides, he had plenty of political clout, more than enough, to get the government to do this. Old and sick, Edgar Mount would no longer be a risk to the youth of St Charles. But Lewis needed to stall Mount until he could get the Great House repaired. It had fared badly since Mount had last seen it. So he told Mount that he needed medical proof of his condition. Once Lewis had the doctor's report, he told Mount, there should be no problem getting the government to lift the ban.

"Suddenly the resort was looking better than ever to Lewis. He expanded the project, now calling it the Savannah Project, but it had become too big a financial obligation for him to handle all alone. He brought in local investors, among them the richest people on the island, probably many of the same people you saw at the Garrison Club. Also some Canadian and British investors.

"They had a survey done and developed an ambitious plan. To make it all work, financially, they were advised to include a gambling casino. It would be the first such on the island and it would probably make them a fortune. Lewis and his backers knew there would be fierce opposition to the casino from the churches. So they initially announced that their plans were to build a golf-oriented resort. Only later, after everyone had got enthusiastic about that idea, was the gambling idea put forth.

"You cannot believe how much money could be made from the gambling," Ollie said in an aside. "And with a portion of the gambling revenue going to the government, it would also mean a lot of money for the country. It could and probably would change Barbados. That was why many politicians were for it and why others were opposed."

I assured Ollie that I did appreciate the profit potential for professional gambling. Legal or otherwise, gambling is a big and profitable business in the States. Not always a nice business, a clean business nor a crime-free business, but profitable for its owners and, as a result, also profitable for the politicians who allowed it to exist.

"As expected, there was a lot of opposition to the Savannah Project from the churches, but it was not just the ministers, there were others. Not the least of them, the Prime Minister. He was not against it strictly on moral grounds. Hell, we've got lots of gambling in Barbados already with the slots, racing and Lotto. He was concerned that the kind of people involved in casino gambling, the kinds of tourists it would attract and the amount of money it would throw off, would change Barbados for the worse. He let it be known quietly that he would support Savannah as a golf project but not if gambling was included.

"But Lewis and Goody had done their dirty work. The majority of the Prime Minister's own political party was pro-Savannah, including the casino. As you can imagine, a lot of money had changed hands with even more promised when the project got through.

"Although little was said publicly, this became the number one issue in Barbados. You were either pro-Savannah or you were not. The majority of both major political parties were pro. It looked like the PM would have to step aside. The groundwork was set for him to resign and for Goody to take over and call a new election. Incidentally, this is not common knowledge, so you mustn't tell this to anyone."

"How do you know all this?" I was impressed by Ollie's knowledge of the inside workings of government and politics.

"We make it our business to know what's going on. We have to, we're the police. Also, I have become close to the Prime Minister. And if I need to know something about Savannah, I can always ask Annie. She either knows it or she will find it out for me from Lewis, from Goody or some other source. And if I ask her, she tells me; after all, I am her brother.

"However, even though we know about things, the police can't always do anything, even if something involves an illegal activity, like the bribing of elected officials. These people, Lewis and the other big landowners, they're too powerful and too politically connected to be stopped by minor concerns with the law."

I urged Ollie to go on with what had happened to the Savannah Project.

"In September 1995 the Water Board – a new authority which had been created to advise the government on water resource issues – commented on the Savannah Project. The Water Board was a non-political, quasi-public entity, made up of public-minded citizens and outside consultants knowledgeable about water-related issues. They released their conclusions about the Savannah Project simultaneously to the government and to the press. They had learned the hard way that if government got their report first, their recommendations had a way of being changed.

"The report stated conclusively that the Savannah Project would draw too much water from the public aquifer, particularly in its first five years. Longer term, the hotel and golf course could get by on their wells plus desalinated and catchment water, but even the most optimistic forecast was that, if Savannah went ahead as planned, one third of the homes in St Charles and St Philip would be without water for up to four months a year.

"Understandably, public support turned against the project. Political support dried up as well; even Goody assumed a low profile. Lewis and his group were devastated, they looked into various alternatives. It was too late to buy off the Water Board, even if they could, so they had to either modify their plan substantially or find another water source. If they eliminated the golf course, the project would require far less water, but they would never get it approved as just a gambling resort. Then they looked into building a larger desalination plant, converting even more seawater to fresh water, but it was too costly, and in the end it would still not give them the volume of water they would need during the dry season. They were stumped. And that's where the Savannah Project is today, stalled."

"Where do the politicians stand?"

"Well, with the Savannah Project ended, or at least on hold, there was no rush to make the Prime Minister step down before the election. There will be an election before the end of the year anyway. But the Prime Minister has been harmed politically by the whole Savannah thing. It is widely assumed that he will not stand for re-election, and that Goody Griffith will probably be the next PM."

I was learning a lot but I still hadn't heard Oliver explain why he had blocked my efforts to look into Clarence's death. All he had said was that someone had asked him to do it. I strongly suspected that the someone was his sister Annie, but why would Annie do that?

"Ollie, you've told me a lot of useful information, but there's one more thing I must know. Who asked you to limit the inquiry into my uncle's death, and why?"

Oliver put his head in his hands and mumbled a short reply. I couldn't make out what he said, so I asked him to repeat it.

"Annie. Goddamn it, it was Annie," he said in an emotionally-charged voice.

"Why would she want you to do that?" I said gently, in recognition of the stress that he was so obviously feeling.

"The truth is, I don't know why for sure; I just know what she told me."

"And what was that?" I persisted.

"Annie called me at home on the Monday, the twenty-third of December, the day that your Uncle Clarence was killed. She said that a body would probably be found the next morning somewhere along the St Charles coast. She said that an elderly man, a redleg, drunk and mixed-up after having been in a fight earlier in the evening, had fallen from the cliff into the sea. She swore that it was an accidental death. She said that the man the old redleg fought with was an 'associate of my special friend'. Special friend was always Annie's term to me for her keepers – first Aubrey Tudor and then Vincent Lewis. I didn't know who she meant by 'an associate', maybe one of Lewis's overseers? I still don't know who she was referring to.

" I asked her who the redleg was but she swore that she didn't know. She asked me to see that the lid was kept on this man's death. It would be better for everyone, she said, if this was seen for what it was, a simple, regrettable accident. Annie warned me that the man's body might show signs of the beating that he had taken in the fight and it would be a terrible injustice if anyone made any incorrect assumptions about how he had died.

"I told her that it was very difficult for me to interfere with an investigation, particularly one which involves a fatality. She really turned it on, begged me to do her this one favour. She said that she would never ask anything of me again. You know women, they can be very persuasive when they want to be.

"I thought about it. It didn't really seem that bad. The man was already dead and, if he had died like she said, it probably would be better for people not to get stirred up unnecessarily. And remember, I owed and continue to owe a lot to Annie, and this clearly was something very important to her. I promised her that I would do what I could.

"I dropped by District C the next morning, seemingly by chance. The body was just being brought in. I could see that it was an old man but I didn't know it was your uncle until the constable told me who it was.

"I took Constable Greenidge and Sergeant Brathwaite aside and explained that the policy of the department on this death was that there should be no further investigation. They were to report to me if anyone asked them any questions. A funeral director, hired by Goody, then showed up and took the body away. Goody's involvement reinforced my conviction that Vincent Lewis was in back of this. Clarence Glenville was buried on Boxing Day. That seemed like that would be the end of it.

"Then you show up. And you're not only my old friend but you're also with the police in New York. As long as you're just asking questions, it seemed like it would blow over. I knew that you were scheduled to go back on that Monday flight. But when you dug up the grave, it looked to be getting out of hand. I leaned on you to make sure that you left Barbados, as per schedule."

"So why are you helping me now?"

"When Glenville burned and your granny and aunt were killed, I felt real bad. I'd promised you that I would look after them, and I did, but this terrible thing still happened. I hoped the fire was just an accident, but there was a chance, probably a good chance, that it was not. And maybe it was related to your uncle's death. I asked Annie what she knew, but she swore that she knew nothing about it."

Oliver promised to help me any way that he could. It was time for me to go, before I fell asleep. I got up to leave but I was definitely wobbly. I told Oliver that I was concerned about driving, considering how much I'd had to drink.

He laughed and told me not to worry.

"At this hour" – it was around eleven thirty – "two thirds of the people drivin' on the island are drunk. You'll fit right in."

"What about the police?"

"We don't hassle drivers much, as long as they can stay on the road."

I didn't know if this was true or if he intended it as a joke. It sure didn't make me feel any better about getting behind the wheel. But I had to get to bed. I thanked Oliver, told him to say goodbye to Elvira for me, and walked stiffly to my car.

I sat there behind the wheel for a few minutes. My God, I was drunk. Drunker than I was at my retirement party. Frankly, I'm not much for heavy drinking, I don't like the feeling of not being in control. I took several deep breaths and then slowly started for St Charles. Somehow, I found my way to the Wavecrest Hotel. How, I could not tell you.

Daily Report 172

Date of Events: Thursday, 3 July 1997 – small hours
Place: Barbados: The Wavecrest Hotel
Summary: Intruder

I fell asleep right away in my sparsely furnished room at the Wavecrest. Oliver's lethal rum rendered me unconscious almost as soon as I hit the pillow, but wild and terrifying dreams closed in and tried to waken me. It was a fitful sleep, at best.

Annie was in my dreams, sometimes as an innocent young girl and sometimes as she was today, beautiful and alluring. Someone else was there as well, a man, but I could not see his face. People slipped in and out of the shadows around me. I tried to catch them but they always eluded my grasp. Others stood in the shadows, witnessing my failures. Everyone seemed to know what was going on except me. I heard waves crashing. And then, everything burst into flames. I was surrounded by fire and couldn't get away. There was smoke everywhere, I couldn't breathe. I panicked.

I woke up. I was sitting up, covered with sweat. It took me several seconds to orient myself. Where was I? What was going on? Slowly, I reconstructed what had happened. Grandma Dora and Aunt Emily were dead. I was at the surfer hotel, in my room, in my bed. And I was drunk, or something like it.

Damn Oliver's goddamn rum. The room was slowly spinning. I thought for a moment I was going to be sick to my stomach. Briefly, that seemed like a good idea, maybe it would make me feel better. But the queasiness decreased, and I decided to hang on for the moment.

I guess I slept again, but for how long? It might have been for minutes or for hours. I know that when I woke I had a dry mouth, a headache and a compelling urge to relieve my bladder. I wanted desperately to lie back down and go to sleep again, but the uncomfortable feeling within convinced me that this would be a bad idea. I told myself that I had to make the effort to get to the toilet.

I heaved myself upright and lurched forward in the pitch-black room toward the small, odd-smelling bathroom. I knew that the door was somewhere along the wall to my right. I found a door knob but it was the door out into the hall. I moved further along the wall until my hand hit another knob. This was the bathroom.

Without turning on the light, I located the toilet and did what I had come to do. Then I stood at the washbasin and looked into the mirror. There was just enough of a glow from the hotel security light coming through the small window for me to see my face. I have looked better, a whole lot better.

Then I heard a noise. The door to my room was opening. The killer of my father and my family was coming for me! My adrenaline kicked into high gear.

Through the half-open bathroom door, I could see a figure entering the room slowly, quietly. He was fairly tall but not as big as I am. The door closed and the shadowed figure moved slowly across the room towards the bed.

I leapt out of the bathroom and wrapped my arms around the intruder, driving him forward, face down onto the bed. There was a muffled scream as the weight of my body drove the air from his lungs.

Suddenly my senses delivered unexpected information to my brain. I didn't feel the muscular body of the killer of my relatives, rather this body was soft and, I suddenly realised, distinctly female.

Then another of my senses kicked in, my sense of smell. I perceived a musky, vaguely cinnamon-floral scent. But no flower on this earth has ever smelled like this. Then I realised that I had smelled this scent before.

Then, I knew. The person I was holding down on my bed was Annie, my Annie. Annie Shorter Griffith. Wife of Goodman Griffith, the next Prime Minister of Barbados; mistress of Vincent Lewis; sister of Chief Inspector Oliver Shorter; former Miss Barbados, first runner-up for Miss World; the girl of my teenaged fantasies a long time ago and still, occasionally, the girl of my adult dreams.

I rolled her over and held her hands back over her head, keeping her pinned to the bed and said, "Welcome to room twelve at the stylish Wavecrest Hotel."

"You certainly do know how to give a girl a big welcome," she said with a laugh. Then she added, "How did you know I was coming?"

"I didn't. You just appeared. Why are you here?"

I released her hands and sat up.

Annie raised herself on her elbows and looked at me with an amused smile. Then her mood shifted suddenly from flirtatious humour to sympathy as she remembered why she had come.

"Ben, I had to see you. It is because of the terrible things that have happened to your family, your grandmother, your aunt. I wanted you to know how sorry I am, and how much I wanted to see you to tell you that."

"Thank you," I said, "And I'm glad you're here because I need to talk to you, too. I am confused about a lot of things, some of them have to do with you. Let's talk now."

"Fine, let's, but first, may I ask a favour?" She said it plaintively, as if she expected me to say no.

I had no idea what she wanted.

"What do you need?"

She laughed and held the flat of her hand up to her nose.

"Your breath, it smells like the bottom of an old rum barrel. Would you mind brushing your teeth?"

I was floored by her request. I blew into my hand and, for my effort, I got the smell of my own breath. I had to admit, my breath would have stripped paint off a 1983 Camaro.

More than a bit embarrassed, I went into the bathroom, closed the door and turned on the light. Again I stood by the basin, but now I vigorously brushed my teeth. I rinsed my mouth and then I brushed my teeth again. Finally, hoping that I was fit to be in the same room with another human being, I turned out the light, opened the door and re-entered the dark bedroom, my breath smelling of original flavour Crest with only a slight touch of rum.

In the dark I could see nothing. My night vision was temporarily inactive because I had been staring into the harsh light of the sixty-watt bulb above the basin.

"Where are you?" I asked.

"Here. Over here," she answered. It sounded like she was just where I had left her, on the bed.

My eyesight began to adjust to the dark. I could now dimly make out her form, either sitting or kneeling on the bed. I reached out to locate the bed so that I could sit and we could begin our talk. Suddenly two hands grasped my wrists and pulled me gently forward. I felt the back of my hand touched by her lips, and then she slid my hand down and under her chin, and held it against her neck. Then she moved my right hand down onto one of her breasts. Annie had taken off her clothes!

I started to say something, what I couldn't tell you, but she put her other hand upon my lips, sealing them. Then she lay back and pulled me toward her. I was drawn down, falling gently into a pool of softness and sweetness and I was totally engulfed and beguiled by the odour of perfume and Annie's own, very personal woman's scent.

Our lips met and Annie started to tug at my tee-shirt. I rolled to one side and quickly stripped off my shirt and shorts, a manoeuvre which I have perfected over the years. Then our bodies came together.

With Oliver's rum acting as a governor to my passion, our lovemaking went on and on. Annie seemed able to read and slow our passion at just the right moment. Our skins became slick from our mutual perspiration as we glided together on the narrow bed.

Finally, as if by mutual agreement, the tempo of our lovemaking increased. Our bodies began to slap together as the tempo of lovemaking accelerated while we reached for our ultimate goal. A rhythmic noise emitted from deep in Annie's throat, more animal than human.

The speed and pitch of the noise increased until Annie suddenly stiffened, then her whole body shuddered again and again and again. I lay still, awed by her passion. Minutes passed, and our bodies locked together again. Then, slowly, Annie began to move her body against mine.

This time, sooner than before, we reached another crescendo. But this time I was the first to let go.

I slept, dreamless and content. At some point we awakened and talked but I can't remember what we said. Annie cried, something had her upset, but I'm not sure she ever told me what it was. We made love again – or maybe I just imagined it.

The next time I awoke, it was daylight and I was alone.

Daily Report 173

Date of Events: Thursday, 3 July 1997 – later
Place: Barbados: the Wavecrest Hotel; Morgue and Coroner's Court; Barbados Museum Library
Summary: Red tape re bodies and Brodeur's storybook insight

I was very slow getting started this morning. My mind was in a turmoil. I got out of bed and fished my notebook out of my pants, which were lying in a heap behind the chair. I reviewed my notes from my meeting with Oliver, looking particularly at what he had said about Annie's role in squashing the investigation of Clarence's death and about her long-term relationship with Vincent Lewis.

Then I remembered that I had recorded my conversation with Ollie. I played segments of it and compared them with my notes to be sure I could accurately summarise what I had learned at Ollie's. It was a good thing I had the recording because, thanks to the rum, my handwriting had become less and less legible as the night wore on.

Next I reviewed what happened later, here in my room, with Annie and me. It is all a bit of a blur. Did it really happen? Yes, it has to be real. I can smell Annie's perfume on my body, on the sheets, even in the air. And I am a man. You know when you've made love.

Am I being played for some sort of a fool? A distinct possibility, I have to admit. It wouldn't be the first time that my desire for a woman has overwhelmed my better judgment, and it probably won't be the last time either.

I have to face the truth. The woman in my arms last night is implicated to some degree in the death of my Uncle Clarence. Moreover, her long-time lover and the father of her child seems to be the most logical person to be in back of everything that has happened here in Barbados.

But when I allow myself to remember the last few hours, I don't want to believe anything negative about Annie. She has been so sweet, so genuinely caring and sad about what had happened to Grandma Dora and Aunt Emily. And her lovemaking! Well, that was something really special. We did talk at length but, with the rum, the late hour and my memory problem, I can't recall what she said. Something about an accident that was not her fault. She was crying so hard it was difficult to follow. And I was more concerned with trying to console her. Then we made love again.

Am I a fool? Possibly, maybe even probably – but maybe not. I realise that eventually I will find out. For now I think I will just wait to see what happens next.

It was nearly ten o'clock. Breakfast is served at the Wavecrest from eight to ten. I walked through the funky lobby into the large dining room where a modest breakfast buffet had been set. Four blond surfers from California – three male, one female – were having coffee and planning their day. I recognised them as having rooms on my hall, adjacent to mine.

They stood and clapped as I entered. I was startled by their action but then it occurred to me that sounds must carry through the walls at the Wavecrest. It made sense: low rates, thin walls, limited privacy.

I was somewhat annoyed by this attention and the surfers' remarks, good-natured but crude. I tried to ignore them as I selected my breakfast, not even glancing their way. Other late breakfast-eaters looked at me curiously, wondering what I had done to deserve this accolade. Eventually, the raunchy remarks of the surfers made it clear to all.

The others eventually left and I lingered over my coffee, reviewing my summary. Annie was connected with Clarence's death, but how and why? I didn't really believe that she would hurt anyone but I was fully prepared to believe that her keeper Vincent Lewis would. Her involvement must have been at his request. However, I also thought that I was falling in love with Annie, if I had ever not been in love with her. I knew that I had to get to the truth of all this before I had lost all perspective and professional judgment.

My first order of business today would be to drive down to Bridgetown to the morgue. There, I hoped to claim the bodies of Grandma Dora and Aunt Emily.

I finally found the morgue, in the basement of the Queen Elizabeth II Hospital. But, as I should have expected, getting the bodies released was not going to be easy. Forms had to be filled out in triplicate. Then multiple clearances were needed, from officials not readily available to sign off. Then I would have to take the papers over to the courts for the final sign-off.

By twelve forty-five there were no empty signature blocks and nothing more that could be done at the hospital. After several missteps, I finally located the elusive Coroner's Court, but it was closed until two. The release of Eudora and Emily Glenville's bodies to me would have to wait for the signatures of more faceless officials. However, I didn't get the impression that I had been personally singled out for this runaround; I suspect that anyone would have got the same treatment. Bureaucracy is bureaucracy, whether in New York, London, New Delhi or Bridgetown. The order of the day is hurry up and wait, paperwork and meaningless approvals.

Long ago in the US Army and, since then, working with and through the NYPD's bureaucracy, I learned that time is your enemy, patience is your only ally. Anger can occasionally be effective with bureaucrats, if used sparingly. I've had most of my success in this arena by implying to them that I have access to their superiors but not openly threatening them with it.

I went into my act by dropping Oliver Shorter's name shamelessly to the Clerk of the Coroner's Court. How successful was the stratagem? Only time would tell.

I was told to go away and return at four. From the clerk's attitude, I judged that my chances of getting the bodies released today were fifty-fifty, at best.

With time to kill, I drove over to the Barbados Museum, located at the Garrison. Oliver had said that it was an excellent source, in fact, the only source, for information on old Barbados families like mine. I wanted to look into the Glenville family's history at the Museum Library; maybe it would shed some light on why my relations had been killed.

Three people were in the small library. One was familiar; it was the elderly white gentleman who had helped me find the Garrison Club last December. I tried to remember his name. Yes, it was Mr Brodeur. He was totally engrossed, carefully making notes with a pencil in an ancient leather-bound book. A middle-aged woman sat at a desk in the corner, performing clerical tasks. The third, a nice-looking East Indian woman in a sari, was leafing through a stack of editions of an old magazine.

I asked the woman at the desk, "How do I go about researching a subject?"

"That depends," she said, looking at me with some suspicion. "It depends on your subject of interest. But you should be aware that there is a fee for using the library's facilities."

I parted with ten dollars Barbados and we got down to business.

"Now, what is your subject of inquiry?"

From her accent I knew that she was Bajan born. From my accent she would have known that I was "from up north, the US or Canada" and, therefore, not to be trusted.

"I am interested in knowing more about the Glenvilles of Glenville House in St Charles."

I sensed a stir of interest from the elderly man at the table. Mr Brodeur looked up and said, "Perhaps I can help you?"

Then he recognised me.

"It's you, is it? You were in here at Christmas looking for a men's club. What was it? Oh yes, the Garrison Club. Did you ever find it?"

"As a matter of fact, I did, right where you said it would be, in the old infirmary."

"I don't imagine they offered you a membership, did they?"

I laughed. "Not exactly, but I did learn what I needed to know."

"What brings you here now?"

"I am down from New York. I am interested in the Glenvilles of Glenville House in St Charles. They're an old redleg family. I thought that there might be something about them here."

"There probably is. Let me see if I can help," Brodeur said.

He stood and walked stiffly to where I stood. Brodeur was slim, his hair and moustache were trim and white, but his movements seemed slowed by age and its frequent companion, arthritis. His skin had the slightly yellow cast that elderly people sometimes develop, particularly in the tropics. But he seemed mentally alert and was certainly willing to help.

He looked at me over his glasses and said, "That is an interesting family, going back to Frank Glenville in the 1880s and, before him, right back to the very beginnings of Barbados. The Glenvilles were among the earliest redlegs here. I am afraid that we don't have much on the Glenvilles before Frank, other than to see one

Glenville or another's name appearing in the usual sources: church rolls, plantation pay rosters, and militia musters."

I said that I was primarily interested in Glenville House and the present-day descendants of Frank. I said that I had spent my summers there when I was growing up.

Suddenly old Brodeur remembered the recent fire and the deaths of Eudora and Emily and, possibly, the earlier death of Clarence.

"Oh, I am so sorry. That terrible fire, I now understand why you are here in Barbados. My deepest sympathies to you and yours for these unexpected tragedies."

I could see that Brodeur was embarrassed. In his mind the Glenvilles were a white redleg family. Given my skin colour, he had not picked up right away on the fact that I was kin to the Glenvilles.

I told him my name and that my father, Nate Cumberbatch, was Dora Glenville's son.

"So, you are descended from one of the sons of Eudora Glenville who had emigrated?"

Brodeur didn't miss a thing. I was impressed that he knew about the Cumberbatches, the light-skinned offshoots of the Glenville family.

"What might there be on Glenville House? For example, how it came to the Glenvilles, and anything else to do with that era?"

"I have just the thing, if I can find it," he replied.

For the next half an hour I stood and watched as the elderly man looked for a children's storybook entitled *Tales of Barbados*.

At last, in a dusty bookcase in the hall leading to the library, Brodeur found the storybook. He held it up for me to see, a large, thin book with a tattered cover. Then he opened it to the title page.

"It was printed in London in 1901. As a boy growing up in Hampshire, just after the Great War of '14 to '18, this book was one of my favourites. It was my introduction to a magical place called Barbados. This book is probably the major reason why, after university, in the nineteen thirties, I came out here to work for Barclays."

As he spoke, he turned the pages to a story called "Frank Glenville, from Redleg to Landowner". He handed it to me to read.

Essentially, it was the same story that I had heard so often from Grandma Dora. The plucky Frank still fought the three drunken sailors and saved the young mistress from "a fate worse than death". There was an illustration of Frank cutting off the hand of the sailor, just as I had imagined it would be.

But in this version the plantation owner, Augustus Mount, was far more gracious and magnanimous than in my grandmother's story. He generously bestowed the lands and house upon Frank Glenville. There was no mention of his daughter's role in making him do it. I guess in Victorian England rich men were expected to be gracious and benevolent and young ladies were supposed to be seen and not heard.

I preferred Grandma Dora's version and my faith was justified. Its accuracy was confirmed because stuck in the book at the end of the story were several newspaper articles from the *Clarion*, from the year 1883. The first few told of the battle and of Frank Glenville's subsequent struggle for his life. Another described how all segments of Barbados society had been interested in the event and particularly concerned about the reward which Frank Glenville would receive from the Mounts. The final article described the ceremony at which Barbara Mount offered to build what would become Glenville House.

In the margin, at the end of the story, there was a notation for readers to refer to another story in the same book, entitled, "The Wandering Lady and her Daughter".

I turned to that story. The illustration showed a Carib Indian woman with a little girl in tow, wandering through a jungle.

Peering out of the dense vegetation at the brave woman were serpents and large-eyed cats, either lions or tigers; it was left to the reader's imagination. Clearly, the artist had never been to Barbados, which has neither carnivores nor serpents.

This story was much different than Frank Glenville's. It was a fairy tale about a beautiful Indian woman, from a time long before the English came to Barbados in the 1620s. The woman had been falsely accused of having been unfaithful to her husband, the son of the Chief. Her accusers were others in the tribe, jealous of her beauty. Anyway, the Chief declared that she and her daughter had to leave the tribe.

The woman wandered the countryside of Barbados, particularly in the hilly areas on the east coast, the section that later became the traditional redleg area. Her husband could hear his wife crying at night in the woods but he could do nothing for her because his father and the tribal law would not allow it.

The old chief eventually died and the husband became the chief. He then learned that his wife had been falsely accused. Distraught and ashamed, he set out to find her, to beg forgiveness and to bring his wife and daughter back home. But they were nowhere to be found. He did find their campsite, but the wife and daughter were never seen again. A large spring of fresh water flowed at the site of the deserted camp and, not far away, a second, smaller spring was found.

The new chief moved the tribe to where the springs had emerged. However, no sooner had they settled there than the springs disappeared. The wise men of the tribe declared that these springs were the spirits of the chief's departed wife and daughter.

The large spring re-emerged at another site, with the smaller spring nearby. The tribe relocated there and, again, the springs soon vanished. Eventually the Indians left Barbados and never returned. They considered the island to be haunted.

When the English arrived centuries later, two springs, a large one and a smaller one, were found in St Charles parish. The local farmers depended on them as their principal source of "sweet" or potable water during the dry season which, in most years, lasted from December to May. But these springs periodically disappeared and then relocated elsewhere in the parish. These mysterious springs were no doubt the basis of the story of the Wandering Lady and her Daughter.

A notation at the end of the story, written in ink, said, "According to plantation records, the Wandering Lady spring was on the hillside above Savannah Plantation in St Charles for fifty years, from 1680 to 1730. The Daughter spring was on the plantation proper. They both disappeared in 1730 and neither of them has ever been seen again." The writer signed with his initials, "J.T.T.", and the date, "15/10/1923".

I remembered Uncle Clarence showing me a large coral slab at the top side of the garden, which he said had been the site of a well in the distant past. He also said that there had been no water on Glenville land for as long as the Glenvilles had owned it.

It was time for me to get back to see if the coroner was ready to release my relatives' bodies to me. Mr Brodeur was enjoying a cup of tea. I stopped to thank him for his help. For sure, I would never have found the book without his assistance. I asked him some additional questions, thinking that he might well have something to add to my knowledge of what was going on.

You could see that Brodeur was an intelligent, long-time observer of the Barbados scene yet, as an Englishman, he might not necessarily be fully integrated into it. The benefit of this would be that he might have retained a certain objectivity or perspective that a native-born Bajan, black or white, might not have.

I asked him, "Why would anyone want to own a small piece of land, too small to farm economically? And why would they want it bad enough to kill for it?"

Brodeur said that he could not imagine anyone in Barbados killing for land because "there is enough to go around. Basically, Barbados is a very safe place. The people are kind and tend to look out for each other. Usually fights are not lethal and typically they're between men, either young or foolish, who have been drinking too much rum."

He added, "In America, in the early days, people were killed for gold. In South Africa, people were killed for diamonds and emeralds. But, to the best of my knowledge, these precious commodities never have existed here in Barbados."

"But," I said, "Barbados has oil."

I've seen numerous oil rigs pumping as I drive from the airport to St Charles. I've also heard it said that Barbados produces most of its own petroleum from the crude oil drawn from these fields.

"Yes, it does have oil, but no one in their right mind would kill for it. You see, the oil belongs to the government. One of the worst things that can happen to you is to have oil discovered on your property. They do give you some compensation but they come in and set up their oil rigs and catchment tanks and they make a terrible mess."

"So, what could make a small piece of land so desirable?"

Mr Brodeur looked at me carefully and then said, "There is only one thing that is worth killing for on Barbados, the one thing that is even more precious on this island than gold or jewels or oil."

"And what's that?" I asked the old man.

"Water, God's gift to man. Pure, drinkable water available in limitless supply. Whoever had that would control the destiny of this island."

Daily Report 174

Date of Events: Thursday, 3 July 1997 – late afternoon and evening
Place: Barbados: Bridgetown; the Wavecrest Hotel; the casuarina grove
Summary: Annie

To my surprise, the clerk had the paperwork ready and waiting for me to claim the bodies. When I got to the morgue at the Queen Elizabeth II Hospital, the small coffins were sitting on a wheeled luggage carrier. Apparently Oliver's name had done the trick. I opened the coffins to be sure that we had the right bodies. The black and burned bodies of Grandma Dora and Emily were there, contained in airtight plastic bags.

In my line of work I had too often encountered bodies such as these. It both saddened and angered me to think that my sweet, gentle relatives had met their death in this gruesome and terrifying way. Seeing them like this further strengthened my resolve to bring their killer to justice.

A young man helped me wheel the coffins outside and to place them in the back seat of my Moke. We tied them down. It would have been a disaster if the bodies had fallen out on the road as I drove them across town in the low, open car to the freight forwarder.

As it was, drivers' and pedestrians' heads spun around in Bridgetown as I passed with my macabre cargo. What did they think was going on? I couldn't even guess.

The shipper accepted the caskets as they are, for shipment to the NYPD forensics lab. These and the fire debris boxes, which I had delivered earlier, would travel on the same ship. I am not concerned about decomposition en route; the bodies are so burned that they are virtually cremated. Just to be sure, I paid a bit extra to see that they will be carried in an empty frozen food locker. They are due to arrive in New York the first week in August. If all goes as per schedule, I should have the results in hand the third week of August.

I returned to the Wavecrest. I had skipped lunch, so I went right in to dinner. As I entered the dining room I was told that someone was waiting for me in the outer lobby. When I got there, no one was to be seen in the half light of the dingy, gloomy reception. I was about to leave when a short, stocky, broad-shouldered black man, wearing matching grey-green pants and shirt, emerged from behind a pillar to my right. He had been there all the time, waiting, but with my poor peripheral vision I had not seen him in the shadows.

"Cumberbatch? I have message for yuh," he said softly.

"And who are you?" I asked.

"Malcolm Newton. I work for Mistress Annie. Dat's why I am here. She wants yuh to meet wid she tonight."

Good, I wanted to see her, too.

"Where and when?" I asked, trying to appear casual.

"She say yuh know de place. De stand o' mile trees near de cliff, down from Glenville village. She say it de place where yuh tell she goodbye one time."

I knew at once where he meant, it was where Annie and I had said our farewells when I left Barbados in 1972, the casuarina grove out on the cliff, east of Glenville village. Somehow I remembered that "mile tree" is another name used in Barbados for what Annie and I had called the casuarina tree.

Malcolm said for me to be there in an hour, at eight fifteen. He would get Annie and bring her there to meet me.

213

I had a salad and soup for dinner. I left the hotel at eight and drove the few minutes to Glenville, where I parked the Moke by the forlorn wreck of Glenville House. I noted that the rope and other signs of police activity had been removed.

I walked down through the small village past the Shorters' old chattel house, now boarded and empty. It sits crookedly on its foundation, one side of which has collapsed. Behind it, a new cement-block house – a wall house as it's called – is under construction. No doubt, when the new house is finished, the Shorter house will be demolished. One less chattel house. Too bad.

The path was not easy to find. It seemed overgrown and less well defined than I remembered. I walked along the trail but, with the passage of time, trees and plants have grown and died. It didn't look the same. And now that I was there, I was not at all sure how far to go to reach the turn-off to the casuarina grove.

A half-moon had just risen above the sea to my left and it cast a soft glow, barely enough to illuminate the trail. I was carrying my flashlight, but Malcolm had warned me not to use it, unless I absolutely had to. I stumbled on roots and outcroppings of coral but, eventually, my eyes adjusted to the uneven trail in the half-light.

After several minutes, I became concerned that I might have passed the turn-off. I need not have worried. Malcolm stepped out onto the trail in front of me. He must have been standing in the shadows waiting for me to show up. For someone so broad, he certainly could make himself inconspicuous.

He gestured for me to turn to my right, up a small dirt track.

On this trail it was even darker. No moon, no stars. I was at once surrounded by tall plants and trees. The light from the moon didn't begin to penetrate the brush. I felt my way along. Then my hand brushed the soft needles of a tree. I realised that I was at the edge of the casuarina grove.

From a few feet away Annie said, "Ben, thank God you've come. I had to see you."

I could just make out her shape, standing there in a white dress. I reached for her but she didn't move to me. She remained still. I sensed that something was wrong.

"Annie, are you all right?"

She ignored my question and said, "Do you remember this place? I almost lost my virginity to you here, do you remember that?"

I did, of course, remember and I laughed and said, "There should be a monument here. It would say, 'Annie Shorter almost made Ben Cumberbatch the happiest fourteen-year-old in Barbados here one summer night in 1972.'"

Annie didn't laugh. In a sombre voice she said quietly, "I think I know who killed your father and your Uncle Clarence."

"Who? My God! Tell me, Annie, who was it?"

"I don't know his name, but I have seen him. He met with my … with Vincent Lewis, at my house and, based on what was said between them, I think he was the one that did it."

"When did they meet?"

"Today, around noontime."

I didn't feel I had to ask Annie why the meeting had been held at her home. It was obvious that Lewis, since he paid for Annie's upkeep, felt free to use the house for confidential meetings whenever he wished.

"What did this man say that makes you think that he killed my father and uncle?"

"He all but said it more than once. For example, he said, 'I got the two men out of the way.'"

"What did Lewis say to that?"

"He didn't say anything specifically, but he didn't act surprised. Then, they talked about you. They agreed that your being here was a problem and that you might ruin everything."

"What else was said?"

"The man asked Vincent about the fire at Glenville but Vincent said he knew nothing about it.

"It was at this point that they realised that I was sitting out on the porch, within hearing range. I was made to go upstairs to my bedroom so I couldn't hear anything more, but from what I'd heard up till then, I fear that you're in danger. That's why I sent Malcolm to find you."

"What did this man look like?"

"He was light-skinned, tall and thin. I would guess that he was in his late fifties or sixties."

"Anything else?" I probed.

"He had an English accent. Like maybe he was born there or, if he was from the islands, he had spent most of his life in England. But his accent was different. He sounds more like an upper-class Englishman in a movie, not like most Bajans you meet who've come back from there."

"Did you happen to notice if he was left-handed?"

Annie couldn't say. She had seen the man only briefly, and in that time he'd done nothing to reveal his preference for one hand or the other.

I kept asking her other questions, but she had heard nothing more of the two men's conversation. I thanked her for the information and the warning.

Then I asked Annie the question that had bothered me since I had my talk with her brother.

"Oliver told me that it was you who had asked him to be sure that no one looked further into my uncle's death. Why would you do such a thing?"

"I did that because my ... friend, Vincent Lewis, asked me to. I take that back. I did it because he ordered me to. I had no idea it was your uncle who was involved. Vincent said that he had an important business associate who'd been in a fight with a man,

216

an old redleg. He said that his associate had beaten the man badly and that the old man was drunk and later fell off the cliff and drowned. He said that the body would probably be found along the coast on Christmas Eve. Vincent was concerned that it would look bad and, as a result, that there would be unnecessary and unwelcome trouble for his associate. He insisted that I go to Ollie and ask him to see that the investigation was kept low key. I think that this man must be the 'business associate' that Vincent had been talking about."

"Did you believe Lewis's story? Did you ever know my Uncle Clarence to have a drink or to fight with anyone?" My voice rose with indignation and anger.

"Ben, remember I didn't know it was your uncle. But I neither believed nor disbelieved Vincent's story. I don't have that luxury. I've been his kept woman for over fourteen years. I depend on him for every morsel for myself and my daughter. And, until recently, I had never thought of having anything different."

I believed that Annie was telling me the truth. Why else would she have come here to warn me? Of course I wanted to believe her, and what she had said made sense and how she had said it was convincing. I was relieved to know that Annie's involvement with Clarence's death had been no more than what it had seemed. She had been used by Lewis to get to her brother to block the investigation. This, of course, leads to the conclusion that Lewis and this mystery man caused my father's and my Uncle Clarence's death and maybe, despite what they said, one or both of them was responsible for the fire at Glenville and Grandma Dora's and Aunt Emily's deaths.

I reached out to hold Annie in my arms but she pulled back, as if she was reluctant to touch me. Was she ashamed of something? No, that's not Annie. There was something else.

"Annie, are you sure that you're OK?"

Then she came to me slowly and buried the left side of her face against my chest. And, just as she had in this same place, twenty-five years before, she began to weep bitter tears. However, these tears were not for my threatened departure. They had to be for something else.

I placed my fingers lightly upon her cheek to comfort her, but she flinched and drew in her breath.

"Annie, there is something wrong with you. What is it?"

She turned away and didn't reply. I wouldn't be put off. I reached into my pocket for the small flashlight and pulled her gently around to face me. I put the light full upon her face.

Her hands went up to block my view, but not before I could see that her left eye was swollen nearly shut, and that she had several nasty bruises and abrasions on her face and forehead. Annie had been brutally beaten.

I pulled her hands down and directed my light upon her face. She stood stiffly, her arms held tightly to her side. Her eyes were shut and tears of shame and pain streamed down her swollen and discoloured cheeks.

"Who did this to you?" As if I didn't already know.

"I don't want to talk about it. It is my problem, not yours," she said miserably.

"It was that sonofabitch Lewis, wasn't it?"

She said nothing. Finally, she slowly nodded her head.

"Why did he do this? Does he do this to you often? Did it have anything to do with me, with what happened between us last night?"

She didn't answer. I took her silence as confirmation which, if it was so, meant that I was, at least indirectly, to blame for what had happened. I took her in my arms and gently rocked her back and forth, trying to comfort her.

She finally regained some composure. She pulled back and looked me in the face.

"Ben, listen to me, this is my problem. I will handle it. But I am worried about your safety."

"Annie, we're old friends, I love you and I care for you," I said softly. "But don't worry about me, I can look after myself. Please tell me what happened. Why did Lewis beat you like this?"

She was silent, organising her thoughts. Then, with a deep sigh of resignation, she said, "I probably deserved it. No probably, I deserved it. Vincent owns me, lock, stock and barrel. I am his keep-miss, as we say. He bought the house, he pays the upkeep, he buys my food and clothes and he pays for Clara's private school. It was all my fault. I forgot who I am and what I am."

"He should pay for Clara's school, for Christsakes, she's his daughter."

Annie said sadly, "He won't even admit that. It's not that he is afraid of losing his wife and three children. He would have given them up, at one time, if I'd really insisted. The real problem is that he doesn't want to admit to his friends at his clubs and at the fancy parties on the West Coast that he has a mistress and her non-white child stashed away up on the hill. When we get away from this island, like when we went to London, Paris and Rome last year, he was a different person. But here in Barbados, he keeps me hidden away."

She paused and then she continued, "Over the years, Vincent has gone to a lot of trouble and expense for our relationship. He paid a lot of money for the house, he gave me the Jaguar and hired Malcolm as my driver and bodyguard. He even made his trained lapdog Goody Griffith marry me after Clara was born. But all of this really was for Vincent's benefit, not for mine."

"Tell me about Goody Griffith," I said.

"Goody and I are no more man and wife than those two trees. But, in a funny way, we've become friends. For appearances' sake, he stops by the house every now and then and we talk. We have one thing in common: we're both on the Vincent Lewis payroll. Goody owes his whole career to Vincent and, if the Prime Minister steps down, like some say he will, Goody, with Vincent's and his friends' support, could be the next Prime Minister.

"You know about the Water Board and the Savannah Project, we talked about that last night."

We did? News to me, but at least now I knew what it was that we had talked about.

Annie continued, "Goody's first act, you may be sure, will be to somehow overcome the Water Board's objections and approve the Savannah Project, complete with the biggest damn gambling casino in the Caribbean.

"When the Savannah Project fell through the autumn before last, after the Water Board's report, Vincent got really down. He said that he would never become really rich, not like his English and American friends on the West Coast. Not, he said, as a planter here in Barbados. No matter how much land he controls, he'll still be a small fish. The sugar crop varies year to year, and the world price goes up and down. Lately sugar prices have been good but, Vincent says, it won't last. There are too many other low-labour-cost countries that can grow sugar cane cheaper than Barbados, and there are all the alternatives to sugar like sugar beets, corn and synthetics. We only get by now because the English pay us above the world market price for our sugar. And that won't last forever. Vincent says that the only way for real money to be made in Barbados in the future will be from land development, and that the biggest money of all will be made by the first group to bring casino gambling to this island.

"I have been with Vincent for fourteen years. These have been, for the most part, good years for both of us. Obviously his wife has known about me and my place in his life for a long time, but either she doesn't care or they have long since come to some kind of understanding. However, lately things have been going from bad to worse between Vincent and me. In the last six months, he has stopped coming to see me. It used to be two or three times a week plus he'd usually spend at least one night. Now I see him once a week, at the most."

Annie continued, "At first I attributed this to his depression about Savannah, but then I began to think that there was something else, maybe something in addition to Savannah. Like, maybe he's got himself a new lady friend.

"I had no direct evidence of this but I began to panic. It is not like I am a wife, someone he would have to take care of if we part. Vincent could throw me and Clara out on the road tomorrow without a penny, and nobody would know or care. I stopped loving him some time ago, but I still do need him. I have nothing in my own name, not the house, not the car, nothing. And I tell you, the prospects for a cast-off kept woman at my age aren't good. You end up being passed from one rich man to another until you are no longer wanted by anyone.

"I knew that I was best off remaining where I was. I was prepared to do anything I could to keep my relationship with Vincent going. I tried to get back on his good side, to show him how valuable I was to him and that he could count on me. That's why I agreed to ask Ollie to stop the investigation. I didn't want to do it but I felt that I had to.

"In the months that followed I was as obedient as a lapdog. I did whatever he asked but, whatever I did, it didn't work. Our relationship got worse than ever, and now, it's over.

"A month ago I accused Vincent to his face of planning to dump Clara and me, but he brushed me aside, calling me a paranoid bitch. Then, the day before yesterday, I was shopping in Bridgetown and I saw him let a young woman out of his car in the alley beside Barclays Bank. She was white, beautiful and about twenty-three. They kissed goodbye.

"It was a shock to see it right there in front of me, but you know what? On one level I really didn't care. Whatever Vin and I once had, it's been over for a long time for me. I was only staying with him because I had no real alternative.

"My concern has always been for Clara. And after all, she's his daughter. I had hoped that he would eventually see how beautiful and special she is and want to acknowledge her. I know now this will never happen. Besides, it's probably too late; Clara hates Vincent and she can barely stand to be around him. And why not? How much rejection is she expected to take? She goes to her room and locks the door whenever he comes to the house."

"What happened today, why did he hit you?"

"He called this morning and said that he wanted to meet someone at my house. This hasn't happened many times before, but what could I say? One good thing was that Clara would be at school.

"They arrived together in Vincent's car around twelve thirty. I gave them something to drink and then I got out of the room. I went into the kitchen and then out onto the veranda that runs along the side of the house. I sat on a sofa reading a magazine.

"Apparently they didn't realise I was there. I wasn't intending to eavesdrop, but when they started to speak, I couldn't help but hear what they were saying. Then Vincent called for me to get them another drink. They were startled when I came into the room from the veranda. You could see they were worried that I had heard what they had been discussing. When I returned with the drinks, Vincent made me go up to my bedroom and close the door. He knew I couldn't hear them from there.

"They left about one thirty. Then, a little while later, Vincent returned. He asked me what I was doing listening to their conversation. I denied that I had heard them. I said that I had no interest in what he and his friend had to say, but Vincent wouldn't let it drop. He must have feared that I would have something to hold over his head.

"We both got angry. I must tell you I have a temper, and when I get cornered I say things that I shouldn't. Unwisely, I picked this time to confront Vincent about the girl I'd seen him with. This only infuriated him further. He shouted and called me all kinds of names.

"Malcolm, who has a room at the back of the garage, heard us arguing and came to see if I was all right. He's very loyal and protective of me and Clara. Then Vincent shouted at Malcolm and I feared that they would come to blows. But Vincent calmed down, he knew that he shouldn't push Malcolm too hard. There is some history there, I don't know the whole story but Malcolm once nearly killed someone. I assured Malcolm that I was fine, and since in the end it is Vincent who pays his salary, Malcolm had no alternative but to back down and return to his room.

"Vincent then told me that Malcolm would have to go and, since I don't drive, he would be taking the Jaguar, as well. I could see what was coming, the next thing would be me and Clara out of the house. The bastard probably wants to install his new lady friend there, in our place. I was frightened. I am frightened. I own nothing but the clothes on my back, if I can even claim those.

"I shouted at him and accused him of being a coward and a liar. I think it was calling him a liar that set him off. You see, Vincent has always had a reputation for being two-faced, for not ever telling the truth. Even his friends say this about him.

"He hit me. He knocked me over the sofa and against the wall. If I had the brains I was born with, I would have stayed down. But I got up and called him more names and then, to hurt him, I told him about you and me last night. I told him that you were the best lover I'd ever had and that he couldn't compare to you in any way.

"Vincent hit me again. He knocked me to the floor and then he sat on me and punched me again and again. I think I passed out. The next thing I knew, Malcolm was putting iced towels on my face and Vincent had gone.

"When Clara came home, I sent Malcolm to find you so that I could warn you that Vincent might be sending someone to harm you."

"I wish he'd come himself," I said angrily.

"He won't, it's not his style. He uses other people to do his dirty work."

Annie begged me not to tell her brother that Lewis had beaten her. She repeated that it was her problem and that she probably deserved what had happened.

"Annie, nobody deserves what happened to you," I said. "But we have to get you out of there, you can't stay there, at your house, under these circumstances. You must go to somewhere safe, for your benefit as well as for Clara's. Why don't you stay with Oliver and Elvira? You'll be safe there."

"There is no place on this island where I would be safe. Vincent can get to me anywhere. I know, I tried to leave him once before but he found me and made me come back. However, don't worry, I'm OK where I am, for now. He hasn't asked me to go yet. I know Vincent, he's probably regretting what he did and is feeling more than a bit sheepish about now. But I also know that some day soon he will ask me to go so that he can install his new lady."

"There must be some place for you to go," I said.

Annie replied, "One other time, long ago, before I got involved with Vincent, I had to leave this island."

I realised that she was talking about the period after Prime Minister Aubrey Tudor had died. A period of time when even her brother doesn't know where she was.

"Where did you go then?"

She didn't answer for several seconds, then she spoke softly, as if this, her "safe haven", was a secret that she has never told.

"I went to Antigua. I stayed in a small hotel on Willoughby Bay called the Ace in the Hole. It's owned by a countryman of yours, Ace Hoagland. He's a former US Navy SEAL and his hotel caters almost exclusively to divers. Ace also rents out boats and equipment and leads dive operations."

"How long were you there?"

"A year and a half, until I heard from friends that it was all right for me to return to Barbados. Over the years, particularly recently, I have thought about going back. Ace still writes me every year and asks me to come back."

"Why haven't you gone before now?"

"Same reason that I've put up with Vincent; I do it for Clara. The Ace in the Hole is a pretty rough place. What can you expect? It's a divers' hangout. There's a lot of drinking, some drugs and fights. I could probably handle it myself, after all I did once before, but it's definitely not the kind of place in which to bring up Clara. Ben, she is something wonderful. She's been to good schools and has lovely friends. She couldn't be suddenly thrust into a place like that, particularly not at this point in her life."

I found myself saying, "Maybe you two should come to New York to be with me."

What have I done?

I continued, "I'd have to find some place a bit larger than what I have now but we could probably work it out."

I couldn't believe that it was me saying this, but it had just popped out. What the hell, maybe it is the right thing for me to do at this time in my life. Anyway, I had said it. I do love Annie, I've always loved her, she is one of my oldest friends and now she needs my help.

"Oh, Ben, do you think we could?"

I put my arms around Annie and drew her to me gently, mindful of her bruises. Then she pulled back and slid to her knees on the ground. She pulled me down beside her. It was soft beneath us, an accumulation of years and years of casuarina needles. Gently, I helped her remove her clothes. She held her arms up and I slipped her dress over her head. I could see that her arms and shoulders were bruised from warding off Lewis's blows.

We said not a word. The only sound we heard was the tinkling of Annie's charm bracelet as she lifted her arms over her head. She shed her bra and then, her briefs.

I took off my shirt and, in one eager motion, the rest. Then we lay together, our arms cradling each other. I couldn't help but remember that night, twenty-five years ago, when the boys and girls from Morton's Cove had come down the path to interrupt us. I think maybe Annie was thinking of that night too.

Gently, sweetly, we began to make love, lying side by side. I was careful not to put my weight on her battered body. It was even painful for her to kiss because her lips were cut and swollen. Despite these problems, our lovemaking was even better than last night's. Our lips touched lightly, but our tongues glided together. In the place of lust and passion, there was love and tenderness. It was even more satisfying, more memorable, than the fireworks of last night.

When we were finished, we lay as before, arms entwined, her face on my chest. I was content to stay like this forever, but she eventually sat up and said that she had to get home. Clara was alone at the house.

Annie stood and began to dress. I lay on the ground, naked, watching her put on her clothes. It occurred to me that I should dress to take her back to her car. But no sooner had I stood up and grabbed my clothes from the ground than Malcolm stepped into the pale light of the small clearing.

Annie's lips again brushed mine, and then she followed Malcolm as he lit her way back up the trail.

I wondered how long Malcolm had been standing there. I came to the conclusion that he had been there, in the shadows, the whole time.

Daily Report 175

Date of Events: Friday, 4 July 1997
Place: Barbados: Glenville; Ollie's home
Summary: Looking for the well; Ollie

After a sleepless night I finally drifted into a dream-filled sleep at dawn, and didn't wake up until mid-morning. I found that I had missed the breakfast buffet but I was able to beg a cup of coffee and a Bajan salt roll and butter from a waiter. The roll was last night's, stale on the outside but inside still soft and tasty. The coffee, barely drinkable at eight, was poisonous at ten forty-five. I drank it anyway.

It was after noon when I finally got to Glenville. I parked next to the ruined house and walked into the garden to try to locate the old well site. Weeds have taken over the grounds. The orderly rows that Clarence, Grandma Dora and I tended so carefully are nowhere in evidence. Here and there a vegetable grows but, for the most part, you'd have to say that weeds are the principal crop at Glenville these days. I could see where a portion of the garden was being tended by Clarence before his death but, in the months since, that area also has been completely overrun by weeds.

I remembered, or I thought I did, where the coral stone slab was at the back of the property. Clarence had pointed it out and said it covered an old well. It was not far from the coconut palm that I had always imagined was the one from where Frank Glenville spied the sailors and Mistress Barbara Mount.

I couldn't find anything resembling a large slab.

The area was overgrown. Small trash trees – Clarence used to call them bread-and-cheese trees – had taken over. They were so thick you could barely force your way through. Their roots could have been hiding a lot more than just a coral stone slab.

I was about to give up when I noticed that a few of the trees differed from their neighbours. Their branches and leaves drooped, as if they might have been disturbed at some time. I looked at the area around them carefully, but still I could not see a slab.

I put one hand out and pushed one of the trees. To my surprise, the tree nearly toppled over, partially exposing its roots. I grabbed the roots and hauled them to the side. There, underneath, I did see a bit of grey coral stone. I poked around and it appeared that it was a slab several feet wide.

I had neither the tools nor the strength to clear this area, expose the stone and move it aside to see what lay below. The slab must have weighed several hundred pounds. It would take major equipment to move it. But this was good news, it meant that whoever recently disturbed this area wouldn't have been able to move the slab either, not without attracting unwelcome attention. I restored the area as best I could and resolved to come back with help and the proper equipment as soon as possible.

I imagined that if I could magically roll the slab back, the mystical Wandering Lady spring would bubble up. And if others also believed this, as the digging suggested, this could well be the reason that my relatives had been killed: to clear the way for the acquisition of Glenville's land and, more importantly, control of the Wandering Lady spring.

I have to believe that Vincent Lewis and his mysterious friend are the ones in back of it. They have systematically eliminated my relatives and stolen the deeds to Glenville House and Grandma Dora's will. Somehow I must prove what they've done. Then they can be brought to justice and made to pay for their crimes.

I next called Oliver to thank him for the other evening. He said that Elvira wanted me to come for supper that evening. I felt a little sheepish about accepting. The last time, Oliver and I got stumbling, falling-down drunk. I don't think that this was usual behaviour for Oliver and I know it was not for me. Elvira is a good, church-going woman; she was probably not too pleased with my performance. But Oliver insisted that I'd be welcome.

I need not have worried. Elvira was friendly and charming as ever when I arrived. She chided us both a bit about the other evening, but she didn't drive it into the ground as some women would. However, this evening our drinking was confined to Pepsi.

Their two boys, Michael, aged fourteen, and Hudson, twelve, were at the table and they were attractive, intelligent boys, a real credit to their parents. They were just the kind of young men that I hoped my nephew-to-be, Benjamin Cumberbatch Downes, would become. It was also clear that they revered their father and, equally evident, their mother ruled them and the home with a gentle but firm hand.

After dinner, Oliver and I took the dog for a walk around the neighbourhood. I told Oliver about the meeting between Vincent Lewis and the stranger at Annie's house, and that the man had all but admitted that he had eliminated my father and my uncle. I honoured Annie's request and did not tell him about Lewis beating her. I was half afraid that Oliver would go after Lewis, I was reserving that pleasure for myself.

Oliver had some news or, more accurately, hot rumours. He said that the word in political circles was that the Savannah Project was back on. No one seemed to know how they intended to get around the water problem, but the betting now was that it would happen.

"This will set off a whole chain of events, if it is true," Oliver told me. "You already know about the political situation. Lewis and his partners know that the Prime Minister opposes the casino. So if Savannah, with the casino, is to happen, they will force his resignation and the Savannah money crowd will back

Goody Griffith for Prime Minister. And we know where he stands on the issue."

"Can't the Prime Minister stand up to them?" I asked.

"I'm not sure that he has the backing," Ollie said dejectedly. "The Prime Minister is a good man, but he's made enemies by refusing to go along with the usual way of doing business. People will support Goody because he can be counted on to cooperate – for a price."

When we got back to the house, I excused myself. I didn't tell Ollie about the Wandering Lady spring. I need to know a bit more about it myself before I start shooting off my mouth. All I know now for sure is that there is a fairy story involving Carib Indians and that, possibly, a spring once existed where Glenville House was built, but that spring had disappeared from there long before the Mounts gave the Glenvilles the land.

And after all, it may just be a fairy story for children.

Daily Report 176

Date of Events: Saturday, 5 July 1997
Place: Barbados: the surfers' beach, Bathsheba
Summary: Surfing

I had a late breakfast and went down to watch the surfers. Approximately twenty men, both local surfers and offshore visitors, were competing. In addition, there were eight female surfers, all but one of them from abroad. Summer is not the main surfing season in Barbados, that's in October and November, when the big storms roam the Atlantic. But there is a second season and it draws the young up-and-coming surfers who want to gain experience before taking on the top surfers in the world. Barbados, in the summer, is a good place for them to develop their skills.

The Californians, who had given me the standing ovation a couple of days ago, did themselves proud. The woman won, hands down. None of the other competitors could match her skill and athletic ability. The male Californians were second, third and eighth in their competition.

The men's title was won by a young Frenchman, no more than twenty. He looked to be half-Polynesian. He had long curly hair, the South Pacific version of Rastafarian dreadlocks, bleached white at the tips from constant exposure to tropical sun.

The Californians were daring and spectacular, but so was the Frenchman, even more so. He skimmed at the edge of disaster throughout his rides but miraculously never fell. The Californians were probably technically superior, that's what the other surfers said; however, compared to the young French-Polynesian, they seemed almost mechanical. He improvised his moves every second, pushing himself and his board to the absolute limit. Just when you thought he was sure to wipe out, he would shift his board and slide gracefully out of danger.

It was a pleasant break for me. I had been constantly on the go since I arrived with little chance for relaxation and contemplation. Since my injury, I've learned to value stopping and carefully assessing what I know and what I should do next. This has become a necessity for me now, but it is contrary to my basic nature. I have always been one to thrust ahead, no matter what the problem, confident that I could deal with the situation as I found it.

However, I have been moving more cautiously here in Barbados because of my injury, and also because I'm in foreign territory without the benefit of my badge. But the time for decisive action may be fast approaching and, if it does come, I must be prepared to throw caution to the winds, to be more like this young Frenchman. I just hope that in the event I'll be ready and able to do what needs to be done.

Six-Week Report 177

Date of Events: 6 July to 17 August 1997
Place: Barbados: Glenville; Wavecrest Hotel; Annie's house, St Michael
Summary: Waiting period; Ollie; Husbands; Annie and Clara

These last six weeks have flown by as I have waited for the boxes of debris from the ruins of Glenville House to arrive at the NYPD arson forensics lab, and for the corpses of my grandmother and aunt to be examined by the Squad's forensic pathologist in New York. Tom Moran and Norman Price have promised me a quick turnaround and a nice official-looking report to impress the Barbados police and, if it goes that far, the Barbados judiciary.

I located some earth-moving equipment for hire and arranged for it to be brought to Glenville to lift the coral stone cap from the top of the old well, but before I could have that done my plans were frustrated. On the eighteenth of July at the Wavecrest, I was served with a legal document saying, "Benjamin Cumberbatch, a United States citizen and a visitor to Barbados, is hereby informed that he cannot trespass or cause others to trespass upon the property known as Glenville House, Glenville, Saint Charles Parish, until the estate of the deceased, Eudora Glenville, has passed through probate by this Court."

In other words, not until the court had decided who was the rightful heir to Glenville could I enter Glenville to look into the old well.

I didn't want to screw things up and get on the wrong side of the authorities, so I promised Oliver that I would abide by the court's order. However, I did tell Oliver about the old Indian myth of the "Wandering Lady", and of my suspicions that it might be at Glenville. And that my father and uncle may have been killed because of their succession to the ownership of Glenville. Oliver said he would try to find out who had caused the order to be issued by the court.

Oliver learned the name of the attorney, the most prominent lawyer in Barbados, a former minister in several previous governments, but his efforts to find the identity of his client were unsuccessful.

"So where do I stand?" I asked.

"If no will is found, the laws of intestacy will apply and the court will award the estate to the next of kin, presumably your oldest sister," Oliver told me.

"How long will this take?" I asked, fearing the worst.

"Years. Sometimes these things drag on forever, but since you and your sisters are the only known heirs, it should, in theory, move quicker than most," Oliver said.

"Well, there are still some Glenvilles around St Charles, but my grandmother said that most had either died, moved away from Barbados or were ancient. In any case, they should have no valid claim. There is ample precedent that only direct male descendants of Frank Glenville can inherit the land. A woman, like my Grandmother Dora, could only inherit if there was no direct male heir. A person would have to be a direct descendant of Eudora Glenville, a child or, like myself, a grandchild to have a claim. With Uncle Clarence, Aunt Emily and my father dead, it should pass to the next level, where I am the only male heir. Come to think of it, there was an uncle, Thomas I think his name was, but nobody has seen or heard from him in over forty years."

"The smart thing for you to do is to hire a lawyer to represent you," Oliver suggested. "If it was me, I'd get one with some political connections, this always helps."

"Do you know any good ones?" I asked.

Oliver laughed. "That is a harder question than you might imagine. You believe Vincent Lewis and his cronies are trying to get Glenville. Between them, they probably retain every competent attorney on the island. I could suggest several, but my concern would be that they would also be representing the other side."

"Lawyers can't do that, can they?" I asked.

"It is not unheard of in real estate deals, but in a case like this it shouldn't happen. But I wouldn't put it past some of the greedier members of the bar." Then Oliver said, "Wait! I've got an idea. I know a good lawyer who retired a few years ago. He's probably seventy or seventy-five, but he was once one of the best. And as far as I know, he's not involved with Lewis and his bunch. Believe me, if he takes your case, I guarantee that you will be well represented."

His name is George Husbands. He is a heavy-set man with coal-black skin, white hair and a white beard. His eyes reflect intelligence and good humour. It took a little persuading on my part, with Oliver's help, but Mr Husbands finally agreed to represent me in any legal proceedings which might arise concerning my inheritance of Glenville.

Annie did not follow my advice to move in with Oliver and Elvira. She said that it wouldn't protect her from Lewis and it might put Elvira and the boys in danger. Anyway, I don't think that Annie fancied sharing a room with Clara and a bathroom with her two nephews. Therefore, Annie and I have had more time together. I have kept my room at the Wavecrest, but most nights I have spent with Annie and Clara at their home on Thrustons Hill.

Lewis stopped giving Annie money to pay her bills, so I have stepped in to help her out financially. And his lawyer has sent

Annie a letter saying that she will have to be out of the house by September 30. The letter warns that if she has "not vacated the premises by that date, you will be forcibly removed".

Annie cried when she read the letter, then she got angry and tore it into shreds.

"After everything I did for him," she said. I stayed clear of her for a few hours, and eventually her anger and humiliation passed and she was her usual sweet, fascinating self.

Annie informed me that she had reached a decision that when she does have to move, she and Clara will stay with Ollie and Elvira until we are able to "move to New York". At first, I was a bit frightened by the whole prospect. It would be a big step for me, from carefree bachelor to family man in one fell swoop. But, deep down inside, I felt good about it.

And at least when I am with her at her house I can protect her from Lewis. And, most important, Annie and I have really got to know one another. The underlying agenda for this summer, unspoken but agreed upon by us both, or as the Bajans say "all two", has been for Annie and I to see if we are truly compatible; to see if we could be happy together. So far, it has looked very good.

I've known some women in my life, but I'm not like Nate. I have always had just one woman at a time. Admittedly, most of them have been New York women: models, actresses, publicists, copywriters, TV executives, teachers, even a female cop or two. And although the majority of them were white, not all were. I had never settled down with one because I wasn't looking for a permanent relationship and, in truth, for the most part neither were they. But now that I am out of the police, maybe it's time for me to settle down.

I never moved in with any one woman; my job as a detective placed special demands on me and I felt that the job took precedence over my private life. Usually the relationships lasted several months and one lasted two years, but with none of them have I ever achieved the sense of peace and contentment that I've found with Annie.

I've just begun to realise the startling – to me – truth that I am in love with Annie. I thought I had been in love on a couple of occasions but, looking back, compared with Annie, these were something less. She is in my thoughts constantly. When we are not together, I am thinking of her and wondering what she's doing. I even find myself thinking about the "M" word. Me, Ben Cumberbatch, co-holder – with Tom Moran – of the title of New York's Number One Confirmed Bachelor, thinking about marriage.

Sure, there are a few complications. Annie is legally married to Goody, but that can't be hard to dissolve, the marriage has always been a sham and Goody would probably be just as happy to be out of it as Annie. Then there is me, single and available, but to some degree damaged goods, with just an NYPD pension and a small savings account between me and the street. But with every day that passes I am feeling better. The combination of Barbados and Annie is doing wonders and I can feel myself getting better, stronger, sharper. My short-term memory still isn't perfect but I can tell it is better than it was just two months ago, when I said goodbye to the docs at Wickham.

Annie and I haven't discussed marriage yet, but it's obvious that she is thinking of it too. The other day we talked about my attitude toward marriage in general. Annie said she thought that my having grown up with my parents' unhappy marriage, plus having witnessed the failure of so many marriages of other cops, had given me an unfair bias against the institution.

"Well, what about you?" I said with a laugh. "You hardly qualify as an authority on happy marriage."

Annie shook her head and said, in a mock English accent, "How dare you! The Right Honourable Goodman Griffith and I have been happily married for eleven years."

"The marriage of the century, no doubt about that," I said. We both laughed.

Our conversations, when they focus on me, are about my injury, my family, my life as a cop and, especially, my past relationships with other women. Annie's mind is constantly probing, seeking more and more information and developing a greater depth of understanding of me, my likes and dislikes, my hopes, my wishes and my fears. And Annie asks me questions that they never thought of at the Wickham Institute.

Of course, Annie is totally untrained as a therapist or anything like it, but she has a natural curiosity and a genuine warmth which makes her a person with whom you can share your inner thoughts.

She is fascinated by my recurring "false memory" of being shot by my father in an alley. We've talked about this aberration at length. Annie's theory is that my "father" represents all authority figures. I remain unconvinced but, anyway, this memory – if that's what it is – has been coming back to me with increasing clarity and frequency.

Sometimes Annie and I giggle and laugh at silly things. I don't even remember why they're so funny. It might just be the way she says them or the inflection in her voice. She's also a great mimic. When Annie tells a story, she automatically adapts her voice and her body posture to the various characters in her story, old or young, male or female, black or white, Bajan or foreigner. The stage and screen lost a great actress when Annie decided to become a kept woman.

Annie has made me tell her about each of my significant relationships. I have never been the kind that dwells on ancient history. Once they're over, they're over. But under her probing I managed to identify six women, six relationships, that were more important to me than the others. I surprised myself with some of the ones I chose. Annie wanted to know everything: what I liked about each woman, what we did together and – if I even knew – why we had eventually parted. I could feel her absorbing this information and I got the impression that she was preparing herself to be the perfect woman for me. I have never had anyone so totally dedicated to a relationship. It is both exciting and a bit overwhelming.

Of course, during intimate moments I tell Annie that I love her and sometimes, when the thought just becomes so obvious, I will just say it out loud, seemingly for no reason at all. I have said "I love you" to other women – not a lot of them, but probably the six that I identified to Annie and a few others – but, in retrospect, it was not the truth. I didn't know what love was until now.

I can see a big difference in Annie, too. Being "kept" by a man like Vincent Lewis must have been a difficult and tension-filled existence, particularly in these last several months. Annie has relaxed, the tension lines have receded from around her eyes and she may have even put on a pound or two – believe me, not a problem. She has told me several times how happy and content she is and how she believes that nothing could ever come between us.

An added benefit to this arrangement is that I have got to know Clara, who really is exceptional, Annie was right. She has done an outstanding job with her daughter, and not under the easiest circumstances. Not only is Clara as beautiful and well-adjusted as any eleven-year-old child could be, she is extraordinarily intelligent and sensitive to her surroundings. And, fascinating to see, she has either inherited or adopted many of Annie's mannerisms. Maybe she is so much like her mother because of the absence of a meaningful father figure in her life.

Clara, like many racially mixed children, has an exceptional ability to adapt herself to various people and situations. She is at ease with everyone: all races and all social and economic levels, with her school friends and their families, with her teachers and the adults that her mother knows socially and, happily, also with me. But, as I have come to know Clara better, I sense that this is not always as easy for her as she makes it appear.

As a light-skinned person myself, I know the subtle and often unintentional cruelties that Clara has faced and will face as she grows older. I've reacted to these, for the most part, by ignoring them. My sister Margaret reacted by passing herself off as white. And only my sister Elyce – certainly the bravest and most honest of the three Cumberbatch siblings – has dealt with them head on.

At first I thought that Clara was oblivious to the way others, both black and white, looked at and reacted to her. However, I now see that she's in fact very perceptive. She understands people instinctively and has, for someone of her age, an uncanny ability to respond to them in the most effective or appropriate manner. It is impressive to see an eleven-year-old girl-woman make people of all ages, sexes, races and backgrounds, sound smart and interesting, and leave them happy for having talked with her. What a fool her father is.

Lewis, just to be sure that Annie would be out of the house, took the Jaguar and stopped paying Malcolm and the part-time cook as of the end of July. Annie's household allowance was cut off on 15 July. The telephone may be used only locally, within Barbados. Overseas calls have to be collect.

With the cook gone, Annie and I have prepared the meals at home or gone out to eat. Malcolm, ever faithful, has dropped by every three or four days to see that Annie and Clara are all right, but Malcolm and I never exchange a word. A couple of times I acknowledged his presence by saying hello, but he looked right through me. I appreciate his loyalty to Annie and Clara but, to tell the truth, he gives me the creeps.

I have seen some nasty divorces over the years, but in none has the husband ever had the upper hand so completely as

Vincent Lewis has with Annie. Of course, this isn't a divorce. The only trump card Annie has, in theory, is Clara, and by never having acknowledged her as his daughter, Lewis has protected himself from that threat. He is one tough, ruthless bastard. I have vowed to myself that I will get him, if I can. I will make him pay for what he has done to Annie and, quite possibly, to my family.

Annie has been frustrated by her inability to get back at Lewis for the way he has treated her and Clara. She knows that his wife knows all about them, so hurting that unhappy lady again wouldn't do any harm to her husband.

I suggested, "Why don't you speak to a reporter at one of the papers, expose Lewis publicly for what he is."

Annie shook her head.

"In the first place, the media are controlled by the powerful. The papers are happy to print bad news about little people or stupid tourists who get themselves in trouble with drugs or sex, but never a word is written about the plantation owner's accident or the executive's wife's shoplifting or the dangerously incompetent doctor's latest fuck-up."

I laughed, without humour.

"I hate to tell you, it's not always that different up north."

"But here, really powerful people, people like Vincent, are not just above the law, they're beyond the reach of anyone but their equals," she said. "The only way that they can be brought down is by each other. Only when they lose the respect and support of the other rich and powerful people can they be made to pay for what they've done."

Daily Report 178

Date of Events: 18 August 1997
Place: Barbados: Annie's house; Oliver's office
Summary: The Invitation

On Monday morning the telephone rang at Annie's.

"It's for you," she said.

Only Ollie and George Husbands called me at Annie's.

Annie held the telephone and pointed to it with a wide-eyed look of terror. She mouthed the words "Tall man" as she gingerly handed the receiver to me.

"Hello," I said cautiously.

"To whom am I speaking?" a cultured voice inquired.

"This is Ben Cumberbatch."

"Are you Nathaniel Cumberbatch's son?"

I said that I was.

The caller had an English accent. Annie was probably right: this might well have been the man whom she had seen with Vincent Lewis. The man who, Annie said, claimed to have killed my father and uncle.

"I am Winston, Mr Mount's butler, and I am calling you on his behalf. Mr Mount wishes you to join him for supper tomorrow evening at Savannah Great House. Please try to arrive by eight o'clock. Dinner will be informal."

My first thought was that the last living male member of the Glenville/Cumberbatch family had just been invited to be killed, so that the Savannah Project could acquire Glenville and the Wandering Lady spring.

"Why should I have dinner with Mr Mount? Of what possible benefit would such a meeting be to me?" I replied, stalling for time.

"That is a very good question, but it is not one that can be answered at this time. However I assure you that if you do come to Savannah tomorrow evening, you will find all the answers that you seek. Moreover you will personally reap a great benefit from this effort. In addition, of course, Mr Mount will be most appreciative if you do him the honour of dining with him."

What the hell! I accepted the invitation. I accepted despite the fact that Annie has warned me that Vincent Lewis and this man consider me to be a problem, a problem that needs to be eliminated. Annie has no real knowledge of their plans but, given what has happened up until now, an intention to kill me has to be a distinct possibility. Despite this, I would hate to pass up an opportunity to get to the bottom of what has been going on. I believe the man meant it when he said that I will find out what I don't know. They may want me dead and out of the way, but it sounds like I might learn some interesting things before they get an opportunity to try.

Moreover, as I thought about it, it was hard to believe that they would invite me to Savannah for dinner, giving me thirty-five hours' prior notice, during which time I could tell half of Barbados where I'm going, and then do me harm. No, I decided that I will not be in danger at Savannah. It's not a sure thing that I'll be safe there, but to me it's definitely worth the risk.

I thought about the young surfer I had watched compete so successfully at Bathsheba. He had let it all hang out, and because of his skill and because he was willing to risk everything, he had won. At more than one point, if he'd hesitated, he would have been crushed under tons of curling water. He might have been hurt or even killed but he never flinched and, as a consequence, he was the winner.

Definitely, I resolved, I had to go for it.

When I told Annie, she begged me not to go. She reminded me again of what she had overheard.

"They plan to kill you, Ben. I know it!" she said, with tears streaming down her face.

I tried to explain to her why I think it's unlikely that they will harm me at Savannah, and that this might be my best chance, perhaps my only chance, to get to the bottom of everything.

Annie beseeched me not to go. She would not listen to reason.

Finally I promised that I would tell Ollie what I plan to do. But when I declared that no matter what, I was going to go to Savannah, Annie ran to her bedroom in tears, apparently convinced that I was serving myself up to be slaughtered.

I followed her and knocked on the bedroom door.

Annie said in a tear-stained voice, "Ben, if you really loved me, you would not go there."

I tried again to explain to her why I have to go and why I'm sure that there's no danger, but her crying only increased. I knocked again but she would not answer, only sobbing in reply.

I called Ollie. He was not in to take my call, but the sergeant who answered the phone said that the chief inspector had left word that if I should telephone, I was to be told to call him again at three o'clock.

Rather than ringing Oliver, I decided to go to his office. I arrived a few minutes before three and was shown up to his office directly. The door was partially open and through it I could see Ollie at his desk, signing letters and documents as they were being fed to him one by one by a burly sergeant.

I was ushered in and sat quietly as Ollie finished his chores. Paperwork is one of the worst parts of being a policeman. There are lots of positive aspects to the job, but there are three negative ones in my estimation: first, there is the possibility of getting injured or killed; next you have the less than generous pay; and third, the paperwork. It was discouraging to see that even at Ollie's level, even in a small place like Barbados, the system still requires you to read and sign tons and tons of paper.

When Oliver completed his task, I told him of my conversation with Winston and of Edgar Mount's invitation to Savannah Great House for dinner tomorrow night. I said that Annie suspected that Winston was the man who had met with Lewis at Annie's house and had said that he had "taken care of" my father and uncle. I added that I tended to agree with her.

Ollie listened intently.

"It sounds as if you're right about who this is but, of course, you can't go," he said. I started to say something but he held up his hand and continued, "Three people are dead on this island, all relatives of yours, probably at the hand of these people. And that does not even count your father in New York. You would be foolhardy in the extreme if you offered yourself up as the next to die."

It sounded to me like Annie had already spoken to him.

I told him that I didn't see it that way.

"They can't be so stupid as to think that I would go there without having told someone like you where I'm going. Even if they're so arrogant as to believe that they're above the law, why risk everything to kill me? What do they gain?"

I told Ollie that we could learn a lot from the meeting, information that we probably were not going to obtain any other way. At last we might have the whole picture and be able to see justice done, if that was possible on this island.

Oliver saw my point but he was still opposed to me going in there alone. I appreciated his concern; I share some of it and, frankly, I don't want to be shot again. So we reached a compromise: I will go into the Savannah Great House alone, as planned, but he and his men will be right outside, hopefully close enough to help me if I get in trouble.

I showed Ollie the ballpoint pen microphone and the recording device that I carry, and explained how they work. I told Ollie that he will have the receiver and I will have the pen in my pocket so he will hear what is going on inside the house. That way he'll be able to monitor my safety, come to my assistance if necessary, and at the end of the evening we will have a record of everything that has been said or has happened inside the house, for possible use as evidence.

Daily Report 179

Date of Events: 19 August 1997
Place: Barbados: District C Police Station; Savannah Great House
Summary: Winston

The next day, just after dark, Oliver and his team met me at District C police station. Oliver had with him three of his best men, experienced sergeants he trusted, from a special police unit. It was agreed that these detectives, under Ollie's direct command, would back me up while I was inside Savannah Great House.

At the first sign of real trouble, the detectives and Ollie would storm the house. We also agreed that if at any time I felt threatened and needed their assistance, I would say the word "chandelier". When they heard that, they were to come into the house right away.

We tested the microphone and it was working perfectly. Ollie wanted me to wear a bullet-proof vest as well, but I refused. The clothes I was wearing were too lightweight. I was sure that Mount would spot the vest and be put off by it.

Ollie also told me that the word going about was that Edgar Mount is very sick. If Mount was really ill, he insisted, we would have to be careful that our actions could not be used against us in accusations that we had adversely impacted his health. If Mount were to die or take a dramatic turn for the worse while I was inside Savannah, it could make things difficult for Oliver and for me. You could bet that a slimeball like Vincent Lewis would use Edgar Mount's ill health or death to his maximum advantage, given an opportunity.

At five minutes to eight, I turned down the long lane from the main road to Savannah Great House. A single light shone above the front entrance. Only one additional light was visible inside the house. It was a far cry from the blaze of lights that I remembered from when I had first looked down this lane from the donkey cart with Grandma Dora and Uncle Clarence in 1969.

Ollie and his men were already in place on my right, crouched behind the stone wall of the plantation yard, ready to come into the house if and when they were needed. They were no more than twenty yards from the front door. Close, but if it turned out that I was in danger inside the house, they might not be close enough.

I hoped that I had assessed this situation correctly. If I had not, I might not be around to hear people say "I told you so."

I rang the bell and waited. Almost a minute passed. I rang again and this time the door opened at once. A tall, light-skinned man ushered me into the dimly-lit hallway. His face was in shadow, not clearly visible to me in the half-light. I could see that he was thin and, from his stiff movements, he appeared to be older than I had expected. He was dressed in a black suit and a white shirt and a navy blue or black necktie. He looked like he was dressed for a funeral. Not mine, I hoped.

"Mr Winston?" I asked.

He nodded.

"Just call me Winston, please, sir. Welcome to Savannah Great House, Mr Cumberbatch. Mr Mount awaits us upstairs."

He led the way down the hall to the broad, curved stairs. I was struck by how shabby everything was. The carpet was stained and torn. The wallpaper, made of silk, was water-stained and, in a few places, hung loosely from the wall. Wires jutted out from the ceiling where once a chandelier had hung. *Great*, I thought. *If I have to summon Ollie and his boys I can say, "Whatever happened to your chandelier?"*

I had never actually seen a butler, except in movies and on TV, but the tall man in black seemed to have all the right moves and the attitude. He acted like he was in charge but at the same time he managed to come across as slightly deferential. I still had not got a good look at his face.

I reminded myself that, rich man's butler or not, this man was quite probably a killer and I should take care that I was not his next victim.

At the top of the stairs he stopped and gestured, with a sweep of his hand, for me to precede him along the corridor.

He said, "Mr Edgar awaits you. He is inside the third door on the left."

I was quite a bit more apprehensive with him walking behind me. If I had gauged this situation incorrectly, and the intent was to shoot me, this would have been a good time for him to do it. But, I reminded myself, I didn't think that was the agenda.

The upstairs corridor was totally dark, but my companion pressed a switch and a bare overhead bulb partially illuminated the way. This corridor was, if anything, in worse condition than the hall downstairs. One wall had lost not only its wallpaper but also much of the plaster beneath. You could see wooden laths to which small pieces of plaster still clung.

When I reached the third door I hesitated, wondering whether I should knock before entering.

Winston said, "Walk right in, Mr Mount will not mind."

The room was dark. The hairs on the back of my neck stood up. I thought, *this could be it.* Framed in the darkened doorway, backlit by the overhanging hall light, I was a perfect target for anyone in the room, sick old man or not.

I stepped into the dark room and Winston entered behind me. Suddenly, three lights were turned on. The largest, in the ceiling, cast a yellowish light that failed to reach the murky corners of the room. The other two were lamps, one on a massive mahogany bureau to my left and the other on the bedside table.

In the bed, lying quietly on his back, hands folded, I saw a thin, waxy-looking elderly man.

This was Edgar Mount, I presumed. It occurred to me that he appeared to be dead.

Winston spoke behind me.

"As you can see, Mr Mount has recently passed away."

I turned to Winston and he was now holding a revolver in his left hand, pointed right at me. I calculated my best move, my only move, would be to dive behind the bed if it looked like he was going to use that weapon on me. I was about to summon Ollie and his crew, but somehow, looking at Winston's sad face and drooping posture, I still didn't feel that I was in danger. I decided to let it play out a bit longer, hoping that all would be clarified, as had been promised.

Winston stepped forward under the overhead light and his features were, for the first time, visible. He was painfully thin and his eyes were watery. His hands shook and the gun drooped. But I was struck by the fact that he looked a great deal like my father. This might just have been a coincidence but I didn't think so. I concluded that Winston had to be my long-lost uncle, Thomas Cumberbatch. And, if that was correct, that would begin to explain a lot of what had happened in the last fourteen months.

"Don't be alarmed," the man who called himself Winston said in a gravelly voice. "I have no desire to harm you, unless I must. But I hold this, this gun, to make sure that you remain to hear me out. It is important to me, to us both, that you hear what I have to say."

He gestured with the gun for me to move closer to the bed. I did so and could see that Mount's skin was stretched thinly over his bones. Crusty sores were in evidence on his chest and on the backs of his hands.

"Edgar Mount died yesterday morning," said "Winston" sadly. "He was dead when I invited you here. He had finally succumbed to his dreadful disease. The final cause of death was pneumonia but the reason for it was AIDS. I have been with Edgar Mount for many years. Many happy years, I might add, but the last eighteen months, watching him die so painfully from this plague, have been most difficult. Most difficult."

He shook his head sorrowfully.

"Do you know who I am?" he asked.

"If I am not mistaken, your name is Thomas Cumberbatch, not Winston, and you are my uncle." I said this cautiously, still mindful that he was holding a gun on me.

"You are both right and wrong. My name is Thomas Winston but I was once Thomas Cumberbatch. And you are correct – I am your uncle Thomas."

I was silent as I looked the man over. He was quite tall, six foot four or even a bit more. Taller than Nate but thinner. I did see a strong facial resemblance to Pa. But Thomas looked older than Pa had, although he was actually several years younger. And in his suit and tie his appearance was different, more sophisticated than my father's had ever been.

I reminded myself that this man was almost certainly a stone-cold killer. Pa, for all his bluster, would never have harmed anyone except in self-defence. Despite this, I was more convinced than ever that Thomas meant me no harm, but it was also apparent that he was in a highly emotional state. His hand shook and his voice quavered. I cautioned myself not to move too quickly or seem to threaten him in any way, to do nothing that might cause him to use the weapon.

I had come here tonight to learn about the deaths in my family and it now looked as if I would get my answers. I was thinking how best to initiate the conversation, but it was not necessary; Thomas began to tell me all that I would ever have to know.

"Let me start at the beginning. I don't know how much you know about our family. I am Dora Glenville's youngest child. My father, Lester Cumberbatch, died just after my first birthday. In addition to your father, four years older, there were twin girls who died young, before I was born. We were the product of a black father and a white mother. Of course, our mother already had had her first two children, both of them white, Clarence and Emily. They were from an incestuous relationship between my mother and her father. Did you know that?"

I nodded but didn't speak, I did not want to interrupt his narrative.

"I do not say this in criticism of Dora Glenville; she was innocent of any wrongdoing. It was all her ignorant father's fault, stemming from poverty and the tragic history of the poor whites of these shores. But that was long ago.

"Your father and I were far enough apart in age that we did not fight much growing up, but neither were we very close. I always admired Nate. He was my big older brother. I wanted to be closer, to be like him, but Nate always went his own way and, eventually, I had to go mine.

"Our mother worked terribly hard in the garden just to keep us fed and clothed. My favourite family member was my half-sister, Emily. She was always sweet to me and I used to spend a lot of time with her in the kitchen. Her brother Clarence never had much to say for himself and, by the time I was born, he had moved out of the house into his shed in the farm garden. We seldom ever spoke.

"As you might know, we were treated as outcasts by our relatives in the village where we lived. Our Glenville kin were envious of us for having the house and gardens and they and the other redlegs looked down on our mother for having mixed-blood children. They acted as if she had betrayed them. We never did meet our father's side of the family.

"I was rather frail as a little boy and I grew up lonely and unhappy. Nate was always bigger, stronger and more popular with other children at school. I was sickly and had no companions, no friends, not even my own brother."

He paused and seemed to be remembering less than pleasant times. He remained silent, lost in his memories.

Trying to get him going again I said, "It must have been difficult. But surely there were some good times?"

"Yes, there were some, a few, but not many. But then something occurred, the most important event in my life. I met Edgar. I was nine and he was two years older than me and, of course, out of a world very different from mine. Edgar's mother had brought him to Barbados for his health. He could not take the cold and damp of the English countryside where the Mounts resided."

Thomas looked down at the frail body in the bed beside us and touched him with his free hand.

"Edgar was an only child, and he was understandably lonely living at Savannah. So when we met, we naturally gravitated together, and eventually became each other's best friend.

"He was always the big brother, I brought up the rear. When we played Robinson Crusoe, he was the shipwrecked sailor, I was his Man Friday. And strangely enough, even when we played Frank Glenville and the sailors, he was Frank, my ancestor, and I had to be the sailors. I never minded, I was just happy to have him as my companion.

"Edgar went back to England when he was thirteen. His parents sent him away to one of the famous public schools. He hated it, but at that time there was no alternative. In England, in his class and station in life, you went away to school. He was just lucky that, because of his health, he hadn't been sent away at age seven as most of his classmates had.

"When next we met, Edgar was fifteen and I was thirteen. He was just beginning to recognise his own sexual orientation.

English public schools were good for that. If you had any inclination toward homosexuality, they would see that it was developed to its fullest potential.

"I don't know how I would have ended up on that score if I hadn't met Edgar. Certainly Nate had enough heterosexual male drive for the whole family. Anyway, I fell under the sway of Edgar early on. But he introduced me to much more than just sex. He taught me how to speak the English language properly and he taught me the manners that would make me acceptable in a home like his. And when he was here, Edgar had a tutor and I was allowed to sit in his classes and learn what I could.

"The Mounts viewed me as a necessary evil. Edgar's parents, particularly his father, were racist, as were most of the plantocracy. They would not have allowed me in the house if there had been any alternative companion for their son. But there wasn't, so they accepted me as Edgar's friend, and in truth were glad that with me around Edgar was out of their way. Edgar and I were equally happy to be left alone.

"Nate never liked Edgar. My brother thought that Edgar and all the Mounts looked down on us. Then one day Nate followed Edgar and me and caught us in a sex act. He beat both of us brutally. Edgar was furious but he never told anyone what my brother had done. It was a good thing too because, if he had, it would have gone hard on Nate in those days.

"Nate was no fool, he realised his danger, so he told no one of what he had seen; but thereafter he tried to keep me away from Edgar. However, Edgar and I were becoming ever more devoted to one another and we easily escaped Nate's notice, whenever we chose. My mother also tried to discourage my friendship with Edgar, but for different reasons. She felt that it was bad for me to spend all my time with Edgar. She thought that because our stations in life were so different, that my exposure to his wealthy world would ruin me for my humble future.

"My mother was well-intentioned but mistaken. I believe that my knowing Edgar has given me a wonderful life. But that was to be in the future. After two years, Edgar again had to return to England, this time to prepare to take his A levels in order to go to Oxford.

"Meanwhile, when your father turned eighteen he joined the British Royal Navy. He wanted to be like our father, so he became a steamfitter. He was eventually stationed at a naval facility on the Thames near Greenwich, on the outskirts of London.

"When I was barely seventeen, I took passage to England on a tramp steamer. I had grown tall and looked older than I was. I landed at Plymouth and found my way to London. With what I'd learned from Edgar and from observing the Mount household, I was able to gain acceptance into a training course to become a manservant. After several months I was placed with a middle-class family in South Kensington.

"The first chance I had, I contacted Nate in Greenwich. Your father invited me to come down to see him on a Saturday. We were to meet at noon at a pub just outside the gates of the shipyard where he worked."

"Pa told me that he'd never seen you again after he left Barbados to join the Navy," I interjected.

"Interesting, but not exactly true. He did see me once but, admittedly, only briefly," Thomas said, with a discernible sadness in his voice.

He returned to his narrative.

"I waited for Nate at the pub. Something had happened to delay him at work, so I sat at the bar and had a pint or two. I struck up a conversation with a young seaman off one of the boats that Nate's yard was repairing. In England, pubs closed at two and reopened for business later in the afternoon. We had to leave the premises.

"The young sailor suggested that I go with him to a small park nearby, where we could be alone. I had no idea when Nate would come, or indeed if he was coming at all. So I agreed to go to the park. What neither of us knew was that this park was well known as a trysting place for sailors and others, and that the naval police actively watched the area. We were apprehended by them in what they called 'a compromising position'.

"They took us back to the naval base. They asked our names. They found the other fellow's name on the duty roster for his ship and they found Cumberbatch on the permanent roster for the Yard. Of course, what had happened was that they confused me with your father, Cumberbatch being such an unusual name to them. I had no idea that this was what was happening.

"We were placed in the brig overnight and then we were released. I hurried back into London as I was overdue at my place of employment. A few days later, Nate and the other fellow were picked up and brought before a court martial.

"Nate was dumbfounded, he had no idea what was going on. The sailor said that he had never seen Nate, that it was a case of mistaken identity. But the authorities remained suspicious, Nate was confined to quarters and was treated as a pariah by his co-workers.

"By now, Nate had figured it out, that it had been me who had been caught in the park. He tried to tell this to the officers, but no one would believe him and he did not know how to reach me.

"Next time I had a day off, I again called Nate. My hope was that he knew nothing of what had happened on my previous visit, but of course he knew it all. He told me that he was in big trouble and it was all my fault. He asked me to come there to explain to his superiors that it had been I, not Nate, in the park that day.

"I went to Greenwich. Nate was present when I testified and we spoke briefly at the conclusion of the hearing. The military finally believed my story and Nate was absolved. Since I was not one of theirs, the military police had no further need for me. They took my name and said they would turn the matter over to the local authorities. I gave them a false address in Stockwell and that was the last I heard of that.

"Your father thanked me for coming but then he said that he never wanted to see me or hear from me again. I was horribly hurt. Nate was my brother, my only contact with home. But when I pressed him, asking for his forgiveness, he became very angry and said many ugly and unnecessarily crude things about me and others like me."

Pa was a hard egg. I could see him doing something like that. He never was very sensitive or forgiving of Ma for her drinking. What his brother said was entirely consistent with Pa's character.

"Nate and I never did see each other again until we met in Brooklyn just over a year ago," he said, watching me carefully to note my reaction.

I was caught by surprise by the baldness of Thomas's statement, unsoftened by any hint of remorse. It was a virtual admission of guilt. I trusted that Oliver was capturing it all on tape.

Thomas continued, "Nate returned from the Navy to Barbados in January 1955. He did not stay long, but what he did in that time would have a long-lasting effect on my life. He told our mother all about me, about Edgar and me, and what had happened in the park in Greenwich. I don't know what more he said, but when I wrote home that spring saying that I would like to come to Glenville for a visit, my mother wrote saying that I was not welcome in my own home, not until I had 'renounced my evil ways'.

"I wrote and begged her to relent, but she did not respond. The next year I came to Barbados anyway, and stayed in Bridgetown. I came out to Glenville, hoping that my mother would change her mind when she saw me. When I came to the door, she met me there and asked if I had rejected my former self. I told her that I was incapable of doing that but that I felt that I was still a decent person, capable of being a good son to her. She slammed the door in my face.

"I persisted. I walked around the house and called to her to at least speak with me. Emily, sweet Emily, waved at me from an upstairs window. My mother finally sent Clarence out with a club to drive me away."

Thomas paused, seemingly reliving this traumatic and humiliating moment.

"Finally, there was nothing more I could do. I left Barbados and never again saw any of them until I saw Clarence last year."

The second admission of guilt.

I asked him to tell me about his recent encounters with his brothers.

"In a moment," he said. "Let me tell you about the rest of my life. As you will see, it is relevant to why we are here tonight.

"I returned to England, hurt and embittered. I changed my name from Thomas Cumberbatch to Thomas Winston. I worked for several different families. For a few years, in the mid-sixties, I even worked as a chauffeur for the Mounts. When Mr Mount died in 1966, Edgar came into his inheritance and moved here to Savannah. I left the Mounts' employ and went to work for another family in London.

"When Edgar was forced to leave Barbados in 1976, he came to England and looked me up. He asked me to take charge of his household. I was delighted. I was the butler, overseeing the household, and over time Edgar and I became more than just master and servant. We again became each other's best friend. I have remained with him ever since."

Thomas turned and stared at the small, grotesque body on the bed. I could see that this was a very emotional moment for him. That would have been the time, if I had wished, to catch him by surprise and disarm him. But I had put aside any concern for my own safety. Thomas Winston, né Cumberbatch, was not a man intent on killing me.

My long-lost uncle finally turned back and looked at me. He still held the pistol but the barrel was barely pointed in my direction.

"Edgar developed full AIDS symptoms two years ago. We had both known for some time that we were HIV positive. More than anything, Edgar wanted to return to Barbados. He wanted to die here at Savannah. Over the years he had managed to spend most of his considerable family fortune. He had been forced to sell his family home in Berkshire and there was little left for him in England. All that really mattered to him, at the end, was Savannah.

"People like Edgar and myself – we, of course, don't have children. Edgar was the last living member of his family and I was totally estranged from mine. As a consequence, places, homes, possessions take on a greater meaning for us. For Edgar, it was Savannah and, if that was what he wanted, if that was what would make him happy in his final days, I wanted it too.

"For years, the plantation and the house had been under the supervision of Vincent Lewis. Edgar had accepted Vincent's annual excuses for why the plantation had lost money. He would send money year after year to supplement Savannah's operation, and presumably to keep the Great House in good condition. Edgar trusted Vincent and believed his glowing reports about Savannah.

"Edgar trusted him, I did not. I could see Vincent Lewis for what he was, a liar and a cheat. He had been cheating Edgar for years but Edgar did not want to see it.

"Vincent Lewis came to London to speak with Edgar about the Savannah Project in the early spring of 1995. Lewis said that there was no future for sugar in Barbados and that land development was the only way to keep Savannah from falling into ruin. He asked Edgar to let him incorporate Savannah as part of a massive hotel and golf resort. If Edgar agreed, it would be known as the Savannah Project and, eventually, when completed, the hotel would be called the Savannah Hotel and Resort. Lewis said that they might build a casino there as well.

"Lewis asked Edgar to become a major investor. He acted disappointed when Edgar said that he was without funds and was unable to invest or even to continue supporting the upkeep of the plantation. However, you could tell that Lewis wasn't really surprised, he must have already had knowledge of Edgar's financial situation. What he really wanted was for Edgar to grant him control over the future of Savannah Plantation. Lewis said that he believed that he could find other investors, particularly if they went through with the casino. He stated that when the project was complete, Edgar would receive one hundred thousand pounds per year as rent.

"Edgar knew, but of course he did not tell Lewis, that he would not live to see or spend that rental income. What really appealed to Edgar was the idea that Savannah Plantation would continue to exist, albeit as a resort. At least it would not turn to weeds or be swallowed up by other plantations. And, of equal importance, the Great House would be maintained for future generations to see and admire.

"Edgar told Lewis that he could have the control he sought in the short term, together with an option to buy Savannah for a very attractive price, exercisable upon Edgar's death.

"Lewis was obviously delighted; he had the permission he had sought and eventually he would own the entire property.

"Edgar then added, 'There is one small thing.' Edgar told Lewis that he wished to have his banishment from Barbados lifted in order that he would be allowed to re-enter Barbados and to spend his final days living at Savannah Great House.

"Vincent Lewis's political connections were quite adequate to get the ban lifted. We were finally informed that Edgar could re-enter Barbados on December 1, 1995. Edgar then called his solicitors and had them place in his will an option to sell Savannah to Vincent Lewis, as he had promised."

Thomas paused and gestured at the bedraggled walls around us and said, "I cannot tell you what a major disappointment it was when we arrived shortly before Christmas and found the house and grounds looking so neglected. It nearly broke Edgar's heart.

"Lewis offered many different excuses: storms, unfaithful servants, restrictions on the use of truly effective chemicals for termites, and had even tried to have us believe that it was because the old house would be meticulously reconstructed as part of the Savannah Project that he had purposely allowed it to deteriorate.

"The truth was that Lewis had neglected Savannah for years, diverting Edgar's money to his own purposes. He had intended to repair and refurbish Savannah prior to our arrival in December, but when the Water Board report in September seemingly ended the Savannah Project, he had stopped the renovation of Savannah Great House to save himself money.

"When we arrived, Vincent told Edgar that it appeared unlikely that the Savannah Project would go ahead because of the water situation. That was bad news, indeed.

"Seeing Savannah looking like this, and then hearing that it would not be resurrected, had a very negative impact on Edgar's health. He began to decline rapidly. However, in February of 1996, something seemingly miraculous occurred. Some workmen discovered that an old well on the edge of the plantation, one that had been dry for as long as anyone could remember, was brimming with water.

"The amount of water running in this well was impressive. But it was still not sufficient to assure the water supply for the

Savannah Project, given the Water Board's objections. But Edgar remembered as a boy having read a book of stories about Barbados. One of the stories, he said, was an old Indian legend about two springs, one several times larger than the other, that came and went. His father had told him that two hundred and fifty years ago the smaller spring had been here on Savannah and the larger one had been up on the hill, actually on the land that Augustus Mount had given our ancestor, Frank Glenville. There had been no water at Glenville when I lived there but perhaps now it had returned."

I interrupted my uncle to say that I had recently read this story, and what Mount had remembered of the old tale was accurate.

Thomas nodded and then continued.

"We met with Vincent Lewis and some of his investors in April. Edgar said that they were a virtual Burke's Peerage of Barbados business and wealth. Lewis told them that if the well on Savannah had regained its water, the larger one up at Glenville might have as well. Everyone agreed that if this was so, Glenville must be acquired and then the Savannah Project would surely go ahead. We were all sworn to secrecy. Lewis and the investors feared that someone else would find out about this and purchase the Glenville spring and raise the price beyond reason.

"I went to Lewis and said that I remembered seeing large slabs in the back of the garden at Glenville that my mother said had once covered a well. I was sure that I knew where those slabs were located. Lewis asked me to go there to be certain. I went in the middle of the night with a few of his men. We found one of them, just where I had thought it would be, but we had neither the time nor the equipment to shift the slab to ascertain if there was water below."

I commented, "I saw where you had been digging, among a stand of bread-and-cheese trees."

"Clever boy. I thought we had covered our tracks better than that. Anyway," he said, returning to his story, "Lewis then paid a call on my mother to see if she would sell Glenville to him. Of course, he did not reveal the reason for his interest. She said that Glenville was not hers to sell, that it had been left to Clarence. But Clarence, never the brightest bulb, refused even to talk to Lewis.

"Vincent Lewis was convinced that the Glenville source of water was the only way that the Savannah Project would ever get going. He said to me, 'You're a Glenville. You should be able to get control of that water.' Lewis knew I was not close to my family but he did not fully understand the status of our relationship. He said that if I would deliver him Glenville with its water, he would give me a percentage of the Savannah Project. We started our negotiation at five per cent and finally agreed on eight per cent. I would not get any shares until they had the deed to Glenville and the spring was shown to be adequate to the task.

"It is important to me that you know that I was not motivated in any of this by a desire for personal wealth. I am sixty years old and not in good health. My only purpose in seeing the Savannah Project go forward was so that Edgar could die knowing that Savannah would again be the magnificent place it once had been. That was all in the world he wanted and I owed him that.

"I told Lewis that there were four people who potentially stood between me and ownership of Glenville. First, there was my mother, who admittedly was eighty-six and could not be expected to live much longer. Then there was Clarence, whom my mother had already identified as heir to Glenville. Of course, there was Emily. But I told him that I knew my mother would never leave Glenville in Emily's hands. And anyway, as long as there was a male heir, Emily could not inherit Glenville. Lastly there was your father, a male four years my senior.

"And then there was the question, was I still in the succession of inheritance at all or had my mother disinherited me? I did not mention this to Lewis but it did make me a bit nervous. However, I doubted that she would have gone to the trouble and expense of having her will altered and, knowing my mother, she probably hoped I would someday return and say that I had changed my ways," he said with a pained grin.

"I told Lewis that my family kept the deed and wills in an iron strongbox in my mother's office. He said that we had to get our hands on the box, to know for sure what the will said. I agreed, I wanted to see it, too.

"Clearly, Clarence had to be dealt with. I had no affection for him, we had never been close growing up and, as I told you, he had rejected and beaten me brutally when I had tried to go home. And now he was our major stumbling-block. There was nothing else to be done, Clarence had to be eliminated. It was agreed that I would do it.

"Lewis believed that with Clarence out of the way he would gain control of Glenville, since my mother wouldn't be able to cope with the garden and would have to sell the property.

"I feared he underestimated my mother, she was made of stern material. Rather than meekly selling her heritage, I feared that she would try to hang on and would offer it to Nate. However, to claim it, Nate would have to move to Barbados. I had no idea whether or not he would do this but if he did, your father, who had wronged me so often in the past, would be doing so once again.

"I decided that before eliminating Clarence, I had to go to New York to speak with Nate, to explain to him that if we co-operated we could share a considerable fortune. All he had to do was to agree not to return to Barbados and instead to urge our mother to sell Glenville. Then with Lewis in control of Glenville, presuming that the spring had indeed reappeared, I would receive a sizeable stake in Savannah which I would share with Nate.

"I hoped that Nate would agree but I must admit, knowing your father, I wasn't at all sure that he would, even though it made very good sense. So I was prepared to deal with this eventuality.

"I went to New York through Montreal on the twenty-seventh of May, entering on false papers that Vincent had arranged. I obtained Nate's address from the phone book and went there to wait for him. Then I followed him through the streets of Brooklyn at a safe distance as he made his rounds of his female friends and took his walks in the park. I did this for several days until I had decided when and where to approach him.

"I didn't go to New York intending to kill your father, I hoped he would co-operate. However, if he did not, I had no option but to silence him. I hoped that, if I had to kill Nate, his death would be counted as just another Brooklyn street crime. And so it might have been, but for one thing. I didn't know that Nate's son was a detective."

He gave me a wry smile.

"You have probably worked out what happened next. I decided that the best time to approach your father would be during his habitual walk after supper, when he was returning home. It would be getting dark and the streets would be relatively deserted. I chose a side street near the park. As I approached him, I couldn't help but be struck by our similarity in appearance. More than most brothers, we looked almost identical twins. Nate didn't look my way; I imagine streetwise pedestrians in New York avert their eyes from strangers, in order not to invite trouble.

"I blocked his path.

"'Nate, it's me, Thomas, your brother.'

"He was astounded; after all, we had not seen one another in over forty years. I didn't waste any time. I explained that there

266

was an opportunity for our mother to sell Glenville for a large amount of money but that Clarence was in the way. Our idiot half-brother would not even hear the proposition. I told him that our mother and sister would be able to live out their lives in comfort. Nate seemed willing to hear me out.

"I then told him that the only solution was that Clarence would have to be eliminated. With Clarence out of the picture, all Nate would have to do was to decline to go to Barbados to run Glenville, and to urge Ma to sell. Then, as a reward for what we had done, Nate and I would share a small fortune. I assured him that it was the best thing for our mother and Emily.

"Nate stared at me in disbelief. He rejected the whole idea and verbally attacked me for even suggesting such a thing. He said that I was mentally unbalanced and had always been so. He alleged that my sexuality, which had so offended him, was just another manifestation of my mental illness.

"His words and his attitude infuriated me. I had come there in good will but, with his attitude, all the old hurts returned from where I had buried them. I became enraged. We both lost our tempers and soon began to fight.

"I drew the pistol that Vincent had given to me but Nate knocked it from my hand with his cane. But I also had a truncheon, a metal pipe, hidden in my coat. I surprised him and struck him. Nate defended himself, in fact he fought very hard, striking me several times with his damned cane. He cracked my ribs and landed a very hard blow on my knee. But I had the superior weapon, the lead pipe, and eventually I knocked him down and then struck him time and again until I heard his skull crack. Our battle must have lasted for five minutes – it seemed like hours – but no one passed our way."

Thomas's words sickened me. My father's killer stood before me describing the act of murder without any apparent remorse. And the man he killed was his brother. Abel and Cain.

Thomas noted my reaction to his words. He raised the gun and pointed it at my chest.

"Let me continue. I had planned to leave New York after I had spoken with or, if it came to that, had eliminated Nate. I had my bag stashed nearby. But after the fight I was in no condition to travel. Nate had cracked two of my ribs. Damned painful they were and my knee was so swollen that I was unable to walk without assistance. I took the cane, picked up the gun, grabbed my bag and hobbled a few blocks away to a small hotel by the park. There I checked in, using the name from my false Canadian driver's licence, Pierre LeBlanc.

"I needed to recuperate for a few days before travelling back to Barbados. I knew that it was dangerous to remain so close to where I had killed Nate but I felt it was unlikely that anyone would look for his killer in a hotel just a few blocks away. I was assuming Nate was dead, but an article in the paper the next day reported that a Nate Cumberbatch was in hospital in a critical condition from a mugging by an unknown assailant. I doubted that he would recover but I resolved to leave just as soon as I was able.

"I soon recovered somewhat, but I felt the need to exercise my knee. I went out late that night, when there were few people on the street, and walked with the cane. No one paid any attention to me.

"The next night, I set out again. When I came out of the hotel there you were, standing across the street. You had found me. How, I don't know."

"I don't know how I got on to you either," I interjected. "I have no memory of that time, thanks to my head injury, but I suspect it may have had something to do with Nate's walking stick. No one else in Brooklyn had one like it. Someone may have seen you with it and called me."

My uncle shook his head, then continued.

"I tried to elude you by slipping down the alley at the rear of the hotel but you followed me. When I got to the end of the alley, I realised that I was trapped. You kept coming at me.

"I did not know who you were but you seemed to think I was Nate. I felt I had no choice but to kill you. I fired at you. Then you ducked and charged towards me, bravely but foolishly. Just as you were about to tackle me, I shot and hit you in the head. Your body crashed into my extremely painful ribs and banged-up knee, it almost finished me off.

"Then, a few minutes later, some boys came and stole your wallet. When they left, I hobbled back to my room, leaving you in a pool of blood, presumably dead. For that I do apologise; but, as you will see, I intend to make it up to you.

"I concluded that if you, whoever you were, had found me, others could as well. I knew that I must return to Barbados at once, taking my chances on Nate's survival. I left the next day for Montreal and then on to Barbados.

"When I arrived in Barbados, I rang the hospital in Brooklyn, claiming to be a distant relative. I knew that if Nate did survive, he would put the police on to me. But I was told that he had died without ever regaining consciousness. Part of me was sad. After all, he was my brother. But remember there had been bad blood between us for years. I will admit I also took some satisfaction from his death. I had come to New York prepared to do just that if I had to. And Nate had left me no choice.

"The hospital switchboard volunteered that Nate Cumberbatch's son, Benjamin, was there in intensive care, suffering from a head wound. That's how I learned who you were. I feared that you would recover and, remembering the family resemblance, identify me as Nate's attacker. But there was nothing I could do about that.

"As time passed and no one came after me, I assumed that you too had died, or had become permanently disabled and could not identify me.

"Now there was the final step, the elimination of Clarence. Nate was out of the way but because of my injuries and a sense of caution arising from your potential involvement, I decided to wait several months before striking. Lewis kept pushing me to act, so I finally promised to kill Clarence before the end of the year.

"We all knew of Clarence's frequent early afternoon walks along the cliffs of St Charles. I decided that this would be where I should attack him. Several times in December I watched my half-brother climbing on the rocks, looking for birds' nests as usual. But although I tried on more than one occasion, I was never able to get behind him at just the right place.

"One day, shortly before Christmas, I saw him walking along the ledge in the deserted area just west of Savannah Plantation. I knew I might never have a better opportunity to do what I had to do. I moved into position and then crept up on him from behind; he could not have heard me because of the wind and the surf. I struck him on the head with a section of pipe. He had no idea who I was or what was happening. He fell forward over the edge of the cliff.

"But Clarence was amazingly strong. He clung to the rocks just below the edge while I rained blows on his head and hands. He still would not go down. I struck him time after time, but he hung on. Not until I pounded his fingers could I force him to release his grasp. Then he lodged again part way down the cliff and hung there beyond my reach. All I could do was hurl coral boulders down upon him. One finally connected and he fell to his death in the turbulent waters below."

Thomas stared at me defiantly. His face and his body language seemed to dare me to stand in judgment of what he had done. By some twisted logic he seemed to believe his actions were justified.

"Then, a few days later, you showed up on the island. Vincent Lewis told me about your meeting at his club. He mentioned the scar in your forehead and said that you had told his lady friend of your memory problems. I assumed that this was why you had never linked me to Nate's death."

I looked at this man who said he was my uncle and shook my head in disbelief. To him, the deaths of his brothers and my shooting had been simple necessities, the ends justifying his despicable acts. I wondered if he would be so coldhearted when it came to the deaths of his mother and his sister Emily.

"What about the women? Why did you have to burn Glenville and cause their deaths?" I asked him sharply, my voice failing to hide the anger that was welling up inside me.

He looked at me intently, his eyes narrowing. He appeared to be greatly offended by my accusation. He slowly raised the gun threateningly, pointing it right at my face. When finally he did answer, it was with emotion equal to mine.

"I did not set that fire. I swear to you that I never would have or could have done anything to hurt my mother or Emily. Their deaths were absolutely unnecessary. With Clarence and your father out of the way, my mother would have had to sell the land to Lewis and I would have realised my piece of the Savannah Project, or if she stubbornly still would not sell, in theory I was next in succession and would eventually own Glenville."

"So, if you didn't do it, who did kill them?"

"It's obvious, isn't it? Vincent Lewis. No one else had motive. I am convinced of it. Shortly after the fire happened, Lewis and I met, at my instigation. I confronted him. But of course the bastard denied that he had done it. However, the man is a notorious liar. He must have done it or, more likely, put someone else up to it. Who else would benefit? If he has in his possession the wills and old deed, it will prove his guilt conclusively. Lewis must have become impatient to control Glenville. He is a bastard, a villain.

"After the fire, Lewis rang me and said I should come forward to the authorities, disclosing that I was Thomas Cumberbatch, the eldest living male heir to Glenville House, and say that I wished to claim my inheritance. He said that either the will would prove my claim or, if it had been destroyed in the fire, I would ultimately have my claim validated.

"I was shocked and horrified by the deaths of my mother and sister, and by his callous suggestion that, after their deaths – deaths that he had caused – I should claim Glenville for his benefit.

"I was furious. I would do anything to stop Lewis. I was able finally to convince Edgar that Vincent Lewis was the despicable scoundrel he is and that he did not deserve Savannah. Moreover, I pointed out, despite his promises, Lewis had done nothing to improve the deplorable state of Savannah Great House and quite probably he never would.

"Edgar, sick as he was, at last had to agree. His solicitor flew out on the Concorde last week from London and Edgar's will was rewritten. What money he had went to charities for AIDS victims and Edgar eliminated Vincent Lewis's option to purchase Savannah Plantation and Great House. Instead, he left them to me, outright.

"But I fear that I will never live to enjoy any benefit from this inheritance. You see, I have known for some time that my own health was deteriorating. I know now that I have gone from HIV positive to an active AIDS status. Having spent these last many months observing my dear friend Edgar descend into his hell, I do not intend to follow in his steps, nor do I intend to spend what's left of my life in prison."

Thomas reached inside his jacket and pulled out a thick envelope. I could see that something was written on it in large block letters. He held the revolver in his left hand and extended the envelope towards me.

"This packet contains a letter which confirms everything that I have just told you, and there is also a copy of my will. Please do me the courtesy of following its instructions."

With that, Thomas Cumberbatch turned the pistol away from me and towards himself.

I shouted, "Chandelier!" and leapt towards him, but it was too late. He had opened his mouth, shoved the barrel of the revolver inside and fired, all in one motion. Blood and brain matter speckled the wall behind him. I stood open-mouthed and in shock as his body slumped back against the wall.

Oliver and his crew arrived several seconds later. Surveying the scene, Oliver said, "Are you all right? We heard everything and, thank God, you were right, he never planned to harm you. And we now know who killed your father and uncle and why. And, if this man is to be believed, we also know who was in back of the Glenville murders."

Oliver knelt down and plucked the envelope from the dead man's hand. I saw my name was written on the envelope. I put out my hand but Oliver placed the envelope in his pocket and said, "This is a police matter, even though it is addressed to you. I will have to take this for now. You can collect it or at least hear what it contains at my office tomorrow."

It was late and I was exhausted from the stress and emotional rollercoaster I had been on. I opted for the Wavecrest rather than taking the long drive back to Annie's house. Plus, I thought Annie would likely be in a highly emotional state about this evening's events and I welcomed a good night's sleep.

Daily Report 180

Date of Events: 20 August 1997
Place: Barbados: Wavecrest Hotel; Ollie's office
Summary: Arson Squad report; Thomas's will

I rang Oliver's office.

He said, "Come by at two today to discuss the contents of your uncle's envelope. I can't give it to you then but at least you deserve to know what it says."

I asked what was in it but Oliver laughed and said, "Wait until we meet, you'll find it very interesting."

"What's so funny?" I persisted, but he only repeated that he would see me that afternoon.

The FedEx man found me sitting in the morning sun on the porch of the Wavecrest. He had the Arson Squad's report. It was a day sooner than they had promised. Thank you, Norman, I said to myself.

Inside the FedEx box there were three copies of a nine-page report and one small box. The report was the usual Norman Price job, thorough and professional. I could tell that Norman had written it himself, not one of his assistants. I appreciate that, too.

The first two pages describe methodology. The next two catalogue the materials the Squad had received from me, and the items which they subsequently found in the ash and debris.

Page five deals with whether the fire was arson or had been started by accident. I'll spare the details. The end result is that they found conclusive proof of arson. The char on the boards which I salvaged from the cistern shows that "a petroleum-based product was present". Further testing disclosed that the product was "high-octane gasoline".

The pattern of charring also indicates that a large quantity of gasoline had been poured on the floorboards and on the bodies themselves. Whoever set this fire had been determined that Glenville and its occupants burned to the ground.

A note from Norman at the bottom of the page states, "Likelihood of arson – 100%."

The last four pages are the autopsy reports from the pathologist, on the charred bodies found at the fire scene. They are identified as "Victim A" and "Victim B".

Victim A is described as a "white female, five foot five to five foot seven, estimated weight when alive, approximately 130 pounds, estimated age, over eighty." Clearly, Victim A is Grandma Dora.

Victim B is described as a "white female, five foot two to five foot three, weight approximately 86 pounds, estimated age sixty to seventy." Although the front of the body had been totally burned, some skin on the back had escaped the fire because there is a comment that the victim appears to have had "little or no skin pigmentation. Had very fair complexion or may have been albino." Victim B is Aunt Emily, for sure.

Victim A died from two stab wounds in the back. One had penetrated a kidney and the other had severed the spinal column. A notation says that the knife wounds had been delivered with "above average force. Death was instantaneous."

Thank God for that.

From the angle of entry, they estimate that the killer was approximately five foot seven to five foot nine and, given the force of the knife wound through bone, almost certainly male.

The weapon appears to have been "a six- or seven-inch blade with a non-serrated edge". They believe that it was either a jackknife – a folding blade – or a small fixed blade like a fisherman's knife. There was no smoke present in the victim's pulmonary system. This led to the conclusion that Victim A was dead before the fire began. Additionally, the front of the body had been "doused with the same accelerant".

Victim B died of a heart attack, "a massive infarction". There were no signs of wounds. Victim B also was dead before the fire reached her. The front of her body, too, had been doused with the same accelerant as Victim A's but a smaller amount.

A memo from Norman addressed to me says that "with two exceptions, all of the items gleaned from the debris are normal household items. The first exception is a Colt revolver, the kind that was commonly issued by the US Navy in World War II. It was not loaded and had not been fired. In fact the gun was badly corroded and the mechanisms were totally frozen. Federal Express would not accept it for reshipment to you in Barbados. If you need to examine the weapon it is being held in the evidence room at the Arson Squad."

He queried, "Did your grandmother have such a weapon in her possession? If not, it may have been carried into the house by the arsonist.

"The second exception is contained in the small box herein. It is a bullet-shaped object made of silver, approximately seven-eighths of an inch long. However, it is not a bullet and may have been an ornament or a piece of jewelry. It is inscribed with a girl's name, GINA, and the date '77.

"Do you know any reason why your grandmother would have had such an item in her home? If not, it too may have belonged to the arsonist."

Well, we knew about the gun. I don't need to see it again to remind me that I should have been more forceful with Grandma Dora about it. If she had not had the gun she might well have still been alive today. I will have to live with that. But, like a lot of things that have happened, it's too late now.

I opened the box and looked at the second item. I didn't recognise it as being from Glenville House, but it was quite small and I might not have ever seen it. The name Gina meant nothing to me. There was no one of that name in our family, as far as I know, nor do I remember anyone named Gina in the village. '77 is almost certainly shorthand for 1977, but I can't think of any reason why that year would have had any special significance to the Glenvilles.

Norman may be right, perhaps that one does belong to the arsonist.

I was right on time at Oliver's office. He gestured for me to be seated and we got right down to business. On his desk was the Thomas Winston/Cumberbatch envelope. I could see my name scrawled in large block letters on the outside, "Benjamin Cumberbatch".

"It contains three items," Oliver said as he opened the manila envelope. "First, is a three-page letter addressed 'To whom it may concern'. Basically, it repeats what Winston told you last night. He admits that he murdered his brother, your father Nathaniel, in a dispute arising from your father's refusal to co-operate with Thomas's plan to kill your uncle Clarence. In addition, he admits that he later killed your uncle, in order to induce his mother to sell Glenville to Vincent Lewis. He says in the letter that Vincent Lewis had prior knowledge of his plans to kill Clarence and had promised him shares in the Savannah Project for doing so. He states that Lewis had no direct part in the death of your father beyond facilitating Thomas's trip to New York to meet with Nate. Lewis also supplied Thomas with a .24 calibre pistol, presumably the weapon which Thomas subsequently used to shoot you."

Oliver turned the page and said, "Thomas Winston denies any role in the deaths of his mother Dora Glenville and half-sister, Emily Glenville, or in the burning of Glenville House. He says that he is certain that this had been done by or, more likely, at the direction of, Vincent Lewis. However, he could offer no proof of this allegation.

"Your Uncle Thomas apologises for having killed his brothers. He says that he had ample reason to be angry with them, but that does not justify his deeds. He also regrets having wounded you but claims that he did it with no malice, it had been in self-defence, and he did not at the time know it was his nephew that he had shot. He accepts that he cannot expect to be forgiven for his acts. He says that he does not believe in a Hell but, if he was mistaken, he fully expects to be there.

"He wants it to be known that his sole purpose for what he did was to have Savannah Plantation restored, in the hope that Edgar Mount's final days would be at peace. His only regret is that Edgar Mount did not live to see this dream come true.

"The second document is addressed to you. Thomas asks you to see that Vincent Lewis and any others involved are held accountable for the deaths of his mother and half-sister. He also asks you to see that he is buried at Savannah, and that his grave be placed as near as possible to the grave of Edgar Mount."

As much as I hate my uncle for the cold-blooded murder of my father and Clarence, I cannot help but feel sorry for him. He'd had a sad and lonely childhood and he had been totally rejected by his brothers and his mother, everyone in the family except Emily.

His relationship with Edgar Mount was all that he ever had. It became the sole focus of his life. But I will never accept or understand how he could have killed his brothers, merely to secure the future of Savannah Plantation as a gesture of affection toward his dying friend. I guess you could see a twisted logic to it but, on balance, I think maybe Pa was on the right track: Thomas definitely had a warped view of life.

Oliver continued, "The third document is Thomas Winston's last will and testament. It is dated a week ago. Apparently it was drawn up by Edgar Mount's solicitor when he came over to redo Mount's will. In it, Winston names you as his sole beneficiary."

I tried to comprehend exactly what it was that Oliver was saying.

"What do you mean, his sole beneficiary?"

"Ben, this means that you are not only the owner of Glenville, you are also the owner of Savannah. You are, that is, if Edgar Mount's last will, leaving Savannah to Thomas, holds up."

Oliver stopped and smiled at me and said, "I'll bet that twenty generations of Mounts are spinning in their graves over that one."

"You've got to be kidding," I interjected. "There is no way that Lewis and his people will ever let me get Savannah. They'll find some way to invalidate either Mount's will or Thomas's. Besides, I am not at all sure that I want the place. It looks pretty run down to me, plus I don't begin to have the money to pay the taxes, much less to fix it up."

"Hell, man," Oliver said. "You don't want to be a sugar-plantation owner, not these days. But you can sell that place for a lot of money. Good growing land is going for five thousand US dollars an acre. Savannah is over 600 acres, that's three million dollars, together with whatever you can get for the house itself. Don't be too quick to walk away from that kind of money."

I saw his point. He continued, "Also, don't overlook Glenville. It's not worth much as it is, but if the Wandering Lady spring you told me about has returned there, as Thomas and others believed, it could prove to be worth a small fortune."

I have to admit, suddenly dollar signs were where my eyelids should have been.

Oliver turned quite serious. He said, "On the other hand, if Savannah Plantation was purchased by the Lewis faction, and the possibility of a nearby source of water confirmed, it would almost certainly resurrect the damned Savannah Project, casino and all. The people who oppose casino gambling are prepared to see that your inheritance is upheld in the courts if you, in return, will commit to keeping Savannah Plantation in agriculture or, at least, not allowing it to become the site of a gambling resort."

"How do you know this?" I asked.

"There have already been discussions about it," Oliver said.

"It sounds to me like you've been talking to the Prime Minister."

I looked at Oliver and he nodded his head in acknowledgement.

"You will have the personal assurances of the Prime Minister. He will promise to remain in office and to stand for re-election. And he will give you a document which pledges his support for your claim to Savannah.

"Also, remember this, Vincent Lewis had prior knowledge of Clarence Glenville's murder. We have a good chance to send him to prison for conspiracy. And if we can prove his involvement in the deaths of your female kin, you can forget about him. He'll be lucky if he is not hanged."

I accepted the proposal. I didn't see that I had any alternative. I could go into the courts on my own to press my claim to Savannah, but I had neither the money for a long legal battle nor did I have any political clout. And I was getting the picture that political clout was what counted in Barbados.

I agreed to meet with the Prime Minister soon to work out our arrangement.

I then told Oliver what I had learned from the NYPD Arson Squad's report. I told him of Norman Price's one hundred per cent certainty that the fire had been arson, and I described the various details of the pathologist's report on the two women. Oliver said that, given these facts, the police would reopen the

Glenville fire case as murder and arson. I promised to give him a copy of the report tomorrow.

However, I didn't tell him about the item which Price had found in the ashes, the small silver bullet-shaped item marked "GINA '77". I decided that I would have to look into that one myself.

Daily Report 181

Date of Events: 20 August 1997 – late afternoon
Place: Barbados: Annie's home
Summary: Silver bullet

I drove up the street to Annie's just as Malcolm was coming across the lawn. He stopped when he saw me and called, "Miss Annie, he here."

Annie came out on the porch and waved cheerily to me.

"Oh, Ben," she called, "I've been worried sick. Why didn't you ring me?"

"I meant to, but I've really been busy."

She walked over to the driveway and stuck her head into my open car, put a hand to my cheek and gave me a long kiss hello.

But, with the unerring radar that women seem to have, she sensed something not quite right in my response to her affectionate greeting.

"Ben, what's wrong? What has happened?"

"A lot. Let's go inside where we can talk and I will tell you everything."

We sat side by side on the sofa in the living room and I told her in detail about what had happened during my visit last night to Savannah Great House and my meeting with her mystery man who, as it turned out, was my Uncle Thomas. I recounted his admission to the murders of his brothers and to shooting me. And then I told her of his suicide and that, possibly, I was heir to Savannah Plantation as well as to Glenville.

But from her reaction I could tell that Annie had already heard much if not all of this from her brother. I was reminded again, should I ever forget, how close these two are. Tell something to one, the other will know it shortly. As close as Elyce and I have been, we have never approached the extraordinary level of brother and sister intimacy and trust that Oliver and Annie share. I am envious of them, and at the same time I have to remind myself it would be wise to never forget the depth of this bond.

"Ben, I'm so happy for you," Annie said, with genuine enthusiasm for my becoming a landowner in Barbados. "We'll make a Bajan out of you yet. How fantastic! And now I don't have to come to New York to be with you, we can be together here. Let's have a glass of champagne to celebrate."

While Annie went to get the glasses and the champagne, I pulled the small, partially melted silver cylinder out of the box in my pocket and looked at it once again, then I put it into my shirt breast pocket. Part of me wanted to leave it there, to never mention it or disclose its existence to anyone. But, deep down, I knew that I could not do that.

There was a good chance that this would prove to be the key to what had happened that dreadful night at Glenville House. With all my soul, I was hoping that my suspicions were unworthy, that it would prove to be nothing. But my commitment to the Cumberbatch family and my pride in myself as a detective meant that I had to follow this lead, no matter what the consequences.

When Annie returned with a tray, two glasses and a bottle of champagne, I was making a notation in my pad.

"Please, put that thing away," she said with a laugh. "You're always writing things down in your little notebook."

I placed the notebook in my back pocket and laid the pen down on the coffee table in front of the sofa.

"To us," she said, raising her glass to mine. "All two of us," she added with a laugh, because she knew how much I enjoyed that distinctive Bajan way of saying "both".

I toasted in response and we drank deeply of the fizzing champagne.

We sat on the sofa, our knees touching. She chattered happily about what a relief it must be for me to know at last who had killed my father and uncle and why.

"To think, it was an uncle that you hardly knew you had. And he probably killed your grandmother and aunt as well, whether he admitted it or not. Or, if it wasn't him, it was someone else that Vincent had put up to it. That's what the police think. Anyway, you now have it off your mind. How difficult all of this must have been for you," she said sympathetically.

I agreed that a great weight had been lifted from me. Annie poured second glasses of champagne. Then she took my hand and placed it, palm down, against her inner thigh. She squeezed her legs together, playfully inviting me to take her to bed.

But not this time. My intentions were different.

I extracted my hand from her legs and grasped her lightly by the left wrist. Under my hand I could feel Annie's charm bracelet. I brought the arm over in front of me and looked at the bracelet as if I had never noticed it before.

I said gently, "Tell me about this, Annie. You must love this bracelet, you always have it on."

"Oh, I know that you've seen this before. I wear it a lot."

"And you must love it but we've never really talked about it."

Annie looked at the bracelet fondly.

"This old thing. It's silly of me, I know, but I wear it for luck and to remind me of happier days. I collected these charms years ago. They were given to the contestants at beauty pageants in the sixties and seventies. Each contestant received a silver charm as a memento from the sponsors and the winner got the same charm, slightly larger, but in solid gold."

She continued, "For two years, when I was young, living with my aunt in Canada, I entered contests all over North America. Later, when I returned to Barbados, I entered contests in the Caribbean and even in South America."

"Let me see," I said, looking at the bracelet more carefully. Some of the charms were gold but more of them were made of silver. They seemed to be in three different designs but the majority of them showed a stylised woman in a bathing suit, her arms raised as if in acknowledgement of the cheers of the crowd.

Annie proudly pointed to her gold charms. Engraved on the back of each was the name of the city and the year that the pageant had been held. She said that there were seven gold charms and twenty-three of silver.

Annie turned over one of the gold charms to show me that it said "Toronto '76".

"I was Miss Ontario in 1976," she said proudly.

"What are your other gold ones?"

She pointed to each and, without looking, in chronological order, she named the pageants. The last three were "Barbados '77, where I won Miss Barbados, Kingston '77, in Jamaica, where I won Miss Caribbean and Rio '77 where I was crowned Miss South and Central America.

"You may have heard that I was a finalist that year for Miss World. I didn't win, but they said I was the first runner-up."

She said this with practised modesty. She pointed to the largest of the silver charms. It was half again as large as the others and the bathing beauty figure was more detailed. On the back it said, "Miss World – Monte Carlo '77".

I told her that I had heard of her success in the Miss World contest in New York – a small white lie – and that it was a great accomplishment and she had every reason to be proud.

Annie fairly glowed with pleasure. Clearly, the beauty pageants were and would always be important events in her life. And she was delighted by my show of interest in them.

"Tell me more," I said, evidencing further interest in the subject. "What about some of the other silver ones?"

Annie began to go through the major ones: "Quebec '77; Minn. Aq. '76" – which she explained was the 1976 Minneapolis Aquatennial Festival, too long a name to fit on the small surface of the charm – "Ottawa in both '76 and '77, I was also a finalist at Ottawa for Miss Canada, the second year."

"You know," I said casually, "the only place I have ever been in Canada is Regina, Saskatchewan. When I was in the military police, they sent me up there with a detail to collect a deserter. I remember it being incredibly cold and windy. Did you ever compete there?"

"Oh yes, in the early spring of 1977, just before I left Canada and returned to Barbados, I went there to compete for Miss Central Canada. I came in second there, as well. And yes, you're right, it was cold and windy," she said, laughing.

"Let me see that one," I said with feigned enthusiasm, my interest in this subject seemingly equal to hers. At the same time, I had a terrible sinking feeling in the pit of my stomach.

Annie riffled through the charms looking for "Regina '77" but she could not find it. Then, with a cry of alarm, she discovered a small empty loop.

"Oh, Ben, I've lost it! I've lost Regina. I can't believe it, this is the first time that I have ever lost one of them. What am I going to do? It is irreplaceable."

"Does it look like this?" I said, as I reached into my pocket and dropped the small silver cylinder on the coffee table in front of her. She eagerly picked it up.

"Ben, where did you get …"

She halted as she saw that the item in her hand was not exactly what she had thought it would be. It was different from the other charms, the upraised arms of the tiny figure were missing. In fact, the top half of the charm appeared to have been partially melted. She turned it over and saw that the first two letters of the city Regina were gone, leaving only GINA '77.

"What has happened to it? Where did you get it? How did it get like this?" She was clearly upset, first by the appearance of her charm, and then with the dawning recognition that somehow this object might link her to the fire at Glenville.

"It looks to me like it's been in a fire, wouldn't you say?"

I spoke very carefully, not threatening or accusing her in the slightest.

"In fact, I am sure it was in a fire, because it was dredged up with the ashes and muck at the bottom of the old cistern at Glenville."

As I spoke, I watched Annie's face carefully. Her expression went rapidly from confusion to realisation to fear. Finally, her eyes began to blink rapidly. She appeared to be trying to think of an explanation of how this charm had got to Glenville.

"Maybe I dropped it at Glenville that night I came to see you there?" Her voice lacked conviction.

I said nothing.

She took my silence as rejection of this theory. She tried another.

"Maybe someone put it there. That's it, someone who was trying to make it look like I had been involved in the fire. Someone like Vincent. He could have taken it there any time."

Again, I said nothing.

An ominous silence filled the space around us. Only the distant traffic noise floating up from Bridgetown below impinged on the stillness. Annie squirmed. Involuntarily, her hand pushed the charm away, as if to distance herself from this incriminating item.

My feelings were only slightly less turbulent than hers. I didn't want to accept what was becoming more and more evident. I had come there with the hope that Annie would be able to prove that this item was not hers or, somehow, would have a plausible explanation for how it had got into the ashes at Glenville.

I am in love with Annie. I was well down the path to asking her to marry me and to spend her life with me and for me to look after her like a man should and become the father that Clara has never had. I would have done anything for her. I was prepared to fight Vincent Lewis and to do whatever it takes to make him pay for his crimes. But as I waited to hear Annie tell me how this piece of silver had got into the ashes of Glenville House, my spirits fell.

Annie stopped and said nothing more. She stared at her hands; her face, her beautiful face, was sad and twisted. I could now see that she knew full well how the charm had got there. And, I feared, so did I. I didn't want to believe it but there seemed to be no other explanation.

In a surprisingly husky voice, dreading the full meaning of my own words, I finally said it.

"Maybe you dropped it there the night you killed my grandmother and my aunt and torched their bodies and the house to cover your crime."

Annie stared at me, her mouth agape. She buried her face into her hands and shook her head, denying my harsh words. After a long pause, she leaned back against the sofa with her head turned away from me.

No matter what my feelings are for Annie, I could no longer avoid the dreadful reality that she was responsible for the deaths of Grandma Dora and Aunt Emily. If I had been in any doubt, her body language now said it was true.

I allowed her to sit there for a while longer, then I reached over and slowly pulled her around to face me. She kept her eyes closed, tears leaking from their corners and running down her face.

"Enough. You must tell me the truth," I said in a gruff voice, betraying not anger but the complex of emotions I was feeling.

She said nothing, eyes still closed.

"Just what happened there that night? Who was with you? And why did you go there in the first place?"

My voice was not harsh, despite my determination to get the answers to my questions. I was fully aware that the answers she was about to give might well alter forever the future course of her life, of my life, and of our life together.

Annie struggled to pull away but I held her firmly, a hand on each shoulder. Her eyes remained shut, avoiding mine, but I did not loosen my grasp.

At last she opened her eyes; they were red, and her misery was evident. Her cheeks were wet with tears – tears of shame and humiliation.

Finally, she spoke. As she did I gradually loosened my hold.

"It was all an accident, a terrible, terrible, unnecessary accident. Ben, you must believe me. And, Ben, I tried to tell you about it, that night before …"

"When?"

"That night when I came to you at the Wavecrest, the night after you had got so drunk with Ollie. But you had your mind on other things, and what with the rum and, I guess, your injury, you didn't seem to remember anything of what I told you. At first, when you didn't mention it, I wasn't quite sure whether you had forgotten or whether you remembered and your silence meant that you had forgiven me. However, soon it became clear that you really didn't remember what I had said. But by then things were going so well between us, I just couldn't bear to bring it up again."

"Well, I am here now and I am sober, tell me about this 'accident'."

"You had been here for a few days at Christmas-time, when Clarence was killed. You and I had met briefly, but I honestly knew nothing about his murder. As I told you, I had done Vincent's bidding by going to Ollie to see that there would be no police inquiry, but I had no other involvement. You went back to New York and I had no reason to think that you would ever return. My whole livelihood, as I've told you, mine and Clara's, depended on Vincent. With things going badly between us, I was desperate to reinstate our relationship.

"Vincent believed that he needed your family's land at Glenville. At first, he had thought he could buy it, but over time he became convinced that your grandmother would never sell him Glenville, even after your father's and Clarence's deaths."

Her voice was tentative and soft, I had to strain to hear her words.

"He was also obsessed, for some reason, with seeing your grandmother's will. I didn't know why, but I assumed that it had something to do with the water problem at the Savannah Project. It didn't matter, I thought that if I could get hold of your grandmother's will, it would be an opportunity for me to get back on an even keel with Vincent.

"It seemed harmless enough, and I knew, from being around the house when we were young, where your grandmother hid the iron box she kept the will in."

"So, what happened?"

"Just Malcolm and I went, nobody else even knew what we intended. I was going to take the box and give it to Vincent as a surprise. I hoped he would be grateful to me and we would be all right again. A day or two later, after Vincent had read the contents, I would return the box to your grandmother's house. Hopefully she would never know it had been gone.

"Malcolm drove to Glenville and hid nearby. He watched and waited until the women went to bed, around nine o'clock, then he came to get me. It was nearly midnight when we got there. We parked away from the village, where no one would see the car.

"The house was dark and everyone was asleep. It was easy to get in. Malcolm just forced the front door. He made a little noise, but no one upstairs seemed to hear. I went right to the room behind the kitchen to look for the iron box. I had just located it in a cupboard when I heard a noise behind me. I turned and saw an elderly white woman, in a pink nightgown, holding a huge pistol pointed at me.

"Of course, it was your grandmother. She may or may not have recognised me, but she never uttered a sound because at that moment Malcolm grabbed her from behind."

Annie paused and shook her head, reliving that dreadful instant, wishing that it had never happened.

In a lower voice she continued, "He put one hand over her mouth. In the other hand he had a knife. He thrust the knife into her back twice, and she fell forward. I rushed to her side but it was too late, she was already dead. I could see that the gun was old and rusted. I don't think it would have worked. Malcolm just stood there, staring at her. He didn't fully realise what he had done.

"Then we heard a noise on the stairs, a muffled cry. Your aunt must have been at the bottom of the staircase watching her mother creep behind me. Malcolm turned and went to get her as she ran back up the stairs. As soon as I realised what was happening, I shouted for Malcolm to stop, not to hurt her. But he continued up the stairs and I followed him to be sure that he didn't harm your aunt.

"However, it made no difference. Your Aunt Emily had collapsed, face down, at the top of the stairs. As near as I could tell, she was already dead. Malcolm swore that he had not touched her. I think she died of fright.

"It was terrible. I swear to you, Ben, we went there with no intention of harming anyone, but suddenly two women were dead. We panicked. We carried your grandmother upstairs and put both bodies in their beds. Malcolm found an empty five-gallon can and some hose on the back porch. He went to the car and siphoned petrol from the tank. We spilled it on the bodies, all over the beds, on the stairs and throughout the house. I went back to the car and waited while Malcolm lit the fire. He ran to join me. Then, there was an explosion. We could see that the house was ablaze as we drove away."

"Who knows you did this?" I asked.

"No one. I've told no one."

"Not your brother?"

"Lord no!"

"Not even Vincent Lewis?"

"Especially not him, he would use it against me."

"What about the iron box? It was missing from the debris."

"We took it with us. I have it upstairs, hidden behind my closet. I never gave it to Vincent because it would have incriminated me in the fire and the women's deaths. Do you want it?" she asked plaintively.

I nodded and Annie ran upstairs. A few minutes later she returned carrying the heavy box, still padlocked.

She placed it on the coffee table in front of me.

"Here it is. It's yours, take it. I wish to God that I had never seen it or heard of it."

She looked at me and said, "Ben, I don't know if you can ever find it in your heart to forgive me but I swear to you, it was an accident. I meant them no harm. I had no idea that Malcolm even had a knife with him and I never would have believed that he would use it like that on a woman."

I said nothing.

"He is so protective of me. I don't think he even thought about what he was doing before he did it. He just reacted when he saw the gun pointed at me."

I remained silent, I had no idea what to say. A flood of emotions was swirling within me. Part of me wanted to rescue Annie from what she had done. To forgive her, to never tell anyone and to get on with our lives together. But could I do that?

I accept that Annie was not fully to blame for what happened. But could this be considered an accident? To sweep it aside that way is in conflict with the policeman in me, with my desire – my *need* – to see justice done. Can Annie and I ever be happy together again? I want to believe yes, but I have my doubts.

I don't have it in me to hate Annie or even be angry with her. I still love her, but I don't know how to forgive, nor could I believe that I would ever be able to forget. This deed would always be there, poisoning whatever chance we might have had for happiness.

Annie began to plead, "Ben, no one has to ever know about this. The police think that Vincent made someone do it but he will deny it and they'll find no evidence of his involvement. No one else will be blamed. Perhaps they will finally assume that your uncle did it or that it was just an accident, after all. Ben, darling, if you think of it, it was what I said, it was just an accident. You've got to understand that it was not anybody's fault."

I was incapable of saying a word. Annie looked into my eyes, trying to see what I was thinking. At that moment, I don't think I had a single coherent thought. I just knew that I had to get away.

I got up, picked up the little charm and put it in my pocket. Then I grasped the handles of the iron box and said, "I've got to go. I've got a lot to think about."

Annie urged me not to do anything right away.

"Ben, darling, think about everything, give it some time. You'll see what I mean."

I mumbled something innocuous and said again that I had to leave. Carrying the box I started towards the door.

Annie picked up my pen from the coffee table and said, "Don't forget this."

Daily Report 182

Date of Events: 20 August 1997 – evening
Place: Barbados: Oliver's office
Summary: Playing the tape

I drove slowly down to Bridgetown. On the seat next to me, the tape recorder was replaying my conversation with Annie. I hate hearing my voice in the conversation. At first I sound so happy to see her – which is genuine – and then, so interested in her bracelet – which is false. And, as her story unfolded, I played Annie along like she was some criminal in a precinct interrogation room. For Christsakes, this is Annie!

Then there's Annie's voice, telling the whole story, and pleading with me to view it as she did, as a regrettable, terrible accident. I want to see it that way but, whether it's the policeman or the Cumberbatch in me, I can't quite bring myself to do it.

I am ashamed of what I did, leading her on and then confronting her like that with the silver charm. However, how else could I have got to the truth of what had happened at Glenville that night? But now that I have the truth, I wish to hell that I didn't.

I played the tape for Oliver. It was hard on him. Tears streamed down his cheeks. He sat at his desk with his hands covering his eyes; then every few minutes he would peer at me from under his hands, hoping that I had some solution, some way for us to avoid the obvious truth: that his sister, his dear Annie, our dear Annie, is implicated in arson, robbery and two deaths.

When the tape was over, Oliver asked me to play the second half of it again. He sat at his desk staring at the small recorder, and shaking his head in disbelief and sadness.

He said, "Why did she lie to me? Why didn't she come forward at once? We could have worked something out."

He looked at me as if he was expecting me to make it right, to make it go away, but he saw that I was as confused and conflicted and as upset as he was.

Finally he said, "There is nothing more that can be done. They must be arrested."

Somehow his declaration sounded less than totally convincing. I am out of my jurisdiction and out of my depth, but I can't see Annie spending much of the rest of her life in prison. However, neither could I bring myself to say that she should just walk away from what she had done. Maybe Oliver is right, Annie and Malcolm will have to accept responsibility for their actions.

After all, Annie intended no harm. Maybe the courts will see that and go easy on her. And of course I know that Oliver has influential friends, and I've observed how vital that is in Barbados. My best chance to save Annie would have been for me to bury the evidence and not to have forced her to face what she had done. Or, having confronted her, to have kept it to myself; but I was unable to carry that burden. It is too much.

Maybe I took the coward's way out when I involved her brother, I will have to live with that. But one thing is clear: if there is going to be a way out of this for Annie it will have to come from Ollie.

Oliver thanked me for bringing the tape to him first.

"It's too late for us to find the right people around here tonight. Meet me here tomorrow morning at nine, and we will get the arrest warrants."

Daily Report 183

Date of Events: 21 & 22 August 1997
Place: Barbados: Annie's house
Summary: Flight and aftermath

After a sleepless night, in which I alternately condemned and then absolved Annie, I went to Bridgetown. I was at Oliver's office door when he arrived at 8:45. He looked like he too had had a sleepless night.

It took two hours plus for us to get the arrest warrants, then we drove up to Annie's house followed by a second car full of constables. As expected, Annie was nowhere in sight. But, disappointingly, neither was Malcolm.

I must admit that my feelings for Annie were – are – in total disarray. I still love her, I think I will always love her, but she was responsible for my grandmother's and aunt's deaths. I fear that this guilt will always stand between us. Maybe time and events will change my perspective, but as I looked at her empty house, I found it hard to believe that we could ever re-establish the love and trust that we had shared there. Something very valuable has been lost.

There is an arrest warrant out for Annie, and she will be put in prison if she is caught, no matter who her brother is. She can expect no help from her so-called husband, Goody Griffith, nor from her ex-keeper, Vincent Lewis. But almost certainly Annie has fled the island by now, left Barbados by ship or private plane or some other way. Her punishment for now is that she is separated from her daughter, her brother and his family, and anyone else in Barbados for whom she cares. And, presuming she still does care, separated from me.

Oliver did me the courtesy of not pretending to be surprised that his sister was gone. He all but confirmed his role in her escape when he said that Clara was staying with him and Elvira, "for the time being". But he did seem to share my disappointment that Malcolm has gone too.

We haven't discussed Annie's whereabouts, but I suspect that she has gone to the same place she went to when she left Barbados for an extended time many years ago. To Antigua, to a place called the Ace in the Hole, a divers' hotel run by an American named Ace Hoagland.

Oliver once told me that he didn't know where she had been. That may or may not have been the truth at that time, but I bet he knows now. However, we haven't spoken of it. We agreed that, wherever she was, Malcolm would not have gone with her. Ollie said Malcolm was probably hiding with friends or relatives in one of the rural parishes.

A brief item referring to the burning of Glenville House appeared in the *Clarion* the next day, but it mentioned only that Annie and Malcolm were wanted for questioning. Annie was referred to as "Annie Shorter, the former beauty queen and model". Her married name Griffith was dropped, presumably to spare the politician any further embarrassment. Nor did the article allude to the relationship between the fugitive Annie and Chief Inspector Shorter.

The article does say that "a massive manhunt is being conducted".

The newspapers here in Barbados, although at times entertaining and always informative on sports like cricket and racing, seem to handle hard news and difficult subjects like murder with kid gloves. Whether this is policy dictated by the government and the powerful, or an editorial reluctance to display this type of news in front of the omnipresent tourists, one can only speculate. If the everyday Bajan had to depend on the news media alone, he or she would have scant knowledge of what is going on.

Fortunately, they don't. This is a small island, just twenty-one miles long and fourteen miles wide, with only 270,000 people. Not much of importance ever seems to escape the public eye for long. The rum shop, the market, the bus stop and the telephone are undoubtedly more effective disseminators of information than newspapers and broadcast media and, thank goodness, they're distinctly not as subject to influence and official censorship.

Six-Week Report 184

Date of Events: August to October 1997
Place: Barbados: Wavecrest Hotel; Supreme Court; Glenville
Summary: Wills and wells

A month and a half have passed. No sign of either Annie or Malcolm. No surprise about Annie, but I would have thought that Malcolm might have been spotted by now. He is too short and too ugly to go long without being noticed. Oliver swears that the police are pulling out the stops to find him, but he says that people in small villages are often reluctant to turn someone in to the police for fear that the relatives of that person might "pay them back". Oliver assures me that Malcolm will be caught.

I have been staying at the Wavecrest full time since Annie left. It feels like I've been here forever. A lot of my time has been spent in Bridgetown, working with my attorney to prove my claims to Glenville House and to Savannah Plantation. George Husbands advises that we not open the iron chest but deliver it untouched to the Chief Justice of the Supreme Court who, incidentally, is a former law partner of George's. Handling the chest in this manner should help forestall any future assertion that we tampered with Grandma Dora's will.

Apparently, this was good advice. The judge was obviously pleased with our action. George and I were present when the chest was opened before the judge in chambers, with his clerk as witness. It was found to contain the original deed to Glenville and all of the wills of subsequent generations, just as I had remembered from those summers long ago.

The one document I had seen the outside of but had never known its contents was Grandma Dora's own will. The judge asked George to read the will aloud in its entirety.

Skipping over all the legal language, I can summarise it as follows: In accordance with her father's wishes, Dora Glenville left Glenville House and lands to the eldest male heir, on the condition that said heir reside at Glenville. It specifically mentioned Clarence Glenville, her eldest son. If Clarence was unable, through death or incapacity, to assume full control of Glenville, it was to pass to her next eldest son, Nathaniel Cumberbatch. If Nathaniel was unable or unwilling to assume full control and move to Glenville, it was to pass to Thomas. If Thomas was unable to meet the criteria it was to pass to the eldest male child in the next generation.

Grandma Dora's will then explains that although she, a woman, had inherited Glenville, it had happened only because there had been no adult male heir at that time. For this and other reasons, which Grandma Dora said had been thoroughly discussed and agreed to by her daughter Emily Glenville, she would continue to follow the original intent of her great-grandfather, Frank Glenville, and Glenville would be left only to the eldest living male.

Probate of my grandmother's will was completed in less than two months. I was told that this was near record time; apparently it was thanks to a few discreet telephone calls from my new friend, the Prime Minister.

The judge declared that, since the house no longer exists at Glenville, the requirement that the inheritor live there is nullified. And, since all of the male heirs specifically named in the will are deceased, the property will pass to the eldest male heir in the next generation. In other words, me.

I asked George to set it up so that Glenville would be shared equally by the three of us – Elyce, Margaret and me. To my great disappointment he informed me that this was not possible. In accordance with the original intent, the property cannot be subdivided and can be passed on only to the eldest surviving male heir, or to the eldest female if no male heir exists. So, like it or not, I am the sole owner of Glenville.

The same judge also handled probate of my Uncle Thomas's will. He declared that I am Thomas's sole heir. However, Thomas left little of value except his own claim to Savannah, and my inheritance of the plantation will depend on the court accepting Edgar Mount's most recent will. This document is being actively contested by Vincent Lewis, and given the stakes, and who is involved, it is far from a sure thing that I will inherit Savannah, no matter what the Prime Minister has promised.

George Husbands warned me that Lewis has a potentially strong case. He said that Edgar Mount may not have been mentally competent when he drew the most recent will. He was elderly and was obviously in very bad health. In fact, he died less than two weeks later. Moreover, it could be said that Thomas, who was admittedly biased against Lewis, had exercised undue influence in this matter upon his lifelong friend, employer and lover. Husbands said that it would take a small miracle for me to inherit Savannah Plantation.

Now that I have inherited Glenville, the Court order restricting me from going there has been lifted. I planned to open the well as soon as possible, to see if the Wandering Lady, the fickle spring that has caused so much death and unhappiness, has indeed re-established residence at Glenville.

I contracted with a local construction company to remove the slab in the back of the garden at Glenville. It took three men, plus a small tractor called a Bobcat, to clear the brush covering the slab – or, as it turned out, five slabs – that covered the old spring. Their work went relatively smoothly. In less than two hours they had uncovered all five coral stones. The total area was approximately thirty feet by forty feet.

Now to look inside. A large tractor hooked a slab with heavy chains and pulled it away from the well site. One by one, each slab was moved to the side. Beneath the slabs we were greeted by the sight of several large coral boulders. They were enclosed by a low-cut block wall approximately twenty-two feet in diameter. The old well appeared to have been filled to its top with coral boulders. The contractor speculated that they had been dug up when the cistern and foundation of the first Glenville House were being built, and had been dumped, for convenience, into the old dry well. Plus, some of the boulders had probably been resting in the fields when the Glenvilles first cleared the land.

It took eight days to remove the boulders from the old well, which was nearly a hundred feet deep. By the time we were halfway down, we pretty well knew that no significant amount of water was there. If the Wandering Lady had moved in, we would have been awash in water by then; but I had them remove all the coral boulders anyway.

Nothing. Dry as a bone. The Wandering Lady, if she ever really did exist, was still out there someplace. Someplace, but not at Glenville.

As I stood and looked down into the empty hole, I could not help but reflect on all that had happened because of the desire to believe that the water was there. People have died, lives and reputations have been ruined, people are in hiding and in exile, and all because of an old tale in a children's book.

Old man Brodeur at the Barbados Museum Library had it right when he said that the only thing worth killing for on Barbados was water. In this instance, the killing was done not for water, but for the mere possibility that water might exist.

Daily Report 185

Date of Events: 22 October 1997
Place: Barbados: Wavecrest Hotel; the Cutter Restaurant; a cave nearby
Summary: The fugitive

It is said that Barbados has the finest weather in the world; the sun generally shines, it is never cold and the constant comfortable temperature is usually modified by a nice breeze and cooling showers. I don't disagree with that opinion but I would not suggest looking for proof of it in September and October. That is the time of year called the rainy season. It doesn't rain every day, but if it doesn't it feels like it should have. The humidity hovers at the theoretical maximum while the temperature stays where it usually is, around thirty centigrade by day and in the mid-twenties by night.

The Wavecrest, fairly dank in the best of times, is now positively dripping. The walls are wet to the touch and small puddles of water have formed at their base. The mirror in the tiny bathroom is always opaque, covered with beads of condensation, as if the shower had been left on. The sheets are slick to the touch and I prefer to sleep on rather than in them, except when the room buzzes with tiny blood-sucking insects.

I know that these conditions will not last. In a few more weeks Barbados will return to what it usually is, weatherwise – almost heaven. But for right now, I would prefer to be back in New York, where October is usually one of the best months. However, things are beginning to happen in the legal world and George Husbands has advised me that my presence is needed here in Barbados for at least the next few weeks.

The Wavecrest is nearly full, as it is the height of the surfing season. Down the way in Bathsheba, at the guest cottages and small establishments nearer the surfers' beach, young men and women from literally all over the world are crammed into narrow beds and in sleeping bags on floors and ledges. Their colourful surfboards, stacked inside and outside chattel houses and tumbledown shacks, signal their presence. As humble as it is, the Wavecrest is a good cut above these accommodations, and from the cost standpoint it is beyond the reach of many of the surfers. It tends to attract the older and more established participants, plus the media and more affluent fans and followers of the sport.

Surfing season or not, the food at Wavecrest is C-minus to D-plus on the chef's best days. I can tolerate the breakfasts, and I am almost always away at lunchtime. I've become a big fan of the fast food chain the Quik Chef, Barbados's more than adequate answer to McDonalds. There they serve a mean barbecue chicken sandwich, and you haven't lived until you have had their all-beef or all-chicken rotis – curried wraps out of India by way of Trinidad. But now that Annie has gone, other than the occasional meal with Ollie and his family I have most of my evening meals here on the east coast, either at the Wavecrest or at one of the other modest establishments catering to surfers and other low budget travellers.

Some of the world's best surfers had come to match their skill and daring with the big rollers that are generated by the storms swinging out of Africa this time of year. The storms, if they are fierce enough, are given either a male or female name. Some go on to achieve immortality. The storms usually swoop past Barbados blowing hard and dumping rain before they enter the Caribbean Sea. There, in the Caribbean's shallower and warmer water, they may gain strength and go on to fulfil their destiny by becoming full-fledged hurricanes.

It was raining fitfully today, but I just couldn't face another meal at the Wavecrest. They have two chefs; one is bad and the other worse. Worse was on duty tonight. So I decided to walk the half mile down the coast to a small restaurant called the Cutter, where the food is sometimes not too bad. They always have a nice pumpkin soup and decent salt rolls. Man could survive on that alone, if he had to.

The rain fell intermittently as I hurried down the road. Waves crashed against huge coral boulders, some thirty feet high, that spill along the beach as if they had been dropped casually by a thoughtless giant. The tide was still high and had just begun to recede. Salt spray leapt high in the air and added effectively to the rain's effort to soak me to the skin. A cool breeze blew into my face.

When I arrived at the Cutter I was chilled and, unusual for me, I had a double whiskey before tackling the tattered menu. I was delighted to see that they had "sea cat" – the local name for baby octopus – on the menu. It proved to be overcooked but it was not a bad choice.

At ten o'clock the Cutter stopped serving food and assumed its second identity, that of a bar and pick-up joint catering to the surfer crowd. Having been witness to a few of these sessions in the past, I knew that the conversation, which ranged from surfing stories to tomorrow's weather and wave action, was less than engaging.

I settled my bill, walked out into the elements and turned left toward the Wavecrest. The wind blew strongly at my back and was laced with a spattering of rain. A coral stone and sand path runs parallel with the road. I chose the path in preference to the poorly-lit road, where one risked being clipped by a speeding car, especially on such a dark, stormy night.

Two hundred and fifty yards down the path from the Cutter, the heavens suddenly opened up. Sheets of windblown rain came pounding down. I briefly considered running back to the Cutter, but it would have been directly into the storm and I would have been soaked by the time I got there.

Usually these showers don't last for long. So I decided to seek refuge in a cluster of large coral boulders to my right. I knew that many of the larger boulders had shallow caves that had been carved out by the sea and that these caves were accessible when the tide was out. If I found the right one it would provide me with temporary shelter.

The first cave I came to was wet and the walls still dripped but, what the hell, at least I was out of the wind and rain. I thought this storm might not last for more than ten or fifteen minutes, then slack off or even stop. With luck, I might make it back to the Wavecrest without being further drenched.

I sat down on a small coral boulder inside the entrance of the cave to wait out the storm. The constant noise of the crashing and pounding of the surf was deafening, probably magnified by the shape of the cave to my rear. However, for now at least, the surf was stopping at the entrance of the cave, which smelled pleasantly of the sea.

It was black as pitch inside, so I fished out of my pocket the small flashlight that Norman and his people had given me, and examined my immediate surroundings. Vienna sausage cans, empty and torn plastic bags and all manner of beer and soft drink bottles, glass and plastic, had been washed into the corners of the cave by the tides. It appeared to be a fairly large cave, going back several feet into the coral, but the small light beam was unable to penetrate the gloom to reach the back wall.

I wedged the flashlight into a niche of the cave wall next to where I was sitting. It served to relieve the darkness somewhat at the cave entrance. Outside rain continued to fall, showing no sign of letting up as yet. I reconciled myself to being there for a while.

I reviewed in my mind, for the umpteenth time, the events of the last hundred days. And, despite myself, I thought of Annie. I wondered how she was faring. I missed her and wished that I could somehow turn back the clock. What if I had been able to remember what Annie had told me that first night at the Wavecrest, would that have mattered? Would I have forgiven her then? Who knows. Probably not. I didn't know her or love her then as I did later, but ...

Just then I saw something moving to my right, at the edge of my limited field of peripheral vision. I turned my head and there, standing a few feet away and holding a well-honed twenty-inch long cutlass, his short, broad body dripping wet, stood Malcolm Newton, the man who had killed my grandmother.

I started to rise but Malcolm slid the sharpened blade against my throat and said, "Sit down, big man, or I jook yo' head clean off wid my cutlash."

As he held the cutlass against my throat, its sharp blade sliced my skin and blood began to drip down onto the collar of my open shirt.

"Malcolm, you don't want to do this," I said as calmly as I could. "You are in some trouble now but Annie explained to us why you did what you did, but if you harm me ..."

"Shud up!" Malcolm's lips curled, making him uglier than usual. "Yuh was de one dat make Miss Annie to go away. Yuh say yuh love she but not true, yuh gonna pay for dat. Yuh come here, all clear-skinned wid blue eyes an' fine talk o' New York so Miss Annie t'ink yuh de man fo she. Malcolm know dat yuh fair words din' prevent yuh from doin' her wrong. She unhappy now. Yuh gonna pay, big man."

"Malcolm, I know that you must miss Annie and Clara. I know that you were a good friend to them and you looked ..."

"Yuh know nutten 'bout Miss Annie an' Malcolm. I did everthin' for she. An' when she look to me, she smile an' I was in goat heaven. Now dat all ruin. Yuh gonna pay, I gonna be cruel. I been followin' yuh for days an' dis is de spot."

It was all clear now. Malcolm was more than just a loyal servant. Poor bastard, he was in love with Annie. His anger at me wasn't just the anguish at having lost his revered employer, it was jealousy, an even more powerful emotion.

This was beginning to look like a very dangerous situation.

Malcolm, wasting no time, drew his arm back to strike me with the cutlass. I swung my right elbow hard into his stomach, knocking him back a few steps and then jumped to my feet. I knew I had to put some distance between him and me or he would quickly cut me to ribbons.

I briefly considered running out of the cave and diving into the surf, but I feared that I might slip and fall on the slippery rocks and that Malcolm would then easily attack me from behind as I struggled to my feet. I decided I stood a better chance if I retreated back into the darkness of the cave.

Malcolm quickly regained his balance and came at me again, with his weapon raised. I ducked left and moved past him into the cave. He swung his blade at me as I slid past him, but the cutlass just grazed my shoulder and did me no harm. I edged further back until my hand touched the back wall. I hoped that there might be an opening there where I could escape from Malcolm, but none was evident. So much for getting out of the cave the easy way. It appeared that the only way out was the front entrance, and a dangerous, determined and armed Malcolm stood between me and ever seeing the outside again.

I could see him standing there, silhouetted by the dull glow from my flashlight. He seemed to be deciding which would be the best way to finish me off. Then it occurred to me that in the dark, if I didn't move, Malcolm wouldn't be able to see me well, if at all.

He moved forward, and seemed to be coming right toward me. I slowly shifted to my left. I stepped on something round and felt down and determined that I was standing among several waterlogged coconuts, pushed to the rear of the cave and abandoned there by the retreating tide. Once again Malcolm moved in my direction. Either he had exceptional night vision or he could hear my breathing. He was now less than ten feet away.

I picked up one coconut. The seawater in it made it heavy. I hurled it at Malcolm as hard as I could but he shrugged and turned easily as it glanced off his shoulder. I picked up two more and hurled one after the other. His cutlass pushed the first aside, but the second struck him in the mouth and chin. He cursed and wiped blood from his lips with the back of his hand.

The coconuts had done Malcolm no real harm, but what they had done was to galvanise him into action. Snarling with pain and anger he rushed at me with his cutlass at the ready, prepared to finish me off. I reached down for another coconut but, instead, I felt the rough edges of a piece of coral. I brought it up just in time to deflect Malcolm's blade. The force of his rush caused us both to crash into the rear wall of the cave. I was knocked to my knees and dropped the coral.

Malcolm also appeared to be stunned briefly but he pulled himself together and stood up before I could get to my feet. He raised his cutlass, ready to crash it down upon my head, but in the dark he was unaware that the ceiling of the cave here in the back of the cave was markedly lower than at the entrance. His blade struck the roof and stopped. Malcolm was surprised and momentarily didn't comprehend what had happened.

I thrust myself forward and tackled Malcolm around the waist, driving him hard into the wall. His head hit the coral with a hollow thump. The stocky man gave a groan and fell limp.

I got down on my knees in the dark and felt around until I had located the cutlass. Once I had it, I used my belt to secure Malcolm's hands behind his back before he could awake and cause more trouble. Then, when he did come to, groaning and cursing, I marched him at cutlass point through the rain over to the surfer bar. From there, I called Oliver.

The surfers were briefly interested in Malcolm and me, then they went back to spinning their tales of past exploits and their prognostications of what the sea would hold for them tomorrow.

The back of Malcolm's head was bleeding from where he had slammed into the coral. The bartender gave me a towel to tie around the wound. Malcolm sat dejectedly on the floor, his back to the bar, with his hands still secured behind him. He muttered to himself and occasionally sent indecipherable curses my way.

An hour later, a police car from District C police station arrived at the Cutter and took Malcolm away.

Daily Report 199

Date of Events: 5 November 1997
Place: Barbados: Wavecrest Hotel
Summary: Annie's proposal

I am scheduled to return to New York tomorrow to get on with my life. The courts are grinding on, deciding whether Savannah passes to me from my Uncle Thomas or if the original will, giving Vincent Lewis control, is still valid. Husbands says that there is little more that I can contribute to that decision.

However, yesterday there was an article in the *Clarion* that said, "Vincent Lewis, a prominent plantation owner resident in St Philip, has accepted a charge of conspiracy to commit bodily harm upon one Clarence Glenville, late of St Charles. Lewis will serve a term of five years in prison. He will begin to serve his sentence on November 15 of this year."

Oliver has told me that part of the government's negotiation with Vincent Lewis was that he had to withdraw his challenge to the Edgar Mount will that left Savannah Plantation and Great House to Thomas Winston. George Husbands assures me that Mount's estate will be settled in a few months' time and, since Thomas Winston will be named rightful heir, and I have already been named Thomas's heir, that Savannah will be mine, in due time. He refuses to speculate on how long "due time" may be.

I had some errands in Bridgetown first thing today. When I got back to the Wavecrest I had a message that a woman had called. She did not leave her name or number but merely said that she would call back at noon.

I had a strong suspicion that I knew who it was that had called.

At noon exactly I was summoned to the phone. I picked up the receiver and said, "Hello."

"Ben, it's me."

It was Annie. Her voice sounded far away.

"I'm sorry I left without saying goodbye, but it seemed like the only thing to do."

Annie sounded subdued, maybe even nervous, not her usual confident self.

"How are you doing?" I asked.

"I'm OK, I guess," she answered, not too convincingly.

"I can understand why you left in a hurry, but if it's any consolation there doesn't seem to be much of a fuss over you here in Barbados. They have Malcolm in custody and now, at last, they're going to put Lewis away for his role in my uncle's murder. Maybe you should come back and face the music. I think that you might well get off pretty easily."

"I would like to believe you're right. I hate being separated from Clara like this but, from what people have told us, if I were to return some people would use me to embarrass Oliver and, indirectly, the Prime Minister. So, for now, they think it's best that I stay away."

"If you say so, but you'll be able to return some day soon."

Annie said nothing. I guess she was not as convinced of this as I was.

I said, "I guess I know where you are, right? How is old Ace?"

"How did you …? Of course, I told you about my staying here before. In truth, it has been difficult and, most of all, I do miss Clara so much, but she is far better off being with Oliver and his family. For a lot of reasons it wouldn't work out for her to be here."

"How come?" I asked.

She paused, collecting her thoughts.

"The principal problem is Ace. When I was here last time, I was twenty-one and Ace was in his forties. I was footloose and I could handle this place. Sixteen years later, I've changed, Ace has changed, only the divers and the Ace in the Hole are the same."

"How has Ace changed?"

"Not for the better. He is sixteen years older in years but this life, with the booze and the drugs and too many dives over 100 feet deep, they have aged him more years than that. I have known some nice-looking men in their sixties but Ace isn't one of them. He is a wreck. And after all the years of telling me how much he needed me and that I could come whenever I wanted, once I got here I found out that he really hadn't meant it."

"That's too bad. You think you can't come back here and you don't want to stay there."

I said it sympathetically, but what I didn't say was what she was hoping I would. So Annie said it for me.

"Ben, that night in the casuarina grove, you said something about my coming to New York. After that, it was always there as an option for us, we used to talk about it. I know that a lot has happened since then but ..."

She paused, hoping for some response from me. I said nothing, so Annie continued.

"I hear you're going back up there soon, what would you think if I came up to New York in a few weeks?"

I didn't know what to say. My mind was wrestling with a million different thoughts involving Annie, me and my new life in New York, Glenville House, Grandma Dora and Emily, and on and on. A part of me wanted to tell her yes, but this was that part of me that I didn't necessarily admire. Would it be weak of me to say yes? Would I be condoning what had happened if I

313

did? And who was I kidding – could Annie and I ever put Glenville behind us?

Annie filled the silence.

"I wouldn't have to stay. I could just come up for a visit. Just to see how it goes. Ben, what do you say?"

I took a deep breath and then I said it, hating my own words.

"Don't. It won't work, too much has happened. I'm sorry, but don't come to New York."

Before she could say anything more, before she could twist and break my heart, before I ended up begging her to forgive me and come to New York, I hung up.

It occurs to me as I write this report that perhaps I am more like Nate Cumberbatch than I would like to think. What was it that Grandma Dora used to say? Oh yes, "A fruit can' fall no further dan de tree." But I should also remember that it was that particular characteristic, the hard side of Nate Cumberbatch, that never did bring him or anyone else any happiness.

Epilogue

Over four years have passed since I finished and put away my account of what happened to me and my family. Where should I start to bring this record up to date?

I might as well start with the good stuff. It took them another two years to settle Edgar Mount's estate, but Mount's will leaving Savannah to my Uncle Thomas was finally declared valid. The prior will, the one granting benefit to Vincent Lewis, was found to have been obtained fraudulently, and thus was held to be null and void. And so, as Thomas's heir, I finally stood to inherit Savannah Plantation.

After Vincent Lewis had gone to jail and, in return for a lighter sentence and certain "privledges" in prison, had withdrawn his suit against the Mount estate, it seemed then that I would have smooth sailing. But that did not happen. On the last day, Goodman Griffith brought suit contesting the will on behalf of the stockholders of The Savannah Project Ltd.

Lewis was not listed as one of the eleven stockholders, but most of the names were easily recognised as people of prominence and wealth on the island. George Husbands speculated that probably Lewis had assigned his shares to Goody for this purpose, although there was no way that could be proved. I needed all the help I could get from Ollie, the Prime Minister and his friends to defeat that challenge. It wasn't until February 2000 that Edgar Mount's second will was again upheld and I finally became the owner of Savannah Plantation and Great House.

The place had deteriorated further during the time the will was being contested; no one had lifted a finger to maintain it.

The worst of it was that people had broken into the house and stripped the place. Not only the furniture and the pictures off the walls but even light switches, counters and toilet bowls. Termites and rainwater had ruined everything else.

The Great House was beyond repair. As soon as I assumed title, it was torn down, the contents that could be salvaged were sold off and what was left was burned.

With Vincent Lewis in jail and with the Wandering Lady nowhere to be seen, the infamous Savannah Project was now a thing of the past. Few people in Barbados even remember it. But there was still the land at Savannah, six hundred and eighty-seven acres of it, plus three good wells. Also, there were several solid outbuildings plus some still useful farm equipment.

So I, Benjamin Cumberbatch, became the proprietor of Savannah Plantation – for two whole weeks! During that time I transferred one third ownership of it to each of my sisters, Elyce Cumberbatch Downes of Freeport, New York, and Margaret Cumberbatch Martensen of Etherington Corners, New York.

Then we sold Savannah to the large Barbados conglomerate that owns a big share of everything of value on the island – hotels, supermarkets, automobile agencies and various businesses, plus thousands of acres of sugar cane land. They were less than generous in their price – typically so, I was told. After all taxes, debts and legal fees were paid, we had 1.8 million US dollars. We set $550,000 aside to jointly rebuild Glenville and then each of us received almost $420,000.

The new Glenville will not be a re-creation of the original, but aspects of it, architecturally, will resemble the old place. For example, it will have a veranda that goes all around, on four sides. The new house will be somewhat larger than its predecessor. It will have four bedrooms and four bathrooms and it will have a swimming pool, built in the space where the old cistern had

316

been. And we have begun to landscape about one acre of the land with tropical plants and citrus trees.

Technically I was the sole owner of Glenville, according to the court, and when I died it would pass to my next of kin. But this was not what I wanted. After all the problems that inheritance had created for our family, I felt that the only equitable arrangement was for all the living grandchildren of Dora Glenville to share the ownership.

George put me in touch with a sharp young lawyer who arranged for us to transfer the ownership of the Glenville land to a British Virgin Islands Corporation which, in turn, was owned equally by Elyce, Margaret and me. Thus, by having the property owned by a corporation, the title would not have to change when one of the owners died. The corporation would continue to own the property.

We have effectively ended the inheritance issue. Somehow, considering what transpired, I don't think Grandma Dora would have objected to what we've done.

Since we're doing the building together – the three Cumberbatch siblings – the final house will be a conglomeration of our tastes. The big surprise has been Margaret. When it comes to decorating, she has some great ideas, really imaginative. In the end, the house will probably be more hers than either Elyce's or mine.

Elyce and I are closer than ever. Margaret and me too, but for a whole lot of reasons I'll never be as close with her as I am with my older sister. Elyce thinks it's partly because I adore her son Ben, which is true, but also I think that I learned something about brother and sister relationships from being with Ollie and Annie. I just hope that we will never have to put ourselves to the test as they have.

Oliver has retired from the police and entered politics. Two years ago, he and his family moved to St Charles and Oliver declared against Goody Griffith. Goody apparently had lost some points with the voters when the courts rejected his effort to take over Savannah. Oliver won the election and now represents St Charles in Parliament.

Clara, now almost sixteen, is so beautiful that she takes your breath away. Oliver and Elvira have done a great job raising her. She is still as sweet as ever and seems to take her looks in her stride. It is the rest of the male population of Barbados that you have to look out for. Oliver and his sons are most protective of Clara. It would be a very bold and unwise young man that tried to take liberties with Clara Shorter. Yes, she has dropped Griffith from her name, most people think that she is Ollie and Elvira's daughter.

Clara has been to Antigua twice to see her mother. Apparently the trips didn't go too well. The second time, Clara came home three days early. Elvira says that Clara refuses to go back to the Ace in the Hole, although Ollie says that she may meet Annie in Grenada or Tobago this spring.

Oliver is guarded with me when we talk about Annie. I guess she's still not too happy with her situation, but he says it is not yet time for her to return to Barbados. Also that he understands why I won't see Annie. I wish I saw it as clearly as he does.

There is a void in me where Annie was. When I think of her a sadness and longing envelops me. I still dream of her, but mostly the dreams are of the young Annie, my idealised version. However, I have not been able to feel any real warmth and affection for another woman since the reawakening of my love for the older Annie.

But, over time, my feelings for Annie are slowly receding. When I am in New York, they're not so intense. But here in Barbados, it is still hard for me to put the memories aside.

Ollie has told me that Vincent Lewis will be getting out of prison a little early, in May or June of this year. There have been articles in the *Clarion* about his stay in prison. He hasn't had to mingle with the other prisoners and has his own cell, double the normal size, fitted out with his own furniture. It has also been rumoured that he receives what the *Clarion* delicately calls "conjugal visits" from a young lady friend. Oliver says that the same young lady lives in Annie's house and drives Annie's Jaguar around town.

Malcolm got twenty years for killing Grandma Dora. And from what Oliver told me, he has been getting the usual treatment at Glendairy.

I guess that about wraps it up. Oh yes, you might want to know about me. I guess I've made a ninety-five per cent recovery from my head injury. Now and then I miss a beat or two, but who doesn't? I still write my notes as I go along and later write a daily summary. It has become a habit and I have found it to be a good way for me to keep on top of things. I still have no peripheral vision in my right eye but I can compensate for it, and the rest of me functions about as might be expected.

I used my part of the money from the sale of Savannah to set up a little private detective business in New York. We're doing OK. A couple of my old friends from the Arson Squad have taken retirement and have joined me. We get a lot of arson-related business from insurance companies, occasional jobs down here in the Caribbean and even some referrals now and then from Tom Moran and our old contacts at the NYPD Arson Squad.

I've had some interesting cases. Maybe I'll write about them sometime.

I'm planning to go over this afternoon to take a walk around Glenville. I like to keep up with how the construction is coming along and how the plants and the citrus trees are doing. I'll also probably look down into the old well. I had them leave a small opening at the top when they put the slabs back. I like to drop a small piece of coral down there, hoping to hear it plop into water.

But so far, it only clatters on to the coral stone below.

The Macmillan Caribbean Writers Series

Series Editor: Jonathan Morley

Look out for other exciting titles from the region:

Crime thrillers:

Rum Justice   *Jolien Harmsen*

Fiction:

Molly and the Muslim Stick: *David Dabydeen*
The Girl with the Golden Shoes: *Colin Channer*
The Roar of Shells: *Dara Wilkinson*
The Festival of San Joaquin: *Zee Edgell*
The Voices of Time: *Kenrick Mose*
She's Gone: *Kwame Dawes*
The Sound of Marching Feet: *Michael Anthony*
John Crow's Devil: *Marlon James*
This Body: *Tessa Mcwatt*
Walking: *Joanne Allong Haynes*
Trouble Tree: *John Hill Porter*
Power Game: *Perry Henzell*

Short Stories:

Catching Crab and Cascadura: *Cyril Dabydeen*
The Fear of Stones: *Kei Miller* (shortlisted for the 2007
    Commonwealth Writers' Prize)
Popo and Stories of Corbeau Alley: *Nellie Payne*

Poetry:

Poems of Martin Carter: *Stewart Brown And Ian Mcdonald (eds.)*

Selected Poems of Ian Mcdonald: *Edited By Edward Baugh*

Plays:

Bellas Gate Boy (includes Audio CD) : *Trevor Rhone*

Two Can Play: *Trevor Rhone*